AND THEN THE END SHALL COME

BOOK TWO - THE QUEST

Thy word is a light unto my path and a lamp unto my feet.
Psalm 119:105 KJV

by Lorraine M. Cafasso

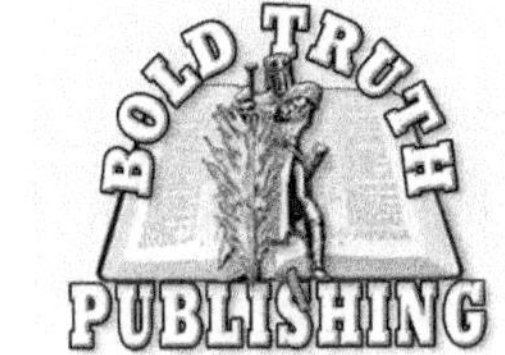

Christian Literature & Artwork
A BOLD TRUTH Publication

THE QUEST

ISBN 13: 978-1-949993-67-7

SECOND REVISED EDITION

BOLD TRUTH PUBLISHING
(Christian Literature & Artwork)
606 West 41st, Ste. 4
Sand Springs, Oklahoma 74063
www.BoldTruthPublishing.com
boldtruthbooks@yahoo.com

Available from Amazon.com and other retail outlets. Orders by U.S. trade bookstores and wholesalers. Quantity sales special discounts are available on quantity purchases by corporations, associations, and others. For details, contact the publisher at the address above.

Overall book design by Aaron Jones.

This book is a work of fiction. All characters in it are a work of the author's imagination.

Poem "The Sands of Time" by Marcella Burnes, used by permission.

Unless otherwise indicated, all Scriptures are taken from the KING JAMES VERSION (KJV) of the Holy Bible. Public domain.

Printed in the USA.
10 20 10 9 8 7 6 5 4 3 2 1

EPIGRAM

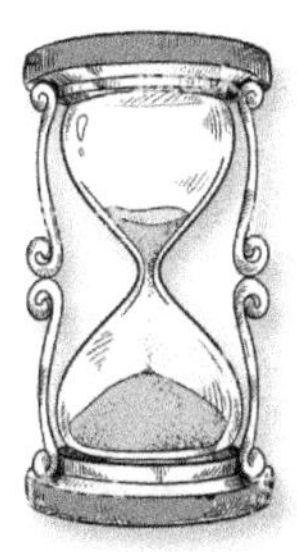

THE SANDS OF TIME

THROUGH THE SANDS OF TIME
I HEAR THE HOURGLASS CHIME.
EACH FALLING GRAIN
COMMANDS A SECOND OF LIFE'S TRAIN.

FALLING SOFTLY, GENTLY, THEN SWIRLING DOWN.
NO MORE TIME HUSHING, NOW POUNDING THE SOUND
A SECOND, A MOMENT, A TINY GRAIN OF SAND,
STACKED UPON HISTORY'S FALLEN MAN.

FROM DUST WE ARE BORN TO DUST WE RETURN,
YET TO OUR MAKER WE ALWAYS YEARN.
KNOWING IS CERTAIN,

A GLOWING OF DUST.
ETERNITIES' MYSTERY?
MAKE HEAVEN WE MUST!!!

Author: Marcella Burnes

TABLE OF CONTENTS

TABLE OF CONTENTS

TABLE OF CONTENTS

TABLE OF CONTENTS

TABLE OF CONTENTS

DEDICATION

The second book of this series is dedicated to two unknowns. Books will probably never be written about them, streets won't be named after them. In fact, except for a select few who knew them, after time, they will be forgotten.

Not so in Heaven. Heaven has a special place for unsung heroes. I am dedicating this book to two of them, both special people, who have gone on to receive their rewards. I'm sure Jesus was waiting for both of them with open arms. His first words to them were probably, "Well done my good and faithful servants".

After a long, hard struggle, Rene Gallo recently went to be with the Lord. Rene came to the U.S. from Honduras as a young man in 1996. He had been in the ministry in one form or another for most of his life. Bringing people to the Lord was his passion in life. He ministered at my church many times, and shared the Word powerfully, but one thing that he had done since the age of sixteen was to interpret for other Ministers.

Without a good interpreter, a Missionary can't get his message to his target audience. No one would be able to tell you who Billy Graham's interpreters were, but it was their skill and anointing that completed the message. It was their voice the people understood. Thankfully, that particular skill won't be needed in Heaven. Everyone there speaks the same language. God bless you Rene for all you did, for being faithful to what God called you to do.

Phyllis Blanton also recently went to be with the Lord at ninety-two years of age. She went to the jail in Jay, Oklahoma for over forty years to minister to those prisoners incarcerated there. After a time she was only allowed to minister to the women prisoners but that did not curtail her enthusiasm. That did not stop her from doing her devil dance every chance she got. She would stomp all over the devil in the Name of Jesus. The prisoners loved to see her coming,

The first time I met Phyllis she came up to me and asked for a hug. She said she collected them. There's no way to count the number of hugs she gave and received in her lifetime. Only God knows, and I'm willing to bet He kept count. Her love and enthusiasm changed the lives of many of the people serving time in that jail, and not just their lives, but their families' lives also.

Not all of us are going to be a Billy Graham, but all of us can be unsung heroes. Ask God every morning what you can do today to enhance and extend His Kingdom and push back the forces of darkness. Most times it may not seem significant to you, but your obedience and willingness is significant to Him. We all want to hear Him say "Well done my good and faithful servant" when it's our time to stand before Him.

ACKNOWLEDGEMENTS

This book was written with the help of a wonderful group of friends and family. Without their help and encouragement I would still be working on The Quest instead of thanking them.

Brenda Livingston was my first critic, but she was a constructive critic who offered her help and expertise to help edit this book.

To my faithful friend Lori Swingle, who has been with me and encouraging me even before I wrote the first word, I offer my deep appreciation and friendship.

To my special friend Elsie Hoffstatter, thank you so much for all your input. There were several mistakes you picked up that the others missed.

My sister Cathy Ryan and her husband Dick worked on the manuscript while they were on vacation. That is diligence. Dick even organized all the separate copies into one final edit.

Finally to my husband's cousin Frank Rattacasa, your constructive criticism and help came from an unexpected source. We went to high school together and I never realized you had these talents. I'm grateful you thought it was important and took the time to do it.

I've learned many things from reading everyone's corrections. Hopefully there will be fewer mistakes in the next manuscript. I also learned that people thought it was important enough to give their time. Time is a valuable, limited commodity—I value that gift.

Lastly, I cannot close my thanking all of you without thanking my husband Mike. He is always there for me, whether it is helping me with a sticky sentence, helping me find just the right word, or vacuuming so I can continue writing. Saying, thank you seems too small an exchange for what all of you did for me. I am truly blessed with wonderful friends and family.

All of you shared in the finished work. I believe that many will read this and come to a personal relationship with God, through His Son, Jesus. Just as you shared in the work, you will also share in the rewards.

ENDORSEMENTS

I grew up reading different tales about characters seeking swords, destroying rings and trying to save the world. I remember watching movies about lost treasure and sacred relics being stolen, then restored to their rightful place.

These stories are brought to mind when I read about the journey of Bekah and those God gathered together to seek the meaning behind the dreams they had been experiencing, and the family heirloom (a Conquistadorian gold and jeweled cross), that now had new meaning to those called on THE QUEST.

I read [these] first two books of the series with anticipation and was not disappointed. I am waiting with bated breath for the last book. The characters, their interactions and the unusual plot kept my interest. I would expect there to be a long line of people waiting to finish the series and experience the excitement of [her forthcoming third book]—The Coming.

Eileen Worthington
M.Ed., English teacher, 16 years

I have been a Pastor for 32 years and in knowing Lorraine Cafasso it has been a pleasure for almost forty years. Lorraine's devotion to God and His Word is sterling. She is a woman of Faith with strong Kingdom convictions based on her solid relationship with Jesus Christ.

I had the pleasure of sitting and speaking with her about her travels to Paraguay and her love for its people. She has vision and writes clearly in conveying her heart, and the heart of God for Paraguay. In addition, I've read her writings and I know her new book will inspire others to be Kingdom-minded and Kingdom Builders along with our Lord Jesus Christ.

Rev. Joseph Catanese
Retired

The urgency of the hour is evident, the sound unmistakable. It is "The Last Call". Lorraine builds upon the story of a nation, and people God is calling for His Kingdom purpose.

In a continuation of "The Call" and "The Quest", [and her upcoming] book, "The Coming", brings an important message for today. What an amazing, God inspired trilogy this series has been.

Pastor David Knox
Grove Christian Center
Grove, Oklahoma

I have known Lorraine Cafasso through many seasons in her life. Then, at the direction of the Lord, she felt compelled to write this three volume work. This captivating, spiritual story is a platform to reveal and demonstrate spiritual reality of prayer, missions, and winning the lost.

I would encourage everyone to read these works, they are filled with very practical wisdom and powerful spiritual insight into both living in the earth and the spiritual warfare from the unseen realm that we all must come to grips with. Great job, Lorraine.

Rev. Ted Estes, D.Min.
Pastor, Lifechanger Church
Claremore, Oklahoma

AUTHOR'S PREFACE

I believe I wrote Book One, The Call, under the leading and guidance of the Holy Spirit. Book Two, The Quest, was written in a similar manner. It picks up where Book One left off. It's my desire, and I believe God's desire also, that these books are to be used as evangelistic tools to strengthen and encourage the believer and to win the lost. Are you lost? It's a question we all need to ask ourselves. Do we have a final destination, and do we know how to get there?

There's a lot of life in this book: happiness and grief, hope and despair, joy and sorrow. Scripture has been scattered throughout the book, giving you an opportunity to read God's Word and discover the answers to the problems troubling you. Many more Scriptures have been footnoted during the numerous times of testing and trials the characters in the book endure. I encourage you to read the footnoted Scriptures and perhaps God will speak to you through one of them and shine a light into your darkness.

My prayer is that your mind be entertained by the story, and your spirit be nourished by the Word of God that is woven throughout the book.

I pray God bless you. "Ñandejára ta nde rovasa" is the Guarani equivalent. (See Chapter 17 for the literal meaning.)

AUTHOR'S PREFACE

CAST OF CHARACTERS

BOOK ONE - THE CALL

Akeem Farzhi – Friend from Iraq, lived with Josh's family thru college

Angie Pritchard – Bekah's lawyer Jim Pritchard's wife

Audrey Hathaway – Jim Hathaway's wife, frequented Bekah's needlework shop

Axel – Member of Manu's tribe, mentored by Daniel

Bekah Ryan – Main character – focal point of dreams

Carlos Rampone – Haydon Carlton's "handyman"

Chabuto – Manu's step-mother

Ciba – Leonardo's wife, seriously gored by wild boar

Constanzia – Edwardo's wife (a.k.a. Connie)

Daniel Albright – Joe's brother, Missionary in Northeast Paraguay

Edwardo – Young Pastor Daniel mentored in Paraguay

Emilio – Baby in basket sent downriver by mother to avoid being burnt sacrifice to evil god

Erecia – Young nursing mother who helps feed Juan

Ernesto – Wild boar hunter

Esteban Montero – Bounty hunter in Paraguay

Fuego Zangersen – Bekah's father's second wife – Bekah's

step-mother

Gabriella Zangersen – Bekah's father's first wife – Bekah's mother

Giancarlo – Member of Manu's tribe – Mentored by Daniel

Haydon Carlton – New York City jeweler

Isaac Klein – C.I.A. operative – friend of Josh's

Jean – Owner of Lobster Pot in Ogunquit, Maine

Jim Hathaway – Sergeant of Maine State Police

Jim Pritchard – Bekah's lawyer

Joe Albright – Roberta's husband – Daniel's older brother

José – Owner of Excelsior – arms store in Asunción, Paraguay

Joshua Randall – Stranger from Claremore, Oklahoma and first to have dream

Juan – Manu and Noemi's newborn son

Juan – Injured wild boar hunter

Kay – Part of large prayer group in Maine

Lara – Connie's twenty-two year old sister

Leonardo – Ciba's husband – Manu's advisor

Luna – Bekah's half-sister, left behind by Fuego, so she could come to U.S. with Bekah's father

Maitie –Young man of tribe mentored by Daniel

Manu – Young Chief of the village

Mara – Riki's wife killed by wild boar

Maria – Edwardo and Connie's three year old daughter

Mario – Young man of tribe mentored by Daniel

Nana Sarah Zangersen – Bekah's late grandmother

Noemi – Manu's wife and baby Juan's mother

Paloma – Village girl sent by Manu to help Sherry with cooking, cleaning and gardening.

Paulo – Edwardo and Connie's six month old son

Penny – Sylvia's granddaughter – works at "Eye of the Needle"

Philippe – Young man Daniel mentored

Renato – Foreman of Bekah's apple orchard, close as a father, originally from Paraguay

Riki – Villager whose wife was killed by wild boar

Roberta Albright – Good friend and part-timer at Bekah's shop, Joe's wife

Sandy – Part of large prayer group in Maine

Sherry Albright – Daniel's wife, Missionary, and closest thing to a doctor for fifty miles

Shirley – Part of large prayer group in Maine

Suma – Village girl sent to help Noemi

Sylvia Jessup – Part-timer at Bekah's shop, close friend

Ted Ryan – Bekah's ex-husband

Young woman – Sent her baby down the river in a basket in response to dream from God

CAST OF CHARACTERS

BOOK TWO - THE QUEST

Alicia Hiccomb – John's wife who frequent Bekah's shop

Alma – Connie's prayer partner

Arandu – Leader of attacked village

Arasunu – Arandu's counselor

Brenda – New member of Maine prayer group

Enrico – Old man in Manu's village (a/k/a Eyo)

Hombrecito (Little Man) – Maria's puppy

Jeruti – Connie's prayer partner

John Hiccomb – Bank President of local bank in Ogunquit, Maine

Josef Muhammad – Leader of Black Death Camps in Paraguay

Kamal – Black Death member, troublemaker

Mehdi – Akeem Farzhi's friend and partner in C.I.A., with him undercover

Pearl – New member of Maine prayer group

Sol – Connie's prayer partner

Susan – New member of Maine prayer group

Tuvicha – Current old shaman of the village

Victoria – Connie's prayer partner

SYNOPSIS

BOOK ONE - THE CALL

God calls two groups of people together as a result of a dream they all had of a remote jungle village under attack. The infant children of that village have been taken from their families and thrown into a roaring fire as a sacrifice to evil gods of the attacking tribe. Then those having the dream see Isaiah in the temple having a vision and God asking, "Who can I send?" Isaiah answers; "Send me."* They see that as a call to them. Through prayer they are finally guided to the country of Paraguay.

The first group is in Ogunquit, Maine and made up of:

Bekah Ryan. She owns a one hundred acre apple orchard outside of Ogunquit, Maine. She came into possession of a jewel encrusted golden crucifix that her grandmother held for her until her death. It was enclosed in a letter which revealed that her biological mother was the daughter of the Chief of the tribe where her father was a Missionary in Paraguay. Her mother had died in childbirth. Six months later her father married Fuego, the daughter of the shaman of the village, and they moved with Bekah to the United States.

Renato is sixty-seven and was also born in Paraguay, but moved with his father to the U. S. when he was thirteen. They started working at the apple orchard. Renato was now the foreman. Bekah was a daughter of his heart, if not by blood.

Sylvia Jessup and Roberta Albright are employees of Bekah's at her needlework store, "The Eye of the Needle". Joe Albright is Ro-

---

* Isaiah 6:1-8

berta's husband. These three stay in Ogunquit to be a base of operations stateside. They also head up a growing prayer team.

Joshua Randall had the dream first and was directed by God to find Bekah. He is a Mission's Director at a church in Claremore, Oklahoma and part-time C.I.A. operative.

Ted Ryan is Bekah's ex-husband. He and Bekah divorced several years ago. One reason God called him was to fund the project.

The second group is in the remote jungles of northeast Paraguay.

Daniel Albright just happens to be the brother of Joe Albright and a Missionary these last four years to a remote village on a river bordering Brazil, known as the "village by the big rock".

Sherry Albright, his wife, is a nurse midwife, and the nearest thing to a doctor within twenty-five miles.

Edwardo is the young Pastor Daniel is working with at the village.

Connie is his wife. She heads up the prayer team in Paraguay, and coordinates with Sylvia and Roberta stateside.

A baby boy is saved from the sacrificial fires in a burning village and sent down river by his mother in a reed basket along with a gold and jewel encrusted crucifix, similar, but larger than the one Bekah has.

Bekah tries to get her crucifix examined and picks the wrong jeweler. Haydon Carlton is motivated by greed and immediately starts trying to obtain the crucifix using whatever means are necessary, legal or not. One of Haydon's employees, Carlos Rampone, ransacks Bekah's house looking for the crucifix, but comes up empty handed.

Prayers are prayed and decisions are made and Josh, Bekah, Renato and Ted head for Paraguay, but the shadow of Haydon Carlton follows them. He has employed Esteban Montero in Paraguay, to find them and get the crucifix, by whatever means are necessary.

During their plane ride to Puerto Bahía Negra, Josh talks to his friend from the C.I.A., Isaac Klein. Josh asks him to see if he can find out any information on Esteban Montero.

They touch down and meet Daniel and four young men of the village who are part of the small group of believers at the village. Several boats have been rented to bring back all the supplies the visitors brought with them to the village. They will spend one day in Puerto Bahía Negra and then head back to the village.

Through supernatural intervention lives are saved and more and more people turn to God. Satan is fighting with all his demonic hoards to stop this move of God; but, through prayer and faith, God's people overcome the wiles of the devil.

PROLOGUE

PARAGUAY
THE JUNGLE

It had been almost a week since the village had been attacked. All the villages in the vicinity feared this large and powerful tribe. They feared their strength and brutality, but they also feared their gods. They were powerful and cruel. They also practiced the dark arts and these infant sacrifices gave them power. When they saw who was attacking, they lost hope. No one had ever been able to force them back, to win the fight. A few warriors fought, but that was because their babies had been taken. They prayed to their god, but it appeared they had been abandoned.

The brutality of the attack had left the remnant surrounded by death and destruction. The fires were finally dying down, but the stench of burnt flesh still hung in the sultry air. It was a constant stench in the nostrils of those left, causing them to relive the moments of that encounter over and over again. No one was exempt from the mental flashbacks.

The noise of the fire had been horrendous, but the screams of the mothers as their infants were ripped from their arms was an unearthly sound that surely had to carry up to the ears of God. The savagery of the attackers was exacerbated by the hideous glee they showed as the infants were thrown into the raging fire, a sacrifice to their evil gods. It appeared as if Satan himself was celebrating.

This particular tribe had been ravaging this area of the jungle for as long as memory lasted. Their last attack on this village had been over ten years ago, and was still remembered with horror. This time, fourteen infants had been sacrificed and it appeared that with their death the hope of the village had died also.

Slowly the survivors came together, seeking the living to help bury the dead. Since the Chief and his son were dead, one of his advisors had assumed leadership. They gathered the injured and treated their wounds. Then they dealt with the task of digging the graves.

It had been almost a week since the carnage had taken place. Those who were going to die had died. Those who were going to live were departing, leaving the burnt-out village deserted. There was no one in sight, but many graves littered the landscape and smoke still rose from the charred ruins. The ground cried out, echoing the screams and replaying the horror that had taken place as the remnant, traveling through the nearby jungle, made an exodus.[1] They left behind their past, all their hopes and dreams, and were walking into an unknown future. The echoes of this calamity would be with them always if they remained. Walking without hope or direction, they put one foot in front of the other, continuing on with no sense of time or distance. Instinct told them to follow the river; it was their lifeblood, whether they realized it or not.

The body of the dead Chief's young wife had been found by the river. The survivors assumed her infant son had fallen prey to the same depraved sacrilege that had claimed the lives of all the other infants of the village. However his mother, prompted by a dream, had fashioned a basket out of reeds and sent him down the river, along with a talisman of the God she prayed to.

Little did the remnant realize that their steps were now being directed by God, one they did not know. God, having heard the prayer of that young mother, determined that the fullness of time had come. He was sending a group of people He had called in a dream,

---

[1] Genesis 4:10

to bring a message of hope to the hopeless, and to engage the enemy, and his forces, in this pivotal battle. It was not for just their village, but for all of mankind.

Eleven people had received an invitation to volunteer in God's army. He was directing all paths to the village by the big rock on the bend in the river. As the crow flies, it was about twenty-five miles north of Puerto Bahía Negra, and twenty miles south of the burnt out village. God was marshalling His forces for an epic battle, and this small village was the staging point. A small army, in the corner of a small nation, would herald in the beginning of the demise of the "prince of this world".[2]

Four people left Ogunquit, Maine to answer God's call to the jungles of Paraguay. Three stayed behind to form a prayer guard, and be coordinators of the quest. Joshua Randall assumed leadership of the group traveling to Paraguay based on his experience and his calling from God. Bekah Ryan was the pivot point of all the dreams. They had been directed to seek her out and offer their help to complete the quest. Renato, the elder of the group, supplied a sense of stability, and Ted, Bekah's ex-husband, had been called to fund the group. These four had been sent to Paraguay, to a native village in which Daniel and Sherry Albright had been missionaries for over four years. Edwardo and Connie were the young pastors of a small group of Christians in the village. God also sent dreams to these four to become part of this quest.

Just as the fullness of time had been necessary to usher in the birth of Jesus, the fullness of time had now been reached to justify His return. When God's plan is completed, the trumpet will sound, and the end will come as promised.[3] There are many ideas and teachings about the end, but we all see through a glass darkly and so the future is still unclear.[4] Certain things have to take place

[2] John 12:31
[3] Matthew 24:14
[4] 1 Corinthians 13:12

before this can happen. We know there will be wars and rumors of war, famine, earthquakes and persecution. We must put our trust in God. We must do the work of God while it is still day for darkness is coming.[5] The enemy is gathering his forces because he knows the final battle is near.

[5] John 9:4

CHAPTER ONE

PARAGUAY, JUNE 12
PUERTO BAHÍA NEGRA

Bekah woke and just for a moment was disoriented. Then she smiled and pushed aside any cares or concerns. They were in Paraguay, and on their way to fulfill the quest that God had called them to. Because it was so late when they had finally unloaded the plane, it was decided to sleep with the supplies that had been offloaded to the side of the runway and transport them to the marina in the morning.

They had already secured three extra boats, but realized last night that at least one more boat would be needed to accommodate all the provisions that had been purchased. Unfortunately, there were no other boats available. It would be necessary for them to wait one more day for a boat to return from upriver.

As disappointing as this was, they decided to put the time to good use. Daniel suggested going through the stores in Puerto Bahía Negra to secure any last minute items. Bekah thought this was a good idea since she had not had much time to shop back in Maine. Their departure had been hurried due to circumstances surrounding the quest. As the sun came up, Bekah looked around the town; there did not appear to be many stores. Daniel saw her look of disappointment and said, “Don’t let the lack of stores fool you. Almost everyone has something to sell. You just need to be a smart shopper."

Ted, Bekah, Renato and Daniel had an adventurous day of shopping. True to his word, Daniel took them into every nook and cranny of the town. Bekah's find of the day was a manual sewing machine and five bolts of cloth that would make wonderful shirts and dresses; she was sure she would be able to teach someone how to use it. She also found two extra pairs of sneakers in her size and a dozen pairs of flip flops.

Daniel mentioned that everyone in the village drank a lot of tea. She found a large case of it to share with the ladies of the village, especially with Sherry. She was looking forward to meeting Sherry. They had talked on the satellite phone a few times, but personal contact with Sherry would carry their relationship to a higher level. She had been in the company of men for the last few days and looked forward to spending time with another woman.

Bekah also thought of the things she had brought down from Maine and a smile bloomed on her face. She brought Sherry several large bottles of quality shampoo and conditioner and several bars of a premium brand facial soap. She brought a case of laundry detergent and dish washing detergent. Even if Sherry was able to get these particular items, it would save her the money. All in all, it was a perfect day. The only flaw was the delay in getting to the village.

They arrived back at the marina to find the rest of the men working hard and sweating freely in the heat and humidity. Bekah felt guilty. She had been enjoying herself while they had been hard at work. No one seemed to begrudge her and they all smiled and waved as the group walked by.

"What are you doing?" she asked Josh as she walked up to him.

He was as dirty and sweaty as the rest of the men, but he grinned at her, "Did you have a good time? Did you find any treasures?"

"Yes I did, to both questions." Bekah's eyes twinkled with

glee as she told him of the special finds.

"Well I hope it won't take up too much room. We may have to build a raft and tow it behind one of the boats," laughed Josh. "We're trying to divide the supplies into five boatloads and we're having a hard time. Luckily, one boat is bigger than the rest and will give us a little more room."

Bekah immediately felt chagrin at herself for not thinking of the already heavy load. She hoped they would be able to fit it all aboard. She saw Josh's head turn as he watched the three large boxes being added to the pile of supplies that still needed to be loaded. If he had a comment, he kept it to himself. She hoped no one was annoyed at her for adding to an already difficult task.

"The men are going to stay on the boats tonight to guard the supplies," said Josh. "We four will have one night in the lap of luxury, figuratively speaking. There is a hotel of sorts here with running water and air conditioning. There's also a restaurant on the ground floor. With God's grace, the food will be good and the shower will be hot. We're almost done here and that shower is already calling my name. The only fly in the ointment is we will have to get up at four to get underway by first light. I'll see all of you at dinner in about an hour. Your bags are in your room."

Josh turned away to finish his work and Bekah, Renato, Ted and Daniel walked to the hotel. Daniel informed them he would be eating with his men and sleeping on one of the boats. "There's still a chance of thieves, especially with the large amount of goods we have. Hopefully our sleeping on the boats will be enough of a deterrent."

After everyone was cleaned up and refreshed, they met at the restaurant. It had a very limited menu – baked chicken and rice. Bekah was unsure whether it was the company or the cook, but it was surprisingly tasty. After dinner they turned in early – morning would come quickly.

CHAPTER TWO

JUNE 13
THE RIVER

Morning had broken on the river, and a cacophony of sound was emanating from the surrounding jungle as five heavily laden boats motored slowly up the river. The howler monkeys were warming up for a rousing chorus as the sun rose above the tree line. Birds of bold color and loud song flew through the branches, splashing their colors all along the meandering river. Insects started to buzz and whine as they prepared for their daily meal. The dinner bell had sounded, breakfast was being served, and anyone unlucky enough to be in the area was on the menu.

Bekah stood on the side of the boat and watched the changing scenery with enthusiastic interest. She felt like a small child who was on her way to Disneyland. At every bend in the river she wanted to ask, “Are we there yet?”

She had sprayed herself with repellent to keep the insects at bay. It helped to some extent. The bugs didn’t bite, but they came close enough to inspect a prospective meal, and to announce their presence with an annoying whine. This elicited the wave of a hand in a fruitless attempt to chase them away.

Yesterday evening they had finished loading Daniel’s boat, and the four extra boats that had been secured to carry their additional supplies. Now, a total of five boats were loaded to capacity and heading upriver. As soon as the sky started to show pink, they embarked. Progress was slow. They were going against a current, and the boats all sat low in the water because of their heavy load.

It became obvious to Bekah after four hours of motoring that the men were taking care of their needs off the back of the boats. It was becoming more and more obvious that hers needs must be taken care of, and that this would require stopping the boat. She went over to Josh and explained her problem. "I was wondering about your bladder capacity," he laughed. "I heard the men talking earlier, making wagers as to how long you would last."

Bekah blushed hotly and said with exasperation, "I hope you didn't participate."

Josh flashed a huge grin and replied, "Everyone did. I'm just sorry to say I've already lost. I hope you will be a good sport about it. They meant no harm."

"Oh I'll be a good sport alright, but I'll find a way to get even. You can count on that." Bekah smiled up at him and it brightened his day. She had been raised by her grandmother on their apple orchard in Ogunquit Maine. After her grandmother had recently died, the family lawyer had delivered a letter to Bekah from her grandmother that he had been holding for over a year with orders to deliver it upon her death. In the letter Bekah discovered she had been born in Paraguay and that her mother had been the daughter of a Chief. There was also a jewel encrusted crucifix on a large gold chain that the letter said came from her mother. Yet, in spite of all the mystery, confusion and pressure, Bekah still had the ability to smile.

The boats signaled to each other and they looked for a stretch of riverbank where they could pull over. It took a few minutes, but a place was found where they could tie up to some overhanging trees and pull up close enough to let Bekah off with a word of caution. "Don't go too far, and don't touch anything," she was told.

She grabbed a vine and used it to help her jump ashore.

The jungle was very dense and she had to push through a tangle of assorted undergrowth. When she did, she felt the jungle close behind her. Immediately she felt cut off from the rest of the group. She felt as though the trees were moving in and cutting her off from the rest of the world. She did not go more than fifteen feet before she stopped and took care of business. Anxious to get back to the security of the boat, she stood up, rearranged her clothes, and turned to retrace her steps. "It would be very easy to lose your sense of direction and get lost in here," Bekah mused. As she started to head back in the direction she had come from, a tall, bearded man dressed in khaki pants stepped out of the dense foliage and blocked her path. His face was blackened with some kind of paint and he carried a machete. Bekah stepped back in surprise as the man reached out and grabbed her; she hollered for help. The man tightened his grip and began to run, dragging her behind him. She got out one more call, before the man turned and hit her on the side of the head. Darkness overpowered her.

Bekah's next conscious thought was, "I smell smoke." Then she heard drums sounding in the distance. "Oh my God," she realized, "this is my dream come to life!" Bekah and all the members of the quest had two dreams. The original dream was of God calling them to help a tribe in the Paraguayan jungle. The second dream was of Bekah being chased in a burning jungle and hearing drums in the background. Bekah was reminded that she had people praying for her, both in Maine and in Paraguay. She thanked God His hand was upon her and determined to not whine or complain, but to put her trust in Him.

She took stock of her situation and saw she was at the side of a small clearing of some kind, whether manmade or natural, she could not tell at the moment. Then she became aware of the burnt smell in the air and realized that a small portion of the jungle had been burnt off to make this clearing. She saw several rakes leaning on a tree nearby. They appeared to have been used to rake away the debris left by the fire.

As Bekah began to move, she also became aware of the injuries she had sustained during her capture and transport to this place. Her left eye was swollen and painful to touch as a result of being hit. The side of her face was throbbing along with the drumbeats. Her whole body was covered in a multitude of scrapes and bruises of varying sizes, and depths. The clothes she was wearing were torn and shredded, and both her shoes were gone. Her long dark hair was matted and dirty, and her throat was sore from the smoke she had inhaled while being dragged to this clearing. She also had a monumental thirst.

Bekah did not know how far she had been dragged, but if the cuts and scrapes were any indication, it had been some distance. She realized that her hands were bound with a vine of some kind, but her feet were free. Judging by the lack of shadows, it looked to be midday. There was still the obvious smell of smoke, and curls of it could be seen in the trees overhead as it rose up into the jungle canopy. From the thickness of it, some burning must still be going on in the surrounding area.

As Bekah contemplated her situation, she thought of Paul and Silas. After they had been beaten and thrown into prison, they were then placed in stocks to further confine them.[6] She thought of what they did in the midst of their situation. They lifted their voices and sang praises to God. Bekah slowly sat up and despite her sore throat, and her current situation, lifted her voice and began to sing. Even though her throat was irritated with the smoke that continued to infiltrate the area, her voice rose soft but clear.

Bekah had started singing when she was a small child. Her voice was known throughout her town and the surrounding area. She was asked to sing at all the local weddings and funerals. It was said she had the voice of an angel. Now she took

[6] Acts 16:22-26

a breath and lifted it, making a beautiful sound that rose up to heaven in a song of praise to a mighty God.

"Amazing grace how sweet the sound, that saved a wretch like me.

I once was lost, but now am found; was blind but now I see.

Through many dangers, toils and snares, I have already come;

Tis grace hath brought me safe thus far, and grace will lead me home." [7]

Bekah took another breath and sang the second verse. The words seemed to encourage her. She was lost right now, but God knew where she was, and He would see to it that she was found. She thanked Him for His grace and mercy, and the strength He gave her to do her part.

Bekah looked around. There didn't appear to be anyone nearby. She heard voices in the distance, but they posed no immediate threat to her. She stood up slowly, careful not to lose her balance, and assessed her situation.

The clearing before her was black with soot. She looked down at herself and saw that she was covered with dirt, but not with soot, which meant she had not been dragged across the clearing, but dropped at its outer perimeter. She assumed this was where they had exited the jungle, and hoped it was the way back; because that was the only clue she had as to which route to take. She was glad the noise she heard was coming from the opposite direction. She couldn't determine where the smoke was coming from; it appeared to surround her.

Turning her back on the clearing, her only recourse was to enter the jungle. As she set out, the multitude of cuts and scrapes that covered most of her body began to burn as she moved, and

[7] Amazing Grace, Public Domain.

her feet screamed in torment, but desperation was an anodyne, and she kept on putting one foot ahead of the other until she had fully penetrated the dense jungle. Struggling with the vine about her wrists, Bekah failed to see the large rock obstructing her path and tripped over it. She landed hard, her bound hands preventing her from deflecting the impact. Bekah clenched her teeth together to keep from crying out. Then, realizing this might be the answer to getting free from the vine, Bekah painfully raised herself up. Using the sharp rock, she began to saw at the vines on her wrists. She bit her lip in pain as the rock also abraded her tender flesh, but she kept sawing, knowing she had to get her hands free in order to have a chance at escape. Finally, the vines snapped, and fell from her wrists. Ignoring the pain, Bekah wiped the blood off on what was left of her clothes and headed further into the jungle. As she moved forward, one thing was made apparent immediately, her insistent thirst. Sweating and breathing smoke for several hours had irritated her throat, and her mouth was so dry it was difficult to swallow. This was just one more reason she needed to find that river.

There had been a light breeze blowing, cooling her face. It abruptly shifted and began to blow from behind her. With the change in direction, Bekah noticed that the smell of smoke had become stronger. Still hearing the drumbeat in the background, she was reminded again of her dream.

Suddenly she became aware of movement around her. Monkeys and other tree dwelling animals were moving hurriedly through the canopy, chattering and screeching as they went. The jungle floor appeared to be alive with animals, large and small, all moving in one direction. They too must smell the smoke and were attempting to escape it. Bekah surmised they were all moving toward the river and she decided to join the exodus. She only hoped that someone was still in the vicinity to come to her rescue.

The wind continued to increase, though the breeze at her back was no longer cool. It was hot, and getting hotter as the minutes passed. She dreaded the thought of what this signified. There was a fire behind her, consuming everything in its path, and it was advancing too fast for her to out run it. She needed to pick up her pace if she was going to have any chance to stay ahead of it. Running in earnest, the pain in her feet was forgotten, now replaced by the fear of the fire. All the animals in the jungle were in full flight and paid no attention to her as they ran by. Given the current situation, the fire was more of an enemy and source of fear than she was.

A wild boar of enormous proportion passed by her without a sidelong glance; focused as he was on his own escape. She saw the large, yellowed tusks on the sides of his head and shuddered, remembering the two women in the village they were heading to who had been gored by the same type of animal. His size left a path as he pushed through the jungle growth, and she decided to follow him, assuming he knew the way to the river better than she did.

Bekah became aware of a growing sound, a loud roar coming from behind her. It was the sound of the fire, and its volume drowned out everything else. She could feel the heat of it envelope her, making it hard to breath. Smoke-filled air burned her already irritated lungs and throat. Burning embers began blowing past her and raining down on her, leaving blisters in their place. Unmindful of where she was stepping, Bekah ran, pulling on all her reserves in an attempt to outdistance the raging inferno. It was moving swiftly across the landscape, but she needed to be faster. She had no idea how far it was to the river, but time was running out.

Abruptly, the trees opened up, and there before her was a gathering of animals standing on a small embankment above the river. Some had already taken the plunge to swim to the other side. Bekah stood there for a moment transfixed, watching them as they all jumped in. The heat and smoke of the fire gave impetus to their flight, and she willingly took the plunge, even though she did not know how deep the water was, or what was on the other side. The water enveloped Bekah for a moment, cooling her overheated body. As she rose and broke the surface, she tried to tread water for a few moments to get her bearings, but immediately, the current captured her and began to propel her downstream.

The water was brown and swirled in several places, making whirlpools that sucked the smaller animals into them just as black holes sucked in space debris. There were all sorts of small creatures surrounding her that she was unable to identify, but her companions in the water were no threat to her at the moment, just as she was no threat to them. They were fixated on the same distant shore she was. She saw the wild boar about twenty feet ahead of her, and heard something large splash into the water at her back. She did not take the time to turn and look; her immediate threat was the fire that roared behind her. The current of the river carried her swiftly downstream, gratefully away from the ravages of the fire, but unfortunately farther and farther away from where she thought the flotilla of boats were and any hope of rescue.

Swimming and praying, Bekah struggled to make headway. The menagerie of animals that surrounded her hindered her progress. The smaller ones attempted to hitch a ride by climbing on her back. The larger ones continually bumped into her as all of them labored to reach the far shore. Adrenalin was wearing off and the trauma of her capture and all the subsequent events was catching up with her, draining what little energy she had left. Looking up, the distant shore seemed no closer, and Bekah could feel exhaustion setting in. The current tugged on her. It would be so much easier to just go with the flow. She felt her body slowly relaxing, letting the cool water cradle her as she sank into its murky depth. Suddenly a powerful arm reached out and grabbed her. Bekah had no more fight left. She just let herself go, too depleted to even offer up a token of resistance. The blessed peace of oblivion took her in its arms and she closed her eyes. Her last thought was, "God, forgive me, I've failed You.

CHAPTER THREE

JUNE 13
THE RIVER

Josh struggled against the current, dragging Bekah with him. He was grateful that Daniel had insisted they tie a rope to him before he dove into the river, only now realizing how powerful the current was as it worked against his progress. He recognized now, in the middle of the river, that trying to resist the pull of the current while dragging Bekah with him would have overwhelmed them both.

He kept a tight hold on her, allowing the rope to tow him to the boat where several people waited to help them. He drew Bekah to him as he grabbed the side of the boat, not wanting to lose her in the process. Josh pushed her toward the lowered arms waiting to lift her out of the water.

Ted stood by with a blanket to wrap around Bekah. Other hands reached down and helped Josh onto the boat. Josh made his way over to where Renato stood praying quietly under his breath, and thanking God for the life of his adopted daughter.

Ted laid Bekah down on the boxes of supplies they had brought from Asunción. He looked down at her pale and bruised face, and said a quiet prayer. He had been married to Bekah ten years ago and let ambition and greed come between them. Looking at her now, he realized there was still some love in his heart for this woman, but a different kind of love.

Now, as a new believer, God had called him to this quest to work alongside Bekah and the rest of the people involved. He realized that he loved all of them. This was a new thing for Ted and he was excited to feel these new emotions. In the past, the only person he had loved was himself. He was also touched by the love these people had for him. He was eager to see God move, leading and guiding them through the labyrinth of challenges that lay before them.

God had called him to finance this project. He was glad to find a way to use what had been weakness and sin in his life previously to now further the Gospel of God. It was the love of money that caused him to lose Bekah and turn from God's gentle tug on his heart. Now, he had a great deal of wealth, but he did not love it. He used it in many ways, one of which was to fund this quest.[8]

Josh came over, dripping water, with a rope still tied to his waist. He grabbed a blanket to dry himself and bent down to assess whether Bekah was breathing on her own.

He took her wrist and counted her pulse, it was racing, but strong. She did not appear to have any broken bones. What she did have were some deep cuts and scrapes all over her body and a large purple bruise that covered most of the left side of her face causing her eye to swell shut.

Most of the afternoon went by before Bekah began to moan quietly and slowly regain consciousness. Suddenly she woke and sat up. She raised her arms in a violent motion, as though warding off an attack. Renato called gently to her and she looked around seeing all the faces staring at her with concern. Tears began to fall down her cheeks and she started to sob in earnest. Renato pushed his way over to her and took her in his arms as a father would his daughter. "Are you hurt badly my

---

[8] 1 Timothy 6:10

sweet girl?" he asked gently. Bekah shook her head, "No," but continued to cry. The stress and trauma of the last several hours had taken their toll physically and emotionally. Renato continued to hold her close, and talk quiet words of encouragement, comfort, and love. After a time, Bekah stopped crying and fell asleep again. Renato gently laid her back down. Josh went and spread another blanket over her. She didn't move one muscle.

Despite what appeared to be a dangerous situation, Josh and Daniel decided to stay tied up to the shoreline. Each boat was assigned a rotating watch during the night. Daniel called Sherry and let her know what had happened and that they were staying where they were so that they could go back through the charred remains of the fire tomorrow. They wanted to look for any signs of Bekah's kidnapper and any camp she might have been brought to. They would be arriving at the village a day or two later than usual, not just because of what had happened to Bekah, but because they were not making good time. The heavily laden boats were sitting so low in the river that they were impeding progress.

Daniel had never taken this much time to travel on the river and he was frustrated wasting a day to search for evidence. He understood that this abduction could be more than just jungle marauders. Josh said that they needed to check that out. Daniel was just impatient to get back to Sherry. He didn't like leaving her under normal circumstances, but given the turmoil in the village and the recent attack on Sherry's life, he was feeling very protective. God was moving in their village, people were turning their lives to God, and the enemy was fighting back. Daniel felt as though his forces were divided. He wanted everyone back together again.

Daniel decided to give the new satellite phone a try and called Sherry. She picked up on the third ring and sounded so happy to hear him. His heart felt full of joy at the sound of her voice. The relationship the two of them had was very special. Daniel knew Sherry felt the same way. They had started dating in high school and that was the end of their dating career. They each knew they had found their soul mate and needed to look no further.

Daniel and Sherry talked for about ten minutes. He gave her an update on Bekah. He had called her earlier to ask for prayer after Bekah had been abducted. They both thanked God for His grace and mercy and asked for His continued guidance and protection. After a tender, “Good-bye”, they both turned in for the night.

CHAPTER FOUR

JUNE 14
THE RIVER

It was still dark, but the eastern sky was awash with the colors of dawn when Bekah next opened her right eye. Her eyes were a beautiful dark brown, but were still red-rimmed from the irritation of the smoke and her left eye was still swollen shut. She had yet to speak, and could feel the pain and burning in her throat, a side effect of the smoke she had breathed and of her raging thirst which had yet to be quenched.

Bekah lay still for a moment. She did not know how long she had slept, but it had been a deep and dreamless sleep. Her body had been battered from the capture and subsequent dragging across the jungle. She could feel every bruise, cut and scrape. Her left eye still hurt, and she raised her hand to touch it. She could feel her hand tremble, whether from exhaustion or pain, both physical and emotional, she could only guess. Though her eye was still swollen, her sight did not appear to be affected in the other eye.

She slowly turned her head to see where she was and what was around her. The muscles in her arms, shoulders, neck and back joined their voices in a crescendo of pain. Bekah grimaced, and let out a soft groan.

At the sound of the groan, a figure emerged from the darkness and moved toward her. It was Josh. He had been sitting on the floor; resting against some of the boxes they were transporting to the village where Daniel had his mission compound. They had five boats sitting heavy in the water packed with building supplies, tools, gifts for the people, and anything else they felt they would need for the next few weeks. They even had five crates holding five chickens apiece that Daniel used for eating, and trading. The eggs they produced also tasted delicious at breakfast time.

Josh came over to her and squatted at her side. He laid his hand gently on her forehead and felt for heat. "Good," he thought, "no heat, no fever." Josh had been awake all night keeping a vigil and watching for any movement in the jungle that might suggest an attack. He had seen nothing, but that did not necessarily mean that no one was there. The jungle hid a myriad of dangers and mysteries; attacks being just one of them.

He had also spent the night observing Bekah. Even in her present condition, she was lovely to look at. She was small framed and slim, but had an attractive figure that curved in the right places. Her face was not one of exceptional beauty, but her inner peace and strength of character, plus a glow that seemed to radiate from within, transformed her into a work of art. Josh felt his heart respond to an attraction he had not experienced in a long time. He pushed that aside, realizing it was not the time or the place to explore those feelings. Bekah attempted to sit up and the movement brought him into focus before his mind could travel back to painful thoughts and times.

As Bekah rose to a sitting position with Josh's assistance, the blanket slid down to her lap and she realized she was only wearing her bra and panties. Bekah grabbed the blanket and pulled it up to cover herself. Josh explained that her blouse and skirt had been torn to shreds, and they had removed them when they treated the cuts and scrapes all over her body. The river had done a good job of cleansing the mud and dirt from the multitude of wounds, but some of them were deep, especially on her feet, and her right shoulder and hip. They must have borne the brunt of walking, and then being dragged through the jungle.

"Sit still now. Don't try to get up unless absolutely necessary. Your feet are a mess. We've put some healing cream on them that the villagers use all the time. Daniel says that even Sherry uses it. She says it has wonderful healing properties. We've also been praying for you, and alerted the prayer army in Maine. The extra satellite phone has already proved its worth. It was a miracle in itself that you came out of the jungle where you did and that we saw you. You must have been a few miles upriver, because the current was fast and carried you down for a distance. We haven't seen where the fire burnt through yet. We should see it shortly after we take off this morning. If possible, Daniel and I are going to backtrack through its path and see if we can find out where you were brought and if anything was left behind; maybe there are some clues as to whom your captors were. Even though the enemy tried to kill you and defeat our quest, God was with us and answered our prayers."

Bekah looked up at Josh and attempted to grasp all he was saying, but her raging thirst was an overwhelming distraction. "Water," her irritated voice whispered. "Can I please have a drink of water?"

Josh reached back behind him and grabbed a bottle of water. He had anticipated that need even before she had awakened. He opened the bottle and gave it to her, propping her up so she could use both hands to hold it. He noticed the quiver in her limbs and realized how weak she must be. Again, Josh had anticipated her need. He reached over to where he had been sitting and grabbed a bowl containing a banana and an assortment of fruit she did not recognize. "You haven't really eaten or drunk anything since yesterday morning. That's probably one of the reasons you're shaking. Try to take a few bites of the banana, it's a good energy food and easy to swallow."

Bekah smiled gratefully. She had already drained half the bottle of water, and the emptiness of her stomach made itself known to those within earshot. She took a bite of the banana, and the sweetness and flavor of it exploded in her mouth. "Tastes good," Josh stated, "doesn't it? We don't get to eat ripe picked fruit very often back home, though you must taste it with your apples, picking them and eating them ripe from the tree."

Bekah owned an apple orchard outside of Ogunquit, Maine. Besides growing apples, she loved to garden. She kept a large one and used the surplus to supply a small food bank she ran out of her needlework shop in town. Bekah was known far and wide for her generosity, and her cooking. She loved to cook, and was very good at it.

"I don't know if I have ever eaten anything that tasted so good," responded Bekah. "I know hunger enhances flavor, but this tastes incredible. " Bekah leaned back against a box and sat quietly for a moment. "I really didn't wander far into the jungle," Bekah said apologetically. "I only went about ten feet. I never even saw where the man came from. He startled me, and I didn't react as quickly as I normally would have."

"Bekah," Josh replied reassuringly, "it wasn't your fault. The native men we are traveling with told me they have had to keep a constant watch for ambush. These warriors watch from the shore for a boat to go by and then follow it up river, waiting for them to tie up on the shore. Then they attack. You're going ashore must have given one of them an opportunity he couldn't refuse. Any one of us could have been the one who needed to go ashore. Surprise gave him an advantage. These are not men of the village, but marauders who roam the shoreline. They are like the highwaymen of old, looking for opportunities to profit in whatever way they can." Josh patted her shoulder reassuringly and reseated himself against the boxes of cargo opposite her. He asked Bekah, "Do you feel up to answering a few questions?"

"Sure," she replied with a strengthening voice, "but let me ask one of mine first." Josh waited for her to go on. "Who was it who pulled me from the water, and how did you all find me?"

Josh replied, "Well I pulled you from the water, only because we determined that I was the best swimmer. We found you only because of the fire. We saw it starting to grow and thankfully, assumed rightly, that anyone alive would try to make their way to the river. As we were motoring up the river, we saw you drifting downriver surrounded by a large collection of other creatures trying to escape the burning jungle and reach the other side.

"Four of us had gone into the jungle and attempted to track you, but the undergrowth was so thick we couldn't find the trail. The stranger must have carried you for a distance. He probably only dragged you after he got tired. We also remembered the dream of you being lost in a jungle fire and prayed God would lead you to safety."

"And He did," Bekah responded. "When all the animals started running, I assumed they were running for the river to get away from the fire. Thank God I was right. When I jumped in the water I didn't see the boats. I was only aware of the roaring fire and all the animals around me. Thank God the river was near. I don't think I could have run much further. When I attempted to swim to the other side, it was a lot further across than I had originally thought. I'm grateful you were there to rescue me because I knew my strength was giving out."

Bekah paused in her narrative. She thought about the quest God had called them to. He asked them to bring a message of hope, the 'Good News' of the Gospel, and of the saving grace of Jesus Christ to Daniel's village, to the village in the dream, and to any other village they might visit.

According to their dream, there was a village living in spiritual darkness, and they had been sent to bring them the Light of the Gospel. Only God could free them from the traps the enemy had put in their paths.[9] Jesus came to set people free, not to ensnare them.[10] He came to destroy the works of the enemy.[11]

God had asked them in a dream to come to Paraguay and be part of His army, fighting physically and spiritually against His enemy, the Devil. Just as God had His army, the people He had called to His quest, the enemy also had an army. Knowing his time was short, Satan was using all his resources to turn the tide of battle in his favor. So far, it appeared as if the enemy had the upper hand, or at least the last word for now, but Bekah wasn't concerned. She knew that if God had called them, He would equip them with everything they needed.

Before they left Maine, Bekah's home had been broken into and ransacked, possibly by someone looking for the golden, jewel-encrusted crucifix Bekah's Nana Sara had held for her since she was an infant. It had been given to Bekah by her mother, who was from Paraguay. In fact, Bekah had only found out in a letter her grandmother had written to her before she died, that Bekah herself had been born in Paraguay, and that her mother had been the chief's daughter.

The man they suspected of being responsible for the break-in was a jeweler and collector of fine arts with a shop in New York City. He was an old friend of Ted's and Ted suggested that Josh and Bekah see him because he was someone they could trust, who would be able to authenticate the crucifix. The jeweler, Hayden Carlton, had shown an unnatural interest in the crucifix once he had seen it. He had attempted to buy it from them, sell it for them, and then, if their suspicions were correct, steal it from them.

When Bekah, Renato, Ted and Josh arrived in Paraguay, they were harassed while trying to purchase supplies for their

---

[9] John 10:10
[10] John 8:36
[11] 1 John 3:8

trip. Thankfully Daniel's name carried some weight, and José, the owner of the store knew him well and respected him. José had taken a shotgun from behind the counter and forced the troublemaker to leave. The trouble maker was well known in the community; his name was Esteban Montero. José warned the four of them that care should be taken, because this man Montero was a formidable enemy.

Josh asked one of his contacts in the C.I.A. to check out the name of Esteban Montero. Josh still worked for the C.I.A. on a part-time basis. He only had a short time left on his commitment and then he would be able to sever his ties with them and be free of that responsibility. His friend, Isaac Klein, who also worked for the C.I.A. put a search out for information on Montero and found he was a bounty hunter with a bad reputation. He only took on "Wanted Dead or Alive" cases, and always returned his captives dead. It appeared that Satan was already hard at work trying to sabotage the quest to which God had called them. Satan had willing pawns in all parts of the earth he manipulated in order to complete his agenda. The most recent attack of the enemy appeared to be this abduction and jungle fire.

As Bekah gave her head a shake and refocused, she announced, "I'm feeling so much better and stronger. Do you think you can get me some clothes to put on so I can get up and walk around? What time is it? When will we start out again? I seem to have hundreds of questions now that I am thinking more clearly."

Josh stood up. He looked down at Bekah and tried to evaluate her alertness. Was she thinking clearly? Just now, she seemed to lose touch for a few moments, but she probably had countless thoughts running through her mind. Every once in a while he had to step back from a conversation to analyze a particular thought or problem. He saw her upturned face. It was eager with anticipation. She wanted to know what was happening, and that was a good thing. It confirmed she was connected with her situation and the circumstances surrounding her.

Josh replied to her excited questions with ones of his own. He felt it better to err on the side of caution right now, rather than let her get up and move around too quickly. "How do you feel? Are you weak or dizzy? How is your eyesight? Do you have blurred vision?"

"I feel fine, my eyesight is great and I'm not dizzy," Bekah replied impatiently. "The only things that hurt are these scrapes and scratches, my feet, and my left eye, and they are feeling much better than they did yesterday. I'll have to start walking sooner or later, so I might as well try now. As far as my eyes go, I have two, and I can see out of the right one just fine. I'm sure as soon as the swelling goes down I'll see out of the left one without any difficulty. My vision isn't impaired. It's only the swelling that is limiting my sight."

Josh informed her, "Your feet were pretty bad. We put some more cream on them and on all the other cuts and scratches while you were sleeping. Some of them were exceptionally deep, and we'll need to have Sherry look at them when we get to the village. We motored up to the place where the fire occurred and stopped there for the night. It was getting late anyway and we wanted to backtrack and see if there was any evidence left where you were held. We're going to do that this morning right after breakfast. Then we are going to continue on to a small supply store and gas station just past halfway. We have to get extra tanks to fill with gas so the men will be able to bring the four boats we rented back to Puerto Bahía Negra. If everything goes as planned, we should get to the village before dark tomorrow. We're not moving very fast because we are sitting very low in the water, the river is against us, and still moving swiftly. Wait here while I get you some fresh clothes."

While she was sitting there waiting for Josh to come back, Bekah looked down and re-evaluated her injuries. She saw bruising and cuts and scrapes all over her body. She was thankful she had been unconscious while she was being dragged. She did not remember the experience at all.

Josh came back in a few minutes with a blouse and jumper and underwear she had purchased in Asunción. She was thankful they were loose fitting and would not irritate her injuries. He also had a pair of soft socks and the spare pair of sneakers she had purchased.

Josh held a blanket up to give her some privacy as she changed. She was expecting the cuts and abrasions to be especially painful, but they were not. Even her feet were not as painful as she had expected. "What's happening?" Bekah wondered. Just a short time ago she was groaning with pain, and now the pain was minimal.

Josh helped her put on her sneakers. This would be the real test of how much pain and discomfort she could stand. She stood gingerly first on one foot, then the other, again surprised at how negligible the pain was. Bekah sat down, took off her sneakers and socks, and grabbed one of her feet to look at the sole. There were still a few scrapes and cuts, but nothing like there had been yesterday afternoon. She grabbed the other foot and it was the same story.

"Josh, come over here and look at this," Bekah called excitedly. "This has to be a miracle. Most of my injuries are almost healed."

Josh looked, and his eyes widened with excitement also, "Yes they are. The native men told us the cream worked very well, but I think God had a hand in this. We prayed for you while you were missing, and after you were recovered. Now we can thank the Lord for answering our prayer." Josh grabbed Bekah's hand and prayed, "We know Lord that Your hand is upon us as we go forth in Your mighty Name, doing what You direct us to do. We thank You that You said Your grace is sufficient."[12]

[12] 2 Corinthians 12:9

Josh gave Bekah's hand a squeeze, looked up at her, and smiled. Bekah immediately felt a response to that smile. Warmth spread through her. She squeezed his hand, and then pulled back. "This is not the time or place for emotional distractions," she said to herself. "I better be careful with this."

Josh moved to the back of the boat to talk with one of the villagers, grateful for his fluency in Spanish. Then he stood and stared out at the river. He felt drawn to Bekah and he also needed to be cautious. Any other time or place he would welcome a warm and tender relationship with a woman such as Bekah. Other than church, he did not socialize a great deal, and in the last few years there had been no one special in his life. He had to admit he was lonely, but he trusted God to provide the person, the time and the place.

Sunrise made its appearance in a majestic display of color. God seemed to continually add new colors to His palette. The jungle began to stir, songbirds started to sing and parrots started to squawk. Insects began to whine and monkeys began to screech. No one needed an alarm clock; nature provided her own.

Josh came over to where Bekah was seated and told her she needed to take care of her personal needs; the boats were going to cast off in ten minutes. Bekah looked up at him in alarm, but he put a hand on her shoulder and said, "Don't worry; I'll go ashore with you. I'll give you privacy, but I won't be more than five feet away, and remember; now we're on the other side of the river."

Josh took her arm and helped her to her feet. Bekah was still somewhat shaky, but she straightened her back, held her head high, and refused to give in to any weakness. Bekah was determined not to be the weak link in this chain. She earnestly prayed there would be no weak links.

Josh took the time to explain to Bekah that he, Daniel, and Leonardo from the village were going to take one boat across the river and backtrack the fire. They wanted to see if they could find where the clearing was she had been taken to, and if any clues had been left behind.

Josh, Daniel and Leonardo motored slowly across the river and up to where the charred remains of the jungle gouged a wide swath. It appeared as though the fire was over one hundred yards in width. After fifteen minutes of walking through the charred jungle, all they had found were the burned remains of many small animals, and a few larger ones. One appeared to be a wild boar. According to Daniel, they were quite common and made up a large portion of the protein in the village's diet.

Most of the foliage had burned completely, but there were several pockets of greenery that had escaped. There were also a number of large trees and pieces of wood that were still smoldering, causing their eyes to burn and tear from the smoke.

Another half an hour went by and they came to what must be the clearing Bekah talked about. It appeared to be devoid of anything showing habitation. Then Leonardo called them over. Sticking out from some ashes were the mangled tines of a rake.

Josh picked it up and turned it over. Nothing was unusual about it except the question it elicited. "What was it doing here?" Maybe if they continued on they would find some answers.

They followed the burned out path for ten minutes more before it opened up into a larger clearing of approximately three or four acres. It looked as though someone was going to use this spot. It had been cleared for a reason.

"Let's spread out and take a look around. Call out if you see anything," Josh said. Then he started off across the smoking remains. They all wandered around the area for about an hour searching for clues. Had someone been living here? If so, what were they up to? So far, they had nothing to show for their efforts. It also appeared as if the clearing was the source of the fire. In walking the circumference, there was no road of ash leading into the clearing, only the one leading toward the river.

Josh called Daniel and Leonardo over. He suggested taking one of the many trails that led out of the encampment and seeing where it went to. He let Leonardo pick since he had the most experience with the jungle.

Leonardo stood for a moment and then turned and took a path to the north. The trail they were traveling had the appearance of being used recently. Its vines were broken and the tall grasses were flattened. “Many people have been down this trail recently,” he stated making further observations as they continued to walk.

About ten minutes down the trail Daniel held up his hand. “It's past noon and we have to get to the supply station today. Given the circumstances, I want to spend the night there. It will give us additional protection. Let’s turn back now. We can come down here another day when we are better prepared.”

They were all in agreement. They arrived back at the boat and motored over to where the rest of the boats were tied up. Everyone was concerned that they had been gone so long. Lunch had been over for an hour, but there were enough leftovers to feed the three of them. There was a short discussion about what they had found. Then with everyone fed and all needs tended to, the five boats cast off.

Bekah sat at the front of the boat, and excitement again bloomed in her eyes. She had a bottle of water at her side that she sipped regularly, since she was still somewhat dehydrated from her ordeal of yesterday. The water flowed down the river, and ever so slowly and the heavily laden boats motored up. The current varied according to the width and depth of the river.

Vines of different thicknesses and lengths hung from the canopy above. Birds of varying size and color landed on the vines and tree limbs that were draped over the river. Bekah kept glancing from one direction to another. The sights and sounds were incredible to behold.

Every bend in the river brought something new to appreciate. Small animals played near the shore, a family of otters swimming in the river, multitudes of large and small animals coming down to the river to drink. All of them took absolutely no notice of the passing boats. The fear of man had not yet been instilled in them.

Bekah wished she knew more about birds, or had a book to help identify them. She had never seen or heard such an abundance of them. Their colors were beyond description. She thought they were the most remarkable creatures she had ever seen. Maybe it was her love of color that caused such an infatuation. When she was a young girl she had saved her money to buy a box of sixty-four crayons. She remembered that she had taken out each crayon and marveled at the intensity of the color and the variety the box contained. She enjoyed that box of crayons until they had all been worn down to nubs.

She recalled her store in Ogunquit, Maine, The Eye of the Needle, and the hundreds of colors and kinds of yarns and threads that filled the shelves. Every time a new color came out, she had to purchase some to add to the constantly growing palette that was already there. Her customers enjoyed the variety also, and the store's reputation drew them in from the surrounding towns.

In season, there were always several-out-of-state customers in the store. Ogunquit was a quaint town on the coast of southern Maine that attracted an ever growing number of tourists in spring, summer and fall. Many of them found their way into her shop. She thought of the small bakery she would stop in on occasion and drink a coffee with a blueberry scone that exploded with flavor. Her mouth watered at the thought of it.

Bekah pulled her mind back to her current situation. She would be forever grateful to God for delivering her out of the snare of the fowler.[13] She felt fear try to rise up in her mind and

[13] Psalm 91:3

sought to remember all the good things God had done for her. Bekah remembered the hymn in which you were told to count your blessings. She sat there and hummed it for most of the afternoon. She thought of all her friends, here and at home. She thought of all the people praying not just for her, but for all of them and the quest God had called them to. Bekah felt peace enfold her like a warm blanket on a cold day.[14]

As dinner time rolled around, a meal of fruit, cold rice, and hot tea, made on a brazier designed to be used on boats, was served to all aboard. The fruit was wonderful, bursting with flavor and juicy, and the tea was hot and steaming. It was welcome. The morning had been cool, the afternoon hot and sultry, but with the sun descending and night approaching there was a chill in the air. Bekah had never tasted this particular kind of tea, and assumed it was some sort of herbal tea made by the people of the village. The rice was sticky and sweet and Bekah ate the whole plateful.

It was almost dark when they pulled up to the station. They tied the boats as close together as possible and commenced fueling them and filling all the spare gas cans. Night fell quickly. Since they were moving so slowly, they wanted an early start to ensure they arrived at the village the next evening, before full dark. Spending another night on the river was not an option anyone wanted to consider.

---

[14] Philippians 4:4-8

CHAPTER FIVE

JUNE 14
THE VILLAGE

It was going to be a busy day for Sherry. With Daniel gone, his chores fell to her. She had asked Manu if one of the young men from the village would see to the water supply and he immediately assigned that task to two of the teenage boys. He also instructed them to see to her wood supply which was also a big chore. All water had to be boiled and that meant having fuel to run the wood stove almost continuously. Since there had been a number of new believers, Daniel also had a Bible study after last meal, but Edwardo was handling that.

Sherry sat down with her first cup of coffee, tired before the day had even started. She knew that it was not uncommon during the first months of pregnancy to be tired, but she was annoyed at herself anyway. She did not have time to spare for napping. There was always so much that needed to be done and less time to handle the extra load accompanying these visitors.

As was their custom, Connie and Edwardo had come up for breakfast along with their family Emilio, Paulo, and young Maria. This time Lara, Connie's younger sister, had come also. Breakfasts together were a tradition they had been following since Daniel and Sherry had been living at the compound. If Sherry remembered correctly, little Maria had been a newborn. Now she was almost four.

After breakfast, Lara carried the two babies back home and Maria followed. Connie, Edwardo and Sherry had a short meeting concerning the Bible study that evening. They had several new converts and they were trying to draw them further into the family of God with love and encouragement.

Tonight's lesson was that God had a plan for our lives. We were not an accident. What we said and did mattered, not only in our lives, but also in the lives of others.[15]

After visiting with Connie and Edwardo, Sherry decided to go and see how Noemi and little Juan were doing. She also wanted to check on Ciba, Leonardo's wife. Ciba and Mara, Riki's wife, had been attacked by a wild boar about a week ago. Unfortunately, Mara had already been dead when they brought her back to the compound. Sherry had worked for several hours on Ciba, sewing up two large wounds in her arm and thigh. Thanks to God's help, she had survived. Riki had been very angry at Sherry because his wife had not survived. He pronounced a curse on her and later attempted to kill her. Thankfully Manu intervened and killed Riki instead. God's protection was always on His people. Satan had tried to attack Sherry through Riki, but it was to no avail.[16]

Sherry went back into the kitchen to clean up breakfast and found Paloma there already doing the dishes and getting food ready for lunch. After God had restored life to Manu's wife Noemi, his heart had been softened. He now wanted to do all he could for Sherry and Daniel. He had asked Paloma to come every day and help cook and clean and tend the garden. Sherry smiled at the thought and decided maybe it was alright to take a nap after all.

Sherry woke to the sound of shouting. She jumped out of bed and grabbed her medical bag. She did not know what

---

[15] Jeremiah 29:11

[16] Isaiah 54:17

the commotion was, but it was important to always be ready for emergencies. Sometimes minutes made the difference between saving a life and losing one. As she ran out of the compound, Sherry could see that something good had happened. The people were happy and energized.

From what she was hearing, several men had been out hunting for extra meat to feed the visitors that were coming. They stumbled upon a wild boar with several hungry juveniles accompanying her. They had a successful pursuit and brought back the sow and five of the juveniles. This much meat would feed the village for two or three days. It would take pressure off the hunters, who were going out continually to feed everyone. The women helped with gardening and gathering and sometimes even fishing, but the protein part of the food supply was mainly the men's responsibility.

Most afternoons someone was in the river fishing. Now what was going to be harvested for the next few days could be dried and kept for times of need. The river was a great source of food, but it was also a great source of danger. The river was inhabited by swarms of piranha and large caiman, both of which had no hesitation attacking a person fishing in the river. Sherry had already had many opportunities bandaging up gaping wounds from the caiman, and numerous bites from the piranha. Everyone fished in groups. There was indeed safety in numbers.

Sherry determined that her services were not needed, but decided to head down to the river to observe the fishing. It was always lively because wagering went on as to who would catch the most or the biggest fish. It seemed fishermen were the same the world over. She remembered Daniel telling stories of when he and his brother Joe went fishing in their boat along the shores of Ogunquit. They usually came home with fish, but there was always talk of the "one that got away." Sherry smiled at the memory.

Since Sherry had her bag in hand she changed her mind and decided to go and see Noemi and Ciba first. They had both been under her care for the last several days. Ciba was recovering from wounds incurred by the attack of a wild boar. Noemi was recovering from what proved to be a miraculous birth after suffering what appeared to be a terminal hemorrhage. God intervened in both instances and their astounding recovery was a sign to the people of the village of God's love and concern for them.

Walking up to Noemi's house, Sherry observed that both Noemi and Ciba were sitting in the sun and talking. Ciba had little Juan in her arms and was talking to him with a tender smile on her face. Noemi was sitting back and enjoying the day and the visit with her new friend. Both Ciba and Noemi had been spending a great deal of time together, healing and bonding.

As Sherry approached she gave them both a clinical once over and concluded they were the picture of health. Sherry looked at Ciba's wounds and asked Noemi some questions. She then sat down and joined them. She enjoyed their company. Ciba was more Sherry's age, so they had that in common. Noemi was still not much more than a girl. They married at a young age in Paraguay. That's one reason for such a high infant mortality rate. The mothers were not much more than children themselves. This fact caused a great number of complications in the birth of their children.

Another problem encountered was that since they were so young they were unprepared for the responsibility of parenthood and had little or no training to help them overcome these obstacles.

Also, Noemi had no mother to share with her the training needed to be a mother. Noemi missed out on all the things a young girl learns at their mother's side. Chabuto, Noemi's mother-in-law, who should have been a help, was jealous of Noemi's place in Manu's heart and house. Instead of trying to help her,

Chabuto tried to harm Noemi and the child by giving bad advice about diet and care during pregnancy and afterward. It was the grace of God that saved Noemi and little Juan's life.

After discovering what Chabuto had done, Manu sent her from his house to care for Riki's six children who had no parents. Chabuto left in anger, but she left, and the important thing was that she was no longer a burden to Noemi. Now Noemi could be Manu's wife and little Juan's mother without the constant scrutiny and animosity of Chabuto.

Realizing that she lacked the skills and knowledge to be a good parent, Noemi asked Sherry if she would be her mother. Sherry's heart was warmed by the request and happily took on that role. Sherry also realized there were other young brides who were ill-prepared for parenthood and started giving a class to instruct them.

Noemi was in charge of organizing it and let Sherry know when she could get several of the young brides and mothers together to go over some fundamentals. They only had one class so far and it was a great success. Noemi told Sherry that there were more people who wanted to attend, even some of the older women. They also wanted to know if God had anything to say about being a parent.

Sherry smiled at the thought of another opportunity to share the Word of God. More and more villagers were showing interest in the things of God and Sherry was bursting with joy at the harvest that was ripening.

Sherry said goodbye to her friends and started down the path to the river. She walked out onto the jetty and sat down in the sun, leaning back against a big rock and watched the people fish. She called out words of encouragement to some of her friends and prayed for a bountiful harvest. As she leaned back again she noticed that the sun had swung down into the western sky and sunset was no more than an hour or two away. She had not eaten since breakfast and was suddenly aware of the emptiness of her stomach. As she rose and turned toward home she smiled. This truly was her home and these people were her friends and neighbors. God had planted her and Daniel into the fabric of this village and they were an integral part of the pattern of life here—they belonged.

Stepping into the kitchen she saw a plate of food Paloma had left her. It was covered by a towel to keep the bugs away. Every house had them, the clean ones and the dirty ones. It was part of living in the jungle; seeing, we were only visitors, they were owners. Everyone dealt with them as best they could. Soap and water and a good fly swatter would keep out most of them. Sometimes there was a larger problem; that was when the chemicals came out. Sherry preferred the natural solutions, but once in a while a can of Raid was needed to determine who would win the battle.

Sherry meandered her way through the plate of food and savored the different flavors and textures. The ripeness and freshness of the food gave it a spice like no other. As you chewed your food the flavor exploded into your mouth setting your taste buds on overdrive. It was an experience she never tired of.

The sun was just beginning to set and Sherry yawned, not once, but twice. She had nothing scheduled tonight. Connie and Edwardo were conducting the Bible study. She felt a slight nudge to attend, but knew she would be there in body only. She would spend most of the time fighting the ever-increasing urge to sleep. Tonight, she would indulge herself and go to sleep with the sun. Hopefully she would have Daniel with her in the bed tomorrow night. She missed him. Before her eyes closed she said a prayer for his safety and all that were with him.

Sherry woke with a start to the sound of a telephone ringing. She did not know how long she had slept. As she got up to answer the phone she realized it could not have been that long.

There were still sounds coming from the village. People were still up and about. Picking up the phone, she smiled when she heard Daniel's voice. "Hello sweetheart," he said in a low voice. "Were you missing me?"

"Of course," Sherry replied. "Not that I would have seen much of you today. I was either sleeping, or out and about in the village. There haven't been any problems. Manu has sent help with water and wood and Paloma has kept me fed. I came home tonight and was in bed as the sun set. In fact, you woke me up; not that I mind. My last thought was of you. Will you be home tomorrow?"

"Yes," Daniel replied, "we should get there late in the afternoon. These boats have been moving so slow, and we wanted to take it easy for Bekah's sake."

"How is she doing? Are her injuries very serious?

"I haven't had much of a chance to talk with her; we've been on different boats. Tomorrow I'm going to ride with her. It will give me an opportunity to get to know her better. She had many cuts and bruises and a very discolored and swollen eye. We've used your jungle cream on her. Between that and prayer she appears to be recovering. I can't believe everything that is happening. I'm glad we serve a mighty God. I'll let you get back to sleep now. I just wanted to let you know our time frame for arrival, and also that I missed you and was thinking of you too. Good night and sweet dreams."

Sherry lay back down and smiled. If time allowed, tomorrow afternoon she would go down to the river and watch for his coming. She closed her eyes and drifted off, feeling his arms around her.

CHAPTER SIX

JUNE 15
THE RIVER

Night passed quickly and Bekah was surprised when she saw Daniel board the boat she was traveling on that morning. For some reason, she had assumed he would stay with the men from the village. Daniel walked over to Bekah and inquired, "How are you feeling this morning? I see that you're up and walking around. How are your feet doing? They looked pretty painful yesterday. Do they hurt much?"

Bekah looked up at Daniel. He stood about six foot, two or three inches, and had pale blond hair which he wore long and pulled back in a ponytail. He had beautiful, bright blue eyes that twinkled when he smiled, and fair skin with more than his share of freckles. He was thin to the point of skinny, but had broad, muscular shoulders.

Bekah was glad they had been able to talk on the satellite phone before coming down to Paraguay. She felt a bond with him even though she had only met him four days ago. She had to tilt her head to look up at him, and answered him with a smile, "I feel so much better, almost back to normal. I'm still just a little sore and a little tired. Actually, my feet are almost well. I was able to walk around with very little discomfort. The thing that bothers me most is that my muscles are sore. That could either be from being dragged, running, or swimming, all of which I do very infrequently. During season, I help in our apple orchard. I lift and drag boxes in my store, and I do a lot of gardening. That's the extent of my physical activity. I understand that my friends in Maine and my new friends in Paraguay were praying for me. I believe I will give God the credit for my quick recovery."

"Well you're certainly right about that," Daniel said with enthusiasm. "He has His hand on all of us. If we continue to allow Him to use us, we will be victorious in this endeavor.

"I called Sherry last night after we finished dinner. I just wanted to let her know our position and that we're all doing well. She told me that several people from the village were praying for you. Even Manu the Chief, who is a new believer, has been praying. Sherry told me they've been having morning and evening Bible studies for the new believers and at every meeting more new people arrive. They always start out with a review. It's a good thing for those new believers to have the lesson repeated. It strengthens their understanding of the Word of God. You shouldn't complain," I told her. "This is what we have been praying for."

"I'm not complaining," Sherry told me. "I just want to prepare you for when you get back home. Our little flock is growing and Manu is our chief Evangelist. He is a different person, always laughing and smiling and telling everyone that Jesus died for their sins and they can be forgiven.

"Sherry's excited," Daniel remarked, "and I can't wait to get home and experience the changes myself. Given our experience in the village these last years, and the hard ground we've had to plow, this is truly amazing."[17]

Bekah smiled and replied, "I'm anxious to get there also. I'm still amazed that God chose me to go on this quest. I don't understand my part in it, except for the fact that I was born in Paraguay and that this golden crucifix surfaced after my grand-

[17] Luke 8:4-15

mother's death. I feel as though I'm reading an adventure novel and I am one of the main characters. I wish I could peek at the last page to see how it ends."

"I can tell you that. The one thing we can be sure of," Daniel said with confidence, "is that God will triumph, and since we are on His side, so will we. Just knowing that helps me keep my confidence in Him. Remember, this applies to all of us; in our weakness, He is strong.[18] Don't let your faith be moved by circumstances.[19]

"I once went to church with a young man who was diagnosed with cancer. I prayed diligently for him. The whole church prayed for him. We anointed him with oil;[20] we prayed healing Scriptures over him.[21] We bound the devil and loosed healing into him and the Word of God over him. We did everything the Bible said to do, and yet he died. I was a new Christian at the time and that devastated me.

"He was married and left a young wife and two small children. Something was very wrong. I thought God was supposed to answer our prayers. The Bible says the thief comes to kill, steal and destroy, but Jesus came to give us abundant life.[22] Where was this man's abundant life? Where was the answer to all our prayers?"

Daniel paused and then said passionately, "I was hurt and I was angry. 'Where were You God? Why didn't You answer our prayers?' I cried out to God and demanded an answer, yet the Heavens were silent. Thank God they were. I realized later, who am I to demand anything from God?

"When I finally got quiet and was willing to hear, He spoke to me in a soft and reassuring Voice. He didn't answer any of

---

[18] 2 Corinthians 12:9
[19] Hebrews 11:1
[20] James 5:14
[21] Psalm 107:20
[22] John 10:10

my questions, but told me that faith was believing, even when it seemed as though it didn't work. It was an answer, but no answer, yet it brought peace to my heart.

"God's ways are always higher, and far better than anything we can figure out.[23] We may have questions about how or why things happen, but God has a plan for us, and it's a good plan.[24] It's to help us, and teach us, and reward us as we diligently seek Him.[25] When troubles happen, we need to remember that all things work together for His good, and ours, if we put our trust in Him.[26]

"A perfect example is your abduction. You could have said, 'Why is this happening to me?' and whined and cried and complained, but you didn't. You gave thanks to God and asked for His guidance. If we could all learn just that one thing, we would all be better for it.

"Now, here you are, a little frayed around the edges, but whole in body and spirit, and stronger in faith. I don't know if I'll ever have the answers to my questions, but it's not important anymore. My faith has moved beyond needing an answer. All I need now is the presence of God in my life."

Bekah looked up at Daniel with a sense of awe. She had never heard someone explain such a gut-wrenching question as, "Why did this happen?" and bring peace without having answered the question. As an awareness of God's presence engulfed her and that peace that passes all understanding rested on her,[27] Bekah bowed her head and absorbed God's grace and mercy.

Some time passed and Bekah raised her head and looked around. Daniel was standing next to her with his hand on her shoulder. He smiled a gentle smile and asked, "Are you feeling better?"

---

[23] Isaiah 55:8-11
[24] Jeremiah 29:11
[25] Hebrews 11:6
[26] Romans 8:28
[27] Philippians 4:6-9

Bekah could not help but smile back. "Yes," she said quietly, not wanting to break the peace of the moment.

Bekah and Daniel sat in companionable silence for a short time, enjoying the presence of God together. Then Daniel looked over at Bekah and said, "I wanted to come over and give you some idea of life in the village and who is involved with our quest. Is it alright if I call Josh over? I sense that he is one of the leaders in our group? We can talk over lunch."

Bekah nodded. She was glad to share this with Josh. She did not want to be a leader, and welcomed a way to divide the responsibility. Daniel went to get Josh from the other side of the boat. He came and sat next to Bekah.

Daniel began, "I'll try to explain what's been going on as simply as possible, but so much has been happening that it isn't simple. You know that four of us had the same dream that all of you did: me, Sherry, Edwardo, my young pastor, and his wife Connie. Connie's dream was slightly different. Like Sylvia, she was called to form a prayer army.

"The morning I returned from getting supplies I was going to tell Sherry about my dream, but I got sidetracked. We found a baby in a basket by the river. We brought the baby and the basket back to the compound. While this was happening, Sherry was just getting off the phone with all of you in Maine. After discussing your phone call, we discovered that the three of us down here had basically the same dream all of you did. We called you back and determined that including all of you, ten of us had received a call from God. It was then we realized that some of you would be coming to Paraguay. Next morning we found the crucifix in the basket, and that Connie, Edwardo's wife, also had a similar dream. That brought the number up to eleven."

Daniel paused and then questioned Bekah, "Did you bring your crucifix with you?"

"Yes, I did. Josh, I wrapped it in a towel and put it in your gun case to keep it safe. Do you want to see it, Daniel?" Bekah asked.

"Yes, I really would. For one thing, I don't want to be surprised if it's not what I expected."

Josh got up and went to retrieve the crucifix. He came back and handed the towel to Daniel.

Unwrapping it, Daniel looked down at what appeared to be a duplicate of the crucifix that Manu had tried to give Sherry. It also matched the one found in the basket with the baby, except the one in the basket was bigger.

Manu's wife, Noemi, and his newborn son, Juan had been saved by Sherry's skill and prayers. Noemi's recovery had been miraculous. She had been hemorrhaging from the birth of her son, and Sherry had no way to stop the bleeding. The small quantity of drugs she had on hand did nothing to stop the deluge of blood. Sherry just held Noemi's hand and prayed that God, in His mercy and grace, and as a sign of His presence and power, would spare this young woman. Sherry sat and watched as signs of life faded. Noemi's vital signs had become undetectable, but still Sherry prayed.

Time passed. Color began coming back into Noemi's face, replacing the ashen features of death. Life and blood appeared to be flowing through her again. As we watched, her chest began to rise and fall, and warmth replaced the previous coldness of her skin. The sounds of the baby's cry caused her to stir. Her eyes fluttered and she asked in a whisper, "Is it a boy?"

Daniel looked up and realized he had been sitting there thinking about the miracle he had witnessed. He gave the crucifix back to Josh and said, "It appears to be a duplicate. When I told Manu about the other crucifix, he became very interested in you, Bekah. When I told him your father had been a Missionary to Paraguay and that your mother was a native, he became agitated and said that he wanted to meet you as soon as you arrived. He didn't appear to be angry, just excited. He wouldn't say anymore. We will have to wait until we get there to solve the mystery."

The afternoon passed as Daniel continued to speak of the village and the people; his love for them shining in his eyes. The shadows were starting to lengthen when Daniel stood up and looked around. "We are almost there," he said, "Maybe another ten minutes."

CHAPTER SEVEN

JUNE 15
THE VILLAGE

Excitement spread from boat to boat. Everyone was standing and craning their necks, trying to see around the next bend in the river. Daniel sounded the horn on the boat several times, to alert the village that he was returning.

When they rounded the bend, they passed the big rock that gave the village its distinguishing name. People started to pour out onto the riverbank and climb onto the jetty that Daniel and Edwardo had built. All the noise and commotion created an air of excitement. Daniel had never experienced such a celebration at any of his previous homecomings. He assumed it was due to the anticipated arrival of the visitors. The five boats tied up to the dock that jutted out into the river.

Daniel had given instructions that the boats be emptied and the supplies brought up to the compound. He put Leonardo in charge of unloading at the dock and Philippe in charge of transporting to the compound. Then he and his four visitors disembarked.

As they walked down the dock toward the riverbank, Manu came down the path from the village. His eyes were riveted on Bekah; an air of eagerness surrounded him. Daniel walked up to him and began to make introductions. In compliance with their culture, he began to introduce the men first. Manu stopped him.

"Daniel, please introduce me to this woman."

Daniel was surprised that protocol was being breached, but he complied with Manu's request. Daniel turned to Bekah. "Manu, this is Miss Bekah Ryan from Ogunquit, Maine. Miss Bekah, this is Manu, Chief of the village."

Bekah extended Manu her hand. He took it with both of his and squeezed it gently. Then he said, "I have been hoping for a long time to meet you one day, and now God has finally brought you here."

Bekah looked at Manu in confusion, wondering what he could possibly mean. Daniel had warned her he had an unusual curiosity about her, but she was unprepared for the extent of it. Daniel finished with the rest of the introductions and Manu welcomed them all to the village. Then he started up the path and called to them, "Follow me. We have prepared a meal for all of you. You must be hungry after your long trip."

Walking back to the village, Bekah noticed that several men separated themselves from the crowd and went down to assist unloading the boats. All the men appeared to dress in colorful printed shirts and loose fitting pants. She noticed it was different from what the man who abducted her had worn. She needed to remember to tell Josh about that.

All the supplies had to be offloaded, carried up to the compound, and stored there until it was decided where everything needed to go. Also, they needed to separate supplies from gifts. She was glad to see these things were being taken care of in an organized manner.

Bekah walked next to Daniel, directly behind Manu, observing her surroundings. The path they were on was narrow, accommodating only two people standing side by side. It appeared there was an ongoing battle with the jungle for control of the path, and that constant maintenance was probably needed to keep it clear. The machetes they had brought would be a gift that could be utilized at once.

As they crested the hill leading to the village, the jungle retreated further and the village spread out before them. The noise level rose as curious people were milling around, wanting to see the newcomers. Daniel and Sherry were probably the only white people some of them had ever seen.

Approaching the village, Bekah observed many small homes clustered together. Near the center was a larger home, approximately double in size from the rest. Next to it was a large covered area that appeared to be a meeting place.

A short distance away, on the side of the village, was a small collection of buildings set apart by a low fence. Daniel pointed to them and said, "This is the compound. One building is our home and attached to it is the clinic. The other building is a new storage shed, which will act as housing for Josh, Ted and Renato while they are here.

"We've had a great deal of construction going on. We've doubled the size of our kitchen and added another bedroom which Bekah will use. It will give her some privacy, which is almost non-existent living as we do. We've enlarged the clinic, doubling it in size also, and decided last minute to add an office. Thankfully, we already had a good supply of building materials on hand. Not everything is completely finished, but everything is useable."

Bekah glanced over her shoulder and saw that her Three Musketeers were right behind her. She had started calling Josh, Ted and Renato that several days ago. Thinking of them elicited feelings of protection and safety. They had discussed it among themselves and determined that safety and protection were what she needed and they assigned themselves to that task. She wished she could stop and ask them what they thought of the current situation, but the momentum of the crowd of villagers behind them kept them moving.

There was a flurry of activity still going on, accompanied

by the sounds of hammers and saws. Two women stood inside the walls of the compound. Connie was identified by the two infants, Emilio and Paulo, she held on her hips. Maria was standing next to her mother with a little brown puppy in her arms. Sherry stood at the entrance with Connie, arms folded and a big smile on her face. Sherry realized that there would be some pomp related to the arrival of their visitors, and stood aside to let Manu enter. "Miss Bekah," Manu said, again breaking protocol by addressing himself to her, "this is our village." He stretched out his arms with pride to encompass all the homes, "and this is our healer, Doctor Sherry, and her medical clinic. Across the path is our meeting area, and there is my house. We sometimes use the meeting area for church and to talk about God and Jesus. As Chief of the village, I want to welcome you and your friends and thank you for what you are doing to help our people, and especially the northern villages that are being attacked."

Bekah was stunned at being made the focal point of this address. She had assumed that Josh would be handling the preliminaries along with Daniel. She quietly thanked Manu. He grabbed her hand again and held it. Then, realizing he was breaking protocol, he let it drop. He turned and started to talk with Daniel.

Bekah immediately reached out and grabbed Sherry's hands. Holding them tightly she said, "I'm so glad to finally meet you. Even with just the few times we've talked, I feel we know each other and are friends. Let me introduce you to the men who are traveling with me. This is Joshua, Ted, and Renato. Smiling, Bekah turned and said, "I assume this is Connie and her ever-growing family. I haven't met Edwardo yet, but I know that he and Connie are somehow part of this quest also."

Manu stood by listening, then turned and started to walk away. "Come," he said. "Food has been prepared. Edwardo and Leonardo will be waiting for us at the meeting area." Bekah thought it prudent to go along with everyone, even though she had questions inside her screaming so loud, she was surprised no one else heard them.

Sherry went over and took Daniel's arm and gave it a squeeze. She put her head briefly on his shoulder and then they started to walk. The Three Musketeers followed. Bekah paused and then turned to Connie and said, "May I carry one of the babies for you. You seem to have your hands full."

Connie smiled gratefully and handed over Emilio. "Thank you, they do get heavy." She turned and spoke to the little girl bringing up the rear, "Come along Maria, and stay with Mama." The little girl looked up with large brown eyes and attempted a smile, but couldn't quite pull it off. Shyness won out over curiosity. She lifted her puppy up and hid behind him. Connie walked next to Bekah, and they brought up the rear. They were an unlikely looking group, but God always knew what He was doing. Every project He started was completed, and in the end, it was always a success.

They arrived at the meeting area and saw that several bowls and platters of food were arrayed on colorful cloths on the ground and mats were spread around for everyone to sit on. There were pitchers of water, juice and herbal tea to drink. Dried gourds were used as cups. Stacks of banana leaves served as plates, and fingers were utensils. Baskets of fruit, some recognizable and some not, brought bright color and sweetness to the food. A type of flat bread was also used as a utensil, and a very aromatic cornbread was used to soak up juices. There was a rich, meaty stew with some root vegetables, and what looked like a bowl of yams.

As they all stood there waiting, Manu asked Daniel to bless the food and everyone bowed their heads. "Heavenly Father, we thank You for a safe end to our journey, for safely delivering Bekah back into our hands and setting her free from her captors. We thank You for bringing us all together with one heart and one mind. We ask for a spirit of unity to bind us together, and above all, that the love of God which never fails will bring this quest to a successful end. We ask Your blessing on this food, and all the hands that prepared it. Thank You for the nourishment, strength, and health it brings to our bodies. We pray all this in the mighty Name of Jesus."

Manu then said, "We all have questions, some more than others, but let us rest and eat, and after we have eaten and the food has been cleared, all questions will be asked, and hopefully, all questions will be answered."

Everyone ate and drank to their fill, savoring the richness of the food and the strange new flavors that tantalized their taste buds. Finally the meal drew to a close and their drinks were refilled. A tall young woman came forward and took the babies from Connie, and the little girl, Maria followed her with the puppy still in her arms.

Daniel sat quietly and watched the interaction between everyone. He was especially encouraged to see that Manu and Leonardo had a greater grasp of English than he had been aware of. Daniel wondered if Manu felt there had been an advantage to keeping their fluency secret. If that was so, Daniel prayed there be no more secrets between them.

Daniel and Sherry had been at the village nearly four years and Sherry, who had a gift for languages, was fluent in Guarani, the native language of Paraguay. She was also fluent in Spanish, which most of the villagers spoke. Unfortunately, that gift had passed Daniel by. He could understand some of what was being said to him in either language if they spoke slowly, but speaking it himself was another story.

Manu stood up and asked if chairs could be brought in for everyone. He said, "Sometimes it's hard to talk when you are sitting on the ground." Ten chairs were brought. Leonardo had stayed at Manu's request.

Manu carried his chair over and sat opposite Bekah. He looked at her searchingly and said, "Before we start talking about anything else, I would like to ask you some questions."

Surprised, Bekah answered, "Certainly, ask whatever you like."

"What can you tell me about your parents?" he questioned.

Caught off guard, Bekah stared at him a moment. "Of all the questions he could ask, why would he ask this?" she thought. Troubled, she replied, "What do you want to know? I was a small child when they died. I don't really remember them."

"I understand you were born in Paraguay. Do you know where and when?" Manu questioned.

"Is this about the crucifix?" Bekah responded, "Because if that's a problem, you can have it back. I never even knew it existed until eight days ago. I brought it here to show you, and if it's yours, you can take it back."

Bekah had a back pack on and took it off. Opening it up and taking out the towel wrapped crucifix, she handed it to Manu. "Before my grandmother died, she wrote me a letter concerning my birth, telling me that my mother was a native of Paraguay, and that she died in childbirth. My father was a Missionary, and my mother gave him the crucifix with the understanding that he was to give it to me when I grew up. For some reason, my grandmother kept it a secret all these years. I only found out about it in her letter to me after she died."

Manu questioned again, "How old are you Miss Bekah," he asked, "and do you know your mother's name?"

I'm thirty-seven," Bekah replied, "And my mother's name was Gabriella."

Manu turned pale. He hesitated for a moment and then said in almost a whisper, "I could be thirty-seven, we don't keep good track of those kinds of things, but my mother's name was

Gabriella and she died while giving birth to a son and a daughter. She was married to a Christian Missionary."

Now it was Bekah's face that turned pale. She felt the blood drain from her face as the implications of his statement penetrated her psyche. She turned to ask how this could be. "Renato," she questioned, "did you know about any of this?"

Seeing his face, she had her answer before he had time to formulate one. "I remember now," Bekah said, "the letter did say she was the daughter of a Chief, and that the Chief gave his daughter the crucifix. Can I see your crucifix?"

Manu turned to Leonardo and asked for the box. Manu removed a cloth-wrapped object, and unwrapping it, placed the one crucifix next to the other. There were minor differences, most likely because they had not been mass produced, but essentially, they were identical.

"Where is the large one?" Bekah asked. "Is it very similar to these?"

"Other than being larger and having more gem stones, it's identical," Daniel said. "I'll go get it. It will only take a minute or two."

As he was leaving, Manu called after him, "Bring back the Book of God with you. I think we need to hear from Him."

Manu turned back to Bekah. "We need to discuss the possibilities of what all this might mean. I think it is very likely that we are not only brother and sister, but twins. My grandfather was the Chief before me. He adopted me when my real father remarried the witch of the village, and left to go back to America. The Chief told my father he could not take both babies, he must leave the son to be Chief in his place, as he had no sons to succeed him. He was also supposed to leave the crucifix, because it belonged not just to his daughter, but to the tribe. The crucifix was to be passed down to the eldest child. Since he had no son, it had gone to our mother. When she died, it was supposed to come to me, since I was the firstborn, but it seems our father had other plans.

"He secretly married Fuego in a ceremony performed by her father, the shaman. Fuego's mother had escaped being burned for witchcraft by fleeing into the jungle. She was never seen again. Fuego appeared to take up where her mother left off. Raised by her father, the shaman, she became a witch also. Fuego had a child, a daughter named Luna, who she left behind, allowing her to go to America with you and your father.

"Luna's grandfather died and with no children to take his place, a new shaman was appointed. Unfortunately, he soon turned to the dark arts and Fuego's daughter Luna followed him down that path. He is Tuvicha, the old shaman we have now. Twenty years ago Luna ran away to escape punishment for witchcraft. She was the same age as you and I. Those were evil times. I thought we had been free of those spirits until a man named Riki placed a curse on Doctor Sherry because she was unable to help his wife who had been injured by a wild boar. His wife was already dead when they brought her to the clinic, but Riki did not want to listen and in anger he cursed Doctor Sherry. It was only because I went to check on her that I was able to stop Riki from killing her. Now Riki is dead, instead of Doctor Sherry.

"This is all ancient history, but it is our history. Somehow God has worked it out Miss Bekah, that we would meet again, and that you would come back to Paraguay and be reunited with me. This crucifix I have was taken from the tribal treasures, because our father and Fuego stole the one you have. After Fuego left, we found out that she had stolen a large quantity of the tribal treasures. Now this can be returned. I have always wondered where the rest of the treasures are that Fuego had stolen. I am also curious to see what other surprises God has for us. Does God like surprises?" Manu inquired.

"I don't know," Bekah said. "They're not surprises to Him,

but we'll have to discuss this more tomorrow, after I've had time to think about it. I don't doubt what you say; I am just so overwhelmed by everything that has taken place in the last several days, not the least what you have just told me. It seems more like a story than real life."

Everyone looked up as Daniel came back to the meeting room. He was carrying his Bible, and a large bundle wrapped in cloth. He opened up the cloth and gave the crucifix to Manu. "This is what was in the basket with little Emilio," he announced to the visitors. "We know he came from upriver and probably traveled for over twenty-four hours. Emilio was wrapped in a wild boar skin, and the crucifix was placed in the basket with him. There were no defining marks on the basket, boar skin or baby to give a clue as to where he came from. All we know is he came from the north."

The crucifix was passed around in order for everyone to see it, and then Manu held it in his lap. Manu thought of the other artifacts that the tribe held sacred. They were hidden in the jungle and only three people knew where they were, himself, Leonardo and the shaman, Tuvicha.

Daniel sat down with his Bible. He opened it up and began to read the Genesis account, starting with "In the Beginning," and ending with:

> "And God saw everything that he had made, and, behold, it was very good. And the evening and the morning were the sixth day.[28]

"God is making a beginning here for us," Daniel said. "We all have new beginnings concerning the quest God has called us to. The people of the village have a new beginning in their relationship with God, and with us. Manu and Bekah have a new beginning, discovering that they are not only related, but also are twins.

---

[28] Genesis 1:1-31 KJV

"Let's be sure to remember what God said when He was finished with creation. He said it was very good. God also said that when we join our lives with Jesus that we are new creations, born of the Spirit of God. All the old is gone, our past sins and our shame. He has made us new again."[29]

They talked for a short time, but Manu observed that his visitors were yawning and working hard to stay alert. He stood up and said, "It has been a long day, and travel is difficult. Let us meet tomorrow here for lunch. We will talk after that." Standing, he said, "I wish you all a restful night." He and Leonardo walked to their homes and the rest of them walked back to the compound.

[29] 2 Corinthians 5:17

CHAPTER EIGHT

JUNE 15
THE VILLAGE

When they all arrived back at the compound, Sherry said, "We don't do this very often because we don't always have it available, but since Daniel just shopped, would anyone care for a cup of coffee?"

Droopy shoulders straightened up and eyes sparkled in anticipation. Everyone said a resounding, "Yes!"

Sherry went about making the coffee and Daniel set out the cups and plates. Paloma had made a cake of sorts and Sherry served that with the coffee. Everyone seemed to pick up a second wind and sat around the table talking. Edwardo and Connie only stayed for a short time; they had family and needed to get home.

"Well Miss Bekah," Renato said, "What do you think of the fact that you are really not alone in the world anymore? You have not just a brother, but a twin brother, and a strong and honorable one I think. It is really interesting how God has orchestrated these circumstances to bring us all together here. I'm sure we don't know the full extent of everything that is going on. God has His plans, and He doesn't always give us all the details concerning them."[30]

"Bekah, did you ever let Sherry look at your injuries?" Josh asked. He knew they had all been busy today, but felt it important that Bekah be given the once over. Some of those cuts and abra-

[30] Isaiah 55:8-11

sions had been deep, and might still need some follow up care.

"No, I didn't," Bekah answered. "There was no time, and they all stopped bothering me. If she wants, she can look at my feet now, they were the worst, but it's been a few days."

Sherry got up from the table and went to the stove. She checked the coffee, and then measured out some hot water in a basin. She added some disinfectant to it, grabbed a towel, and sat on the ground by Bekah. "I guess we could officially call this a foot washing," she said as she smiled up at Bekah. She pulled a pair of latex gloves out of her pocket and put them on. "I'm always prepared," she said as she saw Bekah's surprised expression.

Bekah took off her sneakers and socks and put her feet into the basin. The warm water had a soothing touch after a long and stressful day. Sherry allowed Bekah's feet to sit in the water for five minutes and then she took them out and dried them. She picked up first one, and then the other to examine them, and found no injuries. She looked at Bekah questioningly. "This is truly amazing. What about the rest of your body? I was told you had some pretty deep gashes on your right side."

"Yes," Bekah responded, "They were pretty bad and painful too, but nothing is bothering me now. God seems to have miraculously healed me. How does my eye look? It was swollen shut and a large bruise was forming."

Sherry had to ask, "Which eye was it? I can't tell by looking at them." Sherry felt excitement rising in her as she became aware of another miracle that God had performed.

Bekah put her hand up to her face and felt her eye. "It was the left one, and it's not sore or swollen anymore, and I can see out of it without any difficulty." She began to feel her faith also rise up and her doubts disappear as she realized what God had done for her. She didn't understand why she had been abducted, but she wasn't going to question God. She remembered Daniel's story that faith always believes, even when things aren't going the way you think they should. She felt at peace again, trusting they were all in the palm of God's hand, and He was leading them and guiding them in the way they should go.[31] He would reveal to them everything they needed to know. As awareness of what had transpired spread throughout the room, they all raised their voices in a joyful prayer of thanks.

Suddenly, they were all startled by the sound of the coffee pot boiling over. They looked around at each other and laughed, still caught in the joy of the moment.

Sherry got up, took the basin of water, and emptied it out the door. Then she grabbed the coffee pot and started to pour. The six of them sat around the table, drinking coffee and eating cake. There was a wonderful feeling of camaraderie; a bond was forming between the members of the quest.

Daniel was the first to call them back to the situation at hand. "Bekah, if it's not too difficult for you to recall, can you tell us what you remember of your abduction?"

Bekah's expression sobered and she shivered with a chill that was not due to the temperature of the room. "I've successfully avoided thinking about it all day, but I have to face it sooner or later. Ask me whatever you like, and I'll answer as best I can."

Renato pulled his chair over next to her and took her hand. "It's OK to be uncomfortable or hesitant to talk about something like this. Just remember that we are all friends who love and care for you. It's always easier to deal with something unpleasant if you have someone with you."

Bekah squeezed his hand. "Thank you Renato. I can do this." She turned to the others, "Go ahead and ask your questions."

Josh spoke up first, "Can you describe the man who abducted you?"

Bekah cupped her chin with her hand, and squinted, as if

[31] Proverbs 3:5-6

trying to see him again. "He was about as tall as you Josh, well over six feet. He was dark, but not as dark as the natives here. In fact, I remember he had his face blackened. He had short curly black hair and dark eyes with bushy eyebrows. He had a short, curly beard and was very muscular. Also, he seemed as surprised to see me as I was to see him. Maybe he hadn't been watching the boat," she queried, "in fact, I think he may have been coming from upriver."

Josh was writing all this down on a pad he had pulled from his pocket. "Can you describe what he was wearing? Did he have any weapons?"

Bekah closed her eyes again for a moment, trying to conjure up his image in her mind. "He was wearing camouflage pants. He had on high top boots and a belt across his chest. I think he had a large knife at his waist and a machete in his hand. I didn't see any other weapons. "

"We heard you yell, and then nothing. Did he hit you right away?"

"Pretty much," Bekah answered. "After I yelled, I tried to fight him and that's when he hit me. The next thing I remember was waking up in the clearing."

"Can you describe it, what you saw, the sounds, the smells, even the temperature? Every detail is important. Don't leave anything out, even if it seems trivial."

Bekah heaved a sigh. She spoke haltingly, not wanting to miss a detail. "I remember waking up to the smell of smoke. It was in my nose and the back of my throat burned. As I moved, I realized my hands were tied. I was panicked for a moment.

"My wrists were bound tightly with some kind of vine. I was in a clearing of about an acre or so. It appeared to have been burned to clear it, and all the debris had been raked to the edges. That was something unusual. There were also several rakes lying against the trees, and the smell of smoke was encompassing, but now I remember I also caught a whiff of gasoline. I heard what I thought were drums in the background, but it could have been something else. I tried to determine which direction we had come from and backtracked. I managed to get the vines off my wrists and was hopefully headed back the way I had come. That was when the smell of smoke increased and all the animals were running. I got to the riverbank and jumped in and you know the rest. Does any of this make sense? Is any of it helpful?"

Josh didn't answer Bekah, but turned to Daniel and asked, "Is there any way you can receive a fax or email here? I would like to get some pictures sent here to see if Bekah can identify her abductor? From Bekah's description of him, and of what happened, I think this may have something to do with the secret Black Death training camp the government thinks is out in the jungle. If they came in legally, there would be records of their passports and pictures. If I can, I would like to call Isaac Klein, my friend from the C.I.A. tonight. He might be able to find a way to get those pictures to us."

"Wait a minute," Daniel said. "What are you talking about? What have The Black Death and the C.I.A. got to do with our quest, and how could the C.I.A. possibly be involved?"

"Nothing, I hope," answered Josh. "But I don't want to take any chances. If they're in the area, I want to know about it. Satan uses any tool available to further his causes. The Black Death would be right up his alley."

Josh continued, "We haven't had a chance to talk with you and relay everything that has happened to us while we have been down here. Also I'd like to tell you I'm former C.I.A., but I can't. I still do some part-time work for them, but only for one more month. Then my contract will be up and I will finally be free.

"Isaac is a friend I trust there. I've done some favors for him and he's done some favors for me. While we were shopping in Asunción, we ran into a little trouble at Excelsior when we were purchasing some weapons. A man named Esteban Montero tried to intimidate us and find out who we were and what we were doing in Paraguay. The owner, José, backed him down with a shotgun.

"Montero left the store, mad and threatening. He seemed like a legitimate concern, so I called Isaac to see if he had any information on him. He did, and said he was a really bad dude and to stay out of his way.

"He also warned me that there was rumor of a Black Death training camp in the area, to keep my eyes open, and to let him know if we see anything suspicious. I would say that Bekah's abduction, the description of the person who did it, and where he took her, looked suspicious.

"If something like that is going on around here, we need to know, and we need to let the C.I.A. know. It's not something I would want to deal with on my own. So if it's alright with you, Daniel, I'd like to give Isaac a call and see if he can help us out."

Daniel and Sherry sat there for a moment in stunned silence. He finally answered, "Yes, certainly, but first I'd like to ask a question. Is there anything else happening, or that we all need to know so we won't be surprised again? It's not every day you meet someone who works for the C.I.A. and is ferreting out information on an Islamic terrorist organization. Every time I go down to Puerto Bahía Negra I bring back a stack of newspapers. The Black Death is usually in the headlines at least once a week causing death and destruction in different parts of the world, but I never expected them to turn up in Paraguay."

Josh looked at Daniel awkwardly, sorry that it had been necessary to keep some secrets, and glad now that they were out in the open. "I apologize for the stealth, but in my business, the less people know, the better. Please forgive me."

"Well this quest has had one bombshell after another. I hope this is the last of them, but I somehow doubt it." Daniel went out to get the satellite phone and gave it to Josh.

Looking at the time, Josh wondered if Isaac would still be in the office. It was close to eight, but Isaac liked to work odd hours. Josh decided to give that his first try and dialed the office number. It rang once and was immediately picked up. "Josh, I assume this is you. I can't think of anyone else who would call me from a remote area in Paraguay on a satellite phone."

"Well you're right as usual. I just wanted to update you on what's been happening down here. On our way up the river, we ran into something you might be interested in." Josh related the facts he had compiled about Bekah's abduction. Then he asked, "Is there any way you can get pictures of the men under suspicion for this training center out here to us. We've got a laptop. Can you e-mail them or somehow electronically send them to see if Bekah recognizes her abductor?"

"I think we can probably manage something. Did you bring your laptop? It will make it easier if you did; we have all your info already."

"I'm sure you already know the answer to that," Josh said. "I couldn't find your latest tracking program. I know you hacked into it, so you know my location."

Isaac laughed. "You're always a challenge Josh. I enjoy locking horns with you. I'll get on it ASAP. Meanwhile, I don't have to tell you to keep your eyes and ears open. It wouldn't hurt to set up a perimeter and put out some sentries. Do you want me to send down several men?"

"Don't you dare," said Josh emphatically. "The last time you were going to send me several men, a dozen showed up, and they all stuck out like sore thumbs. Besides, we don't want to draw any attention to ourselves."

Isaac questioned, "Changing tracks, could this have been our friend Montero, trying to use scare tactics and intimidation again? I've been thinking of what you said about the abduction. It seems strange that she was dragged across the jungle, and then dropped in an abandoned clearing with no one guarding her. Maybe they wanted her to escape or maybe they just wanted to scare her."

"That's a possibility," Josh answered thoughtfully. In his mind, he went back over his conversation with Bekah. "I don't think so. Remember, Bekah said the man who captured her appeared to be surprised to see her there. I think it was a chance meeting, and he didn't know what to do with her, so he brought her with him. She just happened to be in the wrong place at the wrong time. I'm just grateful he didn't kill her there and be done with it. He went through a lot of trouble carrying her across the jungle."

"You're right." said Isaac. "For now we'll wait and see what develops. I'll have those pictures to you tomorrow morning. Call me if you need anything else, or if you change your mind about help."

"Thanks buddy," said Josh. "I'll get back with you."

After ending the call Josh turned to look at everyone. They all stared back questioningly. Finally, Bekah voiced what everyone had been thinking. "Can we trust him? How much danger do you think we are in? We're not bringing any danger to the people of the village, are we?"

"The answer to your first question is yes. I have known and worked with Isaac for a long time, and I trust him with my life. Your second question is more difficult to evaluate. There is more danger than we first anticipated. Who and where the danger is coming from will determine what the level of danger is. Montero is a dangerous nuisance. The Black Death is a global threat. If The Black Death is involved, we may need to ask for backup. Let's wait and see what information and pictures Isaac sends us. In the meantime, no one goes anywhere alone. We have four armed men here. Please carry your weapon at all times. We will unpack them in the morning and get them loaded. Daniel, does Edwardo know how to handle a gun? Does he have one of his own?"

"Yes, to both questions. Two years ago we had trouble with

an injured jaguar that was in the area. It attacked one of the women while she was out foraging for food. I killed it with my rifle. Edwardo asked me to teach him to use a gun. He owns a Winchester .22. It's small, but does the job he got it for. When stores are low he brings in some game to supplement our diets. He also owns a Glock 30 with the big magazine. It's good for close quarters. He doesn't have anything big that would handle distance."

"That sounds good," Josh said. "Now, we are only looking out for the safety of the village and surrounding area. Let's get him on board with this tomorrow morning.

"Can anyone else in the village handle a weapon?"

"As far as I know," Daniel said, "most men are very proficient with a knife, spear or machete. A few use poison darts to kill small game, but I don't think anyone else has a firearm of any kind."

"Alright," said Josh, "Forewarned is forearmed. We know some bad guys may be out there. Hopefully, even if they know about us, they will only think we are harmless Missionaries. Let's try and keep it that way. As far as you know Daniel, have they ever interfered with anyone from the village?"

"I don't believe so. If they had it would have been reported to Manu and he would have discussed it with everyone."

Josh thought for a moment and then asked, "Bekah, you are going to be sleeping in the new room that's been added to Daniel and Sherry's house? Daniel has a weapon in his room. I'm trying to figure out how to keep you safe. One of us will have to bunk with you. Would you agree with Renato staying with you? I think he would be the best person if he's in agreement."

Everyone looked to Renato. He drew his thoughts together and then replied. "I have already told Miss Bekah that I would give my life for her. It's right and proper that I stay there, not one of you young men."

"Excuse me," Bekah spoke up. "I'm not quite angry, but

just a little peeved that no one has asked for my opinion or input. If you had, I could have told you that I know how to use a firearm. I took a marksmanship class as an elective in college and did very well. I've kept it up over the years just because it was fun and a challenge, though I never thought I would have use for it. I don't like the big guns with big kicks and big bangs. You can keep your .357 Magnum's and AK-47's. I am more comfortable with a smaller caliber gun. But I know how to fire a big one if I have to. I had a small Glock at home. Come to think about it, it might have been stolen in the break-in."

Bekah considered what to say next. "Renato, I would be honored to have you stay in my room, and I am thankful for your protection." She went over and hugged him and planted a soft kiss on his cheek.

"Bekah," Josh said, "Renato can handle it tonight. I'll get with you tomorrow to see if we have any weapon you feel comfortable with. I don't, but maybe Daniel does. Sherry, can you use a firearm?"

"Just like Bekah," Sherry answered, "I can use anything Daniel has, but I prefer a smaller caliber also."

Daniel spoke up. "Firearms are a hobby of mine. I have always enjoyed owning and shooting them. I have quite a collection I will be happy to show you tomorrow. I have at least ten handguns of various calibers. I have six rifles and several scopes. Three of the rifles are semi-automatic and one is an AK-47. I also have four shotguns and two black powder muskets that I got from a dealer in Asunción. He said they were probably from the late 1600's. They are in pretty poor shape and cannot be fired, but I thought it remarkable they were found in the area. He is a friend and gave me a great price."

"That is quite a collection," Josh responded in awe. "Between the two of us, we could supply a small army. Let's hope it won't come to that. If there are no other issues, let's go to sleep. It's been a long and arduous day." To emphasize that fact, he gave a large, bone cracking yawn. Everyone laughed and the tension was released. "Daniel, do you know where our bags are so we'll have clothes and toiletries for tomorrow?"

"Follow me," Daniel said. "I'll show you what you need and where to go."

CHAPTER NINE

JUNE 15
THE VILLAGE

Just as everyone was getting up to retrieve their belongings and finally go to bed, the phone started to ring. There were very few people who had this number. They had just finished talking to one. The other was Daniel's brother Joe in Maine, who was the stateside leader of their quest. As soon as the phone began to ring Daniel realized that with everything that had gone on, and all the excitement of arrival, they had failed to stay in contact with their very important prayer and supply team.

Joe was Daniel's older brother. His wife Roberta was a good friend to Bekah and was also an employee of Bekah's at her needlework shop. Roberta and Joe were also staying in Bekah's house while she was gone, helping to salvage whatever they could find that was not damaged or destroyed. The house had been broken into and ransacked the night before they left for Paraguay. Someone had been looking for something and had done a very thorough job of searching for it. Basically, everything in the house had been ripped apart and demolished.

They suspected Haydon Carlton was the instigator. He was the jeweler Josh and Bekah had taken Bekah's crucifix to in order to determine its authenticity. As soon as he examined the piece, it appeared his focus changed from helping to identify the background of the crucifix, to wanting it for himself. He said he had many people willing to purchase a piece of that quality, or he could help to place it in a museum. He wanted them to leave it with him and he would handle the transaction. They thanked him for his help, telling him that it was a family heirloom, and that Bekah wanted to keep it. That seemed to start their trouble, and trouble had continued to follow them.

Also stateside was Sylvia, another friend and employee of the needlework shop. She was in charge of prayer for the group. She had recruited three friends, Shirley, Kay and Sandy, to be part of her prayer team, and they would coordinate with Connie, Edwardo's wife. Connie was their Paraguayan prayer counterpart. Their responsibilities were to repel the attacks of their enemy, the Devil, and keep everyone built up with prayer.[32]

Daniel picked up the phone and heard Joe say with some anger in his voice, "Good, you're not all dead. Last we heard from you, Bekah had been rescued from some violent natives along the river. For all we knew, they could have mounted another offense and captured the rest of you. I'm sorry for being so angry, but we were really worried. We've been in almost constant prayer since you called two days ago. I think I used restraint in not calling the C.I.A. to check up on all of you. We've turned Bekah's office into a prayer room, and now have prayer twenty-four hours a day. We have shifts of two people that pray for four hours every day. We've got you covered in prayer, but you have to keep in touch with us."

"You're right," said Daniel apologetically, "We'll do better from now on. You caught us as we were heading for bed, but we're still all here. It's been wild down here with everything that has happened. All the prayers for Bekah were answered. God went above and beyond. All her injuries, even the serious ones were miraculously healed."

Daniel went on to tell Joe, and all those listening, what

[32] Ephesians 6:11-19

had transpired on the boat, and also their suspicions of who the attacker was. Then he recounted the meeting with Manu, and the discovery that Bekah was Manu's twin sister. He told of the revival that was happening in the village and the air of expectancy. God was moving in a mighty way, and they were all part of His plan. Daniel spoke for thirty minutes and then he let Bekah have the phone.

Bekah began by thanking them also for all their prayers. Then she asked Joe, "How have you and Roberta made out in the house? I hated to leave you both in such a disaster. Also, did you discover anything about the key Josh found?"

Josh had spent a few hours going through the shambles of Bekah's house, trying to find anything that might be helpful to them. Nana had kept her desk locked and its contents a secret. Only after Nana's death had Bekah taken the contents of one drawer to her office at the needlework shop and began to go through it. All she seemed to find of any consequence was a book with names, dates and amounts of money listed. Bekah had no clue as to what it concerned. The dates were over thirty-five years old.

While sorting through the rubble, Josh had also found what looked like an old safe deposit box key taped to a piece of wood that he assumed had been part of the desk. They had gone to the bank before they left for Paraguay to determine if it was indeed a safe deposit box key, and if so, what was in the box. They just ran out of time and had left the solving of that mystery with Joe and Roberta.

Joe began by saying, "We found some personal items and mementos of yours. We have cleaned out one room and we are putting everything we find of value in there. So far we have found nothing that seems to be from the contents of Nana's desk. It appears that the desk was destroyed so that everything in it could be packed up and taken away. It was a miracle the key wasn't discovered at that time; then a miracle that Josh found it.

"Roberta and I took the key back to the bank on Monday, and met with John Hiccomb, the bank President. It turns out he knows you through his wife, Alicia, who is also one of your customers. Anyway, we explained the situation to him, told him we had power of attorney, and showed him the papers we got from Jim Pritchard, your lawyer. John looked at the key and verified that it came from his bank, and was from the first group of safe deposit boxes the bank had installed. There were one hundred at the time. That was over thirty-five years ago. He said the records showed it was Joseph, Bekah's father who had applied for the safe deposit box, not Nana Sara. Joe opened it when he came back from Paraguay with his new wife. John went to check the records and they showed only your father had been in it, just once, right before he and your stepmother were killed in the car wreck. In fact he still had a small account open that was used to pay for the box. Jim said he'd forgotten about it, and didn't think Nana Sara was even aware of the box's existence.

"We brought a pad and a camera with us to itemize what was in the box, and take pictures if need be. We were surprised, the box was quite large. Thankfully, we were given a room to examine the contents privately. We were staggered by what we found." At that moment Bekah began to hold her breath. She knew the news was not going to be good. She prayed for strength.

Joe continued talking, "In the box were fifteen other Conquistadorian artifacts of various sizes. Some were jewelry, some were daggers and some were headpieces. There were also three crucifixes and three goblets of varying sizes. All were the same style as the one Nana left you. There was also a letter from your father. It must have been written when he came back, right before his death." Joe paused, waiting for a reply.

There was silence for a moment; no one knew what to say. Everyone's mind was spinning with questions. Finally Bekah spoke up. "Have you read the letter Joe? Does it explain about the contents of the box?"

"Yes," said Joe. "I took the letter; I knew you would want to hear it. I left the artifacts in the box where they would be safe."

Bekah went over and sat by Renato. She needed his comfort and reassurance. She grabbed his hand and told Joe, "Go ahead and read it. I've got my friends around me for support."

"The letter is dated January 4, 1982," Joe said. Then he began to read.

> Dear Mom,
>
> I'm sorry so much time has gone by and we haven't come to visit. I know I haven't called either. My excuse is that I've been too ashamed. I have a confession to make and I hope you can find it in your heart to forgive me. I've asked God to forgive me and He has, but until you do, and I can make reparations, I can't forgive myself.
>
> My first sin was marrying Fuego. I was so lonely after Gabriella died, and Fuego was always there, both comforting me and tempting me. I fell so out of the will of God by giving in to my flesh.[33] I didn't know if I could ever find my way back. I found out Fuego had had a baby also, a little girl around the same age as Bekah. I don't know if she was married or not. I never saw or heard about a husband.
>
> From the first, she convinced me not to tell you that Bekah was a twin. Bekah has a brother named Manu. The Chief told me at his birth that Manu would be Chief one day, and his place was with the people of his village. That's why Gabriella gave him a Guarani name. The Chief said if I wanted to leave, I had permission to take the daughter with me, but I would have to leave the son behind.
>
> Fuego wanted to leave. She wanted to come to the States. She went so far as to sell her daughter to her grand-

[33] Galatians 5:16-21

father the shaman, to get money for her ticket. I went along with all this, almost as if I were under a spell. I turned my back on the villagers, my son, and most importantly on God.

We made the arrangements to leave, and I gave my son to the Chief without a second thought. I just wanted to be married to Fuego. She kept pressuring me for us to leave, almost in a panic each day we were still there. When we were finally ready to go, she had three large boxes that she said were mementoes she could not leave behind. I just put them on the boat. I never questioned her as to what they were. In hindsight now, I can see her conniving and her cunning, manipulating me into doing whatever she asked. My eyes were truly blinded.

I should have been warned by her incessant questioning about Bekah's crucifix. I lied to her and told her I had asked the Chief to keep it until we were ready to leave. I felt I had to keep it from her. In reality, I didn't trust her. She kept nagging me. She wanted to see it. She wanted to wear it. We were already living together and the shaman had blessed our marriage, such as it was. I don't know whose blessing was on it, but looking back, I know it certainly wasn't God's. I didn't see any way I could get out of this situation, so I just went along with everything to keep the peace. If Fuego didn't get her way she went into terrible fits of rage.

When we got to the States, I questioned her about the boxes again. She opened them and showed me the contents, so proud of what she had done. I was horrified to see that they were filled with golden artifacts of varying sizes, fifty-two in all. When I questioned Fuego, she said these were part of the tribe's treasures and that she deserved a share. Somehow she managed to get them through customs undetected. I didn't question her any further about that.

She said when we got to California we would find ways to sell them. Then we could live in luxury the rest of our lives.

After finding this out, I secretly took part of the treasure and opened up a safe deposit box in my name. I put the pieces in there, hoping someday I would be able to return them to the village. I didn't tell Fuego what I had done. That's why we left so quickly. I taped one of the keys to the back leg of the desk, hoping you would eventually find it if I didn't make it back. If something happens to me, will you please see that these artifacts are returned to the village along with my sincere apology? You are my beneficiary.

Things are not going well between Fuego and me. Ever since she discovered that I took some of the artifacts she has become very secretive. She hid the rest of the collection. I've searched the house and can't find them. She must have removed them while I was at work. Also, she has her own bank account. I don't have access to it. The bank is Bank of Los Angeles. She also has a ledger with names and amounts of money. I believe these are people she has sold artifacts to. She keeps it in her desk.

If anything happens to me, please come take Bekah. I don't think Fuego would fight you for her, but I wouldn't be surprised if she tried to sell her to you as she sold her own daughter. She has no love for Bekah at all.

"Don't even ask her about the artifacts; don't get involved with her at all. She is evil and I see that clearly now. I wish I hadn't been so blind before.

I'm sorry. I let God down and I let you down.

If it's any consolation, I'm working at a halfway house for people just out of prison. I feel as though in a way, I'm making restitution for the mess I've made of my life.

I'm coming back to Maine to put this letter in the safe deposit box. I'm sorry, but I can't stop to see you.

I'm trying to get back without Fuego finding out where I've been. I'll just tell her I had a class I had to take for work and would be back the next day. She won't care. I've served her purpose. She's now in the United States and living in the lap of luxury just as she wanted.

Please, at least pray for Bekah. She is the only innocent one in this fiasco. I know only God will be able to work all this out, and get things back the way they should be. I put my trust in Him.

I love you Mom.

Joe

Everyone just sat there astounded, not knowing what to say, or how to respond to such a startling discovery. Bekah just laid her head on Renato's shoulder and wept. He put his arm around her and hugged her close. He looked around at all the people in the room and said, "I think we need to pray for Bekah and also for this situation. The enemy has been working in several areas for thirty-seven years that we know of, maybe more. We need God's strength and guidance to know what to do. Already we can see His hand in calling Bekah to be part of this quest. God knew from the beginning what He would do; we just need to be in agreement with Him in word and deed. We need to take up our weapons and fight the enemy, spiritually and physically.[34] So far we have been fighting a defensive battle. It's time to take the offense."

"Joe," Josh spoke up, "Can you expedite a letter down here with copies of the letter from Bekah's father and also pictures of the artifacts? We can send someone down to Puerto Bahía Negra to pick them up, or maybe you can fax them to us.

"I also think we should come back together an hour earlier tomorrow night and all pray together, your group up there and us down here. Then we can relay what God has said to each of

[34] Ephesians 6:10-18

us. For now, let's close with prayer and then get a good night's sleep." Josh stood up and asked, "Can we all join hands?"

Renato spoke up, "Please pray for Bekah first. This has been very hard on her emotionally, and that can sometimes open the door to an attack from the enemy. We want to cover her with our prayers and deflect his attacks on her mind and body.[35] We know that the Greater One lives in Bekah and that despite what the enemy says or does,[36] he is already defeated."

Josh came over and took Bekah's hands in his. He prayed, "Father, we come to You in the mighty Name of Jesus, asking for Your strength and protection for Bekah. She's had some challenging things revealed to her that normally would be difficult to deal with. But as the Bible says, she has the mind of Christ, and she can renew her mind as thoughts come her way that are not wholesome and Godly.[37] Also we pray for peace for her in this situation. We pray that she thinks on good things, pure things, and lovely things, for Your Word says that then the peace of God will come to her.[38]

"Father, we know that You are with us, that You lead and guide us. We put our trust in You. We won't worry about tomorrow.[39] We ask that You help us to stay in touch with each other consistently, and we pray the Holy Spirit will bring things to our remembrance we might have forgotten.[40] Thank You for good and faithful friends. We put our faith and trust in You Lord. Your Word says that You will renew our strength.[41] Thank You Lord for all You do. We pray all of this in Jesus' Name."[42]

---

[35] 1 Peter 1:13
[36] 1 John 4:4
[37] Romans 12:1-3
[38] Philippians 4:6-9
[39] Matthew 6:25-34
[40] John 14:26
[41] Isaiah 40:31
[42] Colossians 3:17

CHAPTER TEN

JUNE 16
THE VILLAGE

Bekah strained to wakefulness. She felt as a diver does who has stayed underwater too long and was running out of air. She thought her lungs would burst, yet she knew she was dreaming and that her nightmare would be over if she could just reach the surface and take a breath. But as relentlessly as she struggled, she could not break free. Something was restraining her, preventing her from reaching the surface. Then a touch to her arm startled her, she woke and took a convulsive breath, looking around in panic.

Renato stood over her with a look of concern. "Wake up! Wake up Miss Bekah!"

Bekah looked up at him in confusion, the dream had not yet dissolved and her heart was still pounding as though she had just run a race. Slowly the confusion lifted and she took another gulping breath before stating the obvious. "I just had a terrible nightmare."

"I know," said Renato, "I heard you moaning and thrashing about. Are you better now?" Renato looked at his watch. It was only four in the morning, too early for even the birds. "Do you think you will be able to go back to sleep?"

"I don't know. Right now my heart sounds like a jackhammer in my chest. I dreamt I was in a lake or river, I was being held underwater and couldn't make it to the surface for my next breath. I struggled and struggled and knew if I didn't get free soon I would die. The dream was so vivid and terrifying. Renato, please pray for me, I don't want to be afraid."

Renato knelt beside the cot and took both of Bekah's hands in his. "Dear Lord," he prayed, "Your Word says that You haven't given us a spirit of fear, but of power, love, and a sound mind.[43] I pray and agree with Miss Bekah right now that Your Word is true, and that we believe it. Thank You for freeing Miss Bekah from fear and giving her peace. We pray for a restful sleep to all who rest here,[44] in Jesus' Name."

Bekah could already feel herself relaxing and growing sleepy again. It always helped to have someone agree with you in prayer.[45] It also helped to remember that the last dream she had was the dream of being chased in a burning jungle. The knowledge of that dream gave her courage when it actually came to pass. It helped her put her trust in God, Who knows the beginning from the end.[46] She needed to remind herself that God was showing her these things to forewarn her and give her faith when they transpired. In her current circumstances, forewarned definitely needed to be forearmed.

Bekah opened her eyes again to bright sunshine. The birds were on the job, and so were the workmen, if the level of noise meant anything. Looking at her watch, she saw that it was already seven fifteen. They had not agreed on a meeting time for this morning. She still felt guilty about the lateness of the hour, especially when it appeared from the sound of everything around her that she was the only one still in bed. Bekah rummaged through her bags and found something to change into. She would worry about personal hygiene after she spoke with

[43] 2 Timothy 1:7
[44] Psalm 4:8
[45] Matthew 18:18-20
[46] Isaiah 46:9-10

Sherry about what facilities were available and where they were located. She made a quick trip to the outhouse. They all agreed it was not as bad as they thought it would be. Sherry had Daniel dig new holes on a regular basis and Sherry kept it spotless. From what she understood, there was an outdoor shower also. Bekah was curious as to what that entailed. Things were very different from the comforts of home, but she would adapt with a good attitude and a smile on her face.

A wonderful aroma was coming from down the hall. Bekah followed her nose. It led her right to the large coffee pot that sat on an actual wood burning stove that was now in the center of the room. They had knocked down the wall the stove had stood next to, in order to expand the kitchen, but had not yet moved the stove.

Bekah looked around. It appeared the room had been invaded by a large number of people. Daniel, Josh, Ted, Edwardo and Renato were there. Sherry and Connie were at the stove cooking breakfast. Maria was in one corner playing with her puppy, and Emilio and Paulo were on a blanket in the other corner. Manu and Leonardo were talking with four workers who were nailing the planks together to make the new wall. There were several conversations going on at once. It had the sound of an orchestra warming up, organized chaos. Bekah saw cups sitting on the table and went to get one, then followed her nose again to the wonderful aroma wafting from the coffee pot. Bekah loved coffee. There was a Copper Kettle coffee shoppe around the corner from her needlework store, back in Ogunquit. It was her one indulgence for the day.

Even as a little girl, she loved the smell of coffee. Nana Sara consumed copious amounts of it every day, and if Bekah behaved, she would be granted two spoonful's from Nana's cup into her glass of milk at dinner. As she got older, the ratio of coffee to milk increased. Finally, when she turned thirteen, she was granted permission to drink a real cup of coffee. Mornings have never been the same.

Sherry looked up from frying potatoes and said, "Good morning Bekah, did you sleep well?"

Bekah took her first sip and rolled her eyes in appreciation. "I did; but even if I hadn't, this coffee would make up for it. It's wonderful."

"Yes it is," answered Sherry with a grin. "We have a secret source. I hope it's not black market," Sherry rolled her eyes, "but Daniel has a friend."

Bekah laughed, and then asked, "How long have all these people been working?"

"It's nearly eight o'clock, but it appears that everyone slept in this morning. They only started around seven. We don't keep an alarm clock here; time runs by the sun or meals. It's not efficient, but we're not dealing in rocket science."

Bekah observed the crowded room and the several groups of people who were talking. A playbill containing the cast of characters and their corresponding actors and actresses was necessary to follow the plot. She turned in a circle and spotted Manu watching her. She turned back to Sherry and said in a whisper, "Manu is watching me. What should I do?"

Sherry put down her spoon, smiled at Bekah, and gave her a warm hug. "It's OK, really it is. I know this must all seem strange to you, but Manu is a good man. This has to be hard on top of everything else, but just trust that God is weaving a fabric here and Manu is an important color in the palette. He's a very young Christian, and he has been Chief for only five years. He's honest and caring and his people love and respect him. That says a lot. Why don't you go over and say 'good morning'. Knowing him, he is probably waiting for you to make the first move. He is most likely as nervous as you are."

Bekah took a large gulp of coffee, squared her shoulders, held her head up, and pasted a smile on her face as she walked over to him. He smiled a genuine smile at her and she felt her nervousness dissipating. She tried to dredge up an enthusiastic, "Good morning."

"Good morning," Manu returned, "Did you sleep well?"

"Yes I did," Bekah answered; then she remembered her nightmare and a frown crossed her face.

"What is it?" Manu asked with genuine concern in his voice. "Was there a problem?"

Bekah was embarrassed. She felt uncomfortable bringing up another nightmare, especially to a stranger. "I wasn't going to bring it up, but I had a troubling dream last night. I seem to be having them frequently."

"It didn't have anything to do with drowning, did it?" Manu asked with concern, "Because I had one too."

Bekah felt the room begin to swirl around her. The coffee cup dropped from her fingers as she felt herself began to fall. Manu's quick reflexes helped him reach out and catch her before she hit the floor. He sat her down, then he sat down next to her and put his arm around her, gently resting her head on his shoulder. Sherry hurried over, potatoes left to fry themselves. She placed her hand on Bekah's forehead, then knelt down and took her pulse. It was clicking along at a steady pace. Her breathing was normal though her face was pale.

"What happened?" she asked Manu. "What did you say to her?"

"Nothing," he answered indignantly. "Why would I want to do anything to hurt or scare the sister I just found? She told me she had been bothered by a disturbing dream last night. I asked her if it had anything to do with drowning, and she fell to the floor. I had a similar dream about her struggling to get to the surface of the water and take her next breath."

Renato, Ted and Josh had been watching what had taken place from across the room. They all hurried over to her. They had all had their eyes on Bekah since she had entered the room, but each for different reasons.

Renato was watching her because he had the heart of a father and he loved Bekah as if she were his own daughter. When they started this quest, he had vowed that if it were required he would give his life for her, and he was a man of his word. He heard what Manu had said about having the same dream. "What kind of new trouble could this mean?" he thought.

Ted had been watching Bekah also, and for a very similar motive. As a husband he had been a complete failure. He failed to love and cherish Bekah, caring only for wealth; the many ways there were to attain it, and to spend it. Now his goal was to do all he could to make this quest a success. God had asked him in his dream to fund the quest, but he was determined to make sure that nothing bad happened to Bekah, and that they all succeeded in what God had called them to do. He felt he had dropped the ball once when they were married. He was unwavering in his efforts not to fail her again. He also heard what was said about the dream. As a new Christian, he was feeling overwhelmed about the circumstances surrounding them. Everyone kept assuring him that God was in control, but to his way of thinking, God seemed to have dropped the ball a time or two lately.

Josh also had not taken his eyes off Bekah since she entered the room. He found himself watching her quite a bit lately. She seemed to be stirring up feelings in him that had long since grown dormant. Those feelings were wide awake now. This emotion was nothing he was looking for or expecting. "Why now," he questioned God. "This certainly seems like bad timing. I don't need any distractions at this time, and neither does she."

Josh also heard the dream being discussed. He didn't like that either. It appeared that only Bekah and Manu had experienced the dream, and he questioned why God had only given the dream to them. Josh planned to do everything humanly possible to keep everyone safe, especially Bekah. He put his faith in God to do His part and he would handle the rest. He had once heard a preacher say, "If you do the possible, God will do the impossible."

When Josh looked up, he saw Manu watching him. Josh wondered what the Chief had seen on his face in that unguarded moment. Manu stared at him speculatively for a few seconds, pondering that expression. Then he looked back down to Bekah as she began to stir.

Bekah opened her eyes and saw several faces staring down at her. She couldn't have been more embarrassed. She struggled to get up. Manu stood up and gave her his hand. "I'm so sorry," Bekah said. "I don't know why I did that. I'm not generally a weak person."

Sherry led Bekah over to a chair. "Sit down and relax. It's not like you haven't had any stress in your life lately."

Manu came over and pulled up a chair. "I'm sorry I disturbed you. Please forgive me. I don't want our relationship to start out wrong."

Bekah saw the concern on Manu's face, whether for their relationship, her safety, or both, she did not know, but both of those sentiments made her feel cared for. She felt a corresponding sentiment begin to bloom in her heart. She reached out and took both of Manu's hands into hers. With tears in her eyes she spoke from her heart. "I had resigned myself to being alone in this world. I know God is always with me and will never leave me, or turn away from me.[47] Renato has promised to be a father to me, but there was no one of my blood. When Nana, my grandmother was alive..." Bekah stopped, and a look of wonder crossed her face. She paused and looked up at Manu in surprise, then said with emotion in her voice, "She was your grandmother too."

Bekah started to cry, large tears running down her face. The reality of all that had transpired rose up in her and caused her to sob. Manu leaned over and gathered her into his arms. He

[47] Hebrews 13:5

placed a soft kiss on her forehead, as you would a small child to comfort them. He said, “Between Renato and me, we will make sure you are never alone, and that no harm comes to you.”

Bekah gazed at Manu and really saw him for the first time. “We have the same eyes,” she said.

Manu laughed, “My eyes are my best feature.”

They sat in companionable silence for a moment, ignoring the commotion around them. Then Manu asked, “Do you want to tell me about your dream, or is it something we all need to hear?”

Fear tried to rise up in Bekah again, but Manu’s closeness helped keep it at bay. “I think we probably all need to discuss it. It reminds me of the dream I had about the drums and smoke and being chased in the jungle. That dream turned out to be a warning, maybe this dream is also. We can wait until after breakfast. Then while everyone is together, we can discuss this.”

Manu queried, “I do not know about this other dream. Is it something I should be told? Has something happened I am not aware of?”

Bekah looked at him with surprise, “Yes, it appears there are things you don’t know. You do need to know about it, and I’ll tell you about it and the dream I just had after breakfast.”

CHAPTER ELEVEN

JUNE 16
THE VILLAGE

After breakfast, it was decided that they would meet in the gathering area to talk, pray, study and plan. Bekah got herself cleaned up and headed over. She found herself walking with Ted. He had been waiting at the door to escort her. Around his waist was a belt with a gun attached. Bekah asked cynically, "Aren't you a little uncomfortable playing cowboy, and possibly shooting yourself in the foot?"

Ted looked surprised at Bekah's sarcasm, and she immediately felt ashamed for what she had just said. He was quick with a reply of his own. "Well if I'm playing Wild Bill Hickok, you must be playing Annie Oakley."

"I have to admit, you're still fast with the comeback. I want to say I'm sorry for the comment. Please forgive me. I don't know what made me say that. It was inexcusable. I'm not usually so sarcastic."

"I was rather surprised myself, hearing that come from you," answered Ted. "It is a little out of character, but I do forgive you. We'll just chalk it up to the stress that everyone is under. There's a whole lot more happening on this trip than we expected. Last night was definitely an eye-opener. I certainly didn't plan on carrying a gun, but given the circumstances, I'm glad I have it."

Bekah and Ted walked into the gathering place and everyone was there, already sitting on mats in a circle. Bekah smiled and waved at Manu, but she went over and sat by Renato. She still felt safest with him, both physically and emotionally.

Everyone got quiet and Daniel said, "If no one has any objections, let's start with a time of prayer. Let's all pray quietly for several minutes. When we're done, we can talk about the dream, Bekah's abduction, or anything else God may have put on our hearts.

"Manu and Leonardo, I know this is new to you. God has us moving quickly, but He will show you what you need to know. We will try to have at least two Bible studies a day. For now, you can quietly talk to God, thank Him for your blessings, thank Him for sending Jesus to die for us, and ask for His guidance. He likes for you to talk with Him. Sometimes we hear Him talk back. He uses lots of ways to talk with us. Sometimes He uses dreams, as He has with some of us already. Sometimes He speaks quietly in our hearts. Sometimes He uses someone else to confirm what He has said to us. The more we talk with Him, the more He talks with us."

Manu interrupted. "I understand praying is important. Talking to God is a good thing, but I don't feel I can talk to God about the quest if I don't have all the facts. Please tell me what happened on the way up river to Bekah so I can understand all that is happening now."

"Bekah spoke up, "Manu, if you don't mind, I'm going to let Josh tell what happened. I'll fill in if I think something has been left out. Maybe we should cover this first and then pray."

"That's fine," Manu said and turned his attention to Josh.

Josh began to retell Bekah's story, starting first with her dream of being chased in a smoking jungle and hearing drums in the distance. Then he told of her abduction, starting from when they heard her first cry for help and ending with her description of her abductor and the sights and sounds she observed during her ordeal. When he was finished he turned to Bekah and asked if she wanted to add anything.

"Yes I do," replied Bekah. "I just thought of this. Before the kidnapper hit me I thought I heard him use some foul language that is strictly American slang. I've heard it said in anger and frustration, but I don't use that kind of language myself. It definitely isn't a phrase a native or a middle-eastern man would use."

"That's really interesting," Josh replied with surprise, "This is more evidence that there might be a Black Death training camp in the area. They are undeniably drawing recruits from America too. I'm going to have to call Isaac and let him know about this."

Josh turned to Manu and Leonardo and explained, "In addition to being a Missionary and working at my church, I have worked for our government in the past. I have one more month before I can permanently break ties with them as an employer. I have worked with a man named Isaac for years. He's also a friend and I trust him. We had some problems in Asunción, and I asked him to find out about a person who had threatened us. He told us to be careful, that the man was dangerous. Then he told us there were rumors of a Black Death training camp somewhere in the area. Are you both familiar with who or what the Black Death is?"

Manu responded, "We don't hear everything that happens outside our village, but some news gets in. We have been hearing about the Black Death for a year or so. They are very bad people and we do not want them here. We will help in any way we can to get rid of them."

Josh acknowledged the offer of help. "Thank you Manu. I hope that this can be handled without our involvement. Right now most people think we are missionaries, and I'd like to keep it that way. Later today I'll call Isaac and let him know what else Bekah remembered. It may be significant. If that answers everyone's questions for now, let's spend some time talking to God, and listening to what He has to say."

They all became quiet and a peace rested upon them.

Twenty minutes went by and suddenly everyone looked up. Manu jumped to his feet excitedly. "God spoke to me! I heard His Voice," Manu exclaimed with the eagerness and excitement of a new believer. "I didn't hear Him here," he described, pointing to his ears, "But here," Manu said, pointing to his heart. "He told me we need to stop being distracted by everything that has happened and to be busy with what He called us to do. We are to go out and stop the enemy, and bring those under his influence the Word of God." Manu looked around expectantly at everyone, and then sat down.

Leonardo, who had said very little thus far, stood up and said, "I also heard His Voice. It said that I should be busy getting our people ready, and not to worry about anything else. God said we were in the palm of His hand." Leonardo looked to Manu, and Manu nodded. Leonardo sat back down with a look of wonder upon his face. The God of the universe had just spoken to him. That takes a little getting used to. Despite the gravity of the situation, the glow on both their faces brought smiles and words of encouragement from everyone.

Josh stood up and said, "I had a similar word, not to get bogged down in the distractions, but to follow the quest." Josh turned and looked at everyone. "Have you all had a similar message? Did anyone have something different?"

Connie stood up. "God spoke to me to get my prayer team together and get busy. There's a devil out there looking for someone to devour and we need to stay alert, stay in prayer, and stay in touch with our other prayer group in Maine."[48]

She paused for a moment and then continued, "I must ask forgiveness. I have not been doing what God has asked me to do. He asked that I form a prayer army and also said that I have let my family and home duties distract me. I have sufficient help at home and instead of sitting and visiting with them, I

[48] 1 Peter 5:8-9

should be forming my army and praying. God said that His Word would show us what to do and which way to go."

Bekah stood up. "I got a Word of correction and encouragement both. God reminded me that even though Daniel was in the lions' den, He had shut the lions' mouths.[50] Even though Shadrach, Meshach, and Abednego, were in the fiery furnace, they were not consumed by the fire. Only the ropes that bound them were burned.[51] I've already been through some tests and God has saved me. I believe He will continue to save me. I know His Word says that I can do all things through Christ, Who strengthens me.[52] I just need to keep reminding myself of that fact."

Since no one had anything else to add, Josh shared how the group from Maine had called late last night because we had not called them as we had promised. Connie's word was just a reminder that we needed to keep the lines of communication open. Everyone put their thoughts on fulfilling the quest, and obeying the words God had just spoken to them.

Next, Josh brought up the most recent dream Bekah had and asked her to tell everyone what she remembered about the dream.

Bekah stood up and closed her eyes, as if trying to pull the dream from her subconscious to her conscious. "I don't remember much of the dream. It's like watching a ten second clip from a full length film, and then trying to describe what the film was about.

"I remember I was submerged in water. The water was very clear and I could see other people in the water. They also appeared to be struggling. Something had hold of me and I couldn't get to the surface to take a breath. I felt as though I was

---

[49] 1 Peter 5:8-9
[50] Daniel 6
[51] Daniel 3
[52] Philippians 4:13

going to drown." Bekah put her head down and said with frustration, "That's all I remember."

"OK Manu, can you tell us about your dream," Josh requested? "Is it any different from Bekah's?"

Manu responded, "I saw the water and Miss Bekah. It was clear. My dream was very similar to hers. There's a large lake several days north of here. A waterfall feeds the lake and the lake feeds the river. We will probably be going by there when we head out. We just all need to be on alert. Other than seeing Miss Bekah in distress, I don't remember seeing anything else."

"Manu," Josh asked, "Have you heard of any warlike tribes up in that area attacking nearby villages, taking their infants, and sacrificing them to their gods? God told us they were being sacrificed by fire."

Manu responded, "I have heard rumors of such things happening in the northern tribes. They are deep in the jungle and don't see white men very much. They follow the old ways. I think that might have even been where little Emilio came from. Someone may have sent him down the river to save him."

Josh asked, "How many men do you think we would be battling? Do the people from this savage tribe have modern weapons?"

"I do not know how many, they are a big tribe; perhaps seventy or eighty men, maybe more. They do not have modern weapons. Their biggest weapon is fear. All the tribes are afraid of them, afraid it will be their turn next. No one has ever stood up to them or their gods."

Josh responded, "Well I know that our God is greater and more powerful than all their gods put together. He's healed people, cast out devils, walked on water, calmed the storm, fed the multitudes, and even raised the dead. What can their gods do?"

This time Leonardo answered, "They believe their gods gives their tribe power to overcome their enemies."

"That's true," Josh said, "But has any of them ever come up against our God?"

"They probably have never heard of our God. What would happen if we told them of Him? Maybe they would believe and then He would become their God." Leonardo marveled at the thought. "That would be a wonderful thing," he added.

"Yes it would," said Josh. "Maybe that's what we are supposed to do, present the Gospel to them. But how do we go about doing that? In the spirit, we pray and seek God's wisdom and guidance; but what should we do in the natural? Much as I would like to arm everyone and go in fully loaded with as much manpower as possible, I don't hear God saying that. We'd be terribly outnumbered, but that doesn't bother God. He does some of His best work when He's out-numbered. God used Gideon, a man who lived a very long time ago. He was sent by God to fight a large army. God purposely brought down the size of his army from 32,000 to three hundred men fighting against many thousands. His enemies ended up attacking each other and God won the battle.[53] God also told Elisha the Prophet where ambushes were being set up for him so he could avoid them. During one of the battles, God showed Elisha's servant the angelic army that was fighting with them. They greatly outnumbered the enemy.[54] I know that if God has done these things in the past, He can do them again."[55]

Josh paused and was quiet a moment. Everyone waited. Then he spoke with authority, and it was as if the Word of God was coming out of his mouth. "I WANT YOU TO REMEMBER WHO YOU ARE FIGHTING AGAINST AND WHO IS FIGHTING WITH YOU. THE FULLNESS OF TIME HAS COME AT LAST AND SIN AND SATAN WILL BE DEALT WITH. I AM SENDING YOU FORTH TO PROCLAIM THAT THERE WAS A BEGIN-

---

[53] Judges 6 & 7

[54] 2 Kings 6:8-17

[55] Hebrews 13:8

[56] 2 Thessalonians 2

NING AND THAT THERE WILL ALSO BE AN END. PROCLAIM MY LOVE FOR ALL MANKIND, PROCLAIM MY GOODNESS AND MERCY; BUT ALSO PROCLAIM THAT THE TIME OF JUDGEMENT IS UPON US. THOSE WHO BELIEVE WILL BE SAVED AND THOSE WHO DO NOT WILL BE DAMNED.[56] NOW I HAVE CALLED YOU TO WIELD MY WEAPONS OF WARFARE AGAINST THE ENEMY. TAKE YOUR FOOLISH WEAPONS WITH YOU IF YOU WISH, BUT BE STRONG WITH MY WEAPONS WHICH CANNOT BE HELD IN YOUR HANDS, BUT ARE CARRIED IN YOUR HEART AND MIND AND SPIRIT.[57] DO NOT LOOK TO GO FORTH IN NUMBERS, BUT TAKE THOSE WHOM I HAVE CALLED BY THE SPIRIT. WHEN THE MOON IS FULL, I WILL LIGHT YOUR PATH. TAKE THIS TIME TO PRAY AND PREPARE."

They all stood there with eyes closed, listening to the Word of God come forth. For several minutes no one spoke. Then Josh said, "I humbly believe that God has just spoken through me. Before we say anything, let's just take a minute or two to wait and see if He speaks to anyone else."

They all sat there in the gathering place waiting quietly to see if God would speak further. Sensing movement around them they opened their eyes and saw five young men standing in the shadows, Philippe, Mario, Axel, Giancarlo and Maitie. These were the young men whom Daniel had been mentoring. It appeared God had chosen His army. There would be thirteen of them, counting Bekah. They did not count Sherry or Connie. Both of them had been given special orders to prepare things at home, and pray.

The five men slowly entered the meeting place. Mario spoke, "We were out, working down by the jetty, cutting away the tangle of reeds and all of a sudden we all knelt in prayer. After

---

[56] 2 Thessalonians 2

[57] Ephesians 6:10-18

some time passed, we looked at each other and began to talk excitedly. We felt that God had spoken to us to come to the meeting place and tell you we are to go with you."

Josh answered them. "I don't know any of you, and yet I believe that God has called you to come and be part of His army. We will be leaving when the moon is full. Does anyone know when that is?"

Giancarlo, who was the best farmer in the village answered, "It should be in five or six days and it is a good time to travel."

"Yes," Josh replied. We will depart the first night of the full moon. God said He would light our path. I don't know when, or if we will be back, all I know is we are to fight the enemy, and that God always wins. Can we all join hands and dedicate ourselves to this quest?"

Josh prayed, "Father God, we come to You in the mighty Name of Jesus, and consecrate ourselves to this quest. It is now first and foremost in our lives. We will follow where You lead us and not stray to the left or the right. We will work together in unity, and in strength, both physically and spiritually. Lord, just as You strengthened Samson physically in time of need, we pray that You will strengthen us also.[58] Help us keep our eyes and ears open, in order to not lose touch with those around us or with You. Help us to stay close to You Father, close enough to hear Your heartbeat. "

Again Josh spoke. "I feel that tonight we should have a tribal party. Let's invite the whole village. We can have a wonderful dinner, bring out and distribute all the gifts that we purchased in Asuncion, and then tell all those there about the quest. Then we will have another Bible study. I believe that with the telling, more will come to believe in the Father God and His Son Jesus."

Josh asked, "How do we get the word out to all the peo-

[58] Judges 13-15

ple? We don't want to miss anyone. We want everyone at the celebration and we want everyone to have the opportunity to hear God's Word and serve Him."

Manu replied, "For a celebration such as this we let the children do it. They will make sure everyone hears the news. We have three young men; we call them The Young Ring-leaders. They will organize the older children and see to the preparations, setting out mats, gathering banana leaves, making sure there is enough to drink. These three young men are future leaders of the village. I will make any other necessary preparations. I will send hunters into the jungle to bring meat for the dinner."

CHAPTER TWELVE

JUNE 16

ASUNCIÓN, PARAGUAY

Carlos Rampone brought his seat back to the upright position to prepare for landing. He looked out the window and saw the sprawling city of Asunción, Paraguay. He was down here to take care of some unfinished business. He had started to handle this problem back in the states, but before he was through, the participants had all left for Paraguay. Leaving jobs unfinished was not his forte. Carlos had been sent down to finish what he started, and would be working with a man named Esteban Montero. He didn't know much about Montero other than the information Haydon Carlton had provided. Montero was a bounty hunter who always brought in his prisoner. The thing that made him different from other bounty hunters was that his prisoner always came back dead. To Montero, "Dead or Alive," was a choice he got to make; he chose dead because it was more convenient for him. Rampone understood Montero's thinking. A dead body was so much easier to handle than a live one.

Rampone also felt that he had more skill and finesse than this Montero. What did it take to kill someone? No talent as far as he was concerned. But he liked to get the maximum information and the most pleasure out of a job, and simple killing was not the way to do it. He enjoyed playing with his prey as a cat does with a mouse. He had been toying with some ideas for the beautiful Bekah Ryan, and he was anxious to put them into practice. But first he had to pay off Montero, and that might prove to be a sticky situation. Haydon Carlton, his employer, had left things to his discretion, so he proposed to throw out some bait and see what he caught. But first he had some shopping to do. He needed to pick up a few weapons since he didn't want to risk bringing any into the country. After exiting the airport, he hailed a taxi and told the driver the name of a place he had been given to make his purchases.

The taxi pulled up to the Excelsior. It was a fairly large establishment with a shooting range out in the back. When he walked in several people were standing around. They all turned and stared at him. A short, stocky man walked up to the counter and said, "Good morning. My name is José and I am the owner of Excelsior. How may I help you?"

After glancing briefly at some of the other customers, Rampone spoke. "I need to purchase one medium and two high caliber hand guns and a high-powered rifle with a large scope. I want quality. What can you show me?"

"Is there any preference as to make and model?" José questioned.

"No, and cost is not a problem."

After his customer left, satisfied with the selection and performance of the weapons he had chosen, José made a call to a friend. He was worried about another new face purchasing a large amount of fire arms, and wanted to let his friend know what was happening. It was afternoon and he hoped his friend was about. After four rings a voice he recognized answered. "Hello Daniel, my friend," he said.

"José, is that you?" asks Daniel. "I haven't seen or spoken to you in quite a while. I want to thank you for taking care of my friends. They told me you treated them fairly and helped them when Esteban Montero threatened them. I am grateful."

José recounted the incident and then stated, "I was concerned for them, but they handled themselves well. I also want to mention to you that there have been several groups of people come through the store buying large amounts of weapons. Most are in their mid to late twenties and appear to be of Middle-Eastern heritage, but there were a few Americans also. They may try a disguise, but their accent is hard to cover. I am glad for the business, but is there something going on I need to know about? The latest sale was today, to a man of Spanish or Italian descent. He purchased some high caliber hand guns and a high caliber rifle with a large scope. I did not like the look of him. He paid cash and left no name or address, but by his accent, I could tell he also came from the U.S."

Daniel remarked, "I have a friend who might be interested in this information. I'll tell him what you said. Any other strange things happening that I need to know about?"

"I can't think of anything else right now, except the fact that I finally have security cameras. I turn them on when someone comes into the store. I have videos of all these people, including the one today. I will be happy to let you look at them. They are digital now; at last I'm keeping up with technology. I'll e-mail you a copy."

"Thanks José. Send them to me as quickly as you can. This may be important information."

"No problem. I'll send them right now. I've already got them together."

"I'll let my friend Josh know about this and get back with you. He's the one who stood up to Montero. He also has some friends who might be interested in this information. Keep your eyes and ears open." They finished the call and said good-bye. Daniel went looking for Josh to tell him about the phone call. It turns out he did not have far to go. Josh was right outside the door.

As they walked back into the house, Daniel heard the phone start ringing. Before he could even say hello a voice called out, "Is Joshua Randall there?"

Daniel turned and handed Josh the phone. "It's for you," he said.

"Hello, this is Josh."

"Thank God I caught you. News of you is getting around. You're a hot topic right now. Your purchase of weapons in Paraguay was picked up by someone in another department and reported. Your call to me was spotted, and lots of questions are being asked. I got a call from upstairs. I was told to get in touch with you and tell you that you're now on the clock. They said to try not to make your presence known, but snoop around and see what you can find out about these young visitors. Have you found their central location yet?" Isaac asked.

"No, and I don't want to. I want to keep as low a profile as I can here. I am with a bunch of civilians. I'm also staying with people from a rural tribe. Trouble often does have a way of showing up. If it does, we want to be ready for it, but I'm not going to go out looking for it."

Isaac replied, "If your computer is handy, I have emailed you about twenty passport pictures of questionable visitors who entered Asunción in the last few months. Show them to Bekah and see if anyone looks familiar. Is there anything else happening I need to know about?"

"Yes, Bekah remembered one other fact about her abduction. When the man grabbed her and she yelled, she heard him say something no native would say. He swore in English. We may be dealing with an American. We'll need to check this out. Hopefully Bekah will be able to identify her abductor from the passport pictures you're sending down."

"I'll give you a call back later today or tomorrow," Isaac said. "Try and solve some of these mysteries for me today. I have several people breathing down my neck right now. I'd like to make somebody happy."

"Wait, don't hang up yet. Daniel is signaling he has something to say."

Daniel took the phone, "My friend José, who owns The Excelsior, a weapons store in Asunción, called today with some interesting information I think you should know. Lots of weapons are being purchased by several groups of young men, mostly of Middle-Eastern descent. José has security videos of them and has emailed them to us." Daniel handed the phone back to Josh.

"This is really troubling," Isaac stated. "Will you email me a copy of the security videos? Let Bekah look at them too, and have her look at the pictures I sent you. If she recognizes anyone, call me right back. Maybe we might get lucky. Otherwise, I'll probably be calling you. Good-bye for now my friend." Josh ended the call and he and Daniel went looking for Bekah.

They found Bekah sitting in the kitchen with Connie and the children. She was on the floor playing with Maria and the little puppy. As soon as they walked in the puppy started barking up a storm. Josh observed, "He's a feisty little fellow. He's got a good protective instinct." Josh bent down and asked. "What's his name?"

Maria turned and hid her face in Connie's skirts. Connie scolded her. "Didn't you say you were a big girl now, big enough to take care of a puppy?" Maria looked up at Connie and shook her head yes. "Well, if that's the case you are old enough to talk with other people. Answer Mr. Josh; he asked you a question."

Maria stood up and looked at Josh. "His name is Hombrecito."

"Well that is a great name for a puppy, 'Little Man.' I can already see he is going to be a good dog. If you take good care of him, he's going to take good care of you." Josh reached over and scratched the puppy's ears. He looked up at Connie and smiled. Then he turned to Bekah and said, "Would you come with us, we need to ask you a few questions, and we've got some pictures and videos for you to look at."

Bekah sighed and rose to her feet, "I know what you are going to ask me. I've been asking myself the same question. Why didn't he kill me right there? Why did he leave me alone and unguarded? I've been thinking maybe he's not as much of a bad guy as we thought he was. I know he hit me and I was injured. He didn't have to carry me or drag me back to the clearing. He could have just as easily killed me then and there. I can't figure it out. If he was a radical member of the Black Death, I should be dead right now." Bekah realized she was rambling, and paused to regain her composure. "He could have cut off my head just as others have done to their captives. He was carrying a large machete. He also left me unguarded in the burnt-out clearing and only tied my hands. It's almost as if he wanted me to escape."

"It certainly is a mystery," Josh responded, "but one we hope to discover the answers to. Come over here to the computer," Josh motioned. "We have videos José sent us of several groups of men who recently purchased large quantities of weapons and ammunition. See if you recognize any of them."

Bekah sat at the computer with Josh and Daniel behind her. Ted, Renato, Sherry, Edwardo and Connie had all walked in and they looked at the videos together. There were ten very short videos. They were all groups of three or four people. With all their facial hair it was hard to recognize any of them. Also, the lighting was poor. They needed to tell José to have a light at the counter so the videos would show up better. They got to the last video and it was only one person, and he was clean-shaven.

Bekah looked at him thoughtfully. "Does he look familiar to you Josh?"

Josh looked at him for a long moment and then answered, "Maybe, but I can't be sure. My instincts say he's trouble. We know Montero is trouble. Let's just err on the side of caution. Josh paused to think and then turned to Daniel, "We need to tell

Manu there may be trouble. Maybe he can set out some men to keep watch on the jungle trails and the river. I would assume they would be coming by river, but we need to guard all areas of approach. Fortunately, inland is so difficult I don't expect anyone to come that way. The only other way is by air, and that is definitely not feasible.

"Bekah, let's look at these pictures Isaac sent." There were about twenty-five pictures, and Bekah started thumbing through them. She was about halfway through when she stopped. "Here he is!" she exclaimed as she laid his picture down on the table. Everyone gathered around to look.

Josh reached over to pick up the picture and asked her, "Are you sure?"

"I'm positive. I would know that face anywhere. It haunts me."

Josh looked down at the picture and an inkling of recognition stirred in him. "He looks familiar," Josh said. "Why would I know him?"

"Remember," said Bekah. "We think he might be American. Maybe you've seen his picture somewhere else. Do they have most wanted posters where you work?"

Josh laughed, "You've been watching too many movies, and television shows. My office is at the church in Claremore where I'm the Mission's Director. I don't have an office at the C.I.A. I only work for them part time.

"Well whoever he is, we need to call Isaac back and let him know what we've discovered so far. Keeping everyone in the loop is important so no one is taken by surprise. When we talk to Maine tonight, we need to tell them also." Placing the call, Josh continued, "This satellite phone is sure coming in handy. I'm glad we got the extra one. We can take it with us when we head out."

Isaac picked up on the second ring. He laughed. "I knew I'd be hearing from you sooner rather than later, but I didn't expect so soon. Go ahead and make my day. Maybe then I will be able to make someone else happy and they will get off my back for a while. I've been assigned to this case full time now, and anything that comes in concerning it goes right to my desk or cell phone, day or night, weekend or not."

Josh replied, "We're on twenty-four seven down here also, and seven of us are armed. The Chief, Manu, and his advisor Leonardo, are also now part of our group. They don't have firearms, but they have knives and machetes. We just now got a look at those pictures you sent. Bekah identified her captor. There are no names on these pictures, only numbers. He's number C1A4. The strange thing is, when I look at his face, he looks familiar."

Isaac sighed, "I've got permission, but I didn't want to tell you unless I had to. I wanted to be sure of the need before I compromised his cover. C1A is a code for a C.I.A. plant, and it's no wonder he looks familiar. His name is Akeem Farzhi. Do you recognize that name? We recruited him before he went back to Iraq; in fact, he came to us and volunteered before he even finished school. He's provided us with excellent information over the years. Several weeks ago we thought it important to try to get one of our operatives to infiltrate the suspected Black Death camps in Paraguay. We lost contact with him over a month ago. I'm glad it was you who found him. It's good for us, and it's good for you. If things get hot down there, maybe you can help each other. It seems he's already lent you a helping hand."

Josh shook his head. This was hard to believe. "Akeem was my childhood friend. Some of the people here already know this story, but I'll start from the beginning for the rest of you. Akeem moved into our neighborhood when we were in the first grade. He taught me Arabic and I taught him English. We both attended Oral Roberts University together all the way through our Master's Degrees. Akeem's family had a temporary visa. His father had been in the oil industry. He stayed for five years but then had to return to Iraq when his visa expired. He asked my parents if Akeem could stay with us until he finished school. They agreed, and during that time Akeem even became a Christian. I found out later his parents paid for my college education as a thank you for taking in Akeem. After graduation, Akeem said he wanted to return home. He said he missed his family and felt an obligation to them. After he left, I never saw or heard from him again. I tried writing, but the letters all came back."

Josh paused, having so many questions and not knowing which to ask first. "What do you know about his position in the group he's with? Do you have a way to get in touch with him?"

Isaac disclosed what he could, "His cover was that he was a disgruntled member of the elite, tired of the way things were going and wanting to see change quickly. It was a good cover, because it was true for so many young men his age. The trouble is, we haven't heard from him since he arrived in Paraguay over a month ago. Now it appears that he is out in the jungle and unable to get any messages to us. I will notify his contact, José, the owner of the Excelsior in Asunción, to head up to Puerto Bahía Negra. Akeem and his partner Mehdi met Jose when they first arrived in Paraguay. Maybe there will be a way to get a message to Akeem from there. Maybe Akeem will come to town and see José, or maybe you can find Akeem. Unfortunately, it seems there are too many maybes in this scenario. Keep your eyes and ears open. If there's nothing else, I'll call you back tomorrow afternoon."

CHAPTER THIRTEEN

JUNE 16
THE VILLAGE

After ending the call, everyone realized that it was time for the feast. Women from the village had come to escort them to the gathering area. There was a festive atmosphere brought on by all the food, and the large mound of presents that were going to be presented.

Another wild boar had been killed and had been cooking all day. From the sight of it and the delicious aroma permeating the air, it had to be time to eat. Manu announced to everyone that dinner was almost ready. He suggested that this would be a good time to give out the gifts that had been brought.

Josh went over and asked Manu, "We don't know the people. Would it be acceptable to spread out the gifts and you and your counselors can distribute them? But first we have special gifts for you and each of your counselors."

Each of Manu's counselors received a large metal canteen with a leather strap, a fishing pole, and tackle boxes with assorted weights of line and sizes of hooks and lures. They also received fishing nets and gaffs to bring in the catch. A large knife and matching spear with ivory handles had been purchased for Manu. After finding out Manu had a wife, a lovely comb, brush and mirror set was purchased to be given to Noemi.

The gifts for the tribe were distributed and the women especially appreciated the small knives and the scissors. The men were glad to receive the machetes, saws, axes and other farming and building implements.

Ted was eager to present Sherry with part of her wish list. He had purchased an autoclave, a generator, and four large lights. He had plans to purchase some solar panels to put on the clinic roof to provide some electricity. Plans had also been procured for a well to be dug, providing the clinic with a steady supply of water.

Sherry stood there with tears streaming down her face. "I had my faith out for a few of these things, but I had given up hope on the rest. These will all make my job so much easier." Sherry went over to Ted and looked up at him. "I can't thank you enough for all you have done."

Ted stood for a moment and then replied, "I want to thank you for giving me the opportunity to do what God asked me to do. I believe this is part of funding the quest. I'm finally seeing good coming from the money I've made."

People were milling around, talking and examining all the wonderful things that had been given to them. Then Manu called out in a loud voice, "The food is ready. Let us all pray before we eat."

Except for about twenty people who were standing by the shaman, everyone else joined hands and prayed God's blessing on the food. That's when the party really got started. Food and fellowship, no matter what culture, always seem to promote a good time. Torches were scattered around the perimeter of the meeting area and provided bright light for the festivities. The children were playing with their new toys and everyone was enjoying the opportunity to meet and speak with the visitors.

Since everyone was present and most had finished eating, Josh asked Manu if he thought now would be a good time to tell the people about the quest; why they had all come to Paraguay. He also asked if Manu would be willing to share the news of his recently found twin sister and that God seemed to have a hand in bringing them together at this particular time. Manu agreed and said he thought he should speak first as an introduction to Josh's tale of their quest.

Manu shared of the circumstances surrounding his discovery that Bekah was his twin sister. He asked Bekah to come and stand by him and show the people the crucifix her grandmother had given her. As they stood together it was apparent that there were similarities in their appearance. It was also apparent that a bond of love and respect was forming between the two of them. Most of the people were pleased. Again, there was that small group who appeared to oppose anything that had any hint of undermining their influence on the tribe. Finally Manu took Bekah's hand and said to the people, "This is my sister Bekah. Her blood is part of this village. With her permission, we will no longer call her Miss Bekah, but only Bekah, not as a sign of disrespect, but a sign of acceptance and belonging to the heart of this village. I ask that you treat her as one of us, and not just her, but all the visitors and Daniel and Sherry also. They are part of our heart.

"Now I want you to listen to Josh, who wants to tell you why they came, and why they feel that God has sent them here on a quest. You must then judge whether to believe them or not."

Josh came forward and spoke to the people. Manu stood by him translating as Josh spoke. Josh first told of everyone's dream and the call to bring hope through the message of the Gospel to them and the people of the surrounding tribes. Also the message needs to be presented to the large warring tribe who had been attacking these northern villages, taking the infant children they found and sacrificing them in fire to their vicious and evil gods.

The people listened with rapt attention, nodding their heads in agreement. Josh was convinced that some of them were worried that someday that tribe might venture further south and attack them. It would be a good thing to remove that sword from over their heads. When he finished, Josh asked if he could pray for the village, and for the most part, the people were receptive. Again, there was that small pocket of people surrounding the shaman who got up and left the meeting area.

After the prayer was over, Bekah was sitting and talking with Manu when something moving in the jungle caught her eye. It was hard to see clearly because the shadows were lengthening. She looked more intently and then turned back to Manu. "I think I see people standing just inside the jungle. They are watching us," she whispered.

Manu turned around and searched the shadows. Surprised, he saw them also. "I see them Bekah. There seem to be many of them." Manu stood and started walking toward them. A tall man carrying a small, bedraggled child came out from the dense cover of the trees. They spoke together and then Manu reached over and took the child into his arms. The man turned and motioned to the rest of the people to come out of the jungle. As they slowly emerged, it was evident that they had been through a terrible experience. Several of them had injuries ranging from numerous cuts and scratches to burns and possible broken bones. All appeared to be dirty, hungry, thirsty, and just plain tired. They walked with heads hanging and shoulders drooping. Their clothes were in tatters and most appeared to have a layer of soot covering their clothing and their exposed body. They carried no possessions or supplies with them, and advanced, expecting nothing; only hoping for an opportunity to rest, and drink some water. They approached in groups of two's and three's. There was no life or vitality to their step and their eyes were empty, devoid of life or hope.

All talking stopped as everyone from the village turned and observed the travelers coming forward. The laws of hospitality became apparent as several women immediately went in search of wet cloths so that the strangers could wipe off some of the grime they were wearing. Several others went about offering water, tea, and juice to the travelers. Room was made and mats put down so they could sit. Banana leaves were distributed to act as plates for all the food set before them. Because of the generosity of the village, there was more than enough food to go around.

Manu went over to talk with Dr. Sherry, then went and stood in the center of the meeting area and made an announcement in Guarani to the visitors. "There should be enough food and drink for all. You are welcome to spend the night here in our meeting area. We will be happy to provide blankets for those who need them. Also, we have a doctor here who can help those of you who are injured. She is aided by her God who hears her prayers and answers them. I don't know who your gods are, but they do not appear to be taking care of you. If those who are injured will follow me, we will go to our clinic where you will be taken care of."

Renato had translated for his companions what was being said. Bekah said to them, "I'm going with Sherry to see if I can be of any help. I'm not a nurse, but I can boil water or carry instruments and I don't get sick at the sight of blood. This is a way I can personally be involved and I need to do this. These people are my people now." She turned and ran to catch up with the line of injured people.

Sherry turned to Daniel and said, "Now would be a good time for us to get out the cots and blankets you brought back from Puerto Bahía Negra. Set them up in the new room. Get some more hot water going and see if you can find one or two men to help you. We'll probably need a lot of water and wood for the stove."

As Sherry began walking toward the clinic, she counted seventeen people following her. "It was going to be a long night," she thought. Then she saw Bekah running after her and smiled. Even though language might be a problem; a caring smile and helping hand spoke a universal language.

Manu went forward into the group of people that remained behind, “Is the Chief among you?” he asked.

A tall, thin man of about forty years of age answered. “The Chief is dead. I was one of his counselors.” He stood, cradling his left arm and grimacing in pain.

Manu noticed and said, “Those who were injured were told to go with the doctor. Why did you not go?”

“I needed to speak to the Chief and tell him what has befallen us.”

“I am the Chief; my name is Manu. Come, I will walk with you to the clinic and you can tell me your story.”

The man replied, “My name is Arandu. My village is on the river a three day walk from here. Eight days ago our village was attacked by a large tribe led by an evil witch doctor. Early in the morning they came down out of the hills and rushed into our village. There were so many of them we were overcome almost immediately.

“At first they just gathered us all together. Then they began building a large fire. It was at that point we knew what was going to happen and the young mothers tried to escape with their babies. Everyone tried to help them, but many of us were then beaten or killed. I don’t know if any babies escaped. There was so much screaming and fighting going on. The fire had been growing and growing, its flames reaching up into the trees. They did not seem to care if the jungle caught fire; they were so focused on their ritual.”

Arandu’s eyes reflected his despair, and his voice carried the sounds of sorrow. He was not the only one who carried this burden. From the youth to the aged, defeat weighed them down like a millstone. There appeared to be no emotion left in them. They stared blankly ahead with unseeing eyes.

“Then they forced all the mothers of the infants to stand

to one side. We were all aware of what was going to happen because this tribe has been a scourge to the surrounding area for many years. In fact, ten years ago they had previously attacked our village." As they walked Arandu continued to talk, chronicling the horror that had befallen them.

"Most of the warriors stood before the rest of the people with spears and clubs raised. If anyone made an attempt to disrupt the sacrifice, they were killed or seriously injured. One by one the babies were torn from their mother's arms. While they stood there sobbing, the warriors raised the infants to the sky and then callously threw them into the roaring fire. Many died that day trying to save those infants, but there was no escape.

"After they left it took two days for the fire to burn out, and three more for us to prepare to leave. We had to take care of the injured, bury the dead, and gather what food we could find for our journey. There was nothing left to take with us. They had stolen everything of value. All that remains is our tribal treasure, which was buried in the jungle outside our village. If you let us become part of your village, we have agreed to share the treasure with you."

Some pride appeared in Arandu's voice as he spoke of the tribal treasure. That was one thing that had not been stolen from them, but he would have relinquished it all for the life of even one infant. Life, especially young life, was a gift from the gods and something to be cherished. He did not know what god these invaders served, but this loss of life was a sacrilege.

"One thing we did notice before we left was the body of our Chief's wife. We found her by the river. She had been darted by one of the warriors searching the jungle for any who may have escaped. She was also the mother of a small baby. None of the warriors came in with a baby by itself. All were taken from their mothers. We think she was trying to get away. We don't know what happened to the baby."

Manu had listened to everything Arandu had to say without

comment. Now he disclosed some information he had that might be of help. "A few days after your attack, a small baby in a basket drifted down the river and was trapped by the river reeds. He has been adopted by one of our families and is being well-cared-for. After your arm has been taken care of I will introduce you to the family. They are a very good family and are raising him as their own."

Manu and Arandu had arrived at the compound. "Here we are at our clinic. Doctor Sherry will tend to your injuries. I will come back and check on you after we get all your people fed and settled for the night."

Manu turned and asked, "Doctor Sherry, will you need some more help?"

"Yes Manu," Sherry answered in Guarani. "Just at first glance and judging from the extent of the injuries, I'll need at least three people; one more to help me care for the visitors, and two to help get water, wood, and supplies. I'll also need someone to light lanterns and hold them so I'll be able to see. Bekah has come to assist me and Daniel is looking for additional help. If you see him, he can tell you more of what we will need."

Manu thought that Dr. Sherry's ability to speak fluent Guarani was going to be helpful in dealing with this northern tribe. She has a gift for language and was able to speak confidently after only four years in Paraguay.

Sherry had scattered mats on the floor for everyone to sit on. She introduced herself and said, "I'm Doctor Sherry, and this is my friend and helper Miss Bekah. I run the medical clinic here and we will do all we can to take care of you. First, I want to ask my God to help me, and also to help you. I'm going to pray that He strengthen you, help your injuries to heal quickly, and give you hope." With that said Sherry raised her voice in prayer. The people sat there in stunned silence. None of them had ever called on their god for help. Most of the time you didn't want him to notice you for fear he might be angry and punish you just as he had when he sent the evil tribe that had taken their babies.

According to Manu's count, sixty-two people had come out of the jungle; eighteen of them were injured and now sitting here. Sherry went down the line with a pad and made note of obvious injuries, triaging them. Then, starting with the most severe injuries first, she began to minister healing to all of them, physically and spiritually.

Daniel came in with Edwardo, Leonardo, and Giancarlo. He told Sherry he had left Mario in the other room setting up the cots and then seeing to more water.

"I wish we had set up the generator and the autoclave. I could certainly use the light and the sterilized instruments right now," Sherry declared. "But I've managed so far without them; I guess I can manage a little bit longer."

Sherry's most serious injury to tend to was the broken arm Arandu had suffered; but he declined help until all the others had been cared for. Because of his decision, Sherry's first patient was an elderly woman with a large laceration across the right side of her face. It had stopped bleeding, but the wound was dirty, and the edges needed to be trimmed and fastened together. There was a one to two inch gap between the edges, and Sherry washed it out to remove dirt and debris. She then flushed it with an antibiotic solution. She had to trim the dried and dead skin on the sides of the wound to have viable edges to sew together. Finally she began stitching it up. It would leave a large, puckered scar, but there was nothing she could do about that. The emotional scars they would all carry would have a far greater impact. She then applied some antibiotic cream and a bandage.

All through the painful procedure, the woman had not uttered a sound. She sat there, oblivious to her surroundings. Sherry knew she was in shock, not so much physically, but emotionally. It appeared to be a form of post-traumatic stress. Sherry called over to Mario. "See if you can find someone to make some hot, sweet tea for everyone. And bring some food over from the celebration. I think everyone here would benefit from the tea's warmth and comfort. It appears to have been a while since anyone has had anything substantial to eat."

Sherry kept moving down the line of people. She noticed Bekah stopping and ministering a healing touch, or even just a smile to everyone she passed. There were men and women, young and old. They all looked as though they had been through a war zone, and indeed they had. This had been a skirmish, leading up to the final battle: good versus evil, light versus darkness. It appeared the final fragments to the puzzle were being revealed. God was showing them bits and pieces, illuminating an area here and there.[59] Sherry thought, "We don't know all the moves Father, but we know the outcome, and we put our trust in You."[60]

After treating several lacerations, burns, painful bruises and a broken arm Sherry washed her hands one last time. Then she poured herself a cup of the steaming tea from the large pot and sat down amongst her patients. It already appeared they were benefiting from the comfort of the tea, and the platters of fruit and bread that had been brought to them. Bekah was sitting amongst the group with a young girl of about three years old on her lap, rocking her back and forth and singing softly to her. It was amazing what just being in a caring atmosphere could do in situations such as this. Now she was going to introduce them to her God who was the epitome of loving and caring.

Sherry looked at all of them and her heart was grieved at their suffering. Sitting there, she spoke to them in a soft voice. "You won't understand the words, but I'm going to ask my helper, Miss Bekah, if she will sing a song of thanksgiving to our God. Then I will tell you about Him."

Sherry turned to Bekah and asked her if she would sing

---

[59] John 16:13-15
[60] Proverbs 3:5-6

the hymn "Amazing Grace", and let the people experience God's peace as the words invited His presence to come among them.

Bekah was surprised by the request, but was in no way disturbed by it. Bekah had been singing since she was three and knew the power of music.[61] She was confident that even though the people would not understand the words of the hymn, they would be ministered to by the Holy Spirit as he was invited into this gathering of lost and hurting people. He was not hampered by language, His was the language of the Spirit and it was universal.

Bekah began the first verse softly, as a door opening, inviting the presence of God. Slowly the hymn built as the people became more aware of something happening in their midst. As the last verse was sung with power and confidence, it was transferred to the people. An unfamiliar source of hope was in their midst and they were anxious to find out what it was and where it had come from.

When the song ended, Sherry stood up and spoke to those gathered around her. "That song was about my God, and His power to bless you in any circumstance you are in, good or bad. Let me tell you about Him," she said in Guarani. She told them the Genesis story, including the sins of Adam and Eve. "Before sin," Sherry said, "God walked and talked with Adam and Eve in a beautiful garden,[62] but sin separated them from God.[63] A sacrifice needed to be made as a bridge back to God. Man didn't have anything good enough to sacrifice. The blood of animals was not good enough. The blood of man, even children was not good enough, because man was sinful. A pure and holy sacrifice was needed to pay the price for sin. But God, Who is a holy God, loved the people so much, that He sent His only Son Jesus, to die as that pure and holy sacrifice.[64]

"During His life, Jesus did only what was good and pleas-

[61] 1 Samuel 16:23
[62] Genesis 3:8
[63] Isaiah 59:2
[64] 1 John 4:10

ing in His Father's eyes. He healed the sick, fed the hungry, and even raised the dead,[65] yet the rulers of the land killed Him. God allowed this to happen so the sacrifice could be made and the price for sin could be paid. Then God raised Jesus from the dead.[66] Jesus fought Satan, the evil god of this world, and defeated him.[67] Before He went back to Heaven to be with His Father God, He told us to fight against Satan, the god of this world, and keep fighting until He comes back again. Jesus said He would give us the power we needed to fight Satan who is the Devil.[68] He also said He would send us a Comforter Who would not only be with us, but live in us, and help us to serve God, our Heavenly Father, and combat the enemy.[69]

"God knows what it's like to have a child killed and sacrificed to an enemy. Knowing this, He wants to comfort you as only He can. Would you like to know and serve this God?"

Sherry looked at the group and saw them all, men, women and children, nodding their heads. "I'm going to say a prayer to my God and ask you to repeat it." Sherry lifted her face to Heaven and prayed. "Holy Father, You allowed Jesus to be sacrificed for my sin so I could be received by You again as Your child. I am sorry for those things I have done that were not pleasing to You. I ask Jesus to be my Lord and Savior. I ask that He come and live in my heart and help me to serve You with all my heart. In Jesus' Name I pray."

Sherry sat quietly for a while, then stood up and looked around. There was a different Spirit in the room. The atmosphere had changed. The Comforter, the Holy Spirit, had come and applied His balm upon the spirits of the people. Instead of anguish, peace reigned. There were still tears, but now there was hope. In

---

[65] Matthew 11:4-5
[66] Acts 4:10
[67] Ephesians 4:8-10
[68] 2 Corinthians 10:4
[69] John 14:16-21

the dream God had given the group of people He had called to this quest, God said He wanted to send hope to a tribe suffering in the jungle. He was the God of hope and He was fulfilling His Word. He did not want to see anyone suffering.[70]

Edwardo walked in with two other men and brought three large buckets of warm water, towels, soap, and several small basins so the people could wash themselves before they slept. Sherry told them they would also be bringing cots and blankets they could lay on to rest for the night. She assured them the rest of the tribe was being cared for also. She instructed Mario to stay with them and help them in whatever they needed.

Sherry and Bekah left the clinic and saw that most of the people of the village were still at the gathering place, sitting and talking with the people of the tribe from the north. It was much quieter and more subdued than it had been earlier. It was no longer a party, but more like a church service during times of ministry. Here too, hope permeated the atmosphere.

Looking around, Sherry observed that Daniel and Josh were talking with Manu and Arandu. Ted was sitting next to Lara and helping her with the children. Sherry did a double take on that and then smiled. God certainly had a large bag of surprises. She saw Renato on the other side of the gathering place helping one of the older women who had come in from the jungle get to her feet. He had a soft smile on his face and was speaking quietly to her. There appeared to be a young boy with her and Renato had his hand on the child's shoulder. The night was winding down and they were late with the phone call again, but it could not be helped. One person Sherry did not see was Connie and the babies. The coming of this tribe might impact her and Edwardo's adoption of little Emilio. She hoped not, but time would tell. If we trust Him, God will work it out for good.[71]

---

[70] Isaiah 61:3

[66] Romans 8:28

CHAPTER FOURTEEN

JUNE 16
THE VILLAGE

Sherry gathered everyone up and they headed for the house. It was time for their phone call to Maine. She sent Edwardo down to get Connie. Sherry was concerned she might be trying to avoid things by staying out of sight, but that was no way to face a problem.

When Connie arrived Sherry could see that was not the case. Connie was excited and energized. She had been at home for the last three hours praying with her prayer partners Alma, Sol, Victoria and Jeruti. She had brought them with her to the meeting.

"I'm excited that these people have come into our village allowing us to help them. I know they are probably the people little Emilio came from, but I am not afraid. God has asked me to trust Him and He will work it out. He also said our prayers led them to our village so that they would hear a message of hope and come to know and serve Him and His Son Jesus."

Sherry interrupted. "I didn't have a chance to tell anyone, but all those people who needed medical attention listened to the message of salvation and accepted Jesus as their Lord and Savior. So Connie, what you heard in your time of prayer has already come to pass." Then she turned to Daniel with a smile. "Daniel, our church is growing. Edwardo, isn't it exciting what God is doing?"

Daniel nodded and smiled in agreement. "Before we call, does someone want to go and see if Manu and Leonardo are coming?" But that did not prove to be necessary, Manu and Leonardo showed up with Arandu, and also Philippe, Axel, Giancarlo, Mario and Maitie.

Manu declared, "I have told Arandu about the quest. He feels as though he should be involved since it was someone from his village who had been calling out to any god who would listen and our God listened. Now he wants to know more about our God."

Daniel could find no reason to oppose them. So everyone sat and the phone call was placed. "Hello, this is Joe. Is everyone there?"

Daniel spoke up. "Joe, you're not going to believe this, but there are now twenty of us sitting here. I'm sorry the call is late again, but so much is happening. The remnant of the tribe that was attacked came out of the jungle and has asked to become part of Manu's tribe. There are sixty-two of them. Many were killed, eighteen injured, and fourteen infants were taken and sacrificed. They have not yet been able to count all the dead. A few even died in the jungle on their journey here. The eighteen that were injured were tended to by Sherry. Not only did she see to their physical injuries, but also to their spiritual needs. She explained to them the plan of salvation and all eighteen received Jesus as their Lord and Savior."

"That's exciting," exclaimed Joe, "and wonderful news. Not much is going on up here that we can see. No news about Haydon Carlton. He seems to be keeping a low profile, at least as far as we're concerned. Jim Hathaway called and said they haven't made any progress in finding out who broke into Bekah's house. He said he would keep us informed."

"We've had some other interesting happenings," Josh said." While praying God spoke to all of us, even Manu and

Leonardo. He told us to not be distracted by what is happening around us." Josh related the rest of what God had said. "Based on what God said to us, we will be leaving in five or six days, depending on the full moon. There will be eleven of us setting out on the quest."

Josh was interrupted by Arandu. Manu had been translating what was being said into Guarani so he would understand. "No, that is not correct," Arandu stated. "I will also be coming with you, and maybe a few more men from my village. We have been praying and your God answered our prayers. I would like Him to be my God. You must tell all of us about Him because there may be more that feel as I do. You must tell us about this God, and what He requires of us."

Josh spoke to Manu, "Tell Arandu to allow his people to rest tonight. Tomorrow, after breakfast, we will tell them about our God and His Son Jesus. We will tell them about the quest God has sent us on and pray for all who want prayer."

Joe spoke up again. "We will keep all of you in our prayers. Can you work it out that Connie and her prayer team calls us around ten tomorrow morning? Our prayer team would like to talk with them and make sure we are all praying in agreement. Also, you never mentioned whether you got our fax showing all the pictures of the artifacts. We were wondering whether it went through."

Daniel answered, "With everything that has happened today, we haven't even looked. We'll check it after we say goodbye. We are all doing well. God is moving quickly down here and we are following Him as best we can. Don't stop praying. Connie will be calling you tomorrow morning, and we will call tomorrow night. God bless you all."

Daniel spoke to Manu and the rest of the men and women that were here with him. "Do all of you want to come back in the morning for breakfast? We don't have enough chairs, but with the new addition we will have room for everyone to sit on the floor, and we have plenty of mats."

Manu replied thoughtfully, "That's a very good idea. That way I will be able to go now and check on everyone and make sure they are made as comfortable as possible. I will have some extra fruit and bread sent over here tomorrow morning. I will also tell Paloma to come by early so she can help Dr. Sherry. Arandu will spend the night at my house so we can talk a while longer and get better acquainted."

CHAPTER FIFTEEN

JUNE 17
THE VILLAGE

It was a noisy room that Sherry walked into that morning. By the aroma, she could tell that coffee was already brewing and that the tea was steeping. A large pot of rice was on the stove and from the tantalizing smell pervading the room, she knew that chipa, which could only be described as a Paraguayan bagel, was in the oven.

Paloma had brought two other women along to help her with the extra work. They were all busy cutting up bowls of fruit that would be placed between the twenty or so people who would be sitting on the mats scattered on the floor. Food was also being brought back into the spare room that now housed the seventeen injured villagers from of the displaced tribe who had come in last night.

Sherry had just finished examining her patients this morning and was pleased with how well they were recovering. The attention to their injuries, food, hot tea, and a good night's sleep had certainly been beneficial to their improvement. But prayer, God's grace, and their restoration of hope were a far better remedy than anything she could have prescribed. Thank God none of the injuries was life threatening. She was encouraged that the Spirit of God had responded to her prayers and the needs of the injured. His peace still rested on them this morning, helping them to overcome the horrific circumstances they had experienced.

Sherry poured herself a cup of coffee and surveyed the room, searching for Daniel. She spotted Edwardo and Connie sitting with the five young men God had called to go with them on the quest. They were all in their early twenties and Daniel and Edwardo had been mentoring them in the things of God for the last year. Their hearts were tender towards God. They had a genuine desire to serve Him with everything that was in them. Still everyone was experiencing some uncertainty, not knowing exactly what God had planned, and what He would require of them. Sherry placed her hand over her stomach and prayed for the life that was continuing to grow within her. She did not know the future, but put her trust in God, knowing that He would deal with tomorrow. Today seemed to have more than enough challenges of its own.[72]

Sherry spotted Daniel walking into the room with Bekah, Ted, Renato and Josh. They were all in deep conversation and paused as they entered. Josh headed over to where Manu, Arandu and his counselor, Arasunu were sitting. Sherry went over to talk with some of the people who had come in the previous night. She wanted to make sure they were all well, and that there were no other injuries among them.

Josh needed to question Arandu concerning the attack. He had been told that Arandu could speak some Spanish, but it might not be enough to answer the questions Josh wanted to ask. After asking permission, Josh sat down with the three of them. Josh introduced himself and began to speak to Arandu in Spanish, hoping they would be able to converse freely, yet thankful Manu was there to translate into Guarani if needed.

"Arandu," Josh questioned, "Please tell me everything you know about the tribe that attacked you; not just what happened during the attack, but anything you may have heard about them in

---

[72] Matthew 6:25-34

recent years? Even a small detail may turn out to be important."

Arandu conferred with Manu, making sure he understood all of what Josh had asked. Arandu took a deep breath and then spoke of the large warring tribe. He began to speak in halting Spanish. "This tribe has been making war and sacrificing babies since before I was born. Over the years their numbers have grown and their power has increased. They live several days walk northwest of our village. It is always this time of year that they attack. I know of several other villages that have been attacked previously, and I'm sure there are many more villages I am not aware of. They use the power of the gods they serve to overcome their enemies. None have been able to stand against them. The fear of them alone is enough to cause defeat to any tribe they encounter."

Arandu's eyes glazed as the memory of what he had experienced washed over him. He began to relate what he and his village had gone through. Manu was also listening carefully, ready to translate if required. "It was morning when they came. Most families were finishing their meal and making plans for the tasks of the day. The jungle had been unusually quiet that morning, but our tribe had lived in this one region for many years. Most animals, large and small, had left the area due to being hunted continually.

"It was a happy morning for us. My daughter-in-law had just given birth to a strong son two weeks before. This was her first child and my first grandson. There were several of us sitting around the communal fire drinking a last cup of tea when we heard the first cries of alarm. We were attacked on all four sides. Their intent appeared to be to force everyone into the center of the village. As soon as the commotion was heard it was clear what was happening, and the young mothers started to panic, grabbing their babies in an attempt to escape. There were fifteen mothers with young infants who would have been of interest to the attacking tribe and their witch doctor. He did not care about the rest of us. He didn't want to kill us all because that would diminish his continuing supply of infant sacrifices. In addition, given their numbers and strength, we were too weak to offer any serious resistance. He gave orders to kill the most troublesome young men and all who offered opposition. My son was among the young men who were killed. He died trying to save his son from the fire."

Arandu spoke with a mixture of grief and bitterness. He had waited a long time for a grandson. The father of the child was his fourth and only living son. Arandu's wife had given birth to ten live children: four strong sons and six daughters, but accidents and sickness had taken the lives of his first three sons, and one daughter had died in childbirth. Of the rest, one had died on the trip through the jungle. The remaining were young children.

In a low, intense voice, Arandu continued on with the story. "At the orders of the witch doctor, his men went through the village, taking everything of value. They took special care going through the Chief's and the shaman's dwellings, looking for the tribal treasure. Some was stolen, but the people were wise and had kept the bulk of their treasure hidden."

Arandu turned to Manu and declared emphatically, "When we go to avenge our dead and take back what belongs to us, we will dig up the rest of our treasure and bring it back to share with you and your people since we are to be one tribe."

Josh interrupted, "Arandu, you need to realize this isn't a quest to search for vengeance. God has not guided us here to seek revenge, but to bring hope to the tribes of this region, and also the message of the Gospel of Jesus Christ, His Son. We were told this witch doctor sacrifices these babies to his gods for wealth and power. Is that true?"

"Yes," shouted Arandu with great agitation, "And he is going to pay for every life that he has taken. I will see to that." Arandu was breathing heavily and anger emanated from his body like flames from a fire. These flames threatened to burn him up, and anyone else that came within range; not just his enemies, but his own people if they dared to defy him.

"Arandu," Josh called in a quiet voice. "God didn't send us here to wreak vengeance, no matter how much we think it's deserved. God has every right to be angry at us and punish us. We sin against Him continually, but He sent His Son Jesus to be a sacrifice for our sin. He allowed His Son to be killed in order for us to be saved. God sent my friends and me here to bring hope to the hopeless and to bring the Gospel of His Son, Jesus to the lost.

"Arandu," Josh inquired softly, "Are you lost?"

Arandu stared at Josh as tears started to course down his cheeks. "I know where I am, but I don't know where I'm going. I cannot see a clear path before me anymore. Does that make me lost?" Arandu asked.

Despair caused his voice to quaver and his shoulders to droop. He sat there and great sobs wracked his body. Emotion crackled in the air like electricity. Arandu's people sat watching, transfixed by his actions. They had never seen him express these emotions in public before, and were disquieted and confused. Fear knocked on the door of each and every person seated there, an uninvited guest trying to take advantage of the current situation.

Josh sensed this fear in the people, and was reminded of the fact that whenever God intervened in a situation, His first message to His people was "Fear not!"[73]

Josh stood up. He asked Manu to translate into Guarani as he spoke to all who were in the room. He spoke to them of the love and faithfulness of God.[74] He reminded them that God loved them so much He sent His Son, Jesus, to die for

---

[73] 2 Timothy 1:7, Luke 12:6-7

[74] Lamentations 3:22-24

[75] John 3:16

them.[75] He told them that God's love and sacrifice was not just for them, but for all the people of the world, even the people of the evil tribe.

"The Word of God says all of us have sinned and none of us are worthy,[76] yet Jesus died for us while we were all still sinners.[77] God loves all of us with a perfect love we cannot even begin to understand. He loves us from His perspective – not ours. He asks us to forgive those who have sinned against us."[78]

Arandu leapt to his feet with a cry of anger and frustration. "Do you mean God wants me to forgive this tribe and their leaders for what they have done? I don't think a God Who loved me would ask me to do that. It would be impossible."

Josh quietly asked God for His wisdom, and to give him the right words to say. "Arandu, the Bible says we can do all things through Jesus, that He strengthens us.[79] It also says that with God, nothing is impossible.[80] If you ask Him, He will help you."

"I don't want to forgive them," Arandu answered, "their sin is too great."

"The Bible says Jesus' sacrifice paid for the sins of the whole world. They have a right to refuse forgiveness, but you have no right to withhold it. You have asked the Holy Spirit to live in you and lead and guide you. Listen to what He is saying. I will tell you one more thing the Bible says. If you will not forgive others then God cannot forgive you."[81]

Arandu paused at this thought. He knew this God was a very powerful God and he did not want to anger Him. "I don't want God angry at me," he said. "Even if I wanted to forgive these people, I don't think I can. I don't have the strength to do it."

---

[76] Romans 3:23
[77] Romans 5:8
[78] Luke 11:4
[79] Philippians 4:13
[80] Matthew 19:26
[81] Matthew 6:15, Luke 6:37

Josh smiled, "Arandu, you only have to be willing to forgive and God will help you accomplish the rest. As we step out in faith, He meets us. You believe and God is pleased and will reward you.[82] One way He does that is with His help. He will help you forgive if you ask Him. Arandu, will you ask God for His help?"

All eyes turned to Arandu, watching his reaction to the question and waiting for his answer.

Arandu struggled in confusion; thoughts and feelings stirring in his soul. In the darkness of his being he cried out, not knowing if it was in anger, frustration or calling for help. He only knew that he was not capable of forgiving and God had the answer to his problem. Arandu knew he needed God's help, and God in His grace and mercy led him out of the darkness and into His light.[83] A feeling of comfort and protection enveloped Arandu, and not just him, but all who were present.

Manu rose to his feet and went over to stand by his friend Josh. He recognized the presence of God. He had breathed His breath over them and covered them with His peace. As it settled, the pain and fear, the anger, frustration and hopelessness began to dissipate and a refreshing filled all their minds, hearts and bodies. Those whose bodies had been injured felt the pain leave. Those whose spirits had been injured were made whole again.[84]

The refreshing traveled through the whole village and healed and refreshed all those who received it. Chabuto and Tuvicha stood at their door invoking the presence and power of their gods, and refusing to receive the gift of God. The small handful of Tuvicha's followers still resisted the call of the Holy Spirit and clung to their satanic gods of the past.

Arandu's hard heart had been broken before God and forgiveness poured out of his spirit and his mouth. "I know I cannot receive God's forgiveness unless I forgive. I choose to forgive.

---

[83] Matthew 4:16

[84] Isaiah 61:3

I ask God to help me keep on forgiving, even when thoughts come my way of what happened. Please God, keep me in Your thoughts and I will keep You in mine."

Josh spoke quietly to Manu. "These people have been through a terrible situation and God is helping them. Do you remember the time we prayed and God sent His peace?"

"Yes," Manu replied. "It was a wonderful thing. I see He has done it here also. Can He do it again?"

Manu stood up and spoke to Josh excitedly. "Let me talk to the people. Let me tell Arandu and his people the message God has put in my heart. I want to share it."

Josh stood there surprised for a moment and uncertain; then a gentle smile crossed his lips. "Of course you can tell them. That's a wonderful thing. I think God would be very pleased."

Manu stood in the center of the room and gazed out at the large group of people that were sitting there. He experienced the love of God rising up in his heart, and he felt compelled to express to these suffering people the love God had for them. He wanted to tell them all that what God had done in the last few days had changed his life and the lives of so many who lived in his village.

Manu turned and faced Arandu and all his people who were sitting there. He started speaking slowly, in Guarani, but appeared to gain confidence as he continued. Edwardo was translating for Daniel and Sherry if she needed help. Renato was translating for Bekah, Josh and Ted.

"For those of you who haven't talked with me yet, my name is Manu, and I am Chief of this village. First, I want to formally welcome you into our tribe. We will do everything we can to help you overcome the pain of what has happened. We know someone who can take your pain away. He can help with your problems and bring you peace. He is the great God, the one true God. He is above all gods, even the gods you have been serving. You can pray to Him and He will answer your prayers.

"He doesn't want sacrifices, living or dead. He only wants us to serve Him and His Son Jesus. He sent His own Son Jesus to die as a sacrifice for our sins. Then God raised Jesus from the dead and now they live in Heaven together."

Manu paused and looked at the people. They were all listening. "Before I even believed in Him, Dr. Sherry prayed to Him for Noemi, my wife. She was in childbirth and there was too much blood. The baby was born but the bleeding would not stop. We were all just sitting there waiting for Noemi to breathe her last breath, and then something happened. I can't tell you exactly what happened, but it was as if someone breathed on her, and she began to take big breaths. The baby cried and she opened her eyes. The Lord God Almighty fought death and won.

"This God I am telling you about is here right now. We can't see Him, but if we pray, He will somehow answer us." Manu closed his eyes and lifted his voice. "Lord God, I am one of Your people. Jesus died for me and helps me fight our enemies. I know that You also bring peace to those who ask. Please, bring peace to this group of people and show them that You care. Help their hearts to heal. Let Jesus come into their hearts and help them to live and serve You better. Thank you God."

As Manu stood there with his eyes closed, he heard weeping coming from every direction; but it wasn't a weeping of desperation or despair as he had heard previously, but a gentle weeping accompanied by that special peace. Manu looked around in awe. Everyone's eyes were full of tears, even Arandu's. His anger had been washed away by his tears and it appeared that his heart had been changed. Manu smiled. He liked helping God.

Manu turned and beckoned Edwardo. "I don't have the right words to say yet to help the people learn how to serve God. Will you say the prayers with them so they can become part of

God's family?"

Edwardo smiled and began to talk to the people in Guarani. Manu went and sat back down next to Arandu who was like a sail without wind. Arandu didn't know where to go, or what to do when he got there. Manu put his arm around Arandu and said, "Let God's gentle breath bring you back to life, just as it did Noemi; although it wasn't your body that was dead, but your spirit. Listen to Edwardo. He will tell us both things we need to know about God and His Son Jesus."

Edwardo knew he had everyone's attention. A quiet peace pervaded the atmosphere. Edwardo spoke, "We've told you about God and His Son Jesus, but we haven't told you about the Holy Spirit yet. He's the One Who moves all over the earth. He's the One Who makes things happen and gets things done. He's a part of God. You can't see Him; but you can feel His presence. That peace that we are still experiencing is Him. He is sometimes called the Comforter and the Counselor. He brings us peace, and He also reveals and explains things to us. He reveals God to us, and draws us close to Him. He speaks to us in our heart."

Edwardo looked around the kitchen at all the people. Most were from the burned out village, but several people from his village had been standing in the doorway listening. He spoke now with power and authority. "My God is the Lord God Almighty. Your gods cannot stand against Him. He is all powerful and all knowing. Would you like Him to be your God? Would you like to serve Him and leave your old gods behind? You cannot serve both. I must tell you that when you ask my God into your heart you are no longer just His servants, but He makes you His sons and daughters.[85] He adopts you,[86] and He will never turn away from you.[87] You will never be alone. He will always be with you.

[85] 2 Corinthians 6:17-18
[86] Ephesians 1:5
[87] Hebrews 13:5

Now I ask all of you, if this is the God you want to serve, stand up and raise your hand."

Edwardo looked around expectantly, and initially, no one moved. Then, as if someone had thrown a switch, every last person rose to their feet and raised their hand. Even the people in the doorway pushed into the room and stood with the others. God had been moving these past few days and people's hearts were ready. Every meeting they had brought more people into the Kingdom of God. Edwardo asked all of them, "If you want to be a child of God and serve Him, repeat this prayer. Lord God Almighty, I want to be Your child. I want to serve You. I am sorry for all my sins and ask Your forgiveness. Help me not to sin anymore. Thank You for sending Jesus, Your Son to be a sacrifice for me. Help me to serve You with all my strength. Come and live inside my heart all the days of my life."

After finishing the prayer, he looked around at all the people. Instead of the somber group that he had started with, now he was looking at people whose faces showed joy, and above all else hope."[88]

Edwardo continued to talk. "God has a plan for all of us. It's a good plan.[89] It may be difficult, but He said He would always be with us to help us serve Him. He is a good God, and now we are His people."

After all this ministry and prayer, the breakfast was finally served. With the expectation of hope restored, appetites were enhanced and every crumb of food was eaten. It appeared as though a celebration had taken place, and all who had been in attendance had been blessed by the occasion.

---

[88] Proverbs 13:12

[89] Jeremiah 29:11

CHAPTER SIXTEEN

JUNE 17
THE VILLAGE

Up until now the shaman, Tuvicha, had not caused too many problems for the small group of Christians, but he was losing control of the remnant that followed the dark gods. They were slowly being drawn away from him, and he was unable to stop the desertion. The whole tribe was turning to this new God and Tuvicha felt his power dwindling. He felt he needed to make a move before he lost the rest of his followers.

He decided drastic measures needed to be taken to infuse him with the power he needed to fight off these attacks against his gods and hold onto his followers. He would sacrifice one of the small children Chabuto had brought to his house in obedience to the new and powerful god who had recently come to the forefront. Just as the witch doctor he had been hearing about had done to the displaced tribe, Tuvicha too would make this sacrifice to gain the greater power he desired. Then he and Chabuto would leave and join forces with that powerful tribe to the north who still believed in the dark gods. Knowing where the tribal treasure of his village was hidden, Tuvicha would bring a portion of this treasure to gain acceptance from this barbaric tribe and their powerful witch doctor.

He and Chabuto would take the child late tomorrow night to sacrifice him after everyone was asleep. Then they would dig up the treasure and head north. He thought it through once more and could find no flaws in his strategy.

Tuvicha's mind churned in confusion and his heart grew hard against his people. He knew what he was contemplating was wrong, but anger and bitterness strengthened his resolve. Tuvicha sat and discussed his decision with Chabuto. She agreed to help him and accompany him up north. They had today and all of tomorrow to formulate their plans and prepare for tomorrow night's sacrifice and the journey they would be taking. They could use the rest of today to pack what they needed to take north with them.

As Chabuto went to make preparations, she thought of how she had been turned out of her house and lost her important position. She thought of her failed attempt to end the life of Noemi and her son. The more she thought of it the angrier she became. She wanted some sort of revenge. While continuing to brood, thinking evil and destructive thoughts, darkness continued to infect her. Finally, Satan entered her, just as he had entered Judas to betray Jesus.[90] While contemplating her situation, an idea came to her; one so dark and so evil it surprised even her. But as anger and hatred consumed her, the desire for revenge intensified and she began to plot. She would take Noemi's child also. Two babies would mean twice the power. She smiled a wicked smile as she envisioned the pain and anguish this would cause both Noemi and Manu. It would serve them right.

Tuvicha sat in his doorway. He watched the comings and goings of the village, and observed the newcomers and the peace and joy they exhibited. He did not understand how anyone could be joyful after suffering such a catastrophe. In the past he could control the people with fear and threats of retribution, but something had broken his power. He looked at his life and the turn it had taken and he was anything but joyful. His position of importance had been jeopardized by the Christian outsiders, and

---
[90] Luke 22:3-4

he would do his best to bring misfortune upon them.

There were still ten or twelve people who had not succumbed to the call from this strange God. They were comfortable with the old gods and wanted no part of this new God and His strange ways. He would talk with them this evening and see if they wanted to come with him and Chabuto. When he was infused with power, he would call upon his gods to punish the people of this village. He was confident that after the sacrifice, his powers would be enhanced and he would call a curse down upon them. Then, after they had traveled to the northern village and been accepted by the witch doctor and his people, he would lead the witch doctor and his warriors back here to teach them a lesson they would not soon forget.

Tuvicha rose stiffly and called to one of his followers who walked nearby. He spoke to him in a whisper. "Gather all who serve our gods and meet me at the place of sacrifice. I am going there now to offer a small sacrifice. Tomorrow night after full dark, we will offer a special sacrifice. Something very important is going to happen. Do not delay. Chabuto and I will meet you there."

He walked slowly into the jungle, using the path he had taken over many years. It was worn from the many trips taken to the place of sacrifice, but he could see that grasses and vines were starting to assert themselves again because the number of feet traveling on it had decreased. He was old, and his body reminded him of it every waking moment with each movement he made. Pain was a constant companion, and he had allowed anger, envy and jealousy to invade his spirit and take over his life. As a young man, when he had assumed the responsibility of a shaman, he had a concern about the people he cared for. Unfulfilled dreams and expectations and a lack of power from his gods had discouraged and embittered him.[91] Now, instead of embracing this new God, Who seemed to have power and cared

[91] Proverbs 13:12

about the people, he turned away and sought the dark gods with a vengeance.

Tuvicha continued walking until he came to the grove where his gods were kept. It was about a half mile from the village. When he was young it was a short and easy walk, but now as old age overtook him, each time he traveled the path it became more difficult. Putting pain aside, he used his anger and thoughts of revenge to give him strength. As he entered the grove he saw the large fire pit that was used to offer sacrifices. Until now, only animals had been sacrificed, but tomorrow night all that would change. The child would be brought out at the last minute before anyone could object. Once done, the act would bind his followers to him and his increased power would become evident.

He would speak to his followers this afternoon and tell them he was leaving and that he was going to offer a special sacrifice. He would not tell them he was taking part of the tribe's treasure until after the sacrifice. Then he would take some of the shovels the Christians had supplied and dig it up, taking as much as they could carry and still move quickly. He would promise the witch doctor the rest of the treasure when they came and attacked his village, not just the treasure of gold and jewels, but the treasure of infants that were worth more.

Again his thoughts darkened. He could think of at least ten infants belonging to the tribe who were of age to be sacrificed. Not one of their parents had brought them to him after their births for his blessing. He had lost his place of honor. They would regret their lack of adherence to tradition. Tuvicha prayed to his gods, the great ones and the small ones and felt their darkness come and strengthen him,[92] He could already feel strange stirrings in his mind and voices began speaking to him, giving him direction as to what needed to be done.

Feeling this infusion of power, he became more determined

[92] John 1:5

in his resolve to betray the trust of the people. Having chosen the path of darkness, Satan entered him. Tuvicha's countenance changed. He was almost unrecognizable to his followers as they showed up for the gathering. Now there were only ten. Two more had deserted him and had gone over to the Christians. He would remember these betrayals and take revenge when he returned.

Miraculously, Tuvicha felt his pain decrease and strength infuse him. He also felt a strange power flowing through him. He marveled at it and thought, "If this is how I feel before the sacrifice, how much stronger will I feel after it?" Little did he realize Satan used deception to confuse people and cloud their thoughts.

CHAPTER SEVENTEEN

JUNE 18
THE VILLAGE

That morning Connie gathered her prayer group and went into the office to wait until it was time to call their U.S. counterpart, Silvia, Shirley, Sandi and Kay, who were anxious to hear from them. Connie and her group had not had the opportunity to speak to them yet, and were anxious to do so. With everything that had happened, they knew the need for prayer was paramount, and they did not want to be derelict in their obligations.

Daniel had shown Connie how to operate the satellite phone. She followed his instructions closely. She was gratified when she heard the connection being made and a soft voice saying "Hello."

"Hello, this is Connie. Who is this?"

"Oh this is wonderful," said the voice with enthusiasm. "This is Silvia. Shirley, Kay and Sandi are here, along with Susan, Pearl and Brenda. We have a large group of people praying now. Prayer is going on here twenty-four hours a day, so if an emergency comes up that requires extra prayer, you can contact us anytime. We can always call more people in day or night to pray if the need arises.

"How are things going down there?" Silvia asked. "We know that God is moving in a mighty way, but we feel we are missing out. We would love to hear some details. It's very frustrating, not being there."

Connie answered, "I understand what you are saying. I am here with my friends Alma, Sol, Victoria, and Jeruti. We try to spend the days together in prayer while we tend our children, gather food and cook. We don't have the numbers to pray all night, but if God awakens us, we pray. We know you have been told what is going on, but we want to tell you what we see and what we think is important."

Silvia responded, "I think that's a great idea. The others are so involved in what's going on that they don't have the opportunity to pray as much as we do. Because they are so caught up in what is happening they might miss an important fact or circumstance."

Connie spoke up and her voice was filled with concern. "One thing we have noticed that we need to tell the others is something that concerns a small group of people led by the shaman of the village. He has become increasingly upset about the number of people who are turning to God and accepting Jesus as their Savior.

Manu's stepmother, Chabuto, moved in with the shaman and she is not happy either. She lost her place of honor living with Manu and his family when she tried to do harm to Noemi, Manu's wife, and Juan, his newborn son. I feel in my heart that they are going to try to bring injury to Noemi and Juan, to my people, and to my village."

Sandi spoke up. "I haven't said anything because I wasn't sure it was God, but hearing what you are saying makes me think it is. Are there any children who might be in jeopardy?"

Connie answered, "Chabuto took Riki's six children to live with her and Tuvicha when Manu made her leave his house. They are small children and require care. Neither Tuvicha nor Chabuto have any love for these children. I would hate to see harm come to them at their hands. When we finish our call I will talk with Edwardo about this, and if he thinks it necessary, he can tell Manu.

"Also," Connie added, "Bekah and Manu had similar dreams two nights ago about Bekah being in a river or lake and being trapped underwater and unable to get to the surface. At first she was very fearful about the dream. Then she remembered that God had given her the dream about being captured and chased in the jungle. She understood that if God could free her from one trap of the devil, He could free her from anything the devil might try to use to hurt her or to thwart the quest.

"All of us are coming to see that God has His hand firmly on all the members of the quest. We know that God works everything out to a good ending for those who love Him and are called by Him. That is definitely true here. God called all of us to this quest in one way or another."

Goodbyes were said and assurances were given that they would call Maine again tomorrow morning. Connie pronounced a Guarani blessing on the northern group. "Ñandejára ta nde rovasa", which loosely translated means, 'God Bless you'. But the literal translation is, 'May God caress your face with his hand.' I pray your day goes well. Keep that thought on your mind."[93]

[93] Romans 8:28

CHAPTER EIGHTEEN

JUNE 18
PUERTO BAHÍA NEGRA

Carlos Rampone spent two nights in Asuncion preparing for his trip to Puerto Bahía Negra. Now he stood at the airport with Esteban Montero looking over the large mound of supplies that he had purchased in Asunción yesterday. He had called Montero after securing the supplies, to discuss how they planned to find the lovely Miss Bekah and her companions. Unbeknownst to him, Haydon Carlton, his employer, had made a side deal with Montero to cut Carlos out of the equation. After several hours of what felt like avoidance, Montero finally returned his call. He had, at last met with Montero at the airport in Puerto Bahía Negra the previous evening.

This morning, in addition to the supplies Rampone had secured, Montero was standing there with ten other men. Carlos was angry at himself for underestimating Montero, and at Haydon Carlton for not informing him of the capability of this man. He briefly wondered if Carlton meant to throw him under the bus instead of him eliminating Montero. Maybe Haydon thought they would eliminate, or at least incapacitate each other. Then he would be able to march down and grab the prize without paying either of them the promised wages. This project was becoming very expensive, and Carlton was tight with his money. He was only willing to spend outrageously on things that he valued, and it was becoming increasingly clear to Carlos that he was not one of them.

While the boats were loaded, Carlos spent an uneasy few hours looking for something that would give him an advantage. Unfortunately, nothing was forthcoming and the odds appeared firmly fixed in Montero's favor. When the boats were loaded they began the trip upriver. They were using two boats because of the large number of men with Montero, and the amount of supplies needed to maintain them. At the moment a fragile truce was in effect between the two of them, but there were no guarantees as to how long it would last. Carlos decided to play nice for a while, but also to keep a good watch on his back. He was outnumbered and not on his home ground. These two factors alone put him at a serious disadvantage. He needed to find some way to improve his odds.

Esteban Montero guardedly observed Carlos Rampone. He was aware that he was being observed also, but was indifferent to the scrutiny. He had a sixth sense that told him Rampone was trouble. He had been on alert ever since Haydon Carlton had informed him of Rampone's arrival. Montero was disturbed by the intrusion into his territory. Having handled interlopers in the past, dealing with this one would not be a problem. But before disposing of Rampone, he wanted the full story of what was transpiring here. Things were not as they appeared. He did not like secrets, especially when he was in the dark.

Through his contacts, Montero had obtained information as to where his quarry had traveled. He had called ahead and employed several people to keep them in sight. He did not want his prey to elude him. Obviously, they were not aware they had been followed. The trail that they left had been a mile wide. Five overloaded boats had left Puerto Bahía Negra to go upriver. There were not many ports of call along the way and Montero had no doubt that he would be able to track them to their destination.

Montero had decided that he would bide his time in dealing with Rampone, and would coerce the information he needed from him. Extracting information from unwilling victims was one of Montero's specialties.

His quarry was four to five days ahead of him. Given their cumbersome weight and the large number of boats that were traveling together, he was sure he would make better time than they had. The only fly in the ointment was Rampone. Montero was sure he could turn the tables and make him a positive presence as opposed to a negative one.

Having landed in Puerto Bahía Negra yesterday evening; they rented two boats. This morning, with everyone onboard and all supplies loaded, they set off upriver. The current had slowed and the motors were powerful. They made good time.

The slow hours passed and Carlos Rampone sat at the bow of the first boat facing towards the stern of the boat, making sure no one was able to get behind him. From this viewpoint he could observe everyone on the first and second boat. His dark eyes glittered with malice if anyone dared to head in his direction. He had a sinking feeling he would not be returning from this excursion. He felt like one of the loose ends he usually took care of; as though Haydon Carlton was disposing of him as he would an empty ammunition cartridge that had served its purpose.

Rampone was offered something to eat and drink, but refused, not wanting any distractions. He kept his mind alert and focused. It would be very easy for someone to get a shot at him from the second boat if he didn't keep attentive on the whereabouts of all the passengers.

Suddenly the tone of the engine changed. It appeared they were slowing down. He noticed a dock protruding out into the river. Montero had mentioned they would be refueling about halfway. Looking up at the sun, he estimated it to be mid-afternoon. They would not reach the village today unless they traveled in the dark. Considering the conditions of the river, that did not seem wise. The river was full of sandbars and debris ranging in size from small sticks and branches to whole trees. Rampone decided to bide his time by learning about his enemies, while looking for opportunities to even the odds.

Pulling up next to the dock, everyone disembarked except Montero and Rampone. Montero walked to the bow of the boat, approaching his opponent as a fox would approach his prey, with cunning and respect.

Rampone could see no weapon in Montero's hands, but he was smart enough to know that several weapons were probably aimed at him, only requiring a nod from Montero to finish him off.

Montero stopped about three feet away from him and looked down. "You and I have some issues we need to discuss. You have information I want. Haydon Carlton has left me out of the loop. He has not been forthcoming with all the material concerning this assignment. In order for this venture to be successful, I think we need to pool our resources and perhaps help each other."

Rampone listened, and paused to let the ramifications of this statement sink in. He realized he was being given some breathing room, a respite of sorts, and he needed to consider carefully before answering. As tempting as it would seem, now was not the time to make snap decisions. "How can I use what I know to my best advantage?" he thought. He did not want to fool himself into thinking he could trust Montero, but possibly he was buying some time.

Realizing that presently he was in no position to bargain, Rampone decided to play his wild card. "Alright, I'll tell you what I know. Haydon has me following a group of people who claim to be Missionaries. As you are aware, they purchased a large number of weapons and supplies and headed upriver. What you may not be cognizant of is that Bekah Ryan is in possession of a priceless gold and jewel encrusted crucifix dating from the sixteenth or early seventeenth century, which she said came from her grandmother.

"You also don't know that during the late sixteenth century the Spanish Missionaries had converted a large segment of the local population and had used their help in building their cathedral up river near a waterfall. The natives had been treated with kindness and respect until gold and precious stones had been found in the area. When word of these riches got back to Spain an army was sent to establish control and forced the native population into bondage. This river has been used to transport large amounts of gold and jewels that were mined. After years of oppression, the natives rebelled and massacred the inhabitants of the city, destroying it and the cathedral. They removed all the wealth of the city and all the religious artifacts in the cathedral and carried them into the jungle.

"Every so often, a piece or two shows up. No one has ever been able to discover the location of the bulk of this treasure. Haydon suspects this group may be mounting an expedition into the jungle for just that purpose. Joining forces, we can cut Haydon out of the picture. If we can find this group and keep our eyes on them, we can let them do the work for us. Then we can move in, eliminate them, and keep the treasure for ourselves."

Now it was Montero's turn to consider his options. This was more than just one crucifix; this was the pot of gold at the end of the rainbow.

Montero deliberated on his response. What he said and did now would either establish Rampone's cooperation or insure his elimination. He watched Rampone's face and tried to evaluate his intent. "Carlos my friend, it appears that a unique opportunity has presented itself to us. We can choose to work together, ensuring that things go smoothly, or we can oppose each other and walk a rocky path. This whole scenario is taking a different direction than I expected; one that can benefit both of us." Montero extended his hand. "Why don't you call me Esteban? I propose a sixty/forty split. What do you say to that?"

Carlos, having expected extermination, almost jumped up and shouted, but judgement overcame emotion and he paused and measured his options. A sixty/forty split was generous. He wondered at Esteban's motives, but realized he was still in no position to bargain at the moment. He breathed a sigh, and for better or worse, grasped Esteban's extended hand and said, "You have yourself a partner." They turned and walked off the boat together.

There was no expectation of how long the partnership would last. They were like two lions that lay down together in the heat of the day, but snarled and fought fiercely with each other over the rewards of a successful hunt. Each was a king in his own right, and each demanded respect from the other and the rest of the pride.

Now that Carlos had made his decision, he shared some of the information he had held back. "Haydon has been researching this crucifix and the circumstances surrounding it. After the Conquistadors arrived, the native population was enslaved and forced to work in the mines. Artisans were sent over from Spain to work with the raw materials, and countless artifacts of exceptional value and rare beauty were crafted. They were stored in the basement vaults of the cathedral until such time as a ship left for the mother country.

"From what few records are left, men, women and children were massacred by the tribal people they had enslaved. A handful managed to flee into the jungle and find their way down river to the coast where they told their story. An army of sorts was put together to avenge those who were so brutally killed, but the bulk of the soldiers recruited contained people motivated not by justice, but by greed. They were basically soldiers of fortune, looking for any treasure that might have been left behind.

"A small quantity of this treasure was found, but of course, it only caused more fighting and death. The whole incident took on the nature of a curse. It appeared that whenever an artifact showed up, jealousy and greed also showed up and brought with them death and destruction. Many people have followed the lure of unimaginable wealth, only never to return. This was the quest Haydon sent you out on. I have a feeling we are both expendable to him. He keeps his hands clean and expects us to do all the dirty work. We take the risk, and he gets the prize."

Sharing this information placed Carlos and Esteban in the same boat. They were both pawns being used by Haydon Carlton. Neither one was happy about it, but both found that at the present time there was little they could do to change their circumstances, other than join forces and use their combined cunning and experience against a common enemy.

Esteban gave instructions for everyone to board and continue to motor upriver. Carlos and Esteban, having formed a tentative coalition, started working out a strategy on how to put their plan into motion. They continued to talk all afternoon. They decided to stop about five miles from the village and camp on the boat. Sunset came early and they wanted to find a good place to tie up the boats before darkness settled in. Not wanting to betray their presence to the villagers, they gave the village a wide berth. Tomorrow, they would send out six men to head upriver through the jungle and take a look at the village. They were only to observe; no contact was to be made.

After preparing a quick meal, they turned in for the night. Guards were set up on each boat, appointed to four hour shifts. They had not seen any activity in the area, but everyone knew it paid to be careful. They had discussed the extra work and danger with the men. But along with the danger came unimaginable rewards. They were after a big payoff, and no one complained about a little extra duty. Their piece of the pie had just gotten a lot bigger.

CHAPTER NINETEEN

JUNE 18
THE VILLAGE

Life in the village revolved around hunting, gathering, meals and chores, and the day was divided up accordingly. The hunters went out before breakfast and sometimes after last meal if there was need. Gathering took place between breakfast and lunch. Chores were necessary all day long. Rest came after last meal, although in the heat of the day many took a siesta. It was good to rest for about two hours, but since winter was approaching and the temperature had cooled, it wasn't a necessity.

After breakfast, Connie spoke with Lara about the day's chores. Lara was such a big help, Connie liked to give her a choice. She could either go gathering with the other women and older girls in the jungle or stay and take care of the children. Today Lara chose to stay at home with the children.

After Connie left, Lara helped Maria cleanup after her puppy. When they were through she told Maria, "Take your puppy outside for a while and see if he will do his business there and not in the house. He must learn the rules of the house if he is to be allowed inside." As she watched Maria head toward her friend next door, a shadow crossed the doorway. It was the American, Ted. She felt color rise to her cheeks and started to turn away. He called out to her.

"Hello Lara, I came by to check on the water supply. Everyone seems busy doing something, and I don't seem to have any real purpose here. I know everyone is always carrying water. I filled up Daniel and Sherry's water barrels early this morning, I thought I would come and check on yours. If you give me your buckets, I'll get to work."

Ted followed Lara back into the house and watched as she went to get the water buckets. Ted was not adverse to a pretty face which Lara had, but it was her quiet grace that impressed him. She also had very sad eyes, which intrigued him. He wondered what it was that caused such a heaviness of heart. He assumed that at her age, maybe it was a dating problem. Then he wondered if these young women were even allowed to date, and if they did, what did they do for entertainment. He had not observed much free time. Everyone seemed to be busy all day long. He wondered if they still had arranged marriages. Ted had not seen Lara interacting with any of the other young people of the village. He had started watching her in the last day or two.

Lara walked back into the room carrying the two water buckets. "How many barrels do you have?" Ted asked. "How much does it take to fill them?"

"We just got an extra one because of the two babies. They require a lot of water. It takes five trips with the two buckets to fill one barrel," she responded. She watched the smile on Ted's face start to droop. She smiled a slow smile. "Don't worry, one barrel is already half full."

Lara went back into the house and Ted walked down the well-worn path that led to the river. It was approximately a quarter mile to the river, then a quarter mile back carrying two heavy buckets of water. His muscles started protesting after the third trip, and he sat down on a stump in the yard to take a break. Lara brought him some of the herbal tea all the villagers seemed to drink. It wasn't bad, just different. She stood there for a moment with one of the babies on her hip as though she was going to say something, but then she appeared to change her mind. She turned and walked back into the house.

Ted watched her go and sat there; then he got up and began to follow her. He paused at the door and thought, "This probably isn't a very good idea." With a frown on his face, he turned and started back down to the river. Almost three hours later, with arms feeling like lead, his chore was finished. He called Lara to let her know he was leaving but no one answered.

Feeling dejected, he turned to go back to the compound. Hearing voices, he looked up and saw Renato and one of the men from the village coming his way. Renato was carrying two rifles, and the villager had a small spear and a bow with a quiver of arrows. Renato called to him. "Ted, Giancarlo and I are going to do some hunting. I told Josh I would take you along to get some experience and maybe in the process bring home something for dinner. Giancarlo is going to be our guide."

Ted grinned. Taking one of the rifles he responded, "That sounds like a great diversion, and I need some practice. What are we hunting for, anything in particular?"

"No," Renato replied, "whatever presents itself."

Renato and Ted followed Giancarlo into the jungle on a barely discernable path. Other than the modern weapons they were carrying, all vestiges of the twenty-first century faded the further out they walked. There was no sound except for the incessant buzz of the insects and the chatter of the animals that inhabited the area. The further away from the village Ted and Renato traveled, the greater the sense of isolation. On an occasion such as this, it was important to be fully persuaded that you were a child of God and that His protection went with you.[94]

There was little talking as they traveled, Giancarlo kept his eyes on the trail and Ted and Renato kept their eyes on

[94] Psalm 91

Giancarlo. After walking for over an hour Giancarlo suddenly held his hand up and they all stopped. He put his finger to his lips and whispered, "Someone else has been here recently and they didn't come from the village; they came from the river. It's not far to the river from here. Let's go take a look and see if anyone is there." He motioned to them to follow.

As they walked forward Renato kept his mind clear and his thoughts disciplined. There was no point in thinking the worst. They would find out soon enough who had been there and what was going on.

On the other hand, Ted's mind was in turmoil. He was thinking of his inexperience with weapons and that maybe he should have stayed back in Ogunquit. Feelings of inadequacy and insecurity bloomed as his mind dwelt on the lack of experience he had in everything that pertained to this quest. He didn't even have a long standing relationship with God. That was one of his biggest worries.

"God, what am I doing here?" he asked.

His body actually jumped in surprise when he heard a Voice answer, "I called you here. Do you not think I know what I am doing?"

He had just been whining and complaining as usual and didn't expect a reply. He looked around to see if anyone else had heard the Voice, apparently not. They were both walking with eyes and ears alert, paying attention to the surroundings. Ted took a moment to think about his response. It would not be appropriate to blurt out the first thing that came to mind, or would it?

"I'm sorry God. Please forgive me for my bad attitude, help me to maintain a good attitude, and bring strength to this quest and not weakness." With a new fervor Ted walked on, determination in every step.

They followed Giancarlo for another half mile and he put his hand up again. They all stopped and listened. He whispered they were almost at the river. They moved forward slowly, trying to make as little noise as possible. The trail opened right up on the river bank, and tied up there were two boats, very similar to the ones they had rented, loaded with supplies and people. They counted twelve men. They stood there, just inside the jungle, looking around. Renato whispered to Giancarlo that he recognized one of the men and that he was trouble. Giancarlo nodded and motioned them to turn around and go back. They turned and started quickly retracing their steps.

There was no talking as they walked back to the village. Each of them was thinking of the repercussions this discovery might have. The element of danger had been ramped up another notch. They were questioning their preparedness for what might happen. The enemy's army appeared to be moving in their direction and they were not ready. They had been doing a great deal of talking and very little actual planning. It was time to be doers of God's Word and not just hearers of it.[95]

They had already walked another ten minutes when Renato called out to Giancarlo, "Please stop for a moment and tell us what you saw that made you turn around. I did not see anything except the two boats we were observing and the men on them."

Giancarlo responded, "I am sorry. I just wanted to get us out of the area quickly. There were also several men in the jungle who were observing the men on the boats. Thankfully, because they were watching the boats, they did not see us."

Ted and Giancarlo turned and looked expectantly at Renato. "We need to stop a moment and pray. The enemy is out there like a roaring lion seeking to devour someone.[96] I don't want it to be us. The Bible says the weapons we need to fight with are not man made, but they are spiritual.[97] Let's take some

---

[95] James 1:22
[96] 1 Peter 5:8-9
[97] 2 Corinthians 10:4

time to pray and ask God what He would have us do."

The three of them stood there on that jungle trail with heads bowed. They joined hands and Renato prayed. "Father, we thank You that You have all knowledge of what has happened, what is happening now, and what is going to happen.[98] We don't have that insight, but we serve the God Who does. Right now we speak to the fear and uncertainty trying to rise up in our minds,[99] and we speak Your Word, which is a mighty weapon in the spirit.[100] We say that no weapon will have victory over us because You are in control of our lives and we put our trust in You, no matter what circumstances look like.[101] We thank You for trusting us to complete Your quest, and for leading and guiding us."[102] After praying, the three turned and headed back toward the village with a lighter step and hope renewed in their hearts.

Ted was actually smiling. That special peace that accompanies the presence of God was resting on him and he was no longer walking in fear and uncertainty, but in strength, and renewed faith in God and the purpose God had for his life.

---

[98] 1 Corinthians 2:9-13
[99] Romans 12:2
[100] 2 Corinthians 10:3-6
[101] Isaiah 54:17
[102] Psalms 31:3-4

CHAPTER TWENTY

JUNE 18

THE VILLAGE

Upon arriving at the village Giancarlo told Ted and Renato he would go find Manu and tell him what had happened and ask that he and Arandu come to Daniel's compound to discuss what they had seen. Ted and Renato went to find Daniel, Sherry, Josh and Bekah. It seemed hard to believe that it was only lunchtime; so much seemed to have happened in such a short period.

As they were leaving the compound Connie and Edwardo, Josh, Manu, Arandu and Leonardo were coming towards them. It was as though God had called them together to hear the news. There was already a second group of hunters waiting to give a report, and they all listened as Mario began to speak. He spoke in Guarani and Renato translated. "We discovered a large group of people living in the jungle, downriver, approximately five miles from here. They are well armed with guns, knives and machetes. We did not stay there long because we did not want to be seen. The camp appeared as though it had been there for some time. The vegetation was beaten back and several trails were leading from there into the jungle and toward the river."

Josh questioned, "What did they appear to be doing?"

Mario answered, "They were taking siesta."

Josh asked, "Can you describe them?"

Mario thought for a moment and then said, "Most were

tall like Americans, but most had curly black beards. They were darker than Americans, but not as dark as our people."

When Mario stepped back, Giancarlo came forward. He had listened to the report and wondered if it would have any connection with what they had to say. He had seen Renato translating for the Americans. Out of respect, his people tried to speak Spanish or English in their presence, but excitement had caused a lapse and Mario had spoken in Guarani.

Giancarlo began to speak in Spanish. "We were out hunting for game when we came upon a trail three miles away. I followed it to the river where two boats were tied up. There were twelve men in them. We stood there observing them for a short time, then I realized there were others observing them also. We turned around and came back, not wanting to be discovered."

"Manu," Josh spoke up, "would it be all right with you if Giancarlo, Mario and I went out tonight to find that camp again and see if we can discover something about the people occupying it? They are probably the ones in the jungle observing the men on the boats. Mario, do you think you can find it in the dark?"

Mario answered indignantly, "Do you think I am a young boy and do not know my way around the jungle?" He looked at Giancarlo and said, "It's by the bog on the west side of the small ponds. They will be easy to spot. They are not people of the jungle. They will have large fires."

Manu dismissed both groups and told them he would meet with them later with a decision on what to do. He turned to the rest of them and said, "Let's go to the meeting area. There we can talk and no one will disturb us unless there is an emergency."

As the group of them walked quietly over to the meeting area, each one was immersed in his own thoughts and pondering the significance of these two discoveries. When they arrived, they all felt compelled to spend some time in prayer, seeking out the Father's guidance in what should be done. A silence descended and all that could be heard was the soft murmurings of each one praying. The sounds of the village and the surrounding jungle were silent. A deep peace settled on each one as they reached out seeking the presence of God. Suddenly they were surrounded by a bright light. The intensity of it overwhelmed them and they fell forward. Out of the light they heard a Voice speak. The ground reverberated with the sound of this Voice. The Voice had no direction that it emanated from. It just was. It wasn't loud or booming, but it caused them to quake.

In fear and wonder they listened to what was said. "I AM THE GOD THAT FOREVER WAS. I AM THE GOD THAT FOREVER IS, AND I AM THE GOD THAT FOREVER WILL BE. I AM. YOU ARE MY CHOSEN INSTRUMENTS. THE ENEMY IS GATHERING HIS ARMY FOR THE FINAL BATTLE. HE IS SEEKING WHOM HE MAY DEVOUR, BUT YOU MUST KEEP HIM FROM SUCCEEDING. THERE ARE ENEMIES IN YOUR MIDST SEEKING TO DO GRAVE HARM. THEY MUST BE STOPPED. THE FORCES OF DARKNESS WILL CLASH WITH THE FORCES OF LIGHT. STAY AWAKE, BE VIGILANT. EVEN IN THE DARKNESS I WILL GIVE YOU LIGHT. YOU WILL FIND HELP IN UNEXPECTED PLACES. SEARCH OUT THE ENEMY. HE IS OPERATING IN YOUR MIDST AND YOU MUST FIND HIM. HE CANNOT BE ALLOWED TO SUCCEED. DO NOT BE DISTRACTED."

At that moment there was a loud report that sounded surprisingly like a gunshot. The light was extinguished and the Voice was quiet. Then there was a second shot that catapulted them into action. The sound of it appeared to be coming from Edwardo's house. As they ran toward the house, Lara came out, white as a sheet and carrying Edwardo's rifle.

"I killed it," she stuttered as she stood swaying, "but I think it's too late."

As the rest of them rushed in, Ted grabbed the rifle from Lara and picked her up to keep her from falling. He followed everyone through the door. What they saw gripped their hearts with fear. Little Emilio was wrapped in the coils of a giant boa constrictor. The snake has been shot in the head and was dead, but little Emilio appeared to be dead also. His lips were blue and he was not moving.

Josh went over and knelt by his small body. After unwrapping him from the deadly coils of the snake, Josh examined his lifeless form. The body was limp. Sherry came running through the door to see if she could be of help. After examining him, she raised her eyes, looked at Josh sadly, and slowly shook her head. He was dead.

Josh took Emilio's body into his arms. He felt a strength and a faith he had not felt before. He turned to the crowd and spoke in a powerful voice. "Listen to what the Spirit of God is saying, and observe the power of Almighty God." Then he lifted the lifeless body up towards Heaven and spoke with confidence, knowing that the Spirit of God was empowering him. The people stood in awe for they heard him in their native tongue. No interpretation was necessary.[103] "Spirit of death, I rebuke you! You cannot have this child! God brought him here for a purpose and it was not for you to kill him! I command life to come back into his body!"

Suddenly little Emilio twitched and coughed. The Breath of Life saturated him and drove out the spirit of death. Emilio began to make a soft moaning sound that crescendoed into a lusty howl. There was no doubt life had returned to his body.

Many people had come and gathered around to see what was happening. God had accomplished another miracle and all the people were stunned, not only those who believed, but also those who did not. The doubters could no longer deny the presence of Almighty God. Their gods took life, but never gave it back.

The remnant of ten who had still served the dark gods prostrated themselves in fear and gave their life to the One true

---

[103] Acts 2:6-11

God. In return, He took away their bitterness and fear and instead, gave them peace and joy.[104] They were no longer the people they used to be, but a new creation.[105]

Again, Chabuto stood at the doorway of Tuvicha's house, anger painting its ugly face on her features. She had watched all the events that had transpired, from the return of life to Emilio to the transformation of the last of Tuvicha's followers. Her plan had backfired. She had managed to drag the ten foot long snake into the house when no one was looking. She put Emilio on the floor and cold-bloodedly watched as the snake squeezed the life out of the small baby. But before it was able to eat him, the puppy, Hombrecito came into the room and started barking. She heard someone coming and had to leave.

Lara came in, and in horror saw Emilio in the grip of the snake. She ran and got Edwardo's rifle and shot it. "All would not have been lost," Chabuto reflected, "except those Christians had prayed to their God and He answered them. Now there were only two followers of the old gods left, she and Tuvicha. Two were enough to do what needed to be done tonight, and now there were none left to argue against the sacrifice." Chabuto turned and spit on the ground, uttering a curse as she stormed away from the crowd, feeling so confident she didn't even bother to lower her voice.

Josh looked up upon hearing her and asked Edwardo what it was she had said. Edwardo hesitated, "I don't like to even repeat it. She invoked the spirit of death to run through the village and squeeze the breath out of all the people, just as he had done to baby Emilio."

Josh replied to this statement with the conviction of God, "What she has planned for others will come back on her. There is no protection for those who turn their backs on God time after time."

[104] Isaiah 61:3
[105] 2 Corinthians 5:17

Men from the tribe came to gather up the snake's body and take it to dress the meat. A snake of this size would provide food for the village. Everyone would eat well tomorrow night.

Chabuto hurried over to Tuvicha's and told him all that had transpired. They were the only two left. It would be hard traveling so far and carrying a portion of the treasure tomorrow night, and they could not go without the treasure. It was only the presence of it, the promise of more to come, and the number of infants they could guarantee, for any hope of acceptance into this evil, northern tribe.

Someone came by to relate the news that there would be a tribal dinner celebrating the life of Emilio and the death of the snake. It was the latter that was to be the main course of the feast tomorrow night.

Chabuto told the runner they would rather starve than participate in this Christian celebration. The only thing she would celebrate would be the death of every Christian in the camp and the death of their God also. She did not care what the cost; she was determined to see it happen.

"Why would anyone want to worship someone hanging on a cross?" she thought."[106] Her problem was that she had cut herself off from everyone and never took the time to find out that Jesus was no longer on the cross.[107] Jesus was no longer in the tomb.[108] Jesus had been raised from the dead and was now seated at the right hand of God in heavenly places.[109] If she would only turn and hear, she could be saved.

After a last meal in the meeting area, most people returned to their homes. Just as Jesus had an inner circle, so the village did also. Those who were part of the quest were the inner circle. Sherry had coffee made and juice and water available.

---

[106] 1 Corinthians 1:18
[107] Luke 23:50-53
[108] Luke 24:1-8
[109] Ephesians 1:18-21

She also had fruit and some fresh chipa that Paloma had made earlier. The smell of it baking was still in the air.

Daniel told everyone, "It's time for our phone call to the U.S. We will be speaking in English. Those who need translators get in your groups so you all know what is being said. Josh is going to call and we will put it on speaker phone for everyone to hear."

As always, Joe picked up on the first ring. "We're all here waiting. Good thing this phone is portable, we've outgrown Bekah's office. We are now meeting at the Lobster Pot. Jean still lets us have the back room. There are about twenty of us now, and we eat together whether you call or not. It's a good situation for us and it's a blessing for Jean's business.

"Well do you want to go first or should we?" Joe asked. "Other than prayer we don't have much, but one small piece of information could be important."

"So have at it," answered Josh with a smile, "we're all ears."

Joe began, "It's been pretty quiet up here other than the call from your so-called, long lost cousin. We are praying diligently twenty-four hours a day. Everyone involved is very excited about what God is doing. Like I said, things were quiet until today. Today we received a visit from Haydon Carlton. Your opinion of him was right on, Haydon Carlton is a major sleazebag.

"He had the nerve to come in here and ask where you were in Paraguay. He said he sent people down to negotiate with you concerning the crucifix and he has not heard from them. He knows it's only two days, but they were supposed to call every day. He ranted on about all of you being responsible for their disappearance, and if you didn't cooperate he was going to come down there and deal with you himself. He said he knew you all were nothing but a bunch of treasure hunters and that the government of Paraguay would be very interested in that information."

Josh and Bekah actually laughed out loud. "If we're treasure hunters, what does that make him? He's so blinded by his greed he can't think straight. We're not here to take anything away; we're here to return treasure that had been stolen. As soon as we can, we are going to return the artifacts that Bekah's stepmother took. We just don't want to draw attention to that fact. We don't want a passel of real treasure hunters down here polluting the jungle with all their digging, all the trash they leave around, and all the machines they would be using."

Josh added, "If he can't keep track of his men, how does he expect us to? If he can't find them, maybe they are already on the river. That could be possible. We already have a report of men coming up the river in boats and this might be them. We have positioned two men to watch the boats that were spotted today and let us know if they continue coming this way. We also don't want to be surprised by anyone coming through the jungle. I'll talk to Manu about sending out men to keep a watch on the camp south of us. I'm going to ask Manu if I can go out with a few men to take some pictures of the camp tomorrow morning and e-mail them to my friend Isaac in the C.I.A. We'll let you know what happens tomorrow night when we call. Thanks for the warning and keep praying."

After hanging up, Josh talked with Manu and set it up that Giancarlo and Mario would take him down to the other camp tomorrow morning.

With those decisions made, they prepared for their Bible study. Just as in the last few nights, those new believers who were able came by for what they were calling, Christianity 101. It was a crash course that sometimes lasted until early morning. The people were so hungry for the Word of God they just kept asking question after question. God was teaching His people at an astonishing rate. They were absorbing all they could and kept coming back for more the following morning.

CHAPTER TWENTY-ONE

JUNE 19
THE RIVER

After a quiet night, and a quick breakfast, six men set out, each man armed with a rifle, machete, handgun, two bottles of water each and food provisions. They also were issued one compass, one pair of binoculars and two flashlights, although the binoculars seemed redundant. It was impossible to see very far through the thick foliage of the jungle. The men were somewhat nervous due to the fact that they had never been in the jungle before, but greed bolstered their courage. They had been made aware of the change in plans and knew they were now after a bigger pot of gold. Their slice of the pie was the same, but the size of the pie had grown significantly.

They all took note of the time before setting out. It was seven o'clock and they were to travel until they reached the perimeter of the village. Then they were to circumnavigate it, taking note of anything unusual and keeping their eyes open for any evidence of a large amount of weapons at the ready. They were to stay and observe until they needed to depart to reach the boats before dark.

Carlos and Esteban watched as the groups disappeared into the jungle and settled down for the long wait. This left six men at the boats. Carlos and Esteban were on one boat and four of Esteban's men were on the other. They still did not trust each other completely, but had developed a healthy respect for each other's abilities.

Surprisingly, they were honest and open about their arrangements with Haydon Carlton. Because of this, their animosity was no longer aimed at each other, but had been transferred to Haydon Carlton. He had become their enemy, and all their efforts were now being aimed at thwarting his plan and succeeding in their own.

The group trudged on. They had been walking for over two hours and were already tired, dirty and soaked with sweat. They had seen several snakes of various kinds and were becoming more and more nervous as they traveled further and further into the jungle. They had no experience with the jungle and all its dangers. They were city boys and were completely intimidated by their surroundings. Suddenly the lure of golden treasure had lost its glow.

They had been arguing for over an hour about whether they should turn back or not. The fear of Esteban Montero was waning in comparison to their fear of the jungle. Suddenly they began to hear noise. They all quieted and stopped to listen to where it was coming from. They looked through the trees and overgrowth and saw a young woman, a young girl and a small dog. The young woman was helping the little girl pick up fruit under a big tree.

Suddenly the small dog lifted its head and began barking and running toward the spot they had gathered. They all turned and ran back the way they had come from. Three men came running from the village carrying spears. One of them had a small rifle. They questioned the young woman, but she had not seen or heard anything.

The dog continued barking and the men stepped out into the jungle with the little dog leading the way. About twenty-five feet in, they came upon an area that was beat down and a narrow trail leading back into the jungle. Edwardo patted the dog and turned back. He told the woman and young girl to go back to the village and went to find Josh. Setting up a perimeter had paid off. He did not know who had been there, but it was clear someone had.

Carlos and Esteban spent the morning and into early afternoon strategizing how they were going to outmaneuver Haydon Carlton. Their partnership was becoming more and more cemented.

They were growing concerned because the shadows were lengthening and nightfall would be upon them soon. Suddenly they were alerted to some noise in the distance. It was not gunfire, but yelling or shouting of some kind. Everyone on the boats was standing up with guns in hands. Carlos started to leave the boat and Esteban shouted, "Everyone stay put. There is nothing we can do now. There is no sense in all of us getting into trouble also. It's getting late and we don't want to run in there and get lost. They have the machetes, a rifle, a compass and two strong flashlights. We'll wait here to see it they come back. If not, we will go in at first light tomorrow. From the sound of it they can't be that far away. For now, let's sit tight and stay alert."

A meal was prepared and everyone was quiet until it was finished. The four men left on the one boat got together and began to whine and complain. They said they felt the possibility of danger concerning this trip had been underplayed, and since it appeared to have increased in their eyes, they wanted additional compensation. Dusk was descending and the night took on its own form of silence with the growing hum of insects as they awakened for their evening meal.

Unbeknownst to them, twelve men, very well armed, sat observing them just inside the shelter of the jungle. They kept a quiet vigil all night. They were skilled observers, and noted all their enemy's strengths and weaknesses.

CHAPTER TWENTY-TWO

JUNE 19
THE VILLAGE

That morning another large group showed up at Sherry's. Paloma showed up with more food, and even brought Ciba with her to help. Ciba was Leonardo's wife and had been savagely attacked by a wild boar. She had been severely injured and it had taken Sherry several hours to sew her up. She still had some stitches in her and her arm and leg were stiff, but some exercise was good for her. Thank God no infection had set in. Sherry had only a small supply of antibiotics on hand. But combined with prayer, they appeared to do the trick. If Ciba needed any help, Sherry would be right there.

The morning's breakfast was relaxing to all. Hearts were light, everyone smiled and laughed. People came in, stopped and talked and went on their way. Sherry was watching from her seat at the kitchen table. Paloma had sat her there and told her not to get up, that some of the people wanted to see to her needs. This was difficult for Sherry. She was used to being the servant, not the one who was served, but she knew it was important to let the people bless her.

Ciba served her breakfast personally and Noemi saw to her drink. They were especially thankful to Sherry for all she had done for them. Also, because of the extra time spent in their company, they had all become good friends. Paloma came and took away her empty plate when she was through and Sherry turned her attention to the Bible study that was going to take place.

They were all there to attend what Sherry was calling, Christianity 101. This was the fourth session of intense study for all the new Christians. God was doing a quick work. He needed an army to fight the enemy, and for this battle, spiritual weapons were more important than physical weapons.[110]

All the members of the quest had been sitting in on the lessons. It was open to new and old believers. Hearing the Word again reinforced it in your mind and in your spirit. It was important that everyone had a solid foundation of the Word of God in order to effectively fight the enemy.[111] The battle was not necessarily against the evil tribe who was taking and sacrificing innocent babies. The battle was against Satan, the spirit who was behind them and motivating them to perform these satanic rituals.

Sherry was gratified at the progress that had been made through the Bible studies, but her spirit was heavy, knowing that her friends were going to be heading out into harm's way. The thought that concerned her was not knowing if they would all be returning. The only guarantee any of them had was that God would win the battle. There was no guarantee any of them would survive it.

Sherry looked around. There were about thirty people sitting on the floor, their attention riveted on Edwardo as he continued their study of the Word of God. The people had already been taught the meaning of John 3:16, becoming "born again." They had been taught about becoming a new creation, and that old things were gone and that they were new in God's eyes.[112] Their next lesson was on fear.

Fear was a very serious issue that had affected all the

[110] 2 Corinthians 10:3-5
[111] Hebrews 4:12
[112] 2 Corinthians 5:17

villages in the surrounding area. They had all been dealing with the repercussions caused by this evil and powerful tribe for many years. This tribe was a pestilence that had ravaged most of them continually and they could see no way to defeat them to bring an end to the carnage.

Now that the survivors of Arandu's village had been assimilated into the tribe, Manu and his people understood the fear that they had experienced and wanted to do what they could to stop these attacks. They also wanted to provide shelters for these people where they could live until houses could be built. There was much activity and noise as the jungle was further pushed back to make room for the new members.

The recovery of Noemi and Ciba and the raising from the dead of baby Emilio had pierced the darkness and allowed hope to rise up in the people. Unfortunately, old fears were an unwanted guest that would linger, not leaving without a fight. Fortunately, these new Christians were hungry for the Word of God. The more of it they heard, the stronger their faith became. The Bible says that faith comes by hearing the Word of God.[113]

Sherry felt her head begin to nod. She was extra tired because of the pregnancy and circumstances had given her little time for rest. She closed her eyes, telling herself she would just leave them closed for one minute. Time passed and Sherry opened her eyes. She realized that much more than a minute had gone by. She looked at her watch and realized lunch had come and gone. It was mid-afternoon and preparations would soon be started for last meal. Someone had left a plate of chipa, a local bread which Sherry called a Paraguayan bagel, and a plate of fruit. After eating, Sherry again experienced that same tiredness that could not be ignored. She gave in. She got up from the table and went into the bedroom to lie down.

---

[113] Romans 10:17

Two hours later Daniel gently touched her shoulder. Sherry opened her eyes and smiled. "I just had the best dream." Daniel saw that Sherry looked rested and refreshed and was grateful. Early pregnancy required extra rest and Sherry had been ignoring her body's request for days. Today it finally caught up with her. After a morning and afternoon nap she was ready to go.

Sherry had a sweet smile on her face as she got out of bed. "Let me tell you about my dream," she said to Daniel. "I dreamt I was in a boat floating down an azure blue river. The river was swift but the ride was smooth. Suddenly I began to hear a sound that kept getting louder and louder. It finally became a roar. It was a waterfall. I looked for a way to steer to the side of the river but there were no oars. Despite that I was not worried. I just sat still and watched as events transpired."

Sherry stopped to think a moment and then continued. "The boat began to travel faster and faster. Suddenly a sail appeared in the middle of it. The boat shot out over the waterfall and began to glide above the landscape. I looked down and there were many people in the water. Even though I was far away I recognized them. They were the people of the quest. As I watched, they all went to the side of the waterfall and disappeared. Then I woke up. Isn't that strange? I didn't remember the end of the dream until I told it to you. What do you think it means?"

"I don't know," replied Daniel. "You can tell everyone after dinner. Come on. We don't want to be late."

They walked into the kitchen and it was full again. More and more people were coming, and everyone was bringing something to contribute to the dinner. Just at that moment, a man came into the kitchen who Sherry did not know. She did not ever remember seeing him in the village. She motioned to Manu and he walked over, a big smile on his face. It was so wonderful to see the joy of the Lord bloom in these precious people. She asked Manu, "Who is that man that just came into the kitchen, the one in the tattered green shirt?"

Manu looked where Sherry was pointing and saw Enrico. Manu responded to Sherry's question with one of his own, "What do you know of this man?"

"Nothing," answered Sherry. "I don't ever remember seeing him before."

Manu replied, "I have known Enrico all my life. Unfortunately he had never been an asset to the tribe. He lives on the generosity of the village."

Enrico was a small man with a face so wrinkled it was difficult to see his eyes. He shuffled up to Manu and waited to talk with him. Enrico knew he had very little standing in the tribe, but he hoped that Manu would recognize him.

Manu looked over at him and started to turn away, but then hesitated. Something inside him whispered, "Listen to this man." Manu turned back toward Enrico. He felt pity for the poor man and found two chairs. He thought, according to God's Word we are not to look at someone's appearance, but to treat all people as we would want to be treated."[114]

Manu got the man seated, gave him a drink, but then waited impatiently for him to begin speaking. "Is this the way I act with you when you come to Me with your concerns," God asked?

Manu immediately repented, took Enrico's hand, and asked how he could help. Enrico was so taken back by Manu's attitude he began to cry. Manu patted him on the back and spoke encouraging words. This only caused more tears. Manu waited and Enrico composed himself. Finally he began to speak. "I have some information I think you should know. I believe that Tuvicha and Chabuto mean to bring harm to our village. They have both lost positions of power, Chabuto as your mother, the keeper of your house, and Tuvicha as shaman. None of us believe in his gods anymore.

[114] Matthew 7:12

"I was never much of a follower of the old gods, but they were comfortable and they let me be. But recently something has changed and they became darker and crueler. Yours is not the only new God. Chabuto and Tuvicha have a new god also and he is a hard taskmaster. I have seen him operating in them and I am afraid. I have heard this god crying out through them. He wants a sacrifice and they are planning to give him one. It was to be done late tomorrow night at the grove. They may still attempt to do it even though it is just the two of them."

Enrico shuddered and whispered to Manu, "I am afraid of their new god. I am afraid he will try to take revenge on me and on our village for abandoning him."

Enrico began to weep again as the old tend to do when they feel helpless. Manu leaned down to take him in his arms. He felt the frail body shudder with his quiet sobbing. Tears coursed down his lined countenance. Enrico drew in a deep breath and asked, "I have heard it said that your God, Who is now my new God, answers prayers. Will you pray to Him to protect our village from the attacks of our old gods and of Tuvicha's new god? Our old god was never really a good god, and the new god is very bad. I do not want any of our people to suffer because of his evil."

Manu stood up and placed his hand on Enrico's shoulder. "I will now pray to our God, the One and only God. He is strong and mighty. He will not only protect our village, but will also bring you peace. Put your trust in Him."

Manu closed his eyes and lifted his face to Heaven. "Almighty God," he prayed, "Loving Father. There is great evil about. We stand with You Father in fighting this evil. I am grateful for Your help. I have been told You have a great army. Please position them around our village to keep it safe. Show this evil god that You are the One, true, mighty God and that he cannot stand

---

[133] 2 Corinthians 10:5

against You. In the midst of all this trouble, please bring peace to us all. Please bring peace to my uncle Enrico. I respectfully pray in Your Son Jesus' great Name."

Immediately Manu felt the now familiar feeling of peace and love invade the fear Enrico had been experiencing.[115] Manu felt Enrico's shoulders relax and his body stop shaking. Almost simultaneously, Enrico's head came up and he asked in a surprised voice, "What has happened? Who was here? I did not see anyone, but I felt a presence."

With a soft voice and a smile Manu responded, remembering he had recently asked the same question at one of the Bible studies. "That was God's Holy Spirit. He comes around when you pray, but you can't see Him. Peace is a gift He always seems to bring with Him."

Enrico began to cry again, but for a different reason. His tears were now like rain in the desert that caused things to grow. The lines in his face broke into a smile. It had been many years since they moved in that direction, but they broke free of the frown, and joy bloomed from the inside out. "I feel our God. He has accepted me. Now I know that He is my God." Fresh tears coursed down his face, but never had he looked happier.

"I am not troubled anymore. God has His hand on me. If He needs my help for any reason, I volunteer. I am old, but I can still be of service. My life is drawing to an end. I feel my strength ebbing and the shadow of death drawing ever closer, but now I can die knowing God is in my heart. I am no longer afraid."

Manu listened and felt a greater respect rise up for Enrico. "God can use you no matter how old you are. Age makes no difference. Daniel told me that God says that when we are weak, He makes us strong.[116] He can do that for you. All you have to do is ask Him."

[115] 1 John 4:18

[116] 2 Corinthians 12:9

Manu watched as Enrico walked away. There was a spring to his step and a smile on his face. He was a different man from the one Manu remembered. Manu got up and looked around the room for his friends and advisors. He needed to share this threat with them. Again, 'forewarned is forearmed'. He learned that from his friend Josh.

Noemi, his wife, was sitting there with their infant son Juan. Noemi, whom God had raised from the dead after suffering a massive hemorrhage during childbirth, was flourishing. She was sitting at the table. Manu went over and squatted at her feet. Theirs had been an arranged marriage, but the first buds of love and respect were starting to bloom. He had stood up for her when his stepmother, Chabuto, had wanted to call the marriage off. Even before the wedding Chabuto started to be aware of the attraction between them and felt her hold on Manu begin to slip.

She almost caused Noemi's death by advising Noemi not to eat or drink much during her pregnancy, which could have been a cause for the hemorrhage. Her body had been seriously depleted. Chabuto also lied by telling Noemi that eating and drinking while nursing would cause too much milk to flow and could cause the baby to choke. When Sherry finally saw the baby and realized he was losing weight she intervened with Manu. He sent his stepmother out of his home to care for some orphan children living in the village. Little Juan was now recovering and gaining weight.

Sherry looked over at Ted who was engaging Lara in conversation. She wasn't sure how much Spanish either of them knew, but it didn't appear to make a difference. They were communicating nonetheless.

Next, she observed Renato and one of the older women who had come out of the jungle. He was doing quite a bit of smiling lately and she wondered if that woman was the reason. She understood that his wife had died early in their marriage and he had been alone since then. She agreed with God that man wasn't meant to be alone.[117]

Lastly, she moved further into the room and spotted Josh and Bekah. They were having a serious discussion. Their minds might have been on the discussion, but the attraction of their hearts was apparent for anyone who had eyes to see.

Sherry wondered at the timing of these relationships and also of the new life growing inside her. There were no guarantees that they would live through the coming battle. All that was guaranteed was that God's side won.

Manu decided not to tell of the situation with Tuvicha and Chabuto that Enrico had shared until after they had eaten. There was no sense in letting worry ruin their appetites. Manu asked for quiet and blessed the food. He then looked at the group and noticed that all the people answering God's call were in attendance. There were a few extra men who were members of the displaced tribe and were most likely the men Arandu had asked to join them. Connie and Edwardo had just walked in with the two babies and Maria. They did not want to be separated since the attack, and Sherry didn't mind. Connie was like a sister to her and Connie's children had a place in her heart. There were probably thirty to thirty-five men and women in the room that served as a kitchen. Other than eight of them, all were new converts, but all had a zeal that only the Holy Spirit could impart.

Manu stood after the meal was finished. He looked to Josh and questioned. "We are all now followers of the One true God. Is there anything He requires of us before our battle begins?"

Josh rose up and answered, "Yes. God asks that all believers, as a sign of their faith and commitment, be baptized. Manu, can we gather the whole village and go down to the river tomorrow, after our evening meal? Will you make sure everyone knows about it?"

---

[117] Genesis 2:18

"That won't be a problem," Manu answered. "In the morning I will call together the ringleaders and explain what we want done. They will see to it that everything is handled.

After dinner, they had their phone call. Thankfully, not much had been happening up north. They all knew of Haydon Carlton's treachery, and were surprised he had made no further attempts to secure the golden crucifix. Even though he was on the back burner concerning the events transpiring about them, he was not someone to be ignored. It was expected that sooner or later he would make his presence known.

Everyone headed over to the meeting area, anticipating another great Bible study. When they looked up, they could see that there were about fifty people in attendance already. Excitement spread through them as they realized how many more people were attending this evening. They could see more people walking towards them and waving a greeting. Almost the whole village had been converted.

Josh spoke to Daniel and they decided that since they were to have a water baptism tomorrow, it would be good to teach on it tonight.

As the people gathered, Daniel spoke and Edwardo translated into Guarani for those who needed it. "We are told in the Bible that even Jesus was baptized in a river just like we are going to do tomorrow.[118] Jesus told his followers to go into the entire world and baptize those who believe.[119] Remember when we spoke of God making us new creations and how our sins were forgiven and that now we were different? We now want to serve Him; to do good and to be good. Well, baptism is an expression of that, and something we do to show our faith in God and His work. He tells us in the Bible that baptism demonstrates a believer's new life. It shows that just as Jesus died, was buried

---

[118] Matthew 3:13-16

[119] Mark 16:15-16

and then rose from the dead, through faith in Him, we are buried in the water in baptism and then raised as He was."[120]

Daniel spent some time reading additional Bible verses on baptism and then they closed with a time of prayer. Everyone left excited about the upcoming baptism, and about the morning Bible study. They were in awe and wonder about what they had already heard, and in anticipation about what new things they would learn. Daniel wondered if the new believers in the time of Jesus were as excited as the new believers here were. The group broke up and each sought his own bed.

[120] 1 Peter 3:21-22

CHAPTER TWENTY-THREE

JUNE 20

THE RIVER

The night passed slowly. Esteban and Carlos had the four other men come together on one boat. They set up three hour watches. Most were unable to sleep and spent the night tossing and turning in the dark. Everyone was relieved when the birds began to warm up and night lost its hold. With everything that had transpired, the evening meal had been sparse. Judging from preparations, it appeared breakfast would follow suit. They ate the meager fare with growing concern. No one was paying attention to the shore when suddenly twelve men separated themselves from the dark jungle shadows. They were armed with rifles and had them aimed at the six men on the boat. One of them shouted to the men on the boats to stand up and put their hands in the air.

Suddenly a man on the boat drew his gun. A well-aimed knife sliced through the air and pierced his shoulder. He uttered a shout and his gun fell into the water. One of his companions grabbed him to prevent him from following suit.

The man who had spoken jumped onto the boat and began searching each of his captives carefully as the rest of his men watched from the bank of the river. They all appeared very competent and alert to even the slightest movement. Montero and Rampone looked at each other helpless; anger and frustration growing in them with each passing minute.

The tall man with the dark curly beard who appeared to be their leader spoke to them in English, since he heard them speaking it the previous day. "We have captured the six other men of your group who were wandering around in the jungle yesterday afternoon. We actually did them a favor, for they did not appear to know where they were going. Now I ask, who speaks for your group?"

Montero stepped forward. "I do. What right do you have to attack our men and our boats? We have not interfered with you or your men. We are on a peaceful mission up river." Montero managed to convey this message with as much persuasion as he could muster. Even though he was bluffing, he was trying hard to maintain a self-assured attitude. But he was holding a losing hand, and the stranger behaved as though he knew it.

The tall man responded, "We have had eyes on you since before you set out from Puerto Bahía Negra. Word was sent up river you were coming our way. Bring out the rest of your weapons," he ordered. "We know you have three boxes of them in addition to what you are carrying. Now, what would a nice peaceful group of men need all those weapons for?"

Everyone remained where they were until Montero nodded. He was hoping to salvage something out of this mess, but until he had time to think, or an opportunity presented itself, he would play along as best he could.

The tall man spoke to two of his men and they produced ropes to tie everyone's hands. When that was done, he ordered all of them off the boats. He assigned four men to take the boxes of weapons into the jungle and hide them and to find a tarp to carry all the hand guns and ammunition back to their camp. They would return for the other boxes later.

They had over five miles to travel and it was slow going. The six prisoners were not used to walking in the jungle, let alone with their hands tied behind their backs. After over three hours they were only halfway there. The prisoners were tripping and falling every few minutes and constantly needed help getting up. The last straw for them was when one of them fell again and sliced open his cheek. It bled profusely and probably required a stitch. That was not likely to happen. Finally Montero spoke up. "Men," he called out. "Sit down." He turned to the leader and spoke with anger and frustration. "I've had enough of this. We're in the jungle, there's no place to go, and we're your prisoners. The least you can do is tie our hands in front of us to improve our balance so we can prevent so many falls."

The tall man appeared to consider this request. He gave an order to break for lunch, and tie their hands in front so they could eat. He said he would consider leaving them there if everyone behaved. After the meal, he ordered six men to go back and bring the weapon boxes. The rest of them would wait here and have a siesta.

In two hours, the six men showed up with the three boxes of weapons. He let them rest while the other six men carried the weapons back to their camp. As night began to descend, the line of captives and their jailers were still traveling through the jungle, following a trail only the jailers could see. Eventually they saw the light of a campfire and heard soft voices murmuring just ahead of them. They also smelled fresh meat cooking, which caused them to quicken their steps.

As they entered the camp, several other men came forward to talk with the tall man. Upon looking closer, Montero noticed that few of these men appeared to be natives. They were all slightly lighter and had dark beards. "What was this?" Montero wondered. Then he saw the rest of the men he had sent into the jungle. Their hands were tied also, but none appeared to be injured. Their group was motioned over to join the rest of them.

Montero looked around. He counted thirty or forty of the strangers occupying the camp. From the appearance of the camp, it had been occupied for some time. The tall man stepped into the circle of men, but turned to address the captives. "My name is Jim. I'm in charge here. If you behave and obey orders, you may live a few more days; if not, you will be killed immediately." He looked at the faces before him and saw submission in most, but there were a few that experience had taught him could prove to be a problem. He was not concerned. He was well able to deal with them if the need arose. He had full confidence in his men and their ability to keep order in the camp, but he would keep his eyes on the leader and the one who sat by his side. He ordered all of the prisoners to be given something to eat and drink, then to be taken to the area set apart to take care of their personal needs. All bindings were checked before turning in for the night. Guards were set and everyone quieted down.

Montero lay quiet, deliberating the options that were open to him. Unable to find a single one that satisfied him, he rolled over and went to sleep. Rampone, on the other hand, did not like being restrained and fought the situation physically and emotionally. He continuously strained at the ropes that bound him until his wrists were raw. He tossed and turned most of the night until exhaustion overtook him.

Akeem Farsi, known to the men in the camp as Jim, lay on the hard ground contemplating this new situation. For the last month, since going undercover in Paraguay, he had been spending the better part of the night in prayer. His situation was precarious. He had been out of touch with his contact for over a month. There was only one person in this group he could trust, his longtime friend, Mehdi. He had been trying to think of a way to send him down to Puerto Bahía Negra without arousing suspicion.

Dealing with this group of prisoners might be the answer to his prayer. He would send Mehdi down to Puerto Bahía Negra to report the capture of the prisoners and determine what to do with them. While he was in town, Mehdi could make a call to José, their contact and relay to him what had transpired in the camp. José was the owner of The Excelsior, a large weapons and ammunition store in Asunción. José made regular trips to Puerto Bahía Negra. Maybe they could set up some sort of meeting and brief him.

Akeem had told no one about the young woman he had encountered in the jungle and had left at the edge of their clearing. He did not know who she was, but knew she was with the people from the village on the river by the big rock. He knew that she and her friends were staying there. He had been keeping tabs on the village and had seen them all when they arrived. He had tried to avoid interaction with the village and so far, he had been successful. But he needed to get closer and find out what was happening. Things seemed to be stirred up over there and he wanted to know why. Tomorrow night or the next he would take a reconnaissance trip there to gather information. Akeem felt his mind and body relax as he gave this problem to God. For the last month, Akeem had felt an urgency in his spirit. He felt as though God was bringing things to a climax and, as unlikely as it seemed, somehow he was involved.

CHAPTER TWENTY-FOUR

JUNE 20

THE VILLAGE

Come morning, Manu sent young runners throughout the village spreading the word of the upcoming baptism after last meal. If everyone came, there should be nearly one hundred fifty people being baptized. Manu was not quite sure he understood everything that was taught, but he knew that if God said to do it, he wanted to be first in line. He also knew that as Chief, he was the leader of his village and most people would follow his example. He walked over to the meeting area after breakfast and there was standing room only. Most of the village was there to listen to the Word of God being taught by Daniel, Josh and Edwardo. Josh was already standing in the middle of the group with his Bible open.

"Today I want to tell you about the importance of knowing God's Word. Faith comes by hearing God's Word. If you don't hear it, how can you believe?" Josh continued teaching for a short time and then read a Scripture.

Isaiah 55:8-11 KJV

8 For my thoughts are not your thoughts, neither are your ways my ways, saith the LORD.

9 For as the heavens are higher than the earth, so are my ways higher than your ways, and my thoughts than your thoughts.

10 For as the rain cometh down, and the snow from heaven, and returneth not hither, but watereth the earth, and maketh it bring forth and bud, that it may give seed to the sower, and bread to the eater:

11 So shall my word be that goeth forth out of my mouth: it shall not return unto me void, but it shall accomplish that which I please, and it shall prosper in the thing whereto I sent it."[121]

"When God speaks, things happen. When believers speak God's Word things happen. Peter and John, friends of Jesus, spoke to a lame man and told him to get up and walk and he did. This type of thing happened all through the Bible and it's still happening today. Noemi, Ciba and baby Emilio are proof of that. God is always true to His Word.

"God's Word says that no weapon raised against you will succeed, and every mouth that speaks against you, you will condemn.[122] Remember God's Word is one of the weapons we use against the enemy. Something else God says in His Word is that we can do all things through Him because He gives us strength."[123]

Josh looked around at all the people. They were all listening intently. Josh told them, "I want to pray that all of you remember these sayings from God. They will help you when you are in trouble." Josh prayed, and ended the Bible study reminding the people again of the upcoming baptism this evening, and that it would take the place of the evening Bible study.

As the people started to leave Josh asked Daniel, Ted, Renato and Manu if they would meet with him. "I have something important I need to speak to all of you about. They waited until

[121] Isaiah 55:8-11
[122] Isaiah 54:17
[123] Philippians 4:13

the people had left and then pulled some chairs together and sat down. "Manu," Josh spoke earnestly, "ever since you and Bekah had the dream about her being trapped under water, I have been concerned. I know we should not worry, that we need to trust God, but I feel we should pray together. We all have a special relationship with Bekah. Manu, you are her brother, Ted, you were her husband, Renato, you are like her father, and Daniel and I are the leaders of this group. The Bible says if five can put a hundred to flight then a hundred can put ten thousand to flight. If we join together in prayer, we have greater strength."[124]

Manu needed no further encouragement. He immediately dropped to his knees. Ted was more cautious. "Has something happened?" he asked. "Do you know something we don't?"

"No," Josh answered. "I just know that Bekah seems to be the focal point of our quest and has also been the focal point for several attacks by the enemy. God even seems to be showing us that another one is coming. Manu and Bekah both had a dream that I consider to be a warning. If we have been given a warning, it appears to mean we should be doing something to prepare for the attack. Prayer seems to be our best strategy."

Daniel was slow to reply to the statement. "I'm glad we are doing this. Even if we only take an hour each night, I think the sleep we lose will be more than made up for by the grace of God. Remember, Jesus asked His disciples, 'Could you not pray with me for one hour?'[125] I don't know about all of you, but I don't want Him asking me that question."

The rest of them knelt down and began to pray quietly. Josh did not know when they had stopped actively praying, but he became aware that his mind was quiet as well as his voice. He felt that familiar peace permeate every fiber of his being. Manu stirred. He slowly turned toward them, wanting to speak,

---

[124] Leviticus 26:8

[125] Mark 14:37-38

but unable to utter a sound. Finally his tongue was loosened and he whispered, "God is here." Those three words, whispered in reverence and awe, awakened their senses. Their next breath inhaled the presence of God. He infiltrated their very being. Every cell was infused with His glory and His grace. All the cares and worries of the moment were washed away by His presence. Wave after wave of His glory and majesty continued to roll over them. They were overwhelmed.

Slowly they began to come to their senses. Opening their eyes, they saw a crowd surrounding them, all the people of the quest. Connie spoke up first. "I came back to the meeting area because we couldn't find the puppy and Maria was upset. I realized he probably fell asleep and was still here. As I approached I saw everyone lying down and I was afraid. I thought something else had happened and you all had been attacked by someone. I ran back to get Edwardo. When we got back here, he began to walk toward all of you and he also became weak. He backed up and told me to get everyone accompanying us on the quest to come here. We have been waiting for over an hour. If you look in the corner, there's Hombrecito waking up also. No one and nothing can stand in the presence of God, not even a puppy."

Josh, Ted and Manu made a few unsuccessful attempts to get to their feet and gave up. Daniel and Renato both decided they were going to wait awhile before they made the attempt. Everyone was filled with questions, but they all remained quiet and waited until the five men were ready to tell what had transpired. Finally Daniel said, "Get us some chairs and help us up and we will try to explain what happened. I think each of us should tell his own story and determine if God ministered to us differently. I think we are all in agreement that God was here. We felt His presence in a profound way. He didn't speak out of a burning bush, but He definitely spoke. I don't know whether it was audibly or in my heart, but I definitely heard Him, and I assume the rest of us did too. Manu, why don't you tell us what you experienced."

Manu looked at all the expectant faces and joyfully began to share his experience. His face broke into a smile that lit up the area. "I don't know if I can accurately explain what happened to me. God came. I felt Him, I heard Him, and I even smelled Him. We all initially knelt down and began to pray quietly. I don't know how long we had been praying, five minutes or five hours. Time lost meaning. By the way, what time is it now? How long have we been under the influence of Heaven?"

Edwardo answered. "We have been watching you for over an hour, but you had not prayed very long because it is only eleven-thirty, and the Bible study was over at nine-thirty."

"God came and shared Himself with me. First I recognized His peace. He laid it over me like a blanket. It seemed to block all my fears, worries and concerns. He has done that before; I like His peace. Then I smelled a strange smell. I have never smelled anything like it before. Maybe it was a heavenly flower. Do they have flowers in Heaven? It was a sweet smell that hung in the air. Do any of you smell it? I still do. Finally He spoke to me. It was like no other voice or sound I have ever heard. It sounded like beautiful birdsong. It sounded like a babbling brook. It sounded like a mighty rushing wind. Yet all these sounds had a meaning that I understood. It was like a heavenly language that God was speaking and I understood."

Tears were now running down Manu's cheek. "God took away my doubt and fear. He forgave me for my lack of faith, but commanded me to be strong now because He was with me and would help me do whatever He asked me to do. Now I can rest. All I have to do is thank Him for being God."

Many of the people had begun to kneel while Manu was talking, realizing that the presence of the Lord was still in this place.

Ted began to tell of his experience. "What happened to

Manu is very similar to what I experienced. I too felt His peace, and the aroma that surrounded us smelled like the most fragrant rose you can imagine. I wanted to take giant breaths of it. It seemed to fill me with strength and comfort. I have felt fear during this quest, but have tried to ignore it so far. Another thing I struggled with was insecurity. I didn't know how I could be qualified to do any of the things God would ask of me. During this experience, something seemed to break inside of me, but it was a good thing. It was as if a wall I had built to protect myself had been broken down and God was telling me He was my hiding place. He was my refuge and my fortress.[126] God spoke my name in that beautiful language. To me it was a language of love. This whole encounter with God radiated His love."

Bekah watched Ted's face and listened to his words and she began to cry, but these were tears of joy. Having known Ted for many years, she recognized the wall he was talking about. He had erected one against her also, but she felt its eradication. His spirit was now open to all that God wanted him to do, all that God wanted him to be, and all that God wanted to give him.

Daniel spoke next. He reiterated what had been previously spoken. Then he told of what God had spoken specifically to him. "God told me that even though Josh is the leader of the group, I am to be the spiritual head. My knowledge of His Word will be the weapon we must rely on to fight the battle before us. He also said not to look at my lack of converts in the village over the years as being a failure. They were training for the purpose of being faithful. Remember," He told me, "of all the things I require, it is faithfulness in using the gifts I have given you to promote the Gospel that pleases Me the most."[127]

Sherry observed Daniel as he spoke. He may not have been crying, but her eyes overflowed with tears of joy. She alone

---

[126] Psalm 91

[127] 1 Peter 4:10

was privy to the knowledge that until recently, he counted himself a failure. Even after these breakthroughs were taking place, he did not see his labors as bringing forth fruit. God had shown Daniel that his years of what appeared to be fruitless toil were in fact the seeds of the fruit that was now being harvested.

Renato sat still and gazed quietly all around him. He had a joy that was expressed in the light in his eyes and the glow on his face. "God told me He has given me not just Bekah, but all of you to be a father to. Somehow, I don't see myself going any further on this quest, but staying here and caring for all of you as a flock of sheep. Jesus was called the great Shepherd; I hope He gives me the strength and wisdom to do what He has asked me."

Finally Josh stood up. He looked at the faces of all the people surrounding them. They had an expectancy; a hope that God was faithful and He would do all He promised. "God wanted me to remind you that there may be battles and hardships in this fight, but he will never ask more of us than we can bear, and that there will always be a way of escape.[128] God also showed me many visions of what is going to happen, but they were bits and pieces, and they are buried in the midst of countless other dreams. Maybe they will come into focus when it is necessary."

Josh finished by saying, "God made me the head of the quest, and He made Daniel the Pastor. Now let's all join together in agreement and thank God for His visitation, for leading and guiding us, for protecting us, and finally for giving us victory."

The group broke up excited about what God had done and would continue to do, and also looking forward to the baptism this evening.

[128] 1 Corinthians 10:13

CHAPTER TWENTY-FIVE

JUNE 20

THE VILLAGE

Musing about what had taken place with all her men, Bekah took her Bible and wandered down to the river. She walked out onto the jetty and sat down on one of the large rocks. She felt the warmth of the sun penetrate her body and drive out the chill she had been feeling all day. There were several men and women working at the river with nets, hooks, and spears. It was fascinating to watch them catch different kinds of fish with different types of equipment. It reminded her that God used different means to bring people to Him, but first and foremost, it was His love and kindness that drew people into His net.[129]

Bekah lay back against the rock behind her, a lassitude enveloped her and she closed her eyes and slept. As she lay there, the Spirit of God imparted to her things that would be required of her. Many would stretch her to the limits of her faith, but she remained confident that God would be with her every step of the way, that somehow He would light her path.[130] Just as Mary pocketed in her heart all the marvel that took place concerning the birth of Jesus, Bekah did the same with the revelations of

[129] Romans 2:4
[130] Psalm 119:105
[131] Luke 2:19

her dream.[131] Some things she did not understand. Some she understood very well, and pondered at the outcome of all those embarking on the quest.

Suddenly Bekah was startled out of her sleep by people yelling and crying out. Then she realized they were yelling and shouting at her. She turned and saw a giant tree trunk traveling down the river. It had just rounded a bend and was heading straight for her, its leaves and branches waving like so many people attempting to grab her. In trying to scramble to her feet, her foot slipped between two large wet rocks that were part of the body of the jetty. Bekah struggled with all her strength, but her foot stayed stuck and the tree trunk kept coming. Abruptly, just a short distance from where she was trapped, the tree appeared to hit a submerged rock. It careened to the left, raining down a torrent of loose leaves and branches all over Bekah, and a wave of water washed over her from the surge created by the momentum of the tree. Bekah felt as though she had been submerged in the water and trapped by tree branches. Coughing and sputtering Bekah watched the tree go around the jetty; it missed her with the bulk of its body. Unfortunately, she was raked by all the limbs and branches of the tree as it passed by. As bad as it was, it could have been much worse.

Two of the men had left their fishing and hurried over to help free Bekah. The rest had hurried after the tree to see if they could trap it and bring it to shore. After it was dried out, it would supply firewood in the village for many days. The two men were not able to free Bekah's foot from the trap it was in. They sent a runner up to the village to get more help and to send for Dr. Sherry. She would be able to help with the cuts and scrapes, some of which were bleeding quite freely.

The runner's responsibility had been to go to Manu first as Chief, to alert him of the accident. Manu had then sent him on to Dr. Sherry. Manu ran ahead to see for himself the results of the accident and what would be needed to free Bekah. When Manu reached her, Bekah was quietly sitting on a rock; her left foot bracing her against the current of the river, her right foot stuck about three feet below the surface of the water. She was completely soaked from the splashing of the water as the tree bumped its way by. Now because of her foot being in a submerged hole, she was sitting up to her waist in the river as it swirled its way around her.

Assessing the situation, Manu knew this would be a difficult job because the rocks trapping Bekah's foot were under other large rocks contained in the jetty. Several rocks would need to be moved to free her. He sent men up to bring down whatever metal tools they had, especially some of the picks and axes brought as gifts by their friends. He would need everyone's cooperation to get Bekah out of this dangerous situation. He put his hand on Bekah's shoulder in a gesture of comfort. This was going to take a while and Bekah was going to need all the comfort she could get.

Sherry hurried down with her bag, and several blankets. She noticed that Bekah was starting to shiver, but before she could make any attempt to cover her up, Sherry needed to assess the extent of the injuries Bekah had received. Shivering was not just a sign of cold, but also a sign of shock. Nothing looked life threatening, so she folded two blankets and dropped them on Bekah's shoulders. That was the best she could do. Any lower and they would get wet. Sherry asked Bekah, "Other than the cuts and scrapes, are you hurt anywhere else? Are you in serious pain? How do your leg, foot and ankle feel? Do you think you have any broken bones?"

Bekah laughed nervously. "Other than the cuts and scrapes I'm not hurting. My leg, foot and ankle are cold, and as far as I can tell I have no broken bones." Bekah laughed again and said, "I can't believe this happened. What a crazy thing."

Sherry took hold of Bekah's hand. It was ice cold. She thought some of it was the temperature of the river, but it could also be signs of some shock setting in. Shock was not confined to just bodily injury. An incident that caused emotional distress could also contribute to a diagnosis of shock. Almost being hit by a tree and being trapped in a pile of rocks in moving water just might qualify. Sherry turned to one of the women standing on the shore and asked her to run and get some hot, sweet tea for Bekah. As she turned, she saw Josh, Ted and Daniel come running down, followed closely behind by Renato. All four of them made their way out onto the jetty.

Daniel, Edwardo, and several men from the village had built the jetty. It had taken them over six months to complete it. They had started when the river was low and moving slowly. They laid a foundation of great stones that had to be rolled into the river. It took several men to move one stone. After the foundation, slightly smaller stones had been used. They had been successful in their enterprise. The jetty now served as a fishing platform, clothes washing station, and a barrier for any large objects that came downriver such as that tree. Periodically they needed to remove the debris that collected on the upriver side of the levee. They were able to salvage large amounts of fire wood for the village. It had been difficult in the past to cut up the wood. They only had four axes in the entire village. Now they had ten more thanks to the gifts of the Americans. Hopefully, with the addition of their new tools, they would be able to move some of the stones and free Bekah's foot.

Sherry began to clean Bekah's wounds and apply the local healing salve they had used earlier on her when she had been abducted. As Sherry worked, she prayed for healing, and thanked God for wisdom in how to deal with this situation. She began to ask Bekah other questions. "Can you wiggle your toes?" Bekah nodded. "Can you move your foot and ankle?"

Again Bekah nodded yes. Sherry was trying to gauge the extent of the injury. "I haven't gotten down there to feel it; does any of it feel swollen?"

Exasperated, Bekah answered shortly, "No, nothings swollen, I'm just cold, battered and bruised, and my foot is stuck. Does that answer all your questions?"

Sherry took no offense at Bekah's impatient attitude. People don't always act the way they usually would when they are under physical and emotional stress. She turned away and Josh was right behind her. "Go over and sit next to Bekah and put your arms around her. She's losing body heat fast. I've sent for some hot tea and she has two blankets around her shoulders, but it's not enough. We need to get her out of this mess quickly."

Josh sat behind Bekah and wrapped his arms and legs around her to share his body heat. That meant he was sitting in the water also. Sherry realized this and put two blankets around him also.

The hot tea came and both Bekah and Josh drank it. Some of Bekah's shivering abated. Josh called over to Ted to take his place. He wanted to examine the situation and see if any ideas came to him. He had been praying while he held Bekah and felt confident that there was an answer. He stood up and moved in front of Bekah, looking at where her leg went into the hole. "Bekah," he questioned, "when your foot went in the hole, did it twist? It looks a little misaligned."

"I don't know; it happened so fast. It may have."

"If it went in," Josh observed, "and it's not swollen, it should be able to come out without us having to move a bunch of rocks. Can you stand on one foot while we move you around and try a bunch of different angles. Thankfully, the cold water will discourage any swelling."

Daniel had gone up to the compound to see if he had any tools that would be helpful in freeing Bekah's foot. He came back with a large metal bar with a slightly pointed end. He had used it to dig holes for the foundation of their house. It was five feet long and weighed about twenty pounds. It should be a perfect tool to use to leverage some of these rocks off Bekah's foot.

Josh's face lit up with excitement when he saw Daniel coming. He was convinced this was the tool they needed to get Bekah free. After working for over an hour they were all sweating and covered in scrapes and scratches. They were down to one last rock. This was the one that was entrapping her foot. Unfortunately, they did not have a lot of room to work. Bekah's foot was already occupying most of the hole it was in. They could not get the metal bar in there with it. The good thing was they only needed to move it an inch or two. They decided to position the bar under the rock. The down side to that was that they could not control the way the rock shifted. They needed to be careful it did not shift back onto Bekah's ankle.

Everybody got into position. Four men were on the bar, two were using their hands to pull the rock, and two were at Bekah's shoulders ready to pull her out. It was very crowded and everyone needed to be sure their footing was firm so they did not slip. Suddenly Bekah called out, "Wait!! We need to pray that God is with us and that He will send His angels to help us."[132]

Angels were a new concept to the villagers, but those who had been a Christian for a time knew of them and their purpose, and they all prayed together. Then on the count of three they all strained and Bekah was triumphantly pulled free. A shout went up and everyone clapped their hands.

A grateful Bekah stood up and put some weight on her foot; then she looked up and thanked God for His protection. Other than being numb from the cold, there didn't appear to be any serious injuries, but she did take Josh's arm as she walked back to the village. She was shivering and he was radiating heat. She was

---

[132] Hebrews 1:13-14

anxious to wash up, change into dry clothes, and take a short rest.

Josh turned and saw Manu following. He probably wanted to make sure Bekah was alright. Bekah went back to her room and Josh and Manu went into the kitchen. Josh poured them each a cup of coffee. Lately, there always seemed to be a fresh pot on the stove. It was an indulgence he was grateful for. He was wet and slightly chilled himself. He would change later. Now he was glad Manu was here. He wanted to talk with him about what had happened.

"Manu, do you know what a coincidence is," Josh asked?

"I am not familiar with that word," Manu replied.

"A coincidence is something that happens accidentally or by chance. I don't think what happened here to Bekah today was an accident, or that it was by chance. Too many things have been happening to her on this trip. Also, this reminded me a little of her dream; although here she was stuck in water, just not under water."

"Yes!" Manu exclaimed. "You are right. First her house is broken into, then she is abducted, then the fire, and now this. It is too much coincidence."

"You're right," Josh replied, "and we need to see that it doesn't happen again. For some reason, the enemy seems to be targeting Bekah for his attacks. I don't know why. Other than being born in Paraguay, she is no different from any of the other Americans. Remember, Renato was born in Paraguay also, and nothing out of the ordinary has happened to him. When Bekah gets up we will have a short meeting with everyone before last meal and make some plans."

Voices could be heard approaching the compound. The core group walked in and sat at Sherry's new table. Manu had surprised her with it this morning after breakfast. It also had ten chairs. She put the old one in the corner. It could be used for overflow seating. Sherry looked at the group and decided a fresh pot of coffee was in order. There was some cake leftover, enough for everyone to have a small piece.

While the coffee was brewing Bekah wandered into the kitchen. “I thought I smelled coffee brewing. Is this a private party or is everyone welcome?”

Josh looked over at her, his day brightened and he smiled. She looked at him and returned the smile. Josh felt a warmth envelop him, and long denied feelings again stirred. “Wait a minute,” he reminded himself, “this is not the right time for those thoughts. If we get out of this alive, then maybe I can allow myself to daydream, but not now.”

Bekah helped pass out the coffee and came over and sat by Josh. “She feels it too,” he thought. “Maybe the danger of it hasn’t occurred to her yet.”

While they were finishing up Paloma and Ciba came in carrying trays of food for last meal. It was almost time to eat and then to go to the baptism. It looked like the planning meeting would have to be put off until after the baptism.

After their meal the group began to walk down the path to the river. It felt as if the whole village was on the move. There was a jubilant spirit about all of them. They were all rejoicing over the goodness of God and their new found relationship with Him.

When they reached the river, they waited as more and more people began to follow them down the path. When it appeared that everyone who was coming had arrived, Josh again spoke to the group and read to them from the Bible while Edwardo translated into Guarini. “This is what God’s Word says:

> *Then Peter said unto them, “Repent, and be baptized every one of you in the name of Jesus Christ for the remission of sins, and ye shall receive the gift of the Holy Ghost.”*[133]

“Jesus thought baptism so important that He, Himself,

[133] Acts 2:38 KJV

was baptized. Let me read to you what occurred at that time."

> *And Jesus, when he was baptized, went up straightway out of the water: and, lo, the heavens were opened unto him, and he saw the Spirit of God descending like a dove, and lighting upon him: And lo a voice from heaven, saying, "This is my beloved Son, in whom I am well pleased."*[134]

Josh read the event from the Gospel of Matthew, then went on to explain, "Baptism is an act of obedience symbolizing your faith in a crucified, buried, and resurrected Savior and of your death to sin, the burial of your old life, and the ability to walk in a new life with Christ Jesus. It was so important to our Father God that He spoke from Heaven and confirmed that Jesus was His Son and that He loved Him and was pleased with Him. From what God has said, it appears baptism is important to Him. I want to do anything that pleases God. As a tribe, you followed your old gods and were obedient to them. Now, by being baptized you are washing away their influence on you and showing your faith in Jesus and God, His Father. If you agree with what I have spoken and want to be baptized, please line up here in two lines at the edge of the river, women on the left and men on the right."

As all the people lined up, Josh asked Manu and Mario to help him baptize and then asked Daniel, Edwardo and Philippe to baptize the other line. The six of them walked out into the shallow part of the river and the people started coming down into the water.

Manu held up his hands and stopped anyone from coming into the water. He announced to the multitude, "I am your Chief. I was not the first person to become a Christian in this village, but tonight I think it is important that I be the first to get baptized. If anyone is unsure of this, follow me. God has confirmed this with His Word and we can be assured that God does not lie."[135]

---

[134] Matthew 3:16-17

Manu turned to Josh and Daniel. Daniel asked Manu, "Do you accept Jesus as your Savior and repent for your sins?"

Manu answered loudly so everyone would hear, "Yes, I do."

Daniel answered, "Then I now baptize you in the Name of the Father, the Son and the Holy Spirit." He and Josh both lowered Manu into the water and then raised him up.

Manu, who before had always had a stoic type personality began to jump and shout, expressing his jubilation. The people joined him and the sound of it was heard for a distance.

The next person to come out of the water was Enrico. He shook off the water, raised his hands, and gave a loud cheer. Another shout of joy was expressed by those waiting on the shore. This was continued throughout the whole ceremony. Josh was amazed at the reaction of those being baptized and commented on his observation to Daniel. Daniel responded, "Josh, you need to understand that many people in the U. S. regard baptism as a tradition or custom. Because of what has been happening here, that is not the case. These people expect to have an encounter with God, and He's not letting them down. I have witnessed this before when I baptized several others from the village. I am glad to see their excitement. It encourages me, and it encourages each one of them also."

---

[135] Numbers 23:19

CHAPTER TWENTY-SIX

JUNE 20
THE VILLAGE

While all this was going on, Chabuto and Tuvicha sat in stony silence in the yard of his house as wave after wave of sounds of celebration rose up from the river. The Spirit of God called to them again, presenting His message of love and forgiveness, but they hardened their hearts and refused to listen. They spent their time scheming and plotting their retribution against the village and people they had known all their lives.

Satan continued to lie to them, blinding their eyes and deceiving them. He whispered to them that no one cared about them, when in fact many people were actually praying for them. They, for their part prayed also, but to a different entity, one of evil and darkness. When the people of the village prayed to God and received peace, love and hope, the answers to Chabuto's and Tuvicha's prayers were diametrically different. Instead of peace they received turmoil, instead of love they received hatred, judgement and condemnation, and instead of hope they received despair. Unfortunately, they had been dealing with these spirits for so long that these were the feelings that they fed on. The Bible states that you shall know the truth and the truth shall set you free.[136] Unfortunately, they no longer sought the truth.

---

[136] John 8:32

If truth be told, it was not service to their gods that had held their people together, but fear of them, and especially fear of Chabuto and Tuvicha. Since they had combined forces, their power had increased significantly. Now, with the sacrifice of the baby in their sights they appeared, at least to themselves and their followers, unstoppable. Their last group of followers had changed their allegiance and gone over to the other side, but they still harbored fear in their hearts of Chabuto and Tuvicha. Their former followers realized that an unearthly power was working through them. They feared for themselves and their village.

Finally Chabuto rose to go back into the house where six children awaited her. Already her anger was building against them. She hated them and the responsibility they brought. She hated Manu for burdening her with them. The fact was Chabuto was consumed with hatred. It permeated her very being.

When Chabuto walked into the back room of the house, six children sat together with round eyes open, staring silently at her. They had been relegated to the back room and knew the consequences if they disobeyed. Chabuto knew they were hungry. They had not eaten since breakfast, but she did not care, and they knew better than to ask. They were becoming skinny, and their clothes were filthy. It had been many days since they had the opportunity to wash and they were starting to smell. The baby had nothing to wear and was crusted with feces. Because everyone in the village was so caught up in their new-found faith, the villagers had not noticed the absence of the children. If they had seen them they would certainly have taken steps to help them. The baby knew not to cry, because when he did Chabuto would pinch him. The other children all had their own bruises from the abuse they had received from her.

Chabuto allowed one woman from the village to come and feed the baby in the morning. She had been a friend of Mara's, the baby's mother, and did this as a kindness to her memory. She was aware of the conditions in the house and the lack of care and abuse of the children, but her fear of Chabuto kept her from raising an alarm. Despite losing their followers, Chabuto did not feel their lack of support; Chabuto did not fear anyone or anything.

Presently she was seething with anger because her plan to kill the baby with the snake had been foiled by the God these Christians were following. She was confused as to why their God appeared to triumph over her gods. Surely the combined forces of all her gods should be enough to overcome their one God. There must be some sort of spell they were using; but she would find it out and turn the tables on them.

Right now Chabuto was glad she hadn't been seen. The people were unaware of her involvement and she was glad, but she was coming to the point where she did not care if she were found out. What could they do to her? Her powers were too strong.

Bringing her thoughts back to the children, Chabuto decided she was not going to waste food on them. Tonight they would sacrifice the baby and then they would be gone. Let the children that were left be someone else's problem.

CHAPTER TWENTY-SEVEN

JUNE 20
THE VILLAGE

When they were through with the baptism, Manu asked those personally involved in the quest to meet him up at the compound. When they had all arrived, he asked Edwardo to translate into Guarani while he spoke English to his guests. Manu related the facts he had learned from Enrico. When he was through he asked if they would all pray for Chabuto and Tuvicha and ask the Father God to melt their hearts.

Before they finished praying, a young man from the village came running through the door. "Manu, Manu," he shouted. "Enrico has been killed. It appears to be another wild boar attack. The boar pierced him with his tusks and dragged him into the jungle down by the river. He has a puncture wound in his throat and in his chest. There was much blood. Thankfully, he did not suffer greatly. He died quickly. Witnesses report that he saved little Maria's life. She had been walking back to the village with a group from the baptism. Enrico blocked the wild boar with his body to save her. People are preparing his body for burial." The young man stood there waiting for Manu to respond.

Edwardo and Connie got up and started to leave, wanting to check on Maria. "Where is she?" Edwardo asked.

The young man answered, "We took her back to the

house and Lara is caring for her. She is unhurt physically, but what she saw has brought fear to her."

When Edwardo and Connie entered their house they could hear little Maria crying. She was sitting on Lara's lap and Lara was rocking her gently.

Maria looked up and immediately ran to her parents. "Momma, Momma, Eyo is dead, Eyo is dead," she repeated over and over. "He was my friend. Whenever he saw me he would always come and talk to me. He told me this morning he would be going away and I would not be able to come with him; he said that I had to stay here with you and Papa. When I cried, he said some day I would see him again and that God would be watching over me now. How come God did not protect him?" Maria asked. "Didn't He know Eyo was my friend?"

"I don't know," Edwardo answered. "Maybe Eyo volunteered to save you. Maybe he knew God wanted someone down here to help Him and Eyo volunteered. He was a very brave man." Edwardo and Connie continued to comfort and pray for their daughter. Within minutes she slept.

At the meeting area, Manu hung his head in sadness. An evil spirit had visited his village again and he was unsure of what to do. It was too much of a coincidence that Enrico had just spoken to him of Tuvicha's and Chabuto's plans, and now Enrico was dead. Fear tried to grip him. Did the gods of Chabuto and Tuvicha have power over the wild animals? Had he compelled that wild boar to attack Enrico? So many questions were swirling around in his mind that Manu felt his faith begin to falter.

Josh heard what had happened and observed Manu's reaction. Because of his immaturity in the Word, Manu was unsure of what to do or how to react to such a terrible tragedy. But Manu was not alone in the fight. There were seasoned Christians with him, ones who had not only fought the devil, but who had won the fight.

Josh stood up and raised his voice. He spoke in Spanish and translations were made as needed. "My friends," he called out to the group, "don't let your hearts be fearful.[137] God has His hand upon us. He will never leave us or turn away from us,[138] and God does not lie.[139] He said He would be with us always, even to the end of the world.[140] The situations happening all over the world seem to indicate the end is near. Our adversary, Satan, is using all his resources to stop us from completing the quest God has called us to.

Jesus had a cousin who was a messenger for God. He told all who would listen, that Jesus was the Savior and they should follow His teachings. His name was John and he was arrested and killed because of His faith in Jesus. John's death, though tragic, was not in vain. Many people believed in his message and turned away from their sins. Enrico was a type of messenger also. He told Manu of Chabuto and Tuvicha's plans to offer a sacrifice tonight to their gods. He was concerned it would cause trouble. Not only was he brave to share that information, but he also sacrificed his life to save a little girl. Right now he is in Heaven in the presence of God and he is happy."

Josh paused to appraise the people's attitude and gather his thoughts. Suddenly a hush fell over the building and the walls began to lose their substance. The ceiling opened and a bright light shone among them. A heavenly host could be heard singing praises to God. The very air about them emanated an aroma that was unfamiliar, but strangely soothing to body, soul and spirit. Each person was kneeling with hands raised. Standing was not an option. Even if any of them wanted to, no one could stand in the presence of God. The sounds being heard from Heaven diminished and the Voice of God roared. It was not

---

[137] John 14:26-27

[138] Hebrews 13:5

[139] Numbers 23:19

[140] Matthew 28:20

a still, small voice, but a Voice that resounded in their ears and hearts. As He spoke, He gave them strength and encouragement. They had all been operating on blind faith, but God was now showing Himself to them.

Josh realized what was happening. It was not only the enemy, who was stepping up his pressure, but God was calling His troops to action also. Josh knew that many times God seemed to ask the impossible, but he also knew that if we responded in faith, the impossible happened. God needed them to act in faith, and His appearance in their midst caused their faith to surge. Then God spoke to them.

"LISTEN TO ME. I HAVE SENT YOU ON A QUEST AND YOU MUST BE SURE TO DO ALL I HAVE ASKED YOU TO DO. TRUST ME TO PROTECT YOU, TO LEAD YOU AND TO GUIDE YOU. DO NOT WORRY ABOUT WHAT APPEARS TO BE A MYSTERY TO YOU.[141] IT IS NOT A MYSTERY TO ME. I KNOW THE BEGINNING FROM THE END.[142] I AM THE BEGINNING AND THE END.[143] REMEMBER, LEAVE WHEN THE MOON IS FULL AND NOT BEFORE. I WILL ILLUMINATE YOUR PATH. DO NOT LOOK AT THE CIRCUMSTANCES SURROUNDING YOU, BUT KEEP YOUR EYES ON ME. TONIGHT THE ENEMY WILL CALL FORTH HIS FORCES.THEY WILL BE ON THE MOVE. I KNOW HIS PLANS. WAIT FOR MY COMMAND. I WILL SEND YOU FORTH WHEN THE TIME IS RIGHT. REMEMBER, TRUST ME."

Very slowly the atmosphere around them returned to normal, the sights and sounds around them came back into focus. Everyone who had experienced the presence of God was dumbfounded by what they had seen and heard. It's not always easy to comprehend what God was doing or saying, but He asked for faith and trust and everyone was determined to give it to Him.

---

[141] Ephesians 1:9

[142] Isaiah 46:9-10

[143] Revelations 22:13

CHAPTER TWENTY-EIGHT

JUNE 20

THE BLACK DEATH CAMP

There was great discontent in the camp. Most of the camp wanted to execute the prisoners and seize the boats and supplies, especially the weapons. They had not gotten the truth out of the prisoners and had lost interest in trying. They were honed to seek out infidels and destroy them, and here were twelve just ripe for the picking.

They knew Jim, the leader of the camp, had sent Mehdi downriver yesterday to get orders on how to deal with the prisoners. If all contacts were made he could be back in four or five days. Jim spoke with the men in the camp this morning and told them that this evening he would leave the camp to check the surrounding area. He wanted to get a good look at the village that lay close by. He was unsure whether he had seen some signs in the jungle of their incursion into the area surrounding their camp. Up to this time the people of the village had not been bothersome. He hoped they would remain that way.

Jim, whose real name was Akeem Farsi looked about him; all his men were gathered in groups of three or four and were talking agitatedly to each other. He was fairly certain that if he left the camp this evening his men would take circumstances into their own hands. Their fear of him was short-lived, and only when he was present, but that could not be helped. Akeem's main concern was the Guarani village that lay close by. They were innocents. These prisoners were hardened criminals and the rest of the men in the camp were would-be terrorists. He did not like having to make these types of life and death decisions, but his position had required it time and time again, and his conscience had become seared by having to play god during these circumstances. He still continued to pray to God, even after all these years, but God appeared to have stopped listening.

The afternoon meal had been eaten and the camp settled down to rest in the heat of the day. It was beginning to cool off. Winter was approaching, but hot or cold, siesta was observed. He set up a perimeter and lay down to rest himself. It would be a long night.

Akeem did not know how long he had slept, but when he woke up he knew God had spoken, saying to him, "I HAVE A PLAN AND A PURPOSE FOR YOUR LIFE.[144] YOU WERE FORMED IN YOUR MOTHER'S WOMB TO FULFILL THE QUEST I HAVE CALLED YOU TO.[145] I HAVE BEEN KEEPING YOU IN READINESS FOR THIS VERY TIME.[146] YOU ARE MY JONATHAN, AND YOU WILL SHORTLY MEET YOUR DAVID AGAIN. TONIGHT YOU ARE TO GO OUT AND HEAD FOR THE VILLAGE BY THE LARGE ROCK IN THE RIVER. THE FORCES OF DARKNESS ARE ON THE MOVE AND YOU MUST STOP THEM. MY SPIRIT WILL BE WITH YOU LEADING AND GUIDING YOU. BE SURE TO LISTEN."

Akeem looked up and saw that the sun had reached the treetops and the shadows were lengthening. The men had already begun preparing the evening meal and there was much movement in the camp. The man leaving for Puerto Bahía Negra had left yesterday. A rough trail had been cut through the jungle

---

[144] Jeremiah 29:11

[145] Isaiah 49:1

[146] Esther 4:14

to the bank of the river opposite the supply station. As he'd done on a previous trip, Mehdi would call out to passing boats asking for passage down the river into the town. He had his orders to whom he should speak, and that he should return as soon as possible. Akeem hoped that their contact would be there waiting. He had not been in touch for many weeks and prayed someone would be looking for him.

He was unaware Bekah had picked him out of a photo array of young men entering Paraguay. He was also unaware that Isaac had been in touch with José the owner of Excelsior Armament Company in Asunción, and secret contact for the C.I.A. Akeem had been unable to get back down there to talk with José. He prayed that somehow that when Mehdi got to Puerto Bahia Negra they would be able to get in touch. If he could not find any help locally, he would call the emergency number that would get him immediately in contact with José. José took trips twice a week to Puerto Bahía Negra under the guise of talking to local store owners about stocking some of his wares. The amount of guns and ammunition he sold in the area made it well worth his time. Mehdi knew who to look for. Hopefully they would find each other without too much trouble. Mehdi also needed to contact Josef Mohamed and get instructions on what to do with the prisoners. He had a special number to call if they had any problems or questions. They had contacted him two weeks ago when one of the men had been bitten by a snake and died.

Akeem walked over to the fire and took a plate of food. He ate quickly and quietly, keeping his thoughts to himself. He spoke to one of the men, putting him in charge of the camp while he went out to scout the nearby village. He told them again the prisoners should not be harmed, but wondered if their fear of him would suffice, or if they would succumb to their fanatical desires and kill the infidels. He would find out tomorrow when he returned and would deal with it then.

Akeem got his supplies together, then he turned and started down the trail. By the time he reached the village, everything in the jungle would be black except him. He was unusually light skinned for being Arabic, so he blackened his hands and face to partner with the night. He also wore camouflage pants and shirt and carried his machete and a hand gun in his belt. He had a rifle slung across his shoulder and a powerful, hooded flashlight in his belt. It was unsafe to travel the jungle in the dark. Roles were reversed at night, and instead of being the predator, you became the prey. With a brief backward glance he continued down the trail.

The jungle was in shadows, but he was still able to follow one of the marked trails that led to the village. It was marked so as to be unobtrusive at first glance. He did not want permanent trails to be established and easy for strangers to follow. Thankfully, the jungle cooperated, new growth appeared daily. This would make it difficult to follow at night, hence the flashlight, but he had been to the village to spy many times, and was comfortable in the night jungle. The moon was already up and it was only a few days until it was full.

As he walked, Akeem pondered the dream he had experienced that afternoon. He was firmly convinced it was a message from God. That alone stunned him, especially given the fact that since he had just that afternoon been contemplating that he had not felt the presence or heard the Voice of God in a very long time. He began to pray with fervor he had not experienced in quite a while.

"Almighty God and Father, Whose glory fills the heavens and the earth, Your Name is holy beyond measure. You spoke to me in a dream and said that I was born for the quest You have set before me. In obedience to Your Word, I am setting out for the village by the big rock in the river. I pray that Your Kingdom is being established on the earth according to Your will in

Heaven. Thank You for equipping me with what I need to do the job You have called me to do. Forgive me for allowing myself to stray from Your perfect will. I put my trust in You to keep me safe from the evil forces that are on the move, and to lead me, and illuminate my path through the darkness. Help all my senses to be functioning at optimum levels so that I may be exceptionally aware of my surroundings and able to respond quickly and accurately in whatever task You put before me. I don't understand what You mean about my being a Jonathan, but I trust in You, and that You will reveal to me what I need to know. I pray this all in Jesus' Name."

Akeem continued on the almost obscure path he was following, alert to all his surroundings. The sun had fallen and the short twilight was almost over. He had at least another two hours of walking before he reached the village. Looking at his watch, he estimated he would reach it by 8:30. His plan was to stay outside the village, but close enough to hear and observe what was transpiring there. He needed to stay alert, so as not to be surprised by anything or anyone in the jungle, or in the village. He continued to pray, praising God and thanking Him for His protection.

CHAPTER TWENTY-NINE

JUNE 20

THE VILLAGE

Akeem traveled swiftly and surely through the jungle without incident. He looked up and saw the lights of various campfires in the distance. Glancing at his watch, he was surprised to see that it was almost 9:00, later than he assumed, and wondered if God had a time schedule and had adjusted his path to meet His schedule. Akeem sat down on a rock and focused his senses and his mind on the nearby village. Then he reached out to God and asked for open eyes and ears to see and hear what God was revealing to him.

In astonishment, Akeem realized he was hearing several conversations at once. As he surrendered to the Spirit of God Akeem began to identify each conversation and understood what was being said. Most were talking excitedly about what had happened that day and how Almighty God, the One and only God, had conquered the spirit of death and raised a small baby from the dead. One conversation after another repeated the surprise and wonders of a God doing such a thing, and the enormity of the fact that this God, Who was now their God had done it for them. They had been told that no sacrifice was required other than loving and serving only Him. His Son Jesus had been sacrificed as the one and only sacrifice for the whole world. It was hard to understand, but this miracle had convinced them without a doubt that God loved and cared about them.

Suddenly those conversations faded and he heard the sound of a telephone ringing. He stood, and moved in the direction of the sound. It was coming from a group of buildings that were set apart from the rest of the village. He knew this was where the Missionaries lived. "Hello," an excited voice said, "This is Josh, and I apologize for being late again, but so much has gone on today. We are all here finishing a small supper, and trying to understand everything that has occurred." As usual, Josh had put the call on speaker phone.

"Well this is Joe, and all I have to say is we're not surprised. The Holy Spirit has had us praying intensely up here. Several people showed up unscheduled because they felt God had asked them to come and pray, and by what you're saying that extra prayer power seems to have been needed."

Josh spoke up again and related all that had happened that day. There was a stunned silence on the other end of the phone as the Maine contingent tried to absorb all the events that had transpired. Finally Josh said, "Keep on praying. Things appear to be coming to a climax. We are going to call Isaac next and let him know we seem to have stumbled on a small Black Death camp. I don't know if Akeem is in it. I will have to go with someone and see if I can recognize him."

Akeem's head snapped up at the sound of his name in that conversation. Someone knew about him and the Black Death presence in the area. If they knew his name, they must somehow be associated with the C.I.A. and been on the alert for him. He thought of the man who gave his name as Josh. It seemed so far-fetched that he could be the Josh of his childhood. Yet, God had a plan and could work all things together for His plan and purpose.[147]

Walking slowly toward the group of buildings, Akeem con-

[147] Romans 8:28

tinued listening as Josh got Isaac on the line. "Hello Josh," Isaac answered. "What's happening down there? Do you have any news for me?"

"It would take me an hour or so to tell you everything, but triaging the information, I will tell you what is most important to you first. We think we found a small group of Black Death members operating in a camp about five miles from the village. There appear to be about twenty-five or thirty of them and they have taken ten to twelve prisoners. I don't know if Akeem is a member of that particular group, but I will go out tomorrow morning to see if I recognize him from the picture you sent me."

Listening to this, Akeem decided to take a risk, trusting that God was still leading and guiding him. He walked through the open door into the big kitchen. Approximately twenty people were sitting on the floor listening to the phone conversation. Akeem drew a deep breath and spoke in a strong voice. "I am Akeem Farsi. Who are you and what do you want with me?"

As one, all eyes turned and riveted on him. Several members of the group sprang to their feet in surprise, but no one moved from their place. After a moment, Josh stood up also, and walking forward, let a hint of a smile touch his lips. He held out his hand. "I am Joshua Randall and I am so glad to see my long lost friend."

The two stood there a moment staring at each other, then simultaneously moved forward, shook hands, and then embraced each other like the long lost brothers they were. God had made them brothers in spirit just as He had Jonathan and David. They both took a step back, surprised at the passion of that embrace, but aware also, that God's Hand was upon them. It appeared God was moving His pieces into play, preparing for the final battle.

Finally a voice spoke up over the telephone and broke the spell. "Akeem, this is all truly amazing, but before you two catch up on old times, please give me a report on what has transpired since we were last in touch. It's been weeks since we have heard from you."

Everyone turned back to the telephone, having forgotten about the call. Akeem's sudden appearance had diverted their attention. Akeem walked over to the table the phone was on and began to speak. "Isaac, it's good to hear your voice. Because of the current situation in the village, I've been forced to take more risk than usual. I sent Mehdi down to Puerto Bahía Negra yesterday to try to get word to you, but odds are he won't be there for one or two days. He was going to look around town and see what came to the surface. It has to be a miracle that I am here in this village and have made contact not just with you, but with a long lost friend who is more like a brother to me. We grew up together, went through college together and even became Christians together. I can't imagine what he is doing here, but it seems God has decided to stir the pot, and we rose to the surface."

Isaac questioned again, "Akeem, I appreciate the history lesson, but can we concentrate on current events? Give me a report on what's been happening since you've been in Paraguay. We lost track of you right after you entered the country."

While all this was taking place, Edwardo was attempting to translate into Guarani all that was being said. The room was full, and more and more people were showing up, curious to see what was going on. They crowded into the room and filled the doorway. It appeared to them that God's army was being briefed and His support people were being apprised of the situation.

Akeem stood for a moment, gathering his thoughts; then he began to speak. "I came in with six other men from Iraq. I did not know five of them very long. The sixth had infiltrated with me. He was another C.I.A. operative. We had been together two weeks, planning this trip. It wasn't hard to find groups of disgruntled, idealistic zealots who had been radicalized by their religious leaders. They were all ready to fight and just needed a nudge in the right direction. Word had gone out in Iraq that Paraguay was the place to go, and after we arrived we looked around and visited a few mosques. We found one with the radical views we were looking for and after attending twice, we were approached. We were given the time and place of a meeting the next day and invited to attend. The meeting was just what we were hoping for. Everybody's buttons were being pushed and everyone was ready to sign on the dotted line. We were transported with four other recruits to Puerto Bahía Negra. A plane had been waiting for us and no time was given to leave a message. They were making very sure there were no leaks. I don't know what happened to those who chose not to join. My guess is there was no choice. It was join or else.

"We were put together with other recruits and packed into the plane like cattle, enduring the three hour flight in silence. We were all aware that our lives had changed direction and there was no turning back. We had not even been allowed to return to our hotel to secure our luggage. We were told we had no need of it. I attempted to tell them that my friend and I had purchased some weapons when we first arrived, but no opportunity was given for us to speak. One other young man attempted to speak up and he was bashed in the head with a rifle butt. Unquestionable obedience was demanded and punishment was swift."

Akeem paused in his narrative and gathered his thoughts. He looked around at the faces surrounding him. Some showed interest, some concern, some curiosity, and one in particular showed animosity. Taking note, he continued on.

"There were fourteen recruits on the plane, and when we landed we were divided into two groups. I don't know why, maybe because of my size, but I was put in charge of our group. We were assigned to a waiting boat with two people already aboard. They gave direct orders to me and said I was to be sure they were carried out or I would be disposed of. Five minutes out of port the boat was stopped. I was given the order that everyone was to strip and throw all our belongings overboard. I turned to the other six men who had come on board with me and the two already there and did a quick evaluation. They were all smaller than me, but that wasn't always the winning factor. Mehdi, my friend, would support me, but I didn't know if that would be enough. I decided to lead by example. I told everyone the order and immediately began to strip down. They all looked at me nonplussed, and then slowly began to follow suit, grumbling and complaining as they stripped. After waiting a moment and gauging their attitude, I marched up to the biggest one and planted my fist in his stomach. He immediately doubled over, leaving his four friends to stand alone. The two who had already been on the boat appeared to be brothers and very young, maybe in their late teens. I did not think they would cause trouble. Everyone instantly began shedding their clothes, and stripped down their friend also. He did not give any indication of resistance."

Josh listened to what Akeem was saying. It was mind-boggling to hear how all the pieces to the puzzle were falling into place. Even an unbeliever would have to admit there were too many coincidences, and that it must be God's hand making the moves.

Akeem continued, "We motored up river for several hours, only passing one stopping point that had the look of a small boat supply station, but we had several five gallon containers full of fuel on board and those in charge chose not to stop. After another two hours we were given some loose fitting clothes and sandals to wear and told to disembark. There were several packages of supplies that we unloaded and were ordered to carry. We headed into the jungle, and followed the man giving orders. The other man brought up the rear. They both had rifles, machetes, flashlights and handguns in holsters. I don't know about the other men, but I felt more like a captive than a recruit. We began a march that took us the rest of the day. We stopped once for food and water which one of us had been carrying, and once for personal necessities. They kept us at a good pace, and it was only the rifle prods that kept us going. When we reached our destination, we all dropped like rocks."

Bekah stared expressionlessly at Akeem. Here was the man who had assaulted her; the man who had haunted her dream. She felt anger and resentment build up in her, not just against Akeem, but against God. Bekah reviewed in her mind the wrongs that had been done to her, and realized that no one in the room was even remembering what had happened. This caused her emotions to churn and a seed of bitterness and discontent began to grow.

Unknown to her, Renato had been watching from the other side of the room. He had watched the different emotions cross Bekah's face and was concerned. He started to make his way around toward her.

Akeem continued to talk, unaware of Bekah's inner turmoil. In fact, he was so focused on Josh and the phone call with Isaac that he hadn't even noticed her. "We had entered into an area of approximately an acre, maybe a bit more, that had been cleared of the jungle and its debris. A camp had been set up and there were about thirty men inhabiting the place. I was not aware at that time that a hunting party was out in the jungle. They returned as we were resting with several pieces of small game for our meal. When the meal was over and the remnant picked up, a man introduced himself as Josef Muhammed. Everyone paid close attention. Our fates appeared to be transferred from one person to another and currently, this man held it in his hand.

"He stood up and began to speak in a low voice that slowly escalated as the rhetoric became more fanatical. The men around me began to jump and shout in agreement with what he was saying. I stood, and clapped in agreement, but was more restrained than the rest. Mehdi was somewhere in the middle. Josef's eyes gravitated to us and I wondered if we had made an error in showing restraint. He stepped back and spoke to one of the other guards. Then he held his hands up, prayed a prayer, and withdrew.

"We were then told to go sit down. After a few minutes, Mehdi and I were tapped on the shoulder and the guard told us to follow him. He led us to one of the four tents that had been set up in the clearing. When we entered, Josef was standing there to greet us. He told us all our papers had been checked while we were on the river, and there did not appear to be any problems. He said he was looking for some men to be leaders. He noticed we had some restraint in showing our approval of the movement and wanted to hear from us if it was a response of disapproval or caution. He said, 'Caution is a good thing in a leader. It keeps a person from walking too quickly into danger. It gives them a chance to see the pitfalls before they fall into them.' He looked at me and asked if I agreed.

"I decided to still be cautious and answered, 'A leader needs to be cautious, but at the same time he needs to be daring. As you probably already know, I have been a leader in the past. Circumstances were against me; whether from caution or daring I cannot say. Despite what happened, I am still daring, but caution always rides on my shoulder.'"

Josef smiled. "I need more leaders like you. Fanatics are fine for soldiers, but leaders need to exhibit restraint."

Renato came up next to Bekah and put his hand on her shoulder, startling her. Her nerves were frayed from her emotions, and the battle going on inside her. Seeing the face of her captor dredged up all the fear and trauma of her abduction.

He motioned for her to follow him as he walked out the door and into the darkness. An almost full moon illuminated the night. Renato led her over to one of the benches that was in the middle of the compound and asked her to sit down. He stood there and took her hands in his. "Bekah," he said softly, "I've known you since you were a little girl and have loved you as a daughter. I see thoughts and emotions crossing your face that could be a problem, not just to you, but to all of us if you don't deal with them." Renato took out a small Bible from his pocket and read from it.

"Cain suffered anger and resentment against God and Abel just as you are experiencing against God and Akeem. Cain nurtured his anger and resentment. You know what happened. He killed his brother. Now I don't think you are going to kill anyone, but the enemy is out there tonight roaring like a lion and looking for someone to devour. Bekah, don't let it be you. We'll have to talk this out with Akeem when he is through talking with Isaac, so you can be free of this anguish. Just like Cain, sin is crouching at your door, don't give in to it."[148]

Bekah looked at Renato in surprise. She had not been looking at this from a spiritual perspective. She knew about unforgiveness. She had already dealt with it when she forgave Ted for divorcing her. She had not been aware she was falling into that trap again. She knew she would have to face Akeem again and trust that God would give her the strength and the words to say to break the power of this unforgiveness that she was feeling. She took Renato's hand and said, "Thank you Renato for looking out for me. Let's go back inside and finish listening to what he has to say."

Meanwhile, Akeem had been continuing his story, "For the next three days I met twice a day with Josef. We studied the Quran and also the strategy of the movement called The Black Death. He did not sway me with his teaching, but I felt a connection with this man, and sadness that he was so opposed to the teachings of the Bible and anything that supported a Western way of thinking.

[148] Genesis 4:6-8

"After our last meeting, he told me he was going back to Asunción, and I was to stay with this small group and monitor the surrounding area. He was aware of this village, but at that time saw no reason for bothering with it. He had a larger target in his sight. He took me in his confidence and told me that he had nine other training camps such as this in the surrounding jungle, and so far, over one thousand men had been trained and armed. I was immediately concerned with how to get this information to you, but saw no means of escape at that time. This was the information I sent with Mehdi.

"Josef was taking a contingent of men with him and leaving the nine of us who had just come upriver and twenty more. I was to be in charge. He said there were ten firearms among us to be used sparingly. They were to be kept under guard. Everyone was armed with machetes and knives. In addition, I was to have a hand gun and a rifle. He told me to be firm, and if needed, to make an example of the first person to give me a problem. I told him about the incident on the boat, and said I hoped that was enough."

"As he rose to go, he looked at me with fresh appraisal and said, 'Time will tell.' Then he had someone draw up supplies for him and those who traveled with him. Within an hour they had departed and everyone left behind stood there staring at me expectantly, some with looks of approval, some with looks of defiance, and all with looks of expectation.

"I called Mehdi over and told everyone he was second in command. He's small framed, but he has other attributes that come in handy. He was fast, he was a good shot, and he was a trusted friend I could rely on without reservation.

"I divided the men into three groups, day, evening and night. Then I assigned chores and sentry duty. To my surprise, everyone obeyed immediately. That was around a month ago. People come in and others leave in groups of five or ten every week. I think, as they are trained, they are sent somewhere to take up the cause. No one stays long enough for me to find out any information about them or from them. We are isolated here. Maybe that was why Josef was not afraid to leave me in charge. I don't know the location of the other training camps, but I got the impression they were in this general area of the jungle with several miles between each camp.

"Everything had been going smoothly until yesterday when we took two boatloads of people captive, along with all their weapons. Since then everyone has been worked up into a fanatical zeal and wants to kill all who will not convert to Islam. I left them with orders tonight not to harm the prisoners, but I don't know if I will be obeyed.

"I had to come tonight because I had a dream, and in it God told me the forces of darkness were at work and I must stop them. He said He would lead and guide me and here I am. When I arrived, I heard several conversations going on, then they faded and all I heard was yours.

"Isaac, that's all I can say for the moment. I don't know much else. Right now I feel compelled to go out and search the perimeter. In fact, I think at least eight of us should go, splitting up in groups of two. We will call you when we are satisfied everything is under control."

Isaac said he had more than enough information to keep him busy for the present and that they could call any time day or night with any more information.

As Akeem hung up the phone, Renato and Bekah came back into the room. Akeem looked up and recognized Bekah. "You," he exclaimed with surprise. "I am so glad to see that you escaped. I'm so sorry I had to hit you, but because of the circumstances, I couldn't let you go and I couldn't let myself get captured. I didn't know who you were. If I had known who you were traveling with, we could have met up sooner and you would have been saved a good deal of pain and suffering. Please forgive me.

I tried to leave you in a safe spot where you could backtrack to the river. I just didn't expect a jungle fire to break out. Six men from the camp were lost in the fire. We were farther from the river, and some were not as fast as others. I was on the edge of the fire, along with several others. We were able to run to the side and escape. Most had to try to run ahead of it."

Bekah stood quietly for a moment as several emotions were stirred up inside her. Fear rose up and tried to choke off what she wanted and needed to say. Renato was still holding her hand, and she gained courage from that contact. She looked at Akeem. He seemed genuinely grieved for what he had done. Because of his position in the camp, he couldn't have brought her back as a regular prisoner. They would have wanted to kill her or worse. He had to act quickly and according to him, what he did seemed to be his only path.

Bekah realized she could churn over this for hours or days and still not feel good about it, but she knew she could not let her feelings rule her. She needed to be obedient to the Word of God. It said to forgive so your Father in Heaven could forgive you.[149] It was a bad situation and continuing to withhold forgiveness was a bad thing, not just for her, but for the quest they were on. Something like this could be an open door to let Satan come in and try to thwart God's plan. She must forgive Akeem, but it was difficult.

Bekah looked up and saw everyone gazing at her with expectant faces. Manu came and stood before her. "If what you are wanting is revenge, I will deliver it for you, you just have to ask."

Bekah heard what he said, but she also heard the Holy Spirit speaking to her. "Is this truly what you want? Does it not say in the Bible, 'Vengeance is Mine'?[150] By hesitating and not forgiving whole heartedly, you are a stumbling block to these new Christians."

At once, the necessity of the quest became paramount

[149] Matthew 6:15
[150] Romans 12:19

in Bekah's mind and her feelings of anger and resentment dissipated. She quietly thanked God for His patience with her and for helping her to do what was right. Bekah let go of Renato's hand and smiled at him. Then she took Manu's hand and looked up at his face. "I can't allow that," she said softly. "Whether he handled the situation correctly or not is not for me to judge. It is between him and God. My part in this is to forgive, and to do it wholeheartedly. Just as Josh ministered to Arandu, none of us can harbor vengeance or unforgiveness."

She walked over to Akeem. "Just as God forgives me for sins I do against Him, I forgive you for what you did to me. I can't say I understand everything. Whether you were right or wrong, it doesn't matter. God just says forgive and so I do forgive you. I choose not to let the devil cause division amongst us."

Akeem stood there with tears coming down his face. "I've had to make so many decisions and do so many things I did not want to do, but there never seemed to be an option. I ask forgiveness for all the wrong decisions I've made that caused someone harm. Please pray for me."

Everyone stood and gathered around Bekah and Akeem. They also prayed fervently for God's forgiveness in their own lives for anything that might have caused someone else harm, then they prayed for Akeem. Bekah went over and laid her hand on his shoulder and prayed, "Dear Lord, listen to the prayers of this man as he asks forgiveness. Please reach into his heart and heal the wounds caused by all these decisions. Bring Akeem your peace."

Again, God was faithful as wave after wave of peace washed over everyone standing there. As Bekah was overwhelmed by the presence of God she thought, "It's no accident that Jesus is called the Prince of Peace."[151]

Looking at his watch, Josh was surprised to see that it was just after eleven. "I agree with Akeem, we need to go forth imme-

[151] Isaiah 9:6

diately. Ted and Manu, Daniel and Giancarlo, and Edwardo and Philippe, come with us to guard the perimeter. Take your weapons with you, but use restraint and open your eyes and ears to the Spirit of God. It is His leading and guiding that will give us victory. The rest of you, pray. God's Word says to resist the enemy and he will flee.[152] We want him on the run and out of the area."

With that said, they all rose and went outside. Those who were armed with firearms retrieved them, and each group had at least one handgun or rifle with them. The others had spears, machetes and knives. They split up in four directions and began to walk the perimeter of the village, using several feet of the jungle as camouflage. They agreed that if help was needed a shot should be fired. With unity of purpose, all of them went forth, armed with not only physical weapons, but spiritual ones as well.[153]

Josh and Akeem realized that they were at a disadvantage. Their reunion and all the information and the curiosity it involved, plus a long lost friendship yearning to be re-established could easily divert their attention. They needed to stay focused on the events that were transpiring. It was helpful they had years of experience and discipline to fall back on to keep their minds alert to the situation at hand.

Thankfully, the village was only a half mile in diameter and the eight of them should be able to cover that ground without trouble. They each took in all the sights, sounds and smells of the village, and asked God to help them detect anything out of the ordinary.

---

[152] James 4:7

[153] Ephesians 6:10-18

CHAPTER THIRTY

JUNE 20
THE VILLAGE

Chabuto and Tuvicha sat all evening discussing their plan. They had changed it several times, and then changed it back again. They were uneasy about the mood of the village. Everyone had deserted Tuvicha in favor of the new God and His Son, Jesus. In the past, fear had brought Tuvicha power from his gods and obedience from his village, but fear had dissipated as belief in the strange new God grew. Tuvicha was concerned that he and Chabuto alone would not be able to carry out their plan.

The moon was almost overhead, and the village had grown quiet as night spread its blanket. A semblance of peace and calm pervaded but pockets of evil lurked around them. It was these that Tuvicha and Chabuto sought out and welcomed. They both rose up and started walking toward the place where the greatest evil dwelt, the grove of sacrifice. There, over the years, Satan had occupied a place of honor, and so far, the ground was still his. No cleansing had been done to break his stronghold. A door had been left open, and Satan was not about to leave voluntarily.

Tuvicha stopped and spoke to Chabuto. "Go and get the sacrifice. I will wait here for you. We do not want to go into the grove empty-handed and anger the gods."

Chabuto nodded and hurried down the path that led to the home she shared with Tuvicha. When she arrived, all six children were sleeping on a mat in the corner of the back room. She had been a foster mother to these children after Mara had been killed by a wild boar. Riki, Mara's husband, had been killed by Manu as he was attempting to murder Doctor Sherry. Riki had already placed a curse on Sherry and trusted that the strength of the curse would give him success. He had not counted on the fact that she was under the protection of the Lord God Almighty. God put it in Manu's heart to go and check on Sherry. He arrived just as Riki had his killing club raised to smash Sherry's head. Instead, Manu killed Riki with an accurate throw of his knife.

Chabuto was Manu's stepmother and had been jealous of Noemi, Manu's wife, and her new baby. She had attempted to cause the death of Noemi and her child by lying to Noemi and causing her and the child to become weak and close to death. They had both been undernourished during and after pregnancy because of Chabuto's poor care. Thankfully, Sherry had taken them under her wing and both were gaining weight and doing much better.

Chabuto had taken Riki's six children and moved in with Tuvicha. Tuvicha and Chabuto had no love or affection for each other, but respected each other's power. Neither of them had any love or affection for the children. They fed them grudgingly if at all. Chabuto hoped they would be far away before all they had done was discovered.

Chabuto arrived back at Tuvicha's home and walked quietly across the room. She stood for a moment at the door to the back room staring at the sleeping children. They slept as a litter of puppies, drawn together for heat and comfort. She stooped to pick up the sleeping infant, carefully disentangling him from his brothers and sisters. If they woke and raised the alarm, she was prepared to kill them too. The infant stirred and let out a whimper. She quickly covered his mouth with her hand, standing there a moment to make sure no one else moved. Then she hurried back to the glade where Tuvicha waited. She realized there would be no time to take Manu's son and sacrifice him also. Their time was escaping and they had to be well on their way before dawn. She contented herself with speaking curses over him and his family all the way to the glade.

Tuvicha himself was experiencing a renewal of power and strength. He had drunk a special potion earlier that evening made from a secret recipe passed down from shaman to shaman. It was one whose origins traveled back to a distant time. The Guarani were an ancient tribe of people whose roots could be traced back to before the discovery of the new world. The use of this potion was forbidden except for grave circumstances, and Tuvicha had determined that what had happened this week qualified as grave.

Tuvicha had been feeling the effects of this strange brew for the last two hours. Not only had it renewed his physical strength, but it also improved his sensory perception. Time passed and Chabuto did not come. Tuvicha became impatient. "What if she was caught," he thought? "What if she changed her mind?" While Tuvicha stood waiting, he felt the effects of the potion wearing off. He took the bottle from his pocket, gripping it tightly in his sweaty hands, and drank two gulps. He knew that was a large amount and that the ceremony had not been followed, but he was starting to get nervous and have second thoughts about what he was preparing to do. Left to his own devices, Tuvicha would never have thought to sacrifice the infant, but with Chabuto's encouragement, he was accompanying her down a path of destruction, whether theirs or the child's remained to be seen.

At that moment Chabuto came running down the path. He could already hear the cries of the baby. They had to get to the grove and start the fire. Time was running out, and time was needed for the fire to reach the right intensity. While it was heating up, they would go and dig up the tribal treasure. Empowered again by the potion he had swallowed, he pushed himself and began to run the rest of the distance to the grove.

Suddenly Tuvicha stopped and a whimper escaped his throat. He was seeing loathsome things he had never seen before. There were strange animals and insects roving the area surrounding the grove. Snakes were slithering through the grass and hanging from the trees as they passed under them. There were also strange forms of creatures that were not of this earth. All of them appeared to be communicating with each other, but he only heard a deep rumble that ebbed and flowed. An unpleasant stench in the air was overpowering, and all these sensory perceptions appeared to grow in strength as they approached the grove.

Tuvicha stopped abruptly and grabbed hold of Chabuto. Turning towards her, he perceived she was experiencing some of the same phenomena he was. At that moment, a dark apparition rose before them. Waves of anger, bitterness, jealousy, disappointment and pride appeared to emanate from this creature, but along with those emotions rose the promise of great power, wealth and revenge. The creature held its hands out to them, demanding their obedience. Tuvicha felt a moment of uncertainty, then, with a groan of submission, he reached out and took the hand. Chabuto had no reservation; she grasped the other hand greedily, welcoming the strength and power that emanated from it. Immediately, their past lives fell away, so much so that even physically they would not have been recognizable to others in the village. Just as a Christian is born again to the things of God and changed with a transformation that makes them more like Him;[154] so Chabuto and Tuvicha were born again as subjects of their evil god. Their lives and bodies changed also to pattern after the one they had chosen to serve.

The offer of salvation and eternal life in the presence of God had been made to them on several occasions but they had refused. Tuvicha and Chabuto had turned their backs on

[154] 2 Corinthians 5:17

God and chosen to walk the road to destruction and eternal damnation. The Holy Spirit had been calling to them, showing them God's love and mercy. God had shown Himself stronger than their gods, constantly foiling the devil and his plans and schemes. Unfortunately, they had succumbed to the allure of the devil, the deceiver, the father of lies,[155] who also has powers that he uses to his advantage, deceiving even the very elect.[156] If they had but opened their eyes to see and ears to hear, they would have received the truth and the truth would have set them free.[157]

Tuvicha and Chabuto had succumbed to the allure of power, greed, and pride, just as Satan himself had.[158] They continued walking down the path and entered the grove of sacrifice. Chabuto went to dig up some of the tribal treasure while Tuvicha went to start the fire. They would take what they could carry of the tribe's wealth and go south to the strangers' camp. They would use the promise of wealth to enlist their aid. They wanted them to come and attack their village. They thought it would be quicker and easier to reach the camp to the south. It would take several days to get to the northern village, but only four or five hours to reach the southern camp. They would use the rest of the tribal treasure to lure them to their village. In Tuvicha's experience, most strangers who entered the jungle were looking for treasure, and he would appeal to their greed. What Tuvicha did not know was that it was not greed that motivated this particular group of people, it was religious zeal, and if they did reach them they would not be welcomed no matter how much treasure they carried.

Tuvicha had heard of this camp from some of his followers before they left him for the new God. They told of there being thirty or forty members in the camp, and that they also possessed powerful weapons. It was even said that these people

---

[155] John 8:44

[156] Matthew 24:24

[157] John 14:6

[158] Isaiah 14:12-15; Ezekiel 28:11-19

had taken a group of prisoners.

He and Chabuto would have to walk most of the night, but they were not concerned. They were being shown the way and followed unquestioningly. Their thoughts were only on what their gods were saying. Now these gods were their light and inspiration. Their gods promised them safety with this group. What they failed to understand was that their gods were liars and the truth was not in them. The truth was that if they managed to reach the strangers' camp, in all likelihood, they would be killed.

Chabuto and Tuvicha were turning their backs on their village, severing their ties with their past, and heading toward their future and a path their gods had set before them. The moon may have brightened their path, but darkness flooded their souls. With each step they took, evil engulfed them in its relentless grip.

The place where the treasure was buried was just outside the grove, and Chabuto had brought one of the new shovels to dig it up. She had also stolen two backpacks from the strangers to help carry the treasure.

The village had appeared quiet, except for those in the mission compound. Tuvicha was not worried about them coming down to the grove in the night. He did not think they would start tonight. He had shown Chabuto the spot where the treasure was buried. It was behind a large rock off to the side of the grove. Chabuto had the shovel and was digging, exhibiting strength she did not know she possessed.

Tuvicha went to the pile of wood he had gathered earlier in the day. It was placed before the wooden pole so that their gods could look down on the burnt sacrifices. He began to call out to his gods, raising his voice in exhilaration, still experiencing the aftereffects of the potion he had swallowed earlier. He looked up, and the images on the pole began to transform into hideous beasts. Their evil faces appeared to be contorting and coalescing into one large and dreadful form. Compelled by its presence,

Tuvicha started the fire.

As soon as Tuvicha lit the kindling the fire roared to life, its flames rising higher and higher. As the fire grew, the temperature of it increased dramatically. Tuvicha backed away, suddenly overtaken by fear. He heard someone screaming and realized it was him. Chabuto came over and dragged him to where she was digging.

He and Chabuto continued to dig up the tribe's treasure, plundering it, and taking all they could fit in the backpacks. Then they went back to the fire. It was almost ready. It just needed to burn for a few more minutes and they would be prepared to perform the ceremony. Chabuto threw on a few more large pieces of wood and waited for them to ignite. The baby was quiet again and everything was going as planned. Suddenly the wind picked up and sparks rose like a band of excited fire flies. The smoke billowed and began to blow in the direction of the village. Chabuto watched it swirl and began to worry. Someone might smell it and come to investigate.

Indeed her fears were warranted. Akeem and Josh were closest to the grove and smelled it first, but it wasn't burning wood they smelled, it was the reek of death. Akeem spoke to Josh in a low voice. "This is the warning I saw in the dream. I was warned about evil being abroad tonight. This is what evil smells like."

Just then the rest of the group showed up, also alerted by the stench. Josh put his finger to his lips. He did not want to give away their position to anyone. He whispered, "Is there anything in that direction that could be causing that smell?"

Manu answered, "That is where the grove of sacrifice is. Now it is only Tuvicha and Chabuto who would have any business there. Everyone else has renounced the dark gods and they are following the one true God."

Josh replied, "I think this is why we have been patrolling

through the night. Manu, if you will lead, we will follow. Let's all pray quietly and thank God He has given us power over the devil."[159]

The reek of putrefaction increased as the smoke got thicker. Suddenly someone came running towards them from the heart of the village. It was Noemi. She ran up to them breathing hard. "I had been sitting with the group still waiting at the compound. Suddenly something inside me spoke and told me to go check on Mara's children. When I got to Tuvicha's house it appeared deserted. Because of the moonlight coming through the windows I could see no one was in the main room. I walked through to the back room. When I opened the door the stench of the room hit me. I saw the children huddled together on a mat in the corner, their large eyes staring at me. I immediately noticed the baby was missing. I went back in the other room and saw that Tuvicha's medicine bag and golden bird were also missing. Chabuto and Tuvicha are gone. They are not in their home. Mara's baby is gone and I would say good riddance to them, but I am concerned about the baby. I left Juan with Dr. Sherry to be safe. When I looked up I saw fire coming from the grove and started to run that way when I saw all of you."

Manu told Noemi to go directly back to the compound and tell whoever was still there what she had discovered. He told her to ask them to pray, to call the people up north to pray, and to keep praying until all the guardians who had set out to patrol the village had returned.

The moon was almost full and had risen several hours ago, providing sufficient light to allow them to see the surrounding area. They walked quickly in silence, each man praying and asking God for His wisdom, guidance, and protection. Many of them had never fought this kind of battle. They were used to physical battles, not a battle in the spiritual realm.

---

159 Luke 10:19

The night was unusually quiet. Even the insects were subdued. Each man turned his thoughts toward Heaven, praying diligently and listening not just for the noises of the jungle, but for the sounds from Heaven. God had spoken to them earlier and they kept their inner ears open, anxious to hear His Voice again. All of them wondered what was going to happen. The events of the previous week had rocked their world, and the upcoming days should prove just as momentous.

As they approached the grove the smell was overpowering. The sounds of the night disappeared and different sounds took their place. Screeching, moaning and groaning filled the air. Deep rumbles were heard and felt. The atmosphere was full of movement, but nothing was seen. Fear tried to rise up in them as this attack persisted. They kept moving; praying and trusting God that He was with them.

Suddenly these believers felt the peace of God descend upon them,[160] the assurance of His presence, and a certainty He was with them.[161] The smell of smoke increased and they could see a bright light emanating from the center of the grove. Murmuring and chanting could be heard as they moved forward. Then they saw Tuvicha with his arms extended, holding the baby high before the burning inferno. Manu shouted, but was ignored. Tuvicha was enveloped in the evil of his gods and was no longer aware of his surroundings. Chabuto was standing as a statue, unmoving, despite the interruption.

Akeem immediately began to circle to the back side of the fire. He knew that he would not have long to prepare his shot. The heat emanating from the inferno was forcing him to keep his distance. Not just the flames and smoke were obscuring his vision, but the heat was causing the very air to undulate. The evil forces inhabiting the grove were opposing him also. Akeem

[160] Philippians 4:6-8
[161] Deuteronomy 31:8

was concerned. If he fired from the front of this furnace, Tuvicha might fall forward and the baby would be propelled into the inferno. If he fired from the back of it, Tuvicha would most likely fall back and the baby could be rescued, but if he could not make the shot all would be lost.

Akeem heard God speak to him deep down in his spirit. "It's not by your might or power, but by My Spirit the child will be saved.[162] For My ways are higher than your ways. I have spoken this and My Word will not return without fulfilling its purpose."[163] Akeem was reassured that either way, God would rescue this child. God had protected the three Hebrew children from the fiery furnace.[164] If God did it for the three Hebrew children, Akeem believed He would do it for this child. Akeem felt his faith rise up as he took his position. All at once Chabuto became aware of their presence. Instigated by the forces of darkness, she catapulted forward and tried to shove Tuvicha and the baby into the conflagration, but at the last minute Tuvicha stepped aside and Chabuto herself was propelled forward. She disappeared with the sound of a sickening scream that quickly descended into silence.

Manu hurled himself forward and ripped the now screaming infant out of Tuvicha's hands. Stillness settled over the grove. The forces of darkness had been defeated. Tuvicha crumpled slowly to the ground, just like a puppet whose strings had been cut, all his strength leaving him. He knew he had lost his chance; he would not be able to make the promised sacrifice. He knew his gods would be angry and fear came over him. He began to shake with the knowledge that he was alone. He had no protection, and no other sacrifice. He was destitute, and his gods had abandoned him. Now he was at the mercy of their punishment. He had nowhere to go and no one to help him.

---

[162] Zechariah 4:6

[163] Isaiah 55:8-11

[164] Daniel 3:23-28

He looked up at the angry faces that were before him. "What's left for you?" a voice whispered inside him. "You failed to give the promised sacrifice. Now it is you who must take its place." After a lifetime of obeying his gods, Tuvicha stood up and prepared to join Chabuto in the fire.

Josh watched the tide of emotions wash across Tuvicha's face and knew what he was about to do. Now Josh questioned himself. "Should I stop Tuvicha or let him go? If I stop him, he will always be a liability. If I let him go, will I be responsible for his death because I had the power to stop him." All these thoughts were framed in a matter of seconds, then Josh moved simultaneously with Tuvicha and cut him off while attempting to wrestle him to the ground.

Tuvicha, empowered by the demonic forces inside him, overpowered Josh. Daniel, Leonardo and Ted charged forward to help. Tuvicha fought with the strength of ten men. Edwardo and Mario also joined the battle, concerned that Tuvicha would break free. Tuvicha roared like a lion and writhed like a snake. He seemed to have ten arms and legs instead of two. It took all of them to finally wrestle him to the ground. Daniel began to command the demonic forces to come out of him in Jesus' Name.[165] The Holy Spirit showed Daniel it was indeed the forces of darkness that had been making their home in him and growing in strength all these years. They were the power, motivating Tuvicha to this intensity of resistance.

Tuvicha continued to shriek, fighting them with extraordinary strength. Again Daniel prayed in the Name of Jesus, and Tuvicha screamed and continued to fight, but his strength was showing signs of weakening. As the group regained control they all began to pray for Tuvicha, seeing him for the first time not as an adversary, but as one who was a captive.[166] They remem-

[165] Mark 16:17

[166] Luke 4:18

bered the miracle Jesus performed for the demoniacs who lived in the graveyards and attacked anyone who came near. They remembered that even chains would not hold them, and Jesus had set them free from the demons within them.[167] They began to praise God for His saving power and for setting this captive free.

Suddenly Tuvicha cried out, "Let me go, let me go. I am worthless, of no use to anyone. My gods do not want me, and your God will not have me. I am abandoned by all. Just let me go. Maybe my gods will be appeased by my sacrifice and not punish me too severely."

Manu handed the whimpering infant to Edwardo and approached Tuvicha. "Stand up!" Manu ordered. Tuvicha looked up at Manu, expecting anger and judgement. What he saw was sadness and compassion. Tuvicha attempted to comply, but under his own power, he had insufficient strength to obey. Manu reached down and extended his hand. Tuvicha experienced surprise. Immediately, pride tried to well up inside him and cloud his judgement. Having just lost a battle, the forces of darkness were eager to return and reclaim their territory.[168] Tuvicha had been their property. They had owned him. Even though he was of no further value to them, they did not want to release him.

Manu observed the battle being waged inside of Tuvicha and his compassion increased. Memories of the Tuvicha of the past flooded his mind. Manu remembered Tuvicha before these new gods came to power. He remembered the Tuvicha who loved and cared about his people. He remembered the Tuvicha who gave medicine to those who were sick, comforted those who were in mourning, and encouraged those who had lost hope. It was this man who Manu bent down and lifted up.

Tuvicha struggled and offered weak resistance, but Manu tightened his grip, refusing to let go physically or spiritually. He

---

[167] Mark 5:1-19

[168] Matthew 12:43-45

pulled Tuvicha up and gathered him in his arms. Then Manu began to pray. "Father in Heaven, we give You all the glory for our victory in this situation. We thank You that our quest is going forward and that Your plans and purposes are being fulfilled, even at this very moment. We thank You that You also see to our physical and spiritual needs. Forgive us as we have forgiven Tuvicha.[169] We ask that Your grace and mercy be extended to him." Manu looked down at Tuvicha and asked, "Tuvicha, do you want forgiveness? Do you want to serve the one true God and give Him your life?"

Tuvicha experienced a burning anguish in his heart for all the years he had squandered in search of power and glory. It was revealed to him by the Father, Who draws a person to repentance, that he had been deceived by his gods. They had lied to him, and he had believed the lie. "How can I expect anyone to forgive me for everything I have done or tried to do? It is too terrible. How can I make amends for so great a crime?"

Manu answered him tenderly, "You cannot pay. The sin is too great and the price is too high." Hearing this Tuvicha began to crumble again, trying to pull away, but Manu held tight to him. "Don't lose hope. Someone has already paid for all your sins and mine also. Jesus, the Son of God. He came to the earth in the form of a man and has paid for it all. He died a horrible death, receiving the punishment for the sins of the world, but He didn't just die. Three days later God raised Him from the dead, and then after forty days Jesus rose up into Heaven to sit at the right hand of God, His Father. The demons who dwelt inside you did not want you to know of such a great mystery. 'How can this be?' you ask. Daniel, tell Tuvicha what the Word of God says."

Daniel spoke to Tuvicha. "The Word of God says,

> For God so loved the world that He gave His only

[169] Luke 11:4

begotten Son, that whosoever believeth in Him should not perish, but have everlasting life."[170]

"Tuvicha," Daniel asked, "are you sorry for all the wrongs you have done?"

Tears continued to stream down Tuvicha's face and he nodded sorrowfully. "Yes," his low voice whispered. "I am sorrowful to death."

"Remember what I told you. Jesus has already paid for the sins of the whole world. God only asks that you serve Him and Him alone. He asks that you keep a pure heart before Him and not follow any other gods, for they are not gods at all—but devils.[171] God is a jealous God and He does not want you giving your trust and obedience to any but Him. Do you believe what I told you of God and His Son Jesus, and are you sorry for all your sin?"[172]

Tuvicha looked up at Daniel, and then over to Manu. "Is it that simple?" he asked. "Don't I have to suffer? Don't I have to pay for what I did? My gods demanded suffering and sacrifice."

"Remember, I told you that Jesus paid the price. I know it's hard to believe, but it's a gift from God. We only need to believe and receive it and it will be ours."

Tuvicha's face filled with wonder. Daniel prayed with him to receive Jesus as his Lord and Savior. Again, tears started to fall, but these were tears of joy. Starting with Manu and Daniel, Tuvicha hugged them and thanked them for caring enough to show him the way to salvation. He then reached out and hugged and thanked the others who were with them.

For a moment they all stood there grinning at each other, then the baby started to cry again. The magnitude of the challenge that lay before them caused them to remember their responsibilities to the quest and the call of God on their lives. Most of them

---

[170] John 3:16 KJV
[171] 1 Corinthians 10:20-21
[172] Ephesians 2:8-10

turned and walked back to the compound where people from the village were waiting and praying. Two of them remained behind to rebury the treasure of the tribe that had been unearthed.

The fire died down and an unusual hush settled over the grove. With Tuvicha under the care and ministry of the Christians, those spirits left behind went out in search of other minds to foul and confuse and bodies to inhabit. They didn't have far to go. Just a few miles away were a group of people ripe for the picking. They had no allegiance to God, and they were already filled with anger, greed, and cruelty. All they needed was a match to ignite those emotions into flames of violence.

CHAPTER THIRTY-ONE

JUNE 21
THE CAMP

All night long an argument had been raging as to whether to kill the prisoners or not. Everyone was in agreement that they should die, but most were afraid of Jim, and what he would do when he returned if the prisoners were dead. As the night turned to morning the scales tipped and only two or three showed any restraint. The decision was finally made. All they needed now was to determine the method of death. Most wanted to use their machetes and cut off their heads. A few others wanted to throw them into a raging fire.

While this was being argued, the prisoners began to seriously look for a way of escape. Initially, they had assumed they would eventually be set free, but since the leader Jim had left, their circumstances had deteriorated. They were not heavily guarded which was to their advantage, but they were still bound. A few of them had managed to pick up some sharp rocks and they began to earnestly scrape the ropes that bound them.

Carlos Rampone was the first to free himself. He looked around at the rest of the prisoners and got their attention. Then he motioned that he was going to kill the guard. The guard had been watching the arguments going on in the camp and was not paying attention to the prisoners. He even participated in it from a distance, calling out comments and waving his machete as he cast his vote. Periodically he would turn around and spit at them as he shouted in seething anger. Carlos picked up a heavy rock and silently crept toward the guard; he smashed him in the head with it and he dropped without a sound. When Carlos looked back everyone was free. He motioned for them to follow him into the jungle. He had taken the guard's rifle and machete. They were not armed well, but at least they had something besides their bare hands. Carlos unexpectedly uttered a quiet prayer, asking God for His help.

Carlos stopped abruptly after it was said; astonished that it had come forth from his mouth. The last time he remembered praying was over thirty years ago when his sister had been shot in an exchange of gunfire at a robbery. She had been an innocent bystander, in the wrong place at the wrong time. He had been twelve years old and he remembered the noise, the confusion, and the smell of blood. The fear and helplessness in the people who were there was tangible. To this day he could still see the gunmen, their arms and necks heavily tattooed with symbols of the gangs they represented. He remembered the shouts of the three young men as they spoke to the store owner and demanded the money in the cash register. He remembered the bellows of rage when they discovered all that was there was a mere seventy-four dollars. In a fit of anger, the men started randomly shooting into the group of eight people who were inside the store. Suddenly the police rushed in and quickly subdued the three young men. Two were killed, and one surrendered. When it was over, only Carlos and the one gunman were left alive. Carlos' sister had used her body to shield him. She had given her life for his. He remembered sitting on the ground, holding her as her lifeblood seeped out of the three gunshot wounds in her chest. He fervently prayed with the faith of a child that God would perform a miracle; that He would stop the bleeding and bring her back to life, but He did not.

Carlos fought the ambulance attendants when they tried

to take her from him. He prayed, "God help me. Don't let them take her away." But no one answered. He stood and watched the door shut and the ambulance pull away. He listened to the wail of the sirens and felt as though his heart was crying out also, screaming for someone to do something and screaming against the unfairness of it all. His heart was broken, and his faith shattered, Carlos vowed at that moment to never again call on the Name of God, and from that day to this, he had not.

Carlos shook off a moment of hesitation and then walked blindly into the jungle. He walked with an assurance he did not feel. They needed to put as much distance as possible between them and the camp. It would not be long before their disappearance was discovered. He went about five hundred feet into the jungle and stopped. He turned and beckoned them close. "Even though the jungle is dangerous, the people in the camp are our main threat. We need to break up into groups of two or three and go in different directions to confuse them as to where we have gone. They are not jungle savvy either. Every two or three minutes two of you peel off, first group to left, second to right. After one hour, start making your way back to the main trail. We will wait at the end of the trail one hour for all of you to catch up. Be quick, and be safe."

Suddenly Esteban Montero spoke up. "Who appointed you leader of this group? I am the man in charge and the one to give orders. We will all stay together and head towards the village traveling along the river. We have a weapon, and can intimidate them into submission. We will take hostages and force the others to surrender and give us the golden treasure." Greed had clouded Montero's vision and blurred his judgement.

The men looked at one another in confusion, then their eyes were drawn to the fact that Carlos Rampone carried the rifle. As one, they all went to stand by him. Esteban Montero narrowed his eyes in anger. He said, "Well I guess you have the highest card, but I'm coming with you. I don't trust you."

Carlos replied, "Suit yourself. Let's all get moving. First group take off here. Go left. Next group go right in a few minutes. They walked for another few minutes and heard a loud cry from back at the camp. Their escape had been discovered. Two more took off to the right and the rest began to run. Others cut off every few minutes until just Rampone and Montero were left. They ran on for another five minutes and then stopped, both winded and sweating profusely. Chests heaving, they looked around, taking in their surroundings and listening for any sounds coming from behind them.

During their run they had heard several gunshots, and wondered how many were dead or captured. Self-preservation prevented them from backtracking. Their goal was to get as far away as possible from the threat of recapture or death. Rampone looked at his watch and noted that only twenty minutes had passed since they had left the camp. Carlos then took in their surroundings. It appeared to be impenetrable. Thick vines and tangled roots covered the floor of the jungle and dense foliage blocked the sun from shining thru except for a few spaces where it appeared trees had fallen and windows of light illuminated the shadows. One of these windows fell on a small trail that would have been indiscernible except for the brilliance of the sun as it penetrated the darkness.

"Do you see that?" Carlos asked Montero. "It's almost like the path was lit up for us on purpose. I hope some of the other men are left and find this path."

"Don't worry about them," Montero answered, "with just the two of us it's just a two way split. We won't have to share the treasure with any of them."

Carlos looked at Montero with a look of disgust. Carlos did not know the other men well, but they had been through a difficult time together and a small bond had been formed between all of them. He felt a genuine sorrow for what might have happened to them. Again, he was stunned by this thought. He had not thought about anyone but himself in a very long time. Other thoughts began to plague him. "What's the matter with me? Am I going soft? I've been in tight spots before and have never succumbed to this type of thinking." He tried to put these thoughts away and concentrate on the situation at hand. "Let's keep going. We'll stop in half an hour and wait fifteen minutes. If no one shows up we'll go on."

Montero nodded and they followed the illuminated path, almost like Dorothy following the yellow brick road. It was hot and steamy in the jungle. The air did not stir. They sweated profusely and there was no water to replenish them. Tripping and falling, they finally came to the end of the thirty minutes and stopped. They found some rocks to sit on and prepared to wait. Except for the buzz and whine of the insects, there were no sounds in the surrounding jungle. They tried to rest and conserve their strength.

Just then, a slightly accented voice spoke from inside the forest, "Lay down your weapons and stand up." As they complied, a short man with dark curly hair and a swarthy complexion stepped into view. "Everyone has been caught and killed except for the two of you. Their heads are lying in a heap back at the camp. That is the punishment of all unbelievers. I may not be able to perform that service now, but when we get back to camp, I will have the honor."

In desperation, they tried to think of a way out, but it seemed that luck had failed them. Again, a voice spoke to Carlos. "Take his gun away, his bullets will not hurt you."

Carlos rolled that thought over in his mind. Then he thought, "What do I have to lose? I can die now or be beheaded later." Carlos made a move toward the man with the rifle. He heard it click several times as the man depressed the trigger. Nothing happened. Carlos grabbed hold of the rifle and tried to jerk it out of the man's arms. There was a struggle with both men vying for possession of the rifle. Though Carlos was bigger and stronger, the effects of the run through the jungle had taken its toll. Then the gun fired. Unfortunately, Esteban Montero was in the way. The bullet ripped through his shoulder, shattering bone and tearing flesh as it exited. Montero fell, clutching his shoulder with a groan.

Stunned by the discharge, the man hesitated and Carlos secured the rifle and aimed it at the intruder who immediately raised his hands in the universal sign of surrender. "Why should I show you mercy," Carlos asked? "When was the last time you showed anyone mercy?"

The man got down on the ground and began to grovel. "Please," he begged, "I have family, a wife and two sons. For their sake, don't kill me."

"The men you helped kill today had families also. If you didn't spare them, why should I spare you?"

Carlos looked over at Montero who was writhing on the ground and groaning. "What's your name?" he asked his prisoner.

"Kamal," he answered in a subdued voice.

"Come over here," he motioned toward Montero. "Take his shirt off so I can see the wound." Carlos gave Montero a nudge with his foot. "Esteban, can you move your arm? Are any bones broken?"

Montero groaned again as he tried to move is arm. "I can feel the bones grating together. Why don't you shoot this guy and help me?"

Carlos spoke again, "I need this man's help, and you do too." He turned back to Kamal, "Turn him over and see if the bullet exited."

Kamal did as he was told, biding his time. He grabbed Montero and flipped him over, none too gently. Montero roared in pain and anger. Carlos nudged him again with his foot to get his attention. "What's the matter with you? Lower your voice. Do you want to bring everyone down on us?"

He looked down at Montero and saw the large wound. It

was bleeding profusely, both in the front and in the back. They had to staunch the flow of blood or he would be dead in minutes. Already he was weakening.

Carlos turned to Kamal. “Take off your shirt,” he ordered. “Rip it in half and apply it to both sides of the wound. Hold it there and apply pressure.” Kamal appeared to be taking his time obeying, letting Montero’s lifeblood seep into the ground. “Hurry up,” Carlos said, and emphasized his words with a jab of his rifle into Kamal’s back. Kamal leaned over and groaned for a moment, but then began to move much faster in an effort to comply.

Montero continued to bleed in an ever widening puddle that slowly soaked into the floor of the jungle. He had lost consciousness and his breaths were very shallow. Carlos knew he was slowly bleeding to death and there was nothing more he could do. He looked over at Kamal who was holding his blood soaked shirt against Montero’s shoulder in a half-hearted attempt to stop the bleeding. Kamal appeared to watch the approaching death of a fellow human being with a total lack of pity. Carlos knew that he himself had previously put very little value on a human life, but something had changed his disposition and he was confused as to what it was.

Carlos could not take time to explore his feelings. He needed to stay alert, watch and listen from the jungle, and keep his eyes on Kamal. Suddenly Montero’s eyes opened and he spoke, “I am dying, and I’m not ready to die. Please help me,” he whispered, “I am afraid.

Carlos stood there stunned, staring at a man who was more an enemy than a friend. What could he do to help this man? For the second time that morning he called out, “God please help us.”

CHAPTER THIRTY-TWO

JUNE 21
THE VILLAGE

It was very early morning as they all headed out to the meeting area. Akeem called out to Josh, "I wish I could stay, but I must get back to my camp. I am already gone far too long and it will take a few hours to get back. With everything that has transpired, I don't know how I will be received."

Josh came over and they hugged. They had a fierce joy in their hearts, but a strong concern of being separated again. Josh spoke first, "I have not even had the time to tell you why I am here. It has nothing to do with the C.I.A. God sent us."

Looking surprised, Akeem replied, "Well God sent me also. We must get back together and discuss this. Something amazing must be happening."

Josh answered, "A group of us will be leaving in two or three days to follow a quest God has called us to. Maybe you are supposed to come also. Pray and ask God what His will is. He will make a way if it is supposed to happen."

Akeem stood still a moment, letting all that was said be absorbed. "I believe God has a plan, and if we are obedient, we will be part of it. I trust that I will see you soon. Will you call Isaac and let him know what has taken place?"

"Don't worry," Josh answered, "I'll take care of it." As Akeem turned and entered the jungle, Josh whispered to himself, “May you be safe my friend. May we all be safe.”

It was past dawn and light filtered through the canopy of the jungle. Akeem followed the trail he had come out on. He hurried, aware of the fact that he had been away too long from the camp. His mind wandered, flitting from one subject to another. He had no time to dwell on any one subject, so nothing was settled. He was mystified by what had taken place, and baffled by what might transpire in the near future. He realized that everything that had happened so far was not by coincidence, but that God had a plan and He was moving His pieces into play.

Akeem paused; he thought he heard voices in the distance. He moved forward with stealth, wanting to keep his presence from being known. He assumed it was some of his men coming to look for him, but this was not the case. In a small clearing on the trail were three men. He spotted Kamal, one of his soldiers, but he appeared to be a captive. The others were two of the prisoners they had captured two days ago. One appeared to be seriously injured and the other was holding a rifle. Akeem unslung his rifle and prepared to intervene when the injured man spoke. “I am dying, and I am afraid.”

Akeem stood there a moment and then offered a silent prayer. “Please God, show me what to say and do.” He walked into the clearing with gun pointed. “Put down the rifle and everyone stay where you are.” Slowly Carlos lowered the rifle to the ground. Then Akeem turned to Kamal, “What are you doing here with these two prisoners?”

Kamal responded, “The prisoners escaped. In attempting to recapture these two, I was disarmed and held captive.”

Akeem then turned to Carlos. Something about him looked different. He was not the same arrogant man who had been captured. He looked broken and lost. His face sagged and his eyes looked haunted. Before he had been decisive, now he looked hesitant and afraid, unable to decide what to say or do.

"What do you have to say for yourself?" Akeem asked.

Carlos replied, "We were all sitting in camp listening to your men trying to decide whether to cut off our heads or burn us to death. We made a break for it. Now Kamal tells me that all our men are dead and their heads are sitting in a pile in your camp. My friend was injured when Kamal and I struggled over the rifle. Now he is dying. I don't know why I am bothering to answer you. You and Kamal will probably behead us both, but I don't want to die and I am also afraid."

Akeem was silent for a moment, head lowered in thought. Finally he turned to Kamal. "Leave the rifle. Take your machete and return to camp. When I'm done here I will come back and deal with all of you. You will all be punished for your stupidity and disobedience. Maybe some of your heads will join the pile. Now go! Leave now before I shoot you myself."

With a sullen face Kamal picked up his machete. He knew better than to question or talk back. He valued his life, and now was not the time to push the point. When he got back to camp, he would tell those there his version of what had transpired here. He was certainly going to paint Jim in a very bad light. He had a long walk back to camp. By the time he arrived there his version would paint Jim as a failed leader who had lost the vision for the cause they had sworn allegiance to. "All I've got to say," Kamal thought, "is Jim better watch out for his own head or I will personally put it on a stake in the middle of the pile."

Akeem watched Kamal disappear into the shadows of the jungle. He turned and started over to where Montero was laying and Carlos was standing. Carlos was totally subdued. There was no fight left in him. His plans had failed, in fact, they seemed pointless now. He did not care about the treasure, and the wealth it represented. He just wanted to go home. He didn't even know if he would contact Haydon Carlton. It was Haydon's manic desires that had sent him on this wild-goose chase. Now he found himself lost in the jungle with an enemy who had become not a friend, but a partner, and he was lying on the ground slowly bleeding to death. Who had pulled the trigger? He didn't know for certain if it was him or Kamal. If it was him, here was one more life he was responsible for taking. "Oh God," he called out, "what am I going to do?"

Carlos was unaware he had spoken out loud, but Akeem had heard him and the desperation in his voice.

Akeem began to question Carlos. Carlos responded in a subdued voice, "My name is Carlos Rampone and this man is Esteban Montero. Can nothing be done for this man? He is not a friend, but surprisingly, I have come to care about what will happen to him. I don't want him to die in fear. Can you help him?"

Akeem walked over to where Montero was lying and knelt down putting his rifle beside him. "Keep watch and make sure Kamal does not return; nor anyone else from the camp. I will see what can be done for him."

Akeem laid his hands on Montero and he stirred slightly. "He is still alive, but just barely. I am going to pray for him."

Carlos nodded in confusion. This was not what he wanted. He wanted someone to come along and save Esteban's life, but Jesus would not save him, just like he did not save his sister. Carlos stood there and listened to Akeem pray. "Heavenly Father, You are all wise and all knowing. You know what is in our hearts. This man has not served You throughout his life, but now he cries out for help in fear and desperation. This man's natural life may be ending, but his spirit will live forever. I ask that You grant him an opportunity to accept Jesus as his Lord and Savior so that he may spend eternity in Your presence and not in the depths of Hell." Just then Esteban made a strangled sound and his body stiffened. Then it relaxed. He had breathed his last.

Carlos struggled with his composure. His emotions were churning, but he could not put a word to what he felt. All he was certain of was that he had prayed that prayer also and something was happening inside him. He remembered his sister trying to tell him about Jesus, but he did not want to hear. He had friends to play with and places to go. He told her he would listen another time, but she had been killed and that time had never come. All those years had been wasted. He had lived a terrible life, but he would make up for it.

Carlos turned to Akeem and with a penitent heart said, "I want you to pray for me also. When I was a child my sister tried to tell me of Jesus, but I was not interested. I am now. Please tell me what I must do to follow Him." Akeem turned and looked closely at Carlos. This was definitely not the man he had met on the boat two days ago. Already there had been a transformation. Carlos looked questioningly at Akeem.

Akeem replied, "Carlos, God sent His Son Jesus to pay for not just for your sins, but the sins of the entire world. He paid the price for sin so that we could again become sons and daughters of God.[173] Other than putting our faith in Jesus and what He did for us, there's nothing we can do to be redeemed from our sins. Only a sinless sacrifice could do it and Jesus was that sacrifice. He paid for your sins with His blood and His death. Then God raised Him from the dead and He now sits at the right hand of the Father.[174] For those who believe, He calls them forgiven, and through their belief in Him, worthy to be called a child of God.

"Carlos," Akeem asked, "Do you believe? Do you want to be forgiven and dedicate your life to Jesus?"

Carlos dropped to his knees. With tears streaming down his face he replied, "Yes, with all my heart." Carlos suddenly remembered the story of Scrooge and laughed. That was him. As bad as Scrooge was, he had changed. Carlos determined that he would change also.

---

[173] Romans 8:15

[174] Colossians 3:1

With a look of determination, Carlos decided to tell Akeem what had happened to him. Akeem just stared at him with a look of wonder as he told him what he thought and how he felt. “God is certainly amazing. I can’t go into the whole story now, but God has called a group of people together for a mission, to go on a quest. It appears he has called you also. Come with me back to the village. There they can tell you all that has happened and strengthen your foundation in the things of God. There is another there who has led an evil life whom God has saved. He has just given his life to God. The two of you can experience God’s grace and mercy together.

“It’s about an hour’s walk back to the village. We need to go so I can let them know my camp has rebelled and killed all the prisoners. They must take precautions in the event the members of the camp decide to come this way.”

Carlos’ mind was still in turmoil. This one more decision put him on overload. “Whatever you want to do,” he said.

Thoughts visited him like uninvited guests. He attempted to close the door on them, but they continued to knock. Carlos decided to open the door and deal with them. The more he tried to ignore them the worse they became.

CHAPTER THIRTY-THREE

JUNE 21
THE VILLAGE

Everyone at the compound noticed that Chabuto was absent and a changed Tuvicha was present. He looked taller, younger, and more importantly, a gentle spirit rested upon him. He was not the angry and bitter man they had known. There had been a transformation in him and everyone was curious to hear what had happened to him, and where Chabuto was.

Manu spoke to Leonardo, "Find someone to take care of that baby and to go check on the rest of the children. Make sure they have some breakfast and get cleaned up. Have someone sound the drum. We want everyone to gather at the meeting area. Tuvicha is going to tell what transpired last night, and also what happened to Chabuto."

Manu turned to Tuvicha, "You know what has happened in the lives of the people this last week? The events have caused changes in all our lives. Most of us embraced the change, but you and Chabuto appeared to cling harder than ever to the old gods, resorting to actions that brought harm to some people in the village."

Tuvicha interrupted, "I will not deny responsibility. Chabuto and I were both serving the same gods. We were both motivated by greed and power. Every drop of goodness had been squeezed out of us by our gods, but in our anger, and fear of losing our place of importance, we chose to embrace their promises rather than the promise of freedom offered by the God all of you had come to know. I will confess all we have done and then leave this village. I do not deserve to stay here."

Edwardo stood with Bekah, Josh and Ted, translating everything that was said. He too had observed the changes that had taken place in Tuvicha, but anger against Tuvicha welled up in him. He found it difficult to concentrate on what was being said. His mind began to wander down a dark place. He remembered the limp body of little Emilio after the life had been squeezed out of him by the snake. Then he remembered the grace of God that raised Emilio; that he now slept at home with his brother and sister. He remembered that he needed to walk in forgiveness so as not to impede the grace of God. Suddenly the sound of everyone's voices got louder and his focus returned to what was being said.

Manu declared, "I have not asked you to leave. This decision must be put before the people. They are the ones who suffered the effects of both your and Chabuto's actions. They will make that decision."

Tuvicha bowed his head in sorrow, again reminded of all the evil he had done, and all the good he had failed to do. The voices started to whisper in his head again. "Why humiliate yourself before these people? Why bring more shame on yourself? Why don't you go and finish what you were told to do? End your life, become the sacrifice you promised." The litany went on, over and over, attempting to drag Tuvicha down into the depths. They told their lies to him and he had no power against them.

Daniel watched the glow of God's goodness drain from Tuvicha's face, to be replaced by the darkness of the satanic forces that were oppressing him. He knew that until Tuvicha was rooted in the Word of God, he would be battling with the forces of darkness.[175] He turned to Mario, a young man of the village whom Daniel had been mentoring for over a year.

[175] Matthew 12:43-45

"Mario," Daniel called him over. "Tuvicha is still being taunted by the forces of darkness. Would you be willing to work and pray with him, giving him the weapons he needs to fight those evil forces,[176] standing with him as he begins his journey of faith? Even now I can see that the enemy is trying to drag him back into darkness. In fact, all of us should pray for Tuvicha to break the power of the enemy in his life."

Daniel placed his hands on Tuvicha. Tuvicha was aware that his old gods were speaking to him. After long years in their service, he recognized their voices, and the urge to give in was a great temptation. Tuvicha turned his head away. Daniel, aware of his struggle, asked someone to get his Bible for him.

With Bible in hand Daniel ministered. "Tuvicha, I want to talk to you about a man named Peter who was a friend of Jesus when He was on the earth. Peter had been with Jesus for over three years, and had witnessed His many miracles. He had been taught by Jesus that the thief, the devil, had come to kill, steal and destroy, but Jesus had come to give abundant life.[177] Peter witnessed Jesus healing the sick, giving sight to the blind, opening deaf ears, raising the dead, and setting free those who were oppressed by the enemy.[178] Peter and his companions had even been sent out by Jesus, Who gave them power over the devil to heal everyone with a sickness or disease.[179]

"Jesus also taught his followers that he was to be a sacrifice; that He would be killed, and that His Father, God, would raise Him up from the dead after three days." Tuvicha listened in awe concerning what this great God had done and the sacrifice He had made in sending His Son Jesus to die for our sins.

Daniel continued, "This same Peter, who experienced all these things, argued with Jesus about His being killed. He ques-

---

[176] 2 Corinthians 10:3-5
[177] John 10:10
[178] Luke 4:18-19
[179] Matthew 10:1

tioned the plan of God. Jesus was so upset with Peter He told him to get behind Him, that he was a stumbling block and that he did not care about the things of God, but only his own ideas and concerns. Jesus told Peter that Satan desired him, but that He would pray for him.[180] Jesus told His friends, 'No man takes My life; I lay it down for them.[181] If I wanted, I could call ten legions of angels to my side to defeat the enemy.[182] But all must be done to fulfill the Scriptures.

"When Jesus told his friends that one of them would betray Him, Peter boasted that it would never be him, yet when Jesus was arrested and taken away Peter denied on three separate occasions that he ever knew Him. Jesus knew that Satan was trying to deceive Peter, to pull him away from following Him and serving God. He knew that Peter was in a crisis. He cared about Peter so much that he prayed for him, and even after Peter denied Him, He forgave Him and reinstated him.[183]

"Tuvicha, God has removed you from the kingdom of darkness and welcomed you into His Kingdom of light.[184] If you confess your sins to him, though they are many, He will forgive you just as He did Peter."[185]

Tears were again coursing down Tuvicha's face. "How can God want me? Why would He want me? I am old and set in my ways. The dark forces have had me most of my life. I am too much of a bother for God. He does not need me, I am useless to him."

"That's not true," Daniel replied with conviction. "You are as important to Him as anyone of us who is standing here. God cares for each of us. Jesus tells us the story of the shepherd who had one hundred sheep and one got lost. That one sheep,

---

[180] Luke 22:31-32
[181] John 10:17-18
[182] Matthew 26:52-54
[183] John 21:15-18
[184] Colossians 1:9-14
[185] 1 John 1:9

named Tuvicha, was so important to Him that He left the ninety-nine and went out to find the one. When He found Tuvicha, He rejoiced."

"That's all well and good," Tuvicha argued, "but a sheep is valuable. Of what value to God am I? My life is almost over. What can I do for him?" Tuvicha again put his face in his hands. His sobbing was heard throughout the room. His heart felt repentance witnessed by everyone there. He cried out, "I have sinned so greatly, God could never forgive me."

Again, Daniel countered his argument. "Tuvicha, consider this, would the Devil be trying so hard to convince you that God could not use you if it were true. He is a liar, the master of liars.[187] He has come to enslave you. Jesus came to set you free."[188]

Finally Daniel gathered Tuvicha into his arms and prayed, "Heavenly Father, we pray for my brother Tuvicha, whose heart is heavy with remorse, and sorrow for the things he has done in his life. We pray that he receive the measure of faith needed to receive salvation.[189] We also pray that the Spirit of Peace come and minister to his heart, and to all of us who have been involved in this attack of the enemy. Holy Spirit, bring peace as only You can.[190] Encourage our hearts, and free our minds, from the entanglements of the enemy."

As Daniel finished his prayer, the presence of God again flooded them all with His love and peace. Fears left. Anger, bitterness and resentment left. God's presence saturated them all. Mario came over and took Tuvicha's arm. "Come," he said, "we will walk to the meeting place together. God's hand is upon you and He will take care of you. Don't be afraid. He is with you and so am I."

---

[187] John 8:44
[188] John 8:36
[189] Romans 12:3
[190] Philippians 4:6-8

CHAPTER THIRTY-FOUR

JUNE 22
THE VILLAGE

As dawn approached, the small group led Tuvicha to the meeting area. They were surprised as they observed Akeem walking towards them with another man beside him. "I cannot stay," Akeem explained. "Disaster has struck my camp. All the captives have been killed by the group of fanatics that train there. Only this man has survived. On the way back here we talked and I explained the plan of salvation to him. He has already prayed and accepted Jesus as his Lord and Savior, but he needs much more ministry and teaching. The enemy has had a stronghold on his life, but he has rejected the past and turned his life over to Jesus. God has placed his life in our hands for a purpose we do not yet see. We must walk in faith and accept his conversion. I must go to see if I can salvage anything of my camp. Please place guards around the village. The camp may be too worked up to control and I fear for everyone's safety. Pray for me as I go and I will pray for you."

Carlos watched as Akeem disappeared into the jungle. He then turned back and was surprised to see approximately thirty people standing around him and staring questioningly at him. Finally Josh spoke up. "Who are you and why do you look familiar to me?"

Carlos hesitated. The old temptation to lie rose up, but

something inside of him encouraged him to tell the truth. "My name is Carlos Rampone, and you may have seen me at the jewelry store in New York City. I worked for Haydon Carlton. He sent me down here to work with Esteban Montero to find you and take the crucifix away from you. Montero, myself, and the men with him were all captured by Akeem and his men. Last night Akeem headed out into the jungle to check out this village. He told his men to keep watch and guard the prisoners. He told them none of us was to be harmed. Akeem wasn't gone two minutes before they were all arguing about whether to cut off our heads or burn us alive."

Carlos shook his head as the memory of what had transpired replayed itself again in his mind. Through his life he had been in some pretty tough spots, some dangerous situations, but nothing equal to being burned alive or decapitated. He continued with his story. "We made a break for it. We were all running through the jungle. According to Kamal, the man who caught up with Montero and me, we were the only ones left alive. Montero later died from injuries, but not before Akeem found us and prayed.

"I know it's hard to believe, but something in me cried out to God for help—and He helped me. I've led a terrible life and don't deserve it, but He saved me. I keep thinking of all the awful things I'm responsible for. I've done nothing to earn any forgiveness, but He forgave me anyway."

Bekah spoke up, "I remember seeing you at the train station. I was a little intimidated by you, and then a tall gentleman came over and started to talk to me. I don't know who he was but he made me feel safe. I lost sight of you after that."

Carlos continued to unfold his story. "Haydon wanted me to acquire that crucifix, whatever the cost. I was going to grab the bag and push you onto the tracks. In all the confusion I would make my escape. Unfortunately, I couldn't get close enough, it was too crowded, and you're right, that large man appeared to be protecting you. He certainly intimidated me. I decided I'd bide my time until he left, but he stayed with you until you and Josh were reunited. So I followed you to Paraguay and Haydon teamed me up with Montero. We determined that Haydon had his eyes on bigger game."

Carlos repeated the story Montero had told him. "There is a legend of great treasure dating back to the time of the making of your crucifix. The treasure was supposedly hidden in the jungle north of here near a village by a waterfall. Many have sought it and a few have brought back a piece or two, but the bulk of the treasure remains hidden. Haydon thinks you know where it is. Believe it or not, I am no longer interested in that treasure. I hope you will give me a chance to show that my life has been changed. There's no way I can change my past, but I want to change my future."

A murmur went through all the people there. Most understood what had been said, and Edwardo was translating into Guarani for those who needed it. Manu stepped forward and spoke to Carlos. "We have another here who has led an evil life and God has forgiven him and made him one of His own. The two of you will be mentored by Mario, a young man of our village who is a strong Christian and will teach you the ways of God. Who is to say that you both may have been saved to serve a purpose in the quest God is sending us on? Come with us and you can hear his story and then tell yours."

At that moment the first rays of dawn broke through the jungle canopy and the drum began to sound. The whole village began to stir. The sounds of the drum were a summons for all the people of the village to gather at the meeting place. People started showing up quickly; no one wanted to miss whatever was going to be said. Soon the meeting place was full and people were spilling over into the compound. Before many minutes passed it appeared that every man, woman, and child was waiting expectantly for an important announcement. They knew without being told that something significant was happening. The whole tenor of the village had changed since the strangers had arrived. God had stirred all of them up, and He wasn't finished.

Manu came forward and called for quiet. Silence descended. He spoke loudly in Guarani and asked Edwardo to interpret for their visitors and friends. "I want to thank you all for coming so promptly. As all of you know, there has been much change happening in our village in the last two weeks. A new God has visited us Who we have come to know as the one and only God. We now serve Him, His Son Jesus and His Holy Spirit. Unfortunately, His coming has caused conflict with our old gods, who we now understand were not gods at all, but devils. They tried to kill baby Emilio, they were responsible for the death of Enrico, and attempted to kill Dr. Sherry and my sister Bekah.

"Here are two men who fought against God, yet God in His mercy forgave them when they finally asked His forgiveness and gave their hearts to Him. One of these men you know; he is Tuvicha, who together with Chabuto plotted against God and His people, obeying the instructions of their evil gods. Tuvicha is here now to talk to you and ask your forgiveness.

"The other man is Carlos from America. He has been attempting to find an ancient treasure and has been trying to harm our friends from America. He thinks they know where the treasure is. He says he no longer hungers for the treasure, but hungers for God. He too wants to ask your forgiveness."

Tuvicha came forward and all the people marveled at the change in his appearance. His eyes were clear and he was no longer hunched over but stood tall. Instead of the perpetual whine that had always been part of his conversation, he looked at all the people and spoke in a strong and compelling voice. "My family, I humbly ask your forgiveness. I have betrayed all of you for a place of power. As I became older and felt my power diminishing, a new god spoke to me and promised me greater power if I would serve him and call others to him also. Because of my greed and lust for power, I did not test his call, but succumbed to his promise. I now realize that he was not a god at all, but a devil, and a powerful one. I also discovered that his promises were lies and he never intended to keep them."

Tuvicha paused as a tremor went through him. The voices were calling him again and he looked about in confusion. Manu saw him hesitate and went up and put his hand on Tuvicha's shoulder as a sign of encouragement. Immediately Tuvicha's thoughts became clear and he continued.

"It was not just I who listened to this evil call, but Chabuto also. She was unhappy with her place in the village and sought retribution against those she felt had wronged her. She had attempted to harm Noemi and little Juan by lying to Noemi about how she should take care of herself during pregnancy, and how she should take care of Juan after he was born. Chabuto almost succeeded in killing them both, but Dr. Sherry prayed to God and He helped her to save them.

"When Manu made Chabuto leave his house, the devil beckoned her and she joined me. We plotted to rob some of the village treasure and take it to the camp of strangers as payment. We wanted revenge and we were going to ask them to come and destroy the village, but first we were going to sacrifice Riki's baby son to our god to gain his favor and power."

Upon hearing these things an angry murmur went through the crowd of listeners. For the most part, they were a simple and gentle people. Talk of such evil unsettled them. As Tuvicha watched, fear again showed up as an uninvited guest and circulated through the gathering.

Tuvicha continued speaking, intent on finishing his story. "Chabuto died in the fire we made for the sacrifice. For whatever reason, I was spared. I fought to have the fire take me also. I was a failure to my gods and they demanded my life. Before I could obey, the men of the village and these strangers from America stopped me. They wrestled me to the ground and then prayed for me. There was a war going on inside me. I could feel the strength of my gods as I fought. They were strong and almost won, but then the Name of Jesus was used and their strength began to diminish. These strangers prayed again and the evil within me left.

"I was bereft. All the guilt and shame overwhelmed me. I did not deserve to live. Again they prayed and asked God to heal me of my affliction. They told me of Jesus and how His Father sacrificed Him so that I could be forgiven and set free from a life of bondage to my evil gods. I heard the Word of God and asked Him to forgive me. It was a miracle; He did. Now I humbly ask all of you to forgive me. Chabuto and I have caused much harm. After I gather a few belongings, I will leave, and go live by myself in the jungle. Because of what I have done I do not deserve to be part of this village."

The members of the village were quiet, and stood there in bewildered silence, not knowing what to say or how to respond. Tuvicha had been their shaman for as long as most of them could remember. They knew he had changed in these last years, but none of them realized the extent of his treachery.

Next, Edwardo stood up and spoke with a powerful voice. "Forgiveness is a gift from God. We cannot judge someone else or we will be judged.[191] I ask all of you not to stand in judgement of Tuvicha, but to walk in forgiveness. As we walk out this journey of faith in God, He sometimes asks hard things of us. Remember, He rewards those who truly seek after Him, who believe in Him with their whole heart.[192] I ask you all now to forgive Tuvicha as God forgave you."

Slowly at first, and then more quickly, people gathered around Tuvicha and clasped his hand or gave him a hug. Even

[191] Matthew 7:1-2
[192] Hebrews 11:6

the little children ran up to him and hugged his leg.

A river of tears poured from Tuvicha's eyes. A power rose up inside him he had never experienced before. It was the power of the Holy Spirit. By His power, the love of God poured out through these people onto Tuvicha. If anyone had told him he could be free of all the sin and degradation he had felt before, he would not have believed them; yet now here he was. He had no right to feel this good, but he thanked a merciful God for making it possible.

"Don't go away," the people began to cry out. "Stay with us Tuvicha, we forgive you." Those words continued to increase in volume and intensity.

Manu stood before the village and asked, "Is there any among you who wishes Tuvicha to leave? He has not fulfilled his duties as shaman and now we no longer need the services of a shaman to intercede to the gods for us. We all now believe in and serve the One true God and we can speak to Him ourselves."

An older woman came forward and began to speak. "We may not need Tuvicha to speak to God for us, but he can speak to all of us when we are troubled. Many years ago when my husband died, Tuvicha was there to comfort and encourage me. He helped me through that difficult time with his compassion and understanding. He can also help us to solve differences. He can share with us his medicines. There is still an important place for Tuvicha in this village."

The rest of the people nodded and spoke up in agreement. "We don't want Tuvicha to leave," they continued to cry out.

Tuvicha listened to the crowd and he continued to cry. It had been many years since he had felt such love and devotion from his village. God had worked out a way that was so extraordinary that he was humbled to his core. Tuvicha knew in his heart that he did not deserve this show of love and acceptance, but acknowledged that only a loving God could have worked this out in such a remarkable way.

Tuvicha came forward and held up his hands. "Thank you all for your love and forgiveness. Since you no longer need a shaman, I will try to do what was suggested. I will be a helper to all those who need help, a friend to those who are lonely, and an ear to all who need someone to listen."

Tuvicha went forward and walked among the people of the village. They all reached out to pat his back or hug him. There was jubilation in the gathering.

Next Josh came forward to speak. "Most of you know me and the group that has come from America, but not all of you have heard why we are here and the quest that God is sending us on." Edwardo stood next to Josh, interpreting to his people in Guarani.

Josh proceeded to explain the dreams, the opposition from the devil, their enemy, and the support from God to enable them to fulfill His plan. "You all know of the evil and powerful tribe that has been attacking neighboring villages in the north and sacrificing the infant children of those villages to their satanic gods. What you may not know is that there is a group of violent people living in the jungle a short distance from here. They have been sent here to learn how to fight and make war on all who do not serve their god. The time is coming when our God will send His Son Jesus back to Earth to fight the forces of His enemy, the Devil. Many things are happening now that foretell of His coming. The Bible, God's Word, says that there will be wars all around the world. Where there is no war, there will be talk of war. Strange things will happen in the heavens. The sun will darken, the moon will glow red.[193] Many of these things have already taken place, but one thing must still happen, the Gospel must be preached to the entire world.[194]

God has shown me the reason this quest is so important is that this warring and evil tribe is the last group of people on the

[193] Acts 2:20
[194] Matthew 24:14

earth who have never heard the Gospel of Jesus Christ. When they hear, the return of Jesus is eminent. A group of us are to go in His power and might and present the Gospel to them. God told us He would provide spiritual weapons to fight them and that we could also take our natural weapons with us."

Josh saw that everyone was riveted on what he was saying, even the members of the quest. He had not shared all of this with them. Some of them may have already suspected, due to events and circumstances that had occurred, but now it was all out on the table.

"We go forth on the first night of the full moon, which is only days away. We will bring God's Word to all who will listen, whether to a group of foreign fighters training for war or a powerful tribe rampaging through the jungle. God called us and we are here to fulfill His quest.

"While attempting to come here, the enemy put several obstacles in our path. This man standing before you, Carlos Rampone was one of them. He attempted to stop us by any means he could, but God opposed him and He prevailed. Even now, God is working His plan. The people Carlos traveled with are all dead; killed by the group of foreigners who are training for war. God saved Carlos from death and now Carlos has dedicated his life to God. Both he and Tuvicha will spend time together learning about God and His plan for their lives."

Carlos stepped forward and put his hand on Josh's shoulder. "I would like to address the people if I may," he asked. "I am seeing things and hearing things from a whole different perspective. God has opened my eyes, my ears and my heart. I would like to take this opportunity to share my experience with these people, and to also ask their forgiveness for my former intentions."

Josh turned and impulsively gave Carlos a hug. "My brother," he said, "I can sense your heart. I know whatever you say will bless the people. Please speak to them and Edwardo will interpret for you."

Carlos was stunned by the physical contact. Tears filled his eyes and threatened to overflow. He could not remember the last time he had been hugged. He looked out among the friendly and eager faces and was overcome. He lost the battle and a torrent of tears streamed down his face. It took several minutes before he could speak.

Finally he regained control of his emotions. He smiled at the villagers. First he asked, "May I call you my brothers and sisters, for I have no family other than the one Mario told me I am now a part of. He said that we are all brothers and sisters in Jesus. He said we are all part of the family of God."

It was difficult for Carlos to speak as the waves of emotion continued to wash over him, but he persevered knowing that it was important for him to share what had happened to him. "Years ago, when I was a child, my sister tried to tell me about Jesus, but I refused to listen. I am listening now. God has brought me here in a roundabout way to have His will in my life and I will be forever grateful. I am sorry for my previous intentions to rob you of your treasures and do you harm. Now my intention is only to serve God in any way He asks me.

I have heard it mentioned that God is sending people on a quest to do His purpose. One thing they will be doing is going to a warlike tribe and bringing them the Gospel. If they will have me, I would also like to go with them. I would like the opportunity to bring the message of God's love and forgiveness to them just as it was brought to me."

Josh turned with surprise to Carlos; he was not sure that one so young in the Lord should be accompanying them on their quest, but he trusted that God would clarify who was to set out on the quest and who was to stay in the village.

"I want you to know," Josh said to everyone, "that it is the power of the Holy Spirit of God that has changed the lives of Carlos and Tuvicha. Not only have their lives been changed, but all of you have experienced His power. The Holy Spirit is the One Who brings strength when you are weak, courage when you are afraid, peace in the midst of the storm, and guidance in your confusion.

"The group of us who will set out on the quest is in prayer, and we ask all of you to also pray for our success and protection. If Carlos and Tuvicha are supposed to accompany us on this quest, God will reveal it to us. This whole trip has been put together under His guidance, and I am convinced He hasn't brought us this far to leave us without His love, guidance, and protection."

Josh turned to Manu and asked if he wanted to add anything. Manu shook his head, "No."

Josh turned back to the people and dismissed them with the Guarani blessing, Ñandejára ta nde rovasa."

Josh was again moved by the wonderful, rich meaning of the phrase in Guarani; not just "God Bless you," but, "May God caress your face with His hand."

The people slowly dispersed and went to their homes for breakfast, at peace in the midst of the turmoil of the last two weeks.

CHAPTER THIRTY-FIVE

JUNE 22
PUERTO BAHÍA NEGRA

Mehdi scanned the village square, or what passed for a square. There were many shacks, store fronts and buildings of indeterminate age and use. He decided to sit in the shade of a tree and see if anything or anyone caught his attention.

Instead of walking to the waystation on the river, a walk of several hours, he walked out to the two boats they had captured and took one of them. He risked a night trip down the river because he was going to go with the current and the moon was almost full, helping him to maneuver with minimal difficulty. It was morning when he arrived in Puerto Bahía Negra. He brought the boat back to the marina and received the $200 deposit that had been paid at the time of the rental. The money in his pocket assured him he would be able to find at least some answers to his questions.

Mehdi knew that José, owner of The Excelsior, a weapons store in Asunción, was their C.I.A. contact in Paraguay. He also knew that sometimes business brought him to Puerto Bahía Negra several times a month. Mehdi prayed this would be one of those times.

Mehdi prepared for a long morning and afternoon as he watched the wheels of commerce in Puerto Bahía Negra turn slowly. Several planes landed that morning, but no one of interest showed up. Mehdi purchased three empanadas and a cold drink for lunch. As he was finishing, another plane landed. He couldn't believe his luck, there was José exiting the plane. Mehdi followed him, watching to see where he was headed. He did not want to meet him out in the open.

José walked into one of the huts that Mehdi had learned was the biggest weapons store in Puerto Bahía Negra. Mehdi entered several moments later. José was at the counter in deep conversation with the proprietor. Upon completion of their business they shook hands and José walked toward the door. This was Mehdi's opportunity. He walked up to José and said, "Rook to King one." José looked up in surprise. This was the current C.I.A. password for his contacts in Asunción. What were they doing here in Puerto Bahía Negra?

After a moment he responded, "Queen to Queen two."

Mehdi breathed a sigh of relief. "I know this isn't Asunción, but unforeseen circumstances have forced me to look for you here and God has answered my prayer." Mehdi explained their situation. He told of Akeem's plan to go to the nearby village with the visiting Missionaries to get some idea of what was happening there, and that he was unsure when he would be back. He told of the prisoners their soldiers had taken captive, and that the soldiers were restive, anxious to kill them because they were infidels."

"It is fortunate that you found me," answered José. "How many weapons do you have in the camp? How big a threat are they to the prisoners and the nearby village?"

Mehdi answered, "We were given a rifle and handgun that Akeem carries and a small number of rifles and hand guns to be distributed as needed. Everyone else has a machete. In addition, the prisoners brought several boxes of weapons and ammunition with them that we took possession of. I don't know the exact number of weapons there are, but enough to arm almost everyone in the camp; some of them are assault weapons. I am extremely concerned for not just the prisoners, but the inhabitants of the nearby village. They are helpless as far as I know. "

"Well I can give you some assurance about the village. From what I understand, the group that came down from the U.S.A. came with several weapons, and the local Missionary has quite an arsenal. He is a friend of mine. Collecting guns is a hobby he indulges in. Also, one in the group of visitors just happens to be a C.I.A. operative. They say they are Missionaries, but how much of a coincidence is that? They actually came to Excelsior and purchased their weapons from me. My contact at the C.I.A. says he knows the imbedded agent and that he really is a Missionary and that they have become embroiled in these circumstances through no fault of their own.

José said, "I think we ought to rent a boat and get on the river as quick as we can. I'll call Daniel and tell him we are coming. Thankfully, I have a satellite phone to make calls. I'll see about the boat rental. Would you get us some supplies? The river is slowing down and the current won't impede us as much as it usually does. Also, our boat won't be heavy. I think we might be able to make it by dark if we hurry."

Half an hour later Mehdi came out to the dock and spotted José at the helm of a twenty-five foot boat with two large engines. "They would fly up the river," he thought. "About five miles past the way station is where we took the prisoners. About another five miles is the village. We need to be extra careful there because there might be patrols in the area and we don't want to be stopped."

José responded, "I've brought a few weapons myself, the remnant of what I didn't sell. Mostly they are handguns and rifles, but I even have a grenade launcher. Never know when one of them might come in handy," José laughed.

Mehdi and José pulled out of the dock and then set out upriver at top speed. They were armed and they were planning to cover a significant amount of distance quickly. They were determined that nothing would get in their way.

CHAPTER THIRTY-SIX

JUNE 22
OGUNQUIT, MAINE

Sylvia lived in the last house on a dead end street. The street was lined with ancient elms and maples, birches, alders, oaks and chestnuts. Given their age and girth, they formed a dense canopy over the street and sidewalk giving shade all day long, but letting dappled sunlight through to illuminate the colorful yards and flowerbeds. Today was especially shady because it was overcast and there were no sunbeams peeking through the canopy to brighten the neighborhood.

Sylvia and her granddaughter, Penny, were walking to the Eye of the Needle, the needlework shop that Bekah owned. Sylvia had worked there for over five years, and Penny was helping out for the summer while Bekah was away. Penny was talking animatedly; as was her habit. All the exuberance of youth flowed out of her and her face was alight with enthusiasm. She was telling Sylvia how well Bekah's gardens were doing and that soon produce would be filling the back rooms of the store. Bekah used her immense gardens to supply a foodbank she opened up during the growing season. "I can't wait to put the sign on the door telling everyone the foodbank is open. It's such a blessing to give things away and help other people."

Sylvia smiled, listening with one ear as Penny continued to talk. Sylvia's thoughts were actually focused on Paraguay and what was happening down there. She had been awakened last night with the urge to get up and pray. She didn't know exactly what was occurring at that moment, but she knew there was danger and that God was alerting his prayer warriors and calling them to battle.

That was her job as a member of the quest. God had called her to form a prayer army to surround the members of the quest with the power of prayer. They now had people praying on a rotating basis twenty-four hours a day. Often, in times of peril God called individuals to stand in the gap for those on the front lines.[195] Sylvia was on her way to the shop a little early in order to call Paraguay and make sure everyone was safe and find out what, if anything, had occurred last night.

As they were walking, a dark sedan pulled next to them and the window rolled down. Haydon Carlton sat there with a frown on his face. He had visited the shop once before looking for Bekah and trying to extract any information that might help him in his search. He had been resolute in his quest to secure the golden crucifix that Bekah had been given by her mother when she died. Bekah had been born in Paraguay but until the advent of the quest, had known none of the circumstances surrounding her birth.

Bekah and Josh, at the suggestion of Ted, Bekah's ex-husband, had taken the crucifix to Haydon Carlton, an old friend of Ted's who owned a jewelry store in New York. They wanted to authenticate the crucifix, but from the moment they first showed it to him, all Haydon Carlton's thoughts and efforts appeared to be aimed at gaining possession of the crucifix, whether by legal or illegal means. Today he appeared very different from the sophisticated, well dressed and articulate man they had met previously. "I need to find Bekah Ryan and you're going to tell me where she is."

---

[195] Ezekiel 22:30

Sylvia answered him in an annoyed voice, "You already know where she is. She's still in Paraguay. She hasn't come home and I don't know when she will be returning. You know as much as we do as to where she is. You have caused enough trouble already by having her house ransacked and having Esteban Montero threaten her. Just leave her alone, and leave us alone."

Haydon stopped the car and opened the door. In his right hand he held a gun and pointed it at Sylvia and Penny. "So you know about Montero. What else do you know? Has he caught up with them yet? Have they found the treasure? I think he and Carlos have joined forces and want to cut me out. Well they won't get away with that, I have more means at my disposal than they are aware of. I've been watching you for several days. I know there is no one in the store and that you have the capability of contacting Paraguay. We're going to place a little phone call to Miss Bekah and find out what's been going on. I don't like being kept in the dark. My two men have been unreachable for over four days and I am becoming impatient. Come on, we'll walk the rest of the way to the shop; it's only two more blocks."

Haydon turned and sneered. "And who do we have here Miss Sylvia? Is she someone special?"

Sylvia protectively put Penny behind her. "She's no one you need to be interested in. She doesn't know anything."

"Well I guess we'll have to find that out, won't we? She's such a pretty little thing. I'd hate to see anything happen to her. Both of you start walking and don't try anything stupid."

As Haydon walked, he took Penney's arm in his in what appeared to be a friendly gesture, but the gesture did not correspond with his intent. "Now, Miss Sylvia, you're going to tell me everything you know about what is happening down in Paraguay, and do it quickly, or I might just have to hurt this little lady and that would be terrible."

They arrived at the shop and Sylvia took out her key and

opened the door. The antique bell on the door elicited its friendly jingle, but the answering smile was absent from Sylvia's face when she heard it. From this end of the shop everything looked normal. Carlton steered them into the back and his mouth fell open. Between the board and the paper littered table it looked like a war room. Several names were on the board, but one he recognized immediately, Montero's.

He twisted Penny's arm until she cried out in pain. "All right both of you. I want some answers. What's going on down there? Who are all of you? What are you doing here?" Haydon roughly pushed Penny into a chair and turned angrily to Sylvia. "You better start talking now or this little lady is going to suffer some serious injury and it will be your fault."

Sylvia was shaking, not so much in fear, but in anger. She knew she had God on her side and she prayed that He would show His strength to this unbeliever.[196] Carlton grabbed her arm and pulled her over to the phone. "I know you can get in touch with them. Call Bekah Ryan now and let me speak to her."

Unable to think of anything else to do, Sylvia picked up the telephone and dialed their Paraguay connection. She knew nothing would be decided now by talking to them. She only thought that this call could buy her more time to think of what to do about Haydon Carlton. Sylvia heard the phone ring twice and someone picked up. Of all the people who could have answered, it was Bekah who picked up the call.

"Hello, Hello," she answered breathlessly. "We were in the other room. Boy did you ever pick a good time to call, most of us are here and we have a bunch to tell you."

"Well hello there yourself lovely Bekah, it's so good to hear your voice again. Please put the phone on speaker so I can hear all of you and you can hear me. I'm here with Sylvia and a

---

[196] 2 Chronicles 16:9

lovely young woman who seems to mean a lot to her. Does she mean anything to all of you? If she does, you had all better get ready to start answering some questions. If I don't like the answers, she is going to pay the piper."

There was silence on the other end of the line and then Bekah spoke softly, "What do you want to know?"

Carlton smiled. He liked winning, and he could feel Bekah's grudging cooperation. He was the spider and she was the fly and he welcomed her into his parlor. He felt great delight in achieving the upper hand. He took time answering until he had worked out his strategy to his satisfaction.

Bekah became impatient with his silence and almost made a sarcastic remark but decided that holding her tongue would be to her gain. Clearly he had no recent information about what was happening and his ignorance was also to their advantage.

Carlos was with them and his head jerked up at the sound of Carlton's voice. He got up and came marching toward the phone, speaking out before they could stop him. Sarcasm dripped from Carlos' mouth. "Isn't it interesting that you should call this morning of all mornings. I want you to know that I have given my allegiance to these people and I also now serve the God they serve. I spent most of my life running away from God. Ironically, He caught up with me here in the jungles of Paraguay. You would be best served if you forgot about that crucifix and let these people alone. God is surely on their side and you don't want to have Him against you. He is a mighty adversary and He always wins."

Sylvia witnessed the shock on Carlton's face when he recognized the voice speaking on the phone. He was not pleased. She hoped this situation would work to their advantage. She knew that God worked in strange ways and that He used any means at His disposal to gain His end. She looked over at Penny and gave her a smile. Penny was a young Christian and had not seen or experienced God move in her life or the lives of those around her to any great extent. She was going to be in for a surprise because Sylvia also knew that God was on their side, and if that were the case, no enemy could stand against Him.

"Carlos, what are you doing there, and what has happened to Esteban Montero and all the men he hired? The two of you were supposed to be working together."[197]

Everyone in the room sat back and waited to see what would happen. Bekah took advantage of that lull and went to find her purse. She pulled out Sargent Jim Hathaway's card and phone number which he had given her when he investigated the break-in and ransacking of her home. She quietly left the room and called him on the other satellite phone. He answered the phone and identified himself. Bekah spoke softly. "Sargent Hathaway, this is Bekah Ryan. Do you remember me?"

"Certainly I do Ms. Ryan. Are you back at home?"

"No," answered Bekah. "I'm still in Paraguay. We have two satellite phones down here and I'm on one of them. Right now Haydon Carlton, the owner of the jewelry store in New York is on the other one. He has my friend Sylvia and her granddaughter Penny at gun point in my shop in Ogunquit threatening them and using them to try to get information out of us. Please see if you can help them. I don't want them to be injured."

"I'll call the Ogunquit police and alert them to what is happening, and then I'll head over there myself. He's still under suspicion for breaking into your home and possible theft, and destruction of private property. I've got your number on my phone. I'll call you when Miss Sylvia and Penny are safe."

Bekah went back into the room. Carlton was still shouting at Carlos, trying to intimidate him into submission, but he was getting nowhere. Bekah pulled Josh aside and told him of the telephone call she just made to Maine. He smiled and gave her a thumb's up. Now all they had to do was wait and listen for the

[197] Romans 8:31

police. Carlton had nowhere to go. Several minutes went by. Suddenly they heard the shout, "Police! Put your weapon down!" Then they heard that phrase repeated several times. Finally they heard the phrase, "Turn around and put your hands behind your head."

There was a lot of shuffling and moving around. Then a voice spoke over the telephone. "This is Sylvia and we are all safe. Bekah, that was great thinking on your part, and I'm just so thankful no one was injured. Haydon had a crazy look in his eyes. I don't know if he is all there. Maybe this entire obsession with the crucifix has tipped him over the edge."

Bekah responded, "Sylvia, how did this happen?"

"Penny and I were walking up the street to the shop this morning when he pulled up next to us. He got out of his car and forced us to walk with him to the shop. You know the rest of what happened. This morning I woke up early with a call to prayer. I didn't know why; I just felt I should pray. Now I see the reason."

"Sylvia, there is so much to tell you. A lot has happened here. Finish up with the police and then get everyone together and call us back. We'll tell you all about it then."

CHAPTER THIRTY-SEVEN

JUNE 22

THE BLACK DEATH CAMP

Akeem traveled swiftly through the jungle, all concern for concealing his presence forgotten. Secrecy was no longer an issue. Knowing what he may be facing, speed was paramount. As he traveled, he prayed. He knew he was walking into danger, but trusted that the God Who was leading and guiding him would also protect him. He felt the peace of God upon him, comforting and encouraging him, but there was also another voice that whispered words of doubt, discouragement, and fear.

Akeem fought these thoughts as was his habit, with the Word of God.[198] "Father," he prayed, "Your Word says to trust and I do, but I am weary physically, mentally and spiritually." Akeem traversed the jungle, his head was down, his shoulders drooped, and his feet lagged. That other voice was getting louder and he did not have the strength to counter it. He felt despair wash over him. Suddenly he heard voices in the jungle and knew he was about to be discovered. His last prayer before capture was, "Father please forgive me; I have failed you." Then he was overcome as several men rushed him and tackled him to the ground.

When he regained consciousness he was bound hand and foot and Kamal was standing over him with a leer on his face. "The rest of the men and I didn't think you would be stupid enough to come back, Jim. Your presence is no longer required

[198] Hebrews 4:12

in this camp; in fact, it is unwelcome. We're in control now. We voted that tonight we will go and attack that village you have been so interested in. Maybe after a few examples are made they will be happy to turn to Islam and welcome Allah as their god. As for you, since you are a believer, we will not kill you. We will let the jungle do that for us. This way we can answer honestly when we see Josef and he questions us."

Kamal pointed to two men standing close by. "One of you, grab his rifle, then take him a mile or two south of the camp and tie him to a tree. If he is lucky, a big cat will get him before the bugs do." Kamal pointed to another two men, "You two, see about food for us. How long before you can get everyone fed?"

The men objected. "We have not been on food detail before so we are unfamiliar with what we have and what we need. The two men you picked to take Jim into the jungle were the food detail. Let us take Jim and then they will be able to prepare the food."

Kamal did not like being questioned or disobeyed, but he saw the logic of their suggestion and agreed. The men immediately ran after those who were taking Jim into the jungle. Throughout the camp, people were objecting to their assignments. They were rebelling against Kamal. They had respected Jim, and feared him because of his strength and forcefulness. Also they had seen that Josef had favored him. They had only contempt for Kamal. He had been a slacker who had not done his share. He was always pushing his duties onto someone else, either with a bribe or a threat. The camp was coming to the point that there was no leader and everyone was doing what he wanted to do.[199]

The two men hurried after Jim and his jailors. They followed a well-worn trail into the jungle. They had not gone far when they caught up with them and told the two men of the change in duties and that they would be doing the meals. Unfortunately, the cooks objected. They were tired of being cooks.

[199] Judges 21:25

They had been cooking for the three weeks they had been at the camp and they wanted to be part of the action.

This assignment appeared to be a step in the right direction and they were unwilling to relinquish their new responsibility. After they were overtaken and told the new orders, a shouting match immediately ensued. Every day these men listened to inflaming rhetoric, designed to keep them at a fever pitch. Without a strong leader to keep them under control they were like a wildfire, moving whichever way the wind blew. Jim was watching and listening.

He thought maybe these circumstances would work to his benefit. They had pushed him down when the argument started and were standing around fifteen feet away. Jim's hands were still tied, but his feet were free so he was able to walk. He managed to slither around the back of a tree on the edge of the trail. The shouting was still going on and getting louder by the minute. He wasn't sure what was going to come next, a fist fight or gunshots. Gunshots won. There was a loud report and then stunned silence.

While all this was going on Jim used the confusion and surprise to make his escape, not even turning to see what had transpired. He ran through the jungle, trying to leave as little trail as possible, but trusting that speed would be his best friend. These recruits were not trained in tracking and were unfamiliar with the jungle that bordered them. In the last weeks they had ventured very few times into the surrounding area. Most of their training had been in hand-to-hand combat. The rest of the time was spent in study of the Quran and listening to inflammatory speeches.

A moment later he heard a shout and knew his escape had been discovered. He changed direction and continued to run and then he turned again and backtracked, thinking that they would not expect him to head back toward the camp. Finally after several minutes Akeem stopped and listened. Everything was quiet except for the birds and the insects; a good sign he wasn't being followed. He took this time to free his hands from the ropes that bound him. He had an idea and turned east toward the river. He stopped on the way and picked a banana off a tree; he had not eaten since yesterday and needed to keep up his energy. Akeem thanked God for His protection and followed a familiar trail, reassured that if God was for him, who could be against him.[200] Akeem prayed quietly to himself as he progressed toward the river.

As he came within sight of the river, there as he expected was one of the boats that had been captured from Carlos Rampone and Esteban Montero. He wondered what had happened to the other boat. He hoped Mehdi had thought to take it, but he had too many other things to think about without being distracted by questions to which he had no answers.

[200] Romans 8:31

CHAPTER THIRTY-EIGHT

JUNE 22
THE VILLAGE

Sherry looked around the kitchen. Every seat was occupied and people were sprawled on the floor. It was only nine thirty but it felt as though an entire day had elapsed, especially since no one had slept the night before. Coffee was brewing, but it would take several pots to fill everyone's cup. Thankfully, not everyone drank coffee. Sherry also had large quantities of the special herbal tea that most of the native people drank. Her helpers were busy slicing fruit, and there were four loaves of sweet bread and chipa already on the table. All the members of the quest were present plus others who were interested. The entire village seemed to be interested. There were no secret agendas here. Anyone who wanted to could attend. Sherry knew this meal would be an important time of prayer and fellowship.

With so many people in one room, it was surprising that there was only a low murmur of voices heard. People were talking quietly in groups of three and four. Connie and Ted were the last to arrive. Ted had accompanied Lara home to care for the children, and Connie had made sure her children were settled. The food was placed on bamboo mats on the floor and on the tables. Everyone helped himself.

There was a minimum of talking. It appeared everyone was listening to that inward Voice, seeking direction and faith.

They knew that they had overcome some serious obstacles, but they also knew that more were ahead of them. They knew their enemy was Satan and that he was all in, there was going to be nothing held in reserve. Satan was a gambler. He had no problem dealing with longshots. He had multitudes of lives to spend. To him there was no value to life. If he lost one pawn, he could easily replace it with another.

As they were finishing their meal the satellite phone rang. Josh answered. "Josh my friend," a familiar voice sounded, "it appears you may have stirred up a hornets nest down there," Isaac said. "I just got a call from José the owner of Excelsior. He is one of our local operatives and was the contact for Akeem. It seems José was in Puerto Bahía Negra when Mehdi, Akeem's friend who is undercover with him, showed up. José and Mehdi have teamed up, rented a speed boat, and are on their way upriver. If I were you I would send out several men as interceptors, watching to see if anyone from the Black Death Camp is heading your way. José and Mehdi should be there before dark. José is also bringing the remainder of his shipment of weapons that he did not sell this trip; he's even got a grenade launcher. I've filled them both in on what has transpired as of this morning. Mehdi is concerned Akeem may run into trouble when he goes back to the camp.

The residents of the camp have taken it upon themselves to kill all the hostages. Since Akeem had left the camp, his leadership was questioned. Kamal, a member of the camp, is a known trouble maker, and had challenged Akeem's leadership on several occasions. Akeem being gone from the camp for so long, and the killing of the hostages, may have caused their blood to rise. This may have given them courage to rebel against Akeem's conservative leadership in favor of Kamal's radical views.

"Also, we were in position to take several satellite pictures of the village you are in and the surrounding twenty-five miles or so. We saw a clear picture of the Black Death Camp just over five miles south of you and half a mile in from the river. There was also evidence of a fire that started nearby and ran to the river.

"There were other villages located at the edge of our picture, one about twenty-seven miles north, on the river by a large waterfall, and one about fifteen miles north, on the river. I don't know if that is useful information or not, but just thought I would pass it on. Josh, don't take any chances. Keep a good lookout and call me when José shows up."

Josh thanked Isaac for the warning and hung up. He then turned to Manu, "We need to send out four groups of men with at least three men in each group. Three groups will watch the outskirts of the village, one of the men from each group of four will run back to the village with updates or important news on what is happening, passing on important information and bringing back messages if needed. The final group will go forward and spy on the foreign camp if they can safely get close. We need everyone to be unobserved. We don't want to make our presence known. Everyone needs to be back here by last meal, one way or another. José and Mehdi should be here around that time or a little later. Will you assign men from the village, Manu? Perhaps Leonardo, Mario, Philippe, Axel, Maitie and Giancarlo would be good choices for this assignment."

Manu's answer to Josh was brusque. "Whatever you think is right. Have Leonardo see to it."

Manu turned abruptly and walked away. Josh was surprised at the curt answer, but did not take the time to think about it. His mind was going in twenty different directions and that was just one more distraction.

Manu walked away from the meeting with troubling thoughts on his mind. "Who is Chief of this village?" he thought. "Who has lived here all his life? Who are the outsiders?" As Manu concentrated on those thoughts he became angry. "My people look to the outsiders for answers now and not to me.

I have lost my position in their eyes." Manu continued nursing these thoughts. His face became downcast and his shoulders weighed down.

Daniel had witnessed the interaction between Josh and Manu. He was immediately aware of the attack Satan was launching against Manu. The Holy Spirit spoke to Daniel to start to pray for his friend, and to go and speak with him.

Daniel called out to Manu but he kept on walking. Daniel saw Noemi walking toward him and stopped.

Noemi was watching Manu's approach. She realized he had not seen her. She observed Manu's downcast eyes and the frown on his face and wondered what had happened. As he started to walk past her she reached out and touched his arm. He turned with fists clenched and anger on his face. Startled at his appearance, she stepped back in fear.

Seeing the fear in her interrupted the cycle of Manu's thoughts. Daniel felt this was a good time to intervene. He walked up to Manu and said, "I see you are troubled by something my friend. We all need to be aware of the fact that Satan is using the time he has left to bring attacks against us. I observed your conversation with Josh and wondered what had occurred that caused the anger you are now fighting. Will you let me help you? May I pray with you and ask the Holy Spirit to reveal the problem?"

"I already know what the problem is. Josh is trying to take away my position in the tribe. He is making all the decisions and giving all the orders. Who is Chief here, him or me?" The venom in Manu's voice was disturbing, not just to Daniel, but also to Noemi who was listening to the conversation.

A transformation came over her. She lost her shyness and reserve and boldness rose up in her spirit. Noemi spoke to the spirits that were attacking Manu's mind. She again placed her hand on his arm. "You lying spirits who are trying to cause anger, jealousy, and division, I speak to you in the mighty name of Jesus to be quiet and leave. I pray for Manu's mind to be clear. I pray that he hear the Word of God speaking to him, and the voice of strangers he will not follow.[201] I pray for the peace that God always sends to come and be with Manu. I pray in the Name of Jesus, Who helps us and is with us always."

Noemi looked up at Manu and continued, "My husband, you have been listening to the wrong voices. Let Daniel speak with you. He is a Minister of God and will help you overcome this attack."

"Manu," Daniel asked, "Do you remember the story of Cain and Abel in the Bible? Cain was angry and jealous because he felt that God respected Abel, but not him. God questioned Cain. 'Why are you angry?' He asked. 'Why do you have a frown on your face? If you had done right you would have a smile.' Then God told Cain the problem. 'Because you have done wrong, sin is at your door. It wants to take you over. You must fight it and overcome it.'"[202]

Suddenly Manu became aware of his sinful thoughts and was heartsick at believing the lies the devil had told him. He asked Daniel to forgive him. Daniel told Manu, "None of us are without sin. When we do sin we must ask God's forgiveness and He will make us clean again."[203]

Manu then knelt right there on the path and asked God's forgiveness and His continued help in leading and guiding him. Then he and Noemi walked back to the compound with Daniel. Manu also wanted to ask Josh's forgiveness because of the thoughts he had harbored about him.

---

[201] John 10:4-5
[202] Genesis 4:4-7
[203] 1 John 1:8-9

CHAPTER THIRTY-NINE

JUNE 22
THE VILLAGE

After the first groups of men had gone out, another group of ten men were assigned to walk the perimeter of the village and watch for any signs of intrusion while guarding the village area. Josh suggested the rest of them take the time to rest all afternoon. It had been a long night and it didn't appear as if things would get any easier.

Just then Manu, Noemi and Daniel walked back into the room and Josh was reminded of how upset Manu had appeared the last time they talked. Josh knew the enemy was about looking for ways to divide and conquer. He decided to stop any problems before they happened. Josh walked up to Manu and asked his forgiveness. "Manu, last time we talked I saw that you were upset and did not take the time to find out why. Please forgive me. I don't want anything to come between us."

Manu was surprised. He was going to ask Josh's forgiveness and now Josh had asked his. "Josh I was angry and jealous. I felt I was no longer respected as Chief. I let voices talk to me the same way they had talked to Tuvicha and I became very angry. Daniel and Noemi saw me and prayed for me and I asked God to forgive me. I also ask you to forgive me."

"I do," Josh replied. "I also ask you to forgive me. It was insensitive of me to not be aware of your feelings."

Manu reached over and hugged Josh as he had seen Akeem do earlier. Manu felt a brotherhood rise up between them and was pleased.

As they were all starting to disperse, the phone rang again. Josh rolled his eyes as he picked it up. Everyone else came back into the room and sat down again.

The phone was now always on speaker and they heard Sylvia's voice. "Hello down there. How are you all doing? We're fine and it's nice to know that one bad guy is off the streets. I'm just glad that prayer works, and I believe it's going to continue to work, not just here, but down there in the jungles also. More and more people are being called in to pray. I really believe that things are coming to a turning point. With everyone praying we can be sure it will turn in our favor. Now if you have some time, can you tell us what has been happening down there?"

After Josh finished telling everything that had occurred, all they heard was silence on the other end of the phone. Finally Josh spoke up, "Are you still there?"

Sylvia's voice came back over the line. "Yes Josh, we're all still here. We're just stunned by what you have told us. Satan is really stirring the pot down there. Do you know what you are going to do next? Do you know when you are leaving?"

"Right now we're going to take the remainder of the morning and afternoon to rest, maybe get some sleep. We'll be leaving soon. God told us the first night of the full moon. I think that might be tomorrow night. With so much happening, we haven't had time to look up the exact date of the full moon. I know it's creeping up on us. I should have checked the exact date a long time ago. I let myself get distracted by all the events that were taking place down here."

"Hold on," said Sylvia. "I can look that up for you right now. I have the computer right in front of me."

There was a pause and then Sylvia's voice came back on

the line. "You may not be ready to hear this, but the first night of the full moon is tonight. You better get as much rest as you can. Moonrise is at nine fifty-one."

"That took me by surprise," Josh replied. "I was anticipating a little more time. Rest sounds wonderful, but with so much happening it may not be possible. At last count there were about twenty of us going on the quest. Why don't you call back about nine tonight and you can join with the rest of the village as we leave to embark upon our quest. We'll talk with you more later tonight if there is time. If not, please continue to pray. The enemy hasn't given up. I'm sure he will be fighting us all the way. Remember we can still keep in touch; we have two satellite phones down here. One will come with us and the other will stay at the compound. They are solar powered with backup batteries. All we will have to do is find a sunny spot to have lunch and we're good for the day."

Everyone left and went to their homes to rest as best they could. All that were left were four of them, Josh, Bekah, Daniel and Sherry. Satan still had a few tricks up his sleeve and he was not above using subterfuge. He followed Renato to his room and sat on his shoulder. "Do you really want to go on this quest? You're 67 years old. Are you up to this?"

Renato lay down on the cot. He was exhausted. He felt like he wanted to sleep until next week. His aches and pains intensified as he closed his eyes and tried to sleep. The voice in his head wouldn't be quiet and he was too tired to fight it. Renato began to pray quietly. "Oh God, I'm 67 years old. Can't you find someone younger to go on this quest? Surely there are more qualified men than me to fight this battle. I don't want to be disobedient, but I would just like a way out if one was available."[204]

Suddenly a different Voice spoke to him and reminded him with words from the Bible of what Jesus said when facing the cross. Jesus didn't want to do it, and prayed three times that He

[204] 1 Corinthians 10:13

not have to. But the final statement was what mattered. "Nevertheless, not my will but as Thou wilt."[205] Jesus said it three times, not for His benefit, but for ours. It was always God's will that took precedence. Renato recognized the voice of the devil and repented. He then recalled the Scripture that said, "Let the weak say, I am strong,"[206] and God strengthened him with those words.

Across the room on another cot Ted was fighting his battle. Satan was whispering to him also, but using different ammunition in his attack. "You have certainly spent a great deal of money down here. What do you have to show for it? Are you any wealthier? Hasn't that always been important to you? What's going to happen when you go home? Will any of your friends care what you were doing here? Won't they think this whole trip was foolish?"

Ted groaned in frustration. Renato sat up and walked over to Ted. "Is Satan lying to you?" he asked. "Is the devil trying to convince you this whole trip was a bad idea and you're spending good money after bad?"

Ted sat up and stared at Renato in surprise. "How did you know what I was thinking? Are you a mind reader now?"

Renato smiled, "Satan knows us and tries to take us down with our weaknesses. He just tried to tell me I was too old for a quest like this. He was probably talking to you about your finances, a weak spot for you. Remember money ruled you. In the past it was your god, but now you have overcome that. You no longer love and serve money; you love and serve God, and your money serves you."[207]

Renato sat next to Ted on the cot. "Let me tell you a story. There was a man in the Bible called Amaziah who had spent a fortune to enlist mercenaries to fight. God told him to send them home and to trust Him. Amaziah whined and complained about

---

[205] Matthew 26:38-44
[206] Joel 3:10
[207] 1 Timothy 6:10

the money he had already spent. He asked God, 'But what about the hundreds of talents I paid for these Israelite troops?' God answered through the prophet, 'The Lord can give you much more than that.'[208] Ted, it's all God's money anyway. If you do what He asks you to do you will be blessed beyond measure. Give me your hand and let's pray."

Renato stood and put his hand on Ted's shoulder. "Father, I thank You that we can fight the temptations of Satan just as Jesus did, with the Word of God.[209] I thank You Father that in my weakness You are strong. I thank You also that Ted does not rely on Wall Street or banks for his wealth, but trusts You to provide for him. We thank You now Father for a time of rest. We pray in Jesus' Name."

They both lay down; a blanket of peace rested upon them and they slept.

Josh and Bekah had walked out of the meeting and went and sat down on the bench under the big tree in the clearing by the compound. With the weather getting cooler, the native people had started wearing jackets and sweaters, but Bekah and Josh thought the temperature delightful. Lately they found everything delightful, especially when they were in each other's company. They both realized they were coming to care for each other and had fought the feelings because of the situation they were in. They did not want their feelings to interfere with the quest. Josh took Bekah's hands in his. "Bekah, I know you are fighting the same feelings I am. We need to pray and get God's direction on what we should do. This isn't a bad thing we feel for each other, just poor timing. In any other place at any other time we probably would have taken some action towards what we feel. Because of what is happening around us, we have tried to deny our feelings. Maybe we need to acknowledge them and see what God has to say."

[208] 2 Chronicles 25:9
[209] Matthew 4:1-11

Bekah bowed her head and prayed. “Father, I can’t deny that I have feelings for Josh,” she said as a blush traveled up her cheeks. She looked up at him and smiled shyly. She continued, “I am aware that Josh has similar feelings, and that we are keeping them contained because of the situation we are in. Please give us some direction so that we know how to deal with these feelings. We only want to do what is pleasing in your sight. We pray this in Jesus’ Name.”

They both leaned back against the tree with eyes closed and holding hands. They fell asleep and sat there for most of the afternoon. Josh woke first and looked at his watch. It was after three. They had slept over three hours. He was astounded that he had slept so long, in the yard, with people going by all day long. Also a wooden bench against a tree was not terribly comfortable, but he was not stiff or sore.

He gave Bekah a slight shake and she opened her eyes and smiled at him. “You don’t look too bad as an old guy,” she said with a laugh.

Josh smiled at that comment and said “What do you mean?”

“I had a dream,” Bekah replied, “and in it time had passed and we were old. You still had your boyish figure, and you still had all your hair, albeit white.” Bekah laughed. “It really was a cute dream. We were sitting on a deck and staring out over a lake. It looked like a post card. Do you think the dream has any significance?”

“It could,” he answered. What does it say to you? How does it make you feel?”

Bekah thought a moment. “It made me smile. It made me feel good. It gave me hope.”

“Well,” Josh speculated, “that sounds like a good recommendation for the future. Let’s pray and agree that the dream came from God and that we will have a future together, a happy one. We just need to be patient, obedient, and trust Him to work it out." Josh got up and turned back to Bekah. "Let's go find everyone and see what's happening."

CHAPTER FORTY

JUNE 22
THE RIVER

Akeem had managed to get his hands free and was traveling down a familiar path that led out to the river. As the path opened up to the water he saw that only one boat was tied to the shore. Thinking of where the other boat might have gone, he could only come up with one possibility. Mehdi must have taken it down to Puerto Bahía Negra, which meant he must have already arrived there. Akeem thanked God for the provision and took the remaining boat, heading upriver to the village. He had to warn the village of the planned attack tonight.

It would take him around two hours to get to the village because of all the twists and turns in the river. After about an hour on the river he began to hear the sound of an engine. As it got closer he recognized that it was a very large engine. He looked around the boat he was on. There were no weapons, there was nowhere to turn off the river, and there was no place to hide. Just then the other boat roared around a curve, and on board were Mehdi and José. Akeem said a prayer of thanks and slowed down. He pulled his boat over to the river's edge, tied it up, and jumped into José's boat.

While continuing to travel upriver, Akeem told what had transpired that morning. It seems José was already aware of what had happened last night and he had already told Mehdi all he knew. Isaac kept him in the loop concerning what was happening in Paraguay. José increased the speed in order to get to the village before they were set upon by the Black Death. He was fairly sure a perimeter would have been set up to reconnoiter, and also send word back to the village if needed. Forty minutes later, they were pulling up to the dock. They had made the run in four and a half hours, record time.

The noise of the engines had alerted the guards of someone's arrival and they had sent word up to Manu and Daniel who were coming down the trail as José finished tying up the boat. "I have several boxes of weapons that need to be transported up to the village. I didn't have time to pack much of anything else," José said to Daniel as he gave him a big hug. "It appears you may be attacked this evening and Mehdi, Akeem, and I are the only cavalry in the area. Believe it or not, I even have a grenade launcher in one of the boxes. Mehdi tells me there are about thirty men coming. How many armed men do we have?"

Daniel laughed, "You're always ready for a fight. Be glad God is on our side. Including the three of you we have eight men and two women who are able to shoot. The women are not comfortable with larger caliber weapons, but can use them if the need arises. Come up to the compound and we'll share what we know." He turned to one of the villagers, "Please, have some of the men bring these boxes up to the compound right away." They walked into the kitchen and all those who made up the quest were there waiting. Akeem grabbed some food from the counter and sat down to eat while he listened to everyone talk. Other than a banana, he had not eaten since dinner yesterday. The chipa was from breakfast and a little tough, but it filled an empty spot in his stomach. There was always fresh fruit on the table and it was wonderful. He munched contentedly.

As they were finishing their story two runners came in

from the perimeter. They reported that a group of armed men was coming through the jungle toward the village. At their present rate of speed they should be arriving in twenty minutes. The runners waited for instructions.

Josh directed them, "Go back to the perimeter. Leave a few men there so they can run back to inform us what is taking place. This will allow us what little time we have to get organized."

As Josh turned he noticed Carlos standing in the corner watching the preparations. He walked over to Josh and stated, "If you trust me, I can also handle any of those weapons. I would be proud to serve in the army of God."

In the heat of the moment Josh had forgotten about Carlos. He did not have time to go over instructions with him. He simply said, "Go get a weapon you're comfortable with and stay by me."

Daniel's guns, except for the black powder muskets, were brought out and laid on the table. Josh and Ted went to get their supply. All together they looked like a mighty arsenal; unfortunately, they did not have as many defenders as they did weapons. Having Carlos volunteer gave an added boost to their small group who were protecting the whole village.

Suddenly all the members of the perimeter came into the house. A spokesman said, "The men of the camp are heading here from the trail that is due south of the village; the one that ends at the grove. They are strung out along the path, but they have not sent anyone forward to assess the village. They must not know we have weapons, and that we know they are coming. They will enter the grove in approximately ten minutes."

Manu spoke. "Send runners throughout the village to move the elderly, women and children and any injured back into the jungle at the north end of the village. Tell them to stay there until I tell them it is safe to come out. Have the members of the quest assemble in the grove and carry down what weapons are needed. Daniel and José know what to bring. Follow their instructions."

Daniel had some men carry several of his weapons along with boxes of ammunition to the grove. The only thing José brought from his stockpile was the grenade launcher. If he could get one or two shots of it off, it might surprise their enemy and cause them to disperse.

Edwardo took his 22 caliber rifle and gave it to Bekah to use. It would be easier for her to handle. He picked up one of José's automatic rifles and started walking. Armed and dangerous they all hurried to the grove.

They walked quickly and quietly. This was the spot the Black Death fighters were heading to. With their knowledge of the surrounding jungle, they could catch them by surprise, and possibly be able to disarm them. They took the last minutes to offer up a prayer asking God to be with them and give them victory. Then they waited.

Several minutes went by and still their enemy did not enter the grove. Finally one of the perimeter guards volunteered to go forward and see what was holding them up. After a few minutes he came back. "They turned off the trail shortly before they reached the grove. They are circling around to the north end of the village"

All of them stood there a moment slack with shock. Finally Manu shouted, "Send a runner quickly to the people hiding in the jungle to come back and stay in the center of the village. Everyone grab your weapons and follow me. We will have to follow the edge of the village. We don't know exactly where they are or where they intend to come in. I don't think they knew that our people were hiding in the jungle, they were just using good tactics and we were caught unawares. Now they have the advantage and we are in danger. Is God with us, or have we missed something?"

Suddenly Leonardo spoke up, “Didn’t God say that He would fight for us? Didn’t He say we could bring our foolish weapons if we wanted, but that we should be strong with His weapon, His Word which cannot be held in our hands, but is in our hearts and minds and spirits? We need to be still and let God show us what to do, to let Him fight for us. We have been fighting for ourselves and He is not pleased.” Leonardo dropped to his knees and asked for forgiveness. The rest of them followed. They all knelt there not knowing what to do, but giving God control of the situation.

CHAPTER FORTY-ONE

JUNE 22
THE JUNGLE

Kamal had used good tactics in bringing his soldiers around to the other side of the village. He knew they would surprise everyone. He stayed about a quarter mile outside the village. It was hard to tell exactly where they were because there were no trails. They were running and getting strung out a little and the ground was becoming very wet. It seemed the further they went the wetter it got, but Kamal pushed them. He did not want too much time to go by before they attacked from the other side.

Kamal looked to his left and noticed there was a long footbridge raised up about ten yards away in a small clearing. He wondered why there would be a bridge when there was no evidence of any running water. Just then a cry went out from the front of the group, and everyone else seemed to stop short. Kamal pushed his way to the front and was transfixed by the sight. Several of his men had stumbled into quicksand and were already disappearing below the surface. The rest of them had faltered, realizing that they were in a bog and appeared to be surrounded by the soft and shifting surface. Unsure of where to go or what to do they looked to Kamal for leadership.

Unfortunately, Kamal's only thought was of his own safety. He realized now that the bridge was there to allow the villagers to cross the bog without being trapped in the quicksand. He turned and tried to go back the way they had come, but all signs of their footprints had been erased by the water and soil that had been shifted by the men who had lost their fight in the bog. There were now twenty-one men left who were surrounded by a moving grave and there appeared to be no way out. Kamal ordered one man to test the ground around him, and see if he could find some firm footing. The man refused and told Kamal to do it himself. Kamal lost his temper and pushed the man who fell backward into the gripping quicksand. Before anyone could figure out how to help him, he too disappeared. Now there were twenty.

Suddenly the jungle parted and several men from the village came into view. The man who appeared to be the leader spoke to them. "You all appear to be having some difficulty. Would you like some help?"

Before they could respond Akeem came out and stood with the men from the village. Kamal saw him and in a moment of rage, raised his gun to fire at him. Knowing these people were their only source of help, the two men on either side of Kamal shoved him into the quicksand, and as he screamed, he also disappeared. Now there were nineteen. The odds were becoming better.

Akeem said to the group of men, "If you want our help, throw all your weapons into the bog." Splashes could be heard as rifles, hand guns, knives and machetes disappeared from sight. "Is that everything? Because if anyone is holding out, we will return him to the center of the bog and he can take his own chances." There were a few additional splashes and then it was quiet.

The men of the village laid out several layers of banana leaves and crawled carefully on them as they crossed to where the men waited quietly. Then they showed them how to slither on the leaves one by one, not putting their full weight in any one area. By dispersing their weight they did not sink.

One by one they arrived onto dry ground and their hands

were tied. When all nineteen had been rescued, they were accompanied back to the grove. It was determined this would be the easiest place to keep them all together and carefully guarded. Meanwhile, Josh was on the phone with Isaac telling him what had happened and that now he had nineteen prisoners he needed to have taken off his hands. Also, since regular trips were made to the Black Death Camp, precautions needed to be taken to capture Josef, his crew, and any other groups of men they were planning to bring out to the camp.

When the captives were safely gathered and several guards set up to keep watch, the people of the quest gathered again in Daniel and Sherry's home. It was past dinnertime, and with the attack on the village, no meals had been prepared. Thankfully Sherry had a stockpile of food for situations such as this one. She sent Paloma to get more fruit and then she got out her stash of nuts, cheese and crackers, a large tin of cookies, two boxes of pretzels, and a large can of cheese dip. It seemed more like party food than dinner, but it would fill everyone up and it was most definitely tasty.

Everyone sat on the floor and the food was passed around. There was very little conversation. Most of them were overwhelmed by the turn of events.

When the food was cleared Josh stood up. "I count eighteen people here, called by God for one purpose or another, but I do not see eighteen of us leaving tonight. We are all here to fulfill a purpose God has called us to, but I want to go around and ask you one by one if you are certain you are to go with us tonight or if God has you staying here for a different purpose. Remember, obedience to God is the important thing. You may not be going with us. God may have a job for you here. Every job God asks us to do is important and is for His purpose."

Josh started with Manu. "Manu has God asked you to go forth tonight, not knowing whether or not you will come back?"

Manu answered somberly, "I know He has called me. I would not leave my young wife and son for anyone else."

Leonardo was next and he answered, "I honestly believe I am to stay here and be the leader in Manu's absence. I feel that this is what God is asking me to do. I already talked with Manu about this and he is in agreement."

Next Josh turned to Arandu and Arasunu and spoke to them in Spanish. "Arandu, I know you and Arasunu both want to go on the quest, but I don't believe God called you. Has God spoken to either of you? Has He specifically asked that you go with us?"

Arandu answered. "I feel that I am supposed to go on this quest to represent my village and those killed by the evil tribe. I need to be there."

Josh spoke sympathetically. "Arandu, your needing to go and God calling you to go are two different things. We already discussed that vengeance can't be an issue here. We have to let God determine the outcome of this quest. We all need to be honest and determine if it is God calling us to go or is there some selfish reason motivating us."

Arasunu interrupted. "I do not want to go. I only agreed to go because Arandu asked me to. Now I see that if someone goes who does not belong, they could be a hindrance to the quest and cause it to fail."

Arandu looked up. "You are right Josh. I do not need to go. I will put my faith in God that He will make things right."

Josh turned to Ted and spoke. "Ted, you asked to come with us and fund the trip, but I don't believe you are supposed to go on the quest. Do you feel something driving you to go, like maybe an obligation to Bekah? We don't need to go because we are obligated; we need to go because God called us."

"You're right Josh and I'm glad you saw that. I would not want to go and be a hindrance either. I believe there are things I can do here that will far outweigh any value I would contribute if I went. I remember the Bible says somewhere that obedience is better than sacrifice."[210]

"Tuvicha," Josh questioned. "Are you here to go on the quest, I don't believe that God has called you to go?"

"No," Tuvicha answered. "I am here because I want to see what God is doing. I want to know God better and so to do that, I must be with the people God talks to. I can see that He talks to you, but I will stay here. Maybe I can help Dr. Sherry. I have some knowledge in healing herbs. Also, I know that God talks to Dr. Sherry; she hears His Voice. Dr. Sherry, would you accept my help?"

Sherry stood up and went over to Tuvicha. She put her arms around his shoulders and hugged him. "I would welcome your help. Maybe you can even take over plant preparation. It's getting too much for me to take care of everything, especially since I am going to have a baby in early December." Tuvicha beamed. Being needed was important to everyone.

Last Josh turned to Renato. "You are the hardest one to ask this question. Renato, are you supposed to go on this quest?"

Renato stared first at Bekah and then turned his attention to Josh. "I have been a father to you Bekah most of your life. Since this all began I have been a protector also. As you like to say, I'm one of your "Three Musketeers". But God has already shown me that my place is here, helping those who will be waiting for all of you to return."

Josh smiled. "Renato, God wants you to know that He's not through with you yet. He has things for you to do."

Josh then addressed the whole group. "I also believe that Carlos and Akeem are to accompany me along with Mario, Philippe, Axel, Maitie, Giancarlo, Manu, Edwardo, Daniel and Bekah. We have a short time before we leave tonight and we

[210] 1 Samuel 15:22

have much to do. We leave at nine fifty-one. God said he would light our path and that we should travel at night.

We will need twelve backpacks and twelve sets of hooks and hammocks. We will need four days of clothes and whatever non-perishable food we can find. We need several cans of insect repellent, four flashlights, twelve machetes and twelve pocket knives. Toilet paper and any personal items need to be packed, and two canteens each to carry potable water. We also need two compasses. We need a spare if one breaks or gets wet. We're going to follow the river up and so we will need to bring fish hooks and line. From what I've observed in this village, the river is very bountiful. We'll need matches for a fire and a pot or two to boil water and cook with when necessary."

Josh paused in his list and turned to Bekah. "I think you should wear your crucifix. It seems to have some relevance to this quest."

Josh looked at his watch. "It's almost eight o'clock. Will someone take charge of these backpacks and see they are packed with what we need? We can get our own personal items and put them in on top. Everyone who is going needs to try and rest. Someone will wake us at nine thirty. That will give us twenty minutes to pack our personal items and meet in the compound. We will say our good-byes and leave from there."

Bekah put on the crucifix and lay down, not expecting to sleep, and fearful if she did she would have another dream. At nine-thirty Sherry came in and touched Bekah's arm. Bekah opened her eyes and smiled. She had never felt so relaxed after so little sleep.

She thanked God for the rest and refreshing and walked into the compound with Sherry. She had packed four changes of clothes, toiletries and a bar of soap. She had put her hair up in a clip to keep it out of the way, and packed a hair brush and spare clip just in case one broke. Everyone embarking on the quest was already in the compound. Half the village was there and the rest lined the path down to the river.

Bekah went to Ted and Renato. They stood together, encouraging each other in this time of testing. Bekah hugged them both with tears running down her eyes. “Renato, from now on I’m going to call you Dad. You’re the only one I’ve ever known and even though I haven’t said it, I have thought of you that way my whole life. No more Miss Bekah from you. From now on, I am your daughter Bekah.”

Then Bekah turned her attention to Ted. “Ted, I’m so glad you came. I’m glad we’re friends and that there are no hard feelings between us.”

Bekah looked around, “Where’s Connie?” she asked.

Connie was in the corner of the compound with Lara, the two babies, Maria and Edwardo. They were saying their tender good-byes and she did not want to interrupt, but had to ask, “Connie, you won’t forget to keep in touch with the people in Maine? Also, please pray for us, we’ll be praying for all of you.”

Lastly she looked for Sherry. She and Daniel were sitting on the bench under the big trees in the compound. Daniel had his hand resting on the little mound of Sherry’s tummy. A new life was forming there. They were both praying, but tears streamed down Sherry’s face.

Noemi had been saying her good-byes to Manu. Now she walked over to where Sherry and Daniel were seated. Noemi placed her hand on the top of theirs. “I will pray and watch over Dr. Sherry,” she told Daniel. “Remember, she is now my mother and it will be my turn to care for her.”

Josh gave a whistle and the group formed. He asked the five young men Philippe, Mario, Axel, Giancarlo and Maitie to go first because they were familiar with the area around the village and would be able to lead them on paths they were familiar with. Josh and Bekah came next followed by Manu, Daniel, Edwardo,

Carlos and Akeem.

It was time to start. Twelve set out following the direction of God. They walked down the familiar path that led to the river. Stopping at the edge of the jungle by the narrow path, they joined hands and each prayed a prayer of dedication, first to God, and then to the quest He had called them to. They also thanked God for His direction, grace, peace and mercy. The group all turned to look back at the people lining the path down to the river. There was a somber mood among everyone. Daniel felt compelled to shout up to them, "Do not be afraid for us. God has told us He will illuminate our path.[211] We do not know what will happen, but we know God will be victorious, and so shall we."

Looking up they saw the full moon rising above the treetops in the night sky. All of them stared in shock. It was a blood moon that hung low in the sky. This is what would shine on them all night. Was this another message from God? Was it good news or bad? Disquieted, they resumed walking, everyone keeping their thoughts to himself.

And so the strange parade marched into the jungle that first night, not knowing exactly where they were going or what they would find. Only knowing that Almighty God had called them on this quest, and they would see it through with their last ounce of strength. They wouldn't worry about tomorrow, today had enough problems.[212] They would meet each challenge with faith in their hearts and the Word of God in their mouths.

---

[211] Psalm 119:105
[212] Matthew 6:25-34

EPILOGUE

Jesus looked down from Heaven and remembered another group of twelve He had sent out. He remembered they had returned full of excitement because even the demons had obeyed them.[213] Those men had sat at His feet for three years. Unfortunately, there had been a traitor among them.

This group was made up of matured Christians and very young ones. Sometimes circumstances necessitated that maturity be achieved at a greater speed than normal. He would speak to them in dreams and visions.[214] He would lead and guide them all with the still, small Voice of His Spirit.[215] Their traitor would be dealt with when necessity required it. He felt their hurt at the betrayal even now. When the time came, He would send the Comforter to bring them peace and renewed strength and endurance.

---

[213] Luke 10:17
[214] Job 33:15-16
[215] 1 Kings 19:12;

ABOUT THE AUTHOR

Lorraine and her husband Mike started out as high school sweethearts. They have now been married forty-seven years. They have two children and two grandchildren who help keep life exciting. Lorraine was raised in New Jersey and relocated with her family to Oklahoma in 1977. At that time she hoped there was a God, but had no faith to support that belief. That hope was turned into a firm belief in 1981. She subsequently developed a burning desire to share God's Word with those around her. Unfortunately, she had very little knowledge of the Bible. This prompted her to attend Rhema Bible Training Center where she received a two year degree. She served in her local church in a number of positions and was eventually ordained into the Ministry.

Lorraine has a heart for Missions and has been on several mission trips over the years, including trips to the Philippines and Ivory Coast. Her last was a two week trip to Paraguay at the end of November, 2017. There she got to experience what she had only imagined and meet the people who already lived in her heart.

Lorraine is also a registered nurse. She has incorporated her nurse's training and experience, plus her love of gardening, cooking, and needlework into the tapestry of her books. THE CALL and THE QUEST are Books 1 and 2 of the series, AND THEN THE END SHALL COME

Lorraine is currently working on a third book, THE COMING, which should be out shortly. To order the third book in the series, contact me at: *lmcafasso@gmail.com*

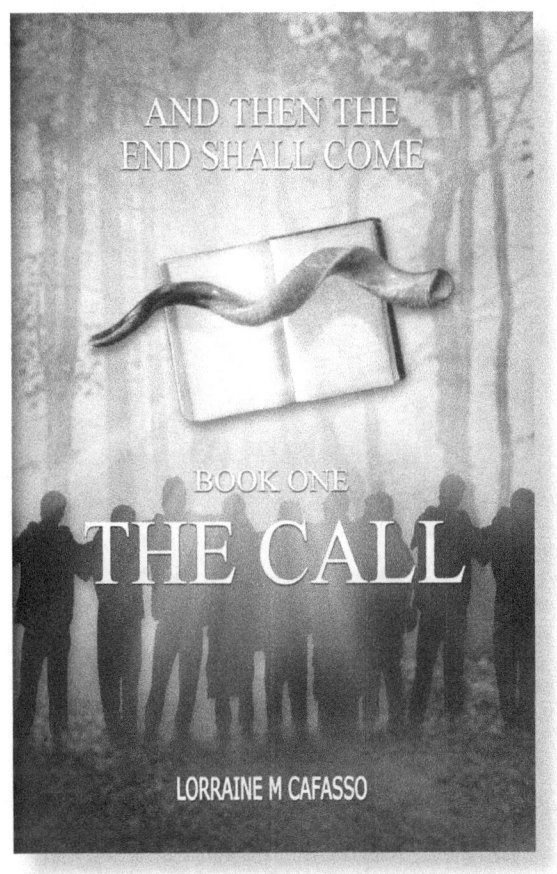

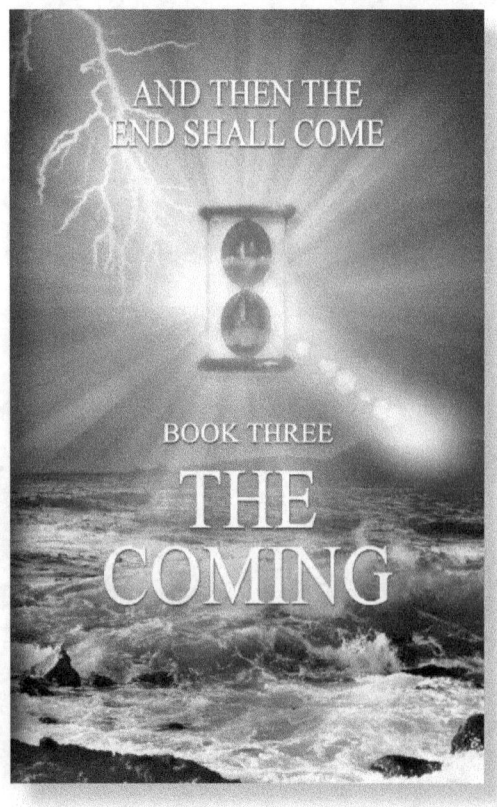

www.ingramcontent.com/pod-product-compliance
Lightning Source LLC
Chambersburg PA
CBHW071156020726
47502CB00002B/437

* 9 7 8 1 9 4 9 9 9 3 6 7 7 *